THE DARK SUN

CRISTINE KELLER

The Dark Sun

Copyright © 2025 by Cristine Keller

This novel is a work of fiction. All names, characters, locations, and incidents are the product of the author's imagination or are used fictitiously. Any similarities to actual events, locales, or persons, living or dead, are purely coincidental.

All rights reserved.

No part of this publication may be reproduced, scanned, uploaded, transmitted, photocopied, recorded, digital or printed, other electronic or mechanical methods, or distributed in any form or by any means without permission is considered theft of the author's intellectual property.

ISBN 979-8-9936111-1-2 (Paperback)

ISBN 979-8-9936111-0-5 (Hardcover)

ISBN 979-8-9936111-2-9 (Ebook)

The Library of Congress Cataloging-in-Publication Data is available upon request.

Cover design by Miblart.com

NO AI TRAINING: Any use of this publication to "train" generative artificial intelligence (AI) technologies is prohibited.

No AI was used to create this publication.

First Edition 2025

I dedicate this book to my husband, Chris, and my daughter.

Prologue

Cannon Hyashi squeezed a few drops of blood from his fisted hand into a tumbler. He then handed it to his servant Tort, who had watched with a bland expression, and took it carefully into his hands. Except for eyebrows, the hairless man wore the appropriate garments that all Cannon's servants wore. The smooth white linen shirt and brown pleated pants were tight on Tort's scrawny frame. Though the look was to keep up appearances, Cannon couldn't have cared less about how they dressed. He only cared that they obeyed him without question.

"Fill the rest with juice and give it to the girl. Make sure she ingests all of it," Cannon ordered.

Just that morning, he had adopted twins from an orphanage, a boy and a girl. *Purchased* was the more appropriate word. They were a year younger than his five-year-old biological son, Stellan, who had thought Cannon bought the twin boy for him to have a brother. That hadn't been his intention at all, but he didn't bother to correct the little shit for assuming as such.

"Yes, Sire."

"And, Tort," Cannon said gruffly, "I've seen the way my son is looking at the boy. Keep him away from both. Inform the other servants of this as well." Normally he didn't care what his son wanted to do to other people, but he obtained the twins for a reason and needed them to be unscathed for the time being.

"Yes, Sire."

After Tort left, Cannon went to the overturned leather chair where he had placed his clothes and began dressing, taking stock of himself as he did. His once brown skin was lighter these days. Whether that was from age or the colder climate, he didn't know, and it didn't matter either way. He had also lost quite a bit of weight. The green satin shirt with gold trim and black leather pants were now looser than they once had been.

He absently ran a hand through his coarse gray hair, startled to find it had grown so long that several strands were tangled. His beard was longer than he remembered as well.

Cannon shrugged and made a mental note to have a servant tend his unruly hair; however, he had the strange sense that he'd concluded this before. He shrugged again, dismissing the thought.

His black leather knee-high boots and black satin robe completed his attire. As Cannon tied his robe, a wooden clock fell from the wall and crashed to the floor, breaking into several pieces. He looked around his study and realized that most of the room was in disarray. The blue fabric wall lining, sprinkled with white dots, was faded and shredded in several places. Against the far wall was a floor-to-ceiling bookshelf. Some of the shelves had collapsed, and books lay in a messy pile by two leather chairs and a low wooden table. A statue that had once stood on a marble column in one corner had also fallen and was broken into numerous pieces. What the statue had once been, he didn't know and didn't care.

The only object Cannon utilized in the room was the oversized mahogany desk on the opposite end. The large open ledger on the surface only mocked him; Cannon loathed this part of being an aristocrat, but his servants needed to be paid. Getting ones who were willing to give a four-year-old his biofluids without questions or morals getting in the way deserved their cost, but he still lacked the motivation to get it done.

Before returning to his desk, Cannon went to the only window within the study, which was so large it was nearly floor-to-ceiling. He grabbed a chunk of the off-white lace curtain obstructing his view and yanked it away. He'd only meant to move the curtain aside, but his strength ripped the entire curtain rod from the wall. Cannon stepped back in time before being hit by the golden bar. Angered, he picked up the heavy metal rod and tossed it to his left.

The lovely, familiar sound of bones breaking drew his attention to where the bar had landed. The remains of two skeletons were sandwiched between the wall and a small couch. He had long forgotten about those. He smiled as he fondly remembered the days when the stench of death had perfumed the study. The glorious odor had died down years ago. He stepped back up to the window, making another mental note to have the servants bring new victims to his room and rekindle his favored smell.

Cannon viewed his property and the land beyond with disgust. Greenery eventually gave way to a lush forest, which eventually gave way to high-rise buildings. The buildings were so tightly packed together that it looked like a barrier from this distance. The planet, Oxtaria, was certainly in its prime for sustaining life. The planet's only moon, Lutania, was full tonight. The light it beamed from the solar system's star, Jua, was so bright it nearly looked like daytime. He hated what he saw, but it would all soon be a dead wasteland. He was quite pleased with the progression toward his end goal.

Oxtaria had five major continents. Of those five, only two were habitable enough for larger Animalia lifeforms to thrive. Theton was presumably the largest continent. Its landmass extended from the northern hemisphere to the southern hemisphere, each end almost reaching the polar caps. Yet humans could only occupy a small portion of the northern region. Cannon had studied how that had come to be and how another continent soon became a lifeline for humankind.

With the right conditions for lifeforms to evolve, Theton's mid-region was the birthplace for many of the world's current species. However, with the planet shifting on its axis, the mid-region soon became too barren and hot to sustain life, which drove surviving lifeforms to the northern area of Theton until the landscape became too steep to climb or too cold to thrive. Millions of years went by, and a primal form of humanoids evolved to a higher consciousness of intelligence. They stabilized their environment by building structures and farming. Thousands of civilizations and languages became refined as the population grew, gaining and occupying every viable piece of land.

Thousands of years had gone by, and humans had either pushed out or killed other competing lifeforms. Provinces formed, giving each tribe the chance to develop their own customs. But with the continual growth of humankind, farmland soon became scarce as concrete and metal took over to accommodate the ever-growing population. Single-family neighborhoods soon became multilayered structures. Dirt roads were now paved for a motorized transportation system. People utilized their roofs for gardens, and animals were raised in specialized multilayered warehouses. But that soon wasn't enough to feed the population. Even the coastal provinces couldn't keep up with the demand. Their only solution was to explore other possible lands.

Theton's mid-region, Xozon, was still hostile and unapproachable. The mountains and the extreme freezing temperatures in the northernmost region gave no hope either. Exploration then turned to the waters. Vessels that ventured to the west never returned. But the ones that went east discovered humanity's salvation. The land they discovered was abundant with life and boosted optimism.

To Cannon's dismay, humans weren't going to be stupid about it this time. The new land was named Shad'Dyn. A representative from each province—all three thousand, eight hundred ninety-two—formed a committee on how to maintain a balanced system to grow and raise food. Laws were put into place to protect the land and the people who volunteered to migrate there. That was roughly twelve hundred years ago.

Shad'Dyn was now a combination of farmland and forested areas, a utopia that differed greatly from Theton's dystopia. The population there were a proud people who took their lineage seriously. The food they grew and raised sustained themselves and the people of Theton. Besides the coastal provinces that had an established fishing industry, Theton was now entirely dependent on Shad'Dyn for the majority of their food.

As Shad'Dyn formed into a fine example of cooperation and a peaceful nation, Theton grew darker in some places, which enabled Cannon to plan his vision for world destruction in the shadows. It was laughable that Theton's modern-day societal practices worked in his favor.

Even though there were thousands of different cultures within Theton, a three-tier hierarchy system governed the provinces. The highest were the aristocrats who ruled over their entire estate. Basic nepotism passed their authority and entitlements onto the next generation within their family. The middle class voted in their elected officials to rule over them for a certain amount of time and then would repeat the process. The lower class provinces consisted of the unwanted or exiled citizens and were ruled by no one. Many orphanages among these communities housed the discarded.

Besides the classes snubbing their noses at each other, there was a balanced system between the three. Aristocrats made their currencies by either mass-producing consumer products or supplying the highest educational services. The middle class mostly depended on tourists or other trivial means. The lower class provided the darker needs that humans obsessed over. Cannon was quick to exploit the provisions the lower class offered for his grand plan. He smiled to the point that it hurt. Now that he had the twin girl, the outcome for his future was on an even better trajectory than he had initially planned. The thought of it all put him in a better mood. He went to his desk and resumed his work.

Sometime later, someone knocked on his door and asked permission to enter. Cannon instantly recognized the voice. It was Vince, his most trusted and rightly titled first commander. It had been nearly fifty days since he had seen the man and was eager to hear news from him.

"Yes, come in."

Vince came in with heavy breaths. His attire—the same as Tort's—was a bit disheveled. Usually, he was just as hairless too, but the man had been away long enough to have some growth. His refined black hair glistened with sweat. On a normal day, Cannon could only distinguish the man by a long scar across his cheek. Without it, he saw no difference between any of his servants.

"Sire," Vince began with a smile. "Pham is requesting your presence. I have steeds ready. We can leave at once if you'd like."

"Yes," he replied, quickly standing up.

The Hyashi province was located in the northwestern area that was annoyingly cold year-round. After putting his oversized leather coat on, Cannon then followed Vince down the wide hallway. Along the way, Stellan ran up to him, babbling about something. Without stopping, Cannon put his hand on the child's face and shoved him between the wall and a tall wooden chest. Stellan fell into a heap and began to cry, but Cannon didn't care for such childish things. He had been waiting impatiently for Pham to beckon him and didn't have time for another one of his son's tantrums.

Now in the stairway, Cannon and Vince went down four flights that led directly to the stables. Two bay horses were saddled and ready with a stable hand holding one each. After exiting the stables, Vince took the lead with a sudden gallop. Cannon kicked his mount to follow and stayed closely behind.

As distance expanded between them and his household, Cannon looked back at the towering six-story mansion. The antique stone-built manor had not been upgraded to modern standards and was starting to collapse in some places. Thankfully the rooms that he and his entourage occupied were holding well for the time being.

Cannon grinned as he remembered the day he and his entourage had taken over the place. He wasn't sure anymore how long ago that had been. Ten years? Twenty? Regardless, it still amused him how he had obtained the prestigious Hyashi property and name. It wasn't in the typical aristocratic way but in the murder-every-living-being kind of way. It had been too easy to take. When the real Hyashi lords opened their doors, they had no idea the glorious suffering that would rain down upon them.

Cannon then glanced over to what was left of the church within walking distance from the manor. Most of the inhabitants had sought refuge inside when the attack began. Though a majority of Theton's population cultivated many different customs, there was still a universal religious consensus in the belief of the Divine Universe. The laughable notion was that it was a magnificent force that created and protected all that it had made. The people of the Hyashi manor certainly thought it would save them from the slaughter. Cannon smiled. The looks on their faces still aroused him to this day. The pathway to the church had once been a disgusting flowered garden but was now an honored yard of bodies. He recalled the lovely stench that had permeated the courtyard. He and his entourage still celebrated that glorious day.

Cannon commanded his horse to keep up with Vince. They rode hard over the vast landscape of rolling hills and jumped over rows of small bushes or old wooden fences. There were very few aristocratic provinces that had open land such as this. Most had converted their land into factories and residential buildings. Why the real Hyashi lords didn't would never be answered. Little did they know their mistake of not doing so would forever end their lineage. The wide-open area was the size of thirty provinces and just what Cannon needed for his grand plan.

They finally reached the tree line that surrounded Cannon's property, which was where his authority ended. The surrounding provinces were not far away and kept a watchful eye on anything suspicious. Gangs within the lower class provinces would attempt to break in to steal food or conduct other nasty crimes. Even though they were given a siphon of rations, they were still the last to receive resources. Most of the time it was whatever higher classes picked over, which was usually rotten food.

Though Cannon applauded the gangs and their efforts, it did make this part of his plan difficult. Most provinces handled their own law enforcement; however, some called upon the Iarothian Military Force. The IMF dominated their standing in the world. They mostly provided land and ocean rescue services or aided in disaster relief, but they were also called to resolve conflicts or investigate where their noses didn't belong. Cannon's entourage that accompanied Pham had to be cautious not to alert nearby locals, who would certainly contact the IMF. Though Cannon could quietly decimate a household, he was not quite equipped to go against the IMF.

Before reaching the tree line, Cannon and Vince slowed their horses. Their charges breathed heavily and were lathered in sweat.

"How much farther?" Cannon demanded.

"Not far, Sire," Vince said as he wiped his face off with a cloth.

Cannon nodded as they rode on in silence. Not long after entering the forest, he spotted a campfire and tents up ahead. His servants were chatting quietly around the fire when they came upon them. After dismounting, Cannon handed the reins to the closest person, uncaring if the servant caught the horse or not.

"Pham!" Cannon shouted. A moment later, a boy he had known for count-less lifetimes emerged from one of the tents.

Unlike the rest of his entourage, Pham was just like him and his son, Stellan. They referred to their kind as Abnormals. Even though they'd been born into this world, they were foreign to it. Their origins were unknown to them. How-ever, their sole nature was to end all life. Their drive to do so went deep down into their core.

Pham was around twelve years old. His ebony complexion shone like obsid-ian rock, making his hazel irises sparkle like gems. His black hair was styled into several pointed spikes. Unable to remember specific moments from their last life, Cannon at least recalled that they both had a reddish, tan skin tone with orange hair and yellow eyes. Just as in previous lifetimes, Abnormals were born randomly by happenstance to whomever birthed them. And regardless of their upbringing, they were evil and no moral compass could deter them from that.

Pham stopped in front of him and spoke quietly. "Sir."

Not needing to go into pleasantries, Cannon got right to the point. "Show me."

Pham turned and began walking away from the campsite. Cannon trailed not far behind. They walked alone in silence for a few minutes before the boy stopped in front of a giant tree that towered its neighbors by almost half and had to be at least a hundred years old as well. Pham stooped down and pointed to an area at the base. Cannon could see well enough that the boy had dug a hole with his bare hands but couldn't see exactly what was inside. Whatever was there, it was something Pham had been searching for.

"Is this what you've been looking for?"

"Yes," Pham said as he pulled out several misshapen, dark, round balls and tucked them into a pouch sewn into his shirt. "'Tis a very rare fungi, only found along the roots of elder trees like this one." He handed over a small one for Cannon to examine.

Pham was a brilliant artist with his gift of destruction, but Cannon hadn't the slightest idea of what the boy had in mind for this lifetime. He rolled the object in his hands. The texture was rugged with tiny indentions.

"And what do you plan to do with them?" Cannon asked.

Pham removed two more balls of fungi, then took the one he had given Cannon. The boy then ate the small morsel, dirt and all, and didn't so much as grimace as he chewed and swallowed. After licking his lips clean, he held up a hand and slowly wiggled all five fingers. This was his way of indicating to wait a few minutes.

Cannon had forgotten that Pham was a light talker. Most Abnormals were, he supposed. It was hard to remember such small details from their past lives. The human mind they occupied couldn't handle the enormity of all the information gained from the countless lives they'd lived. However, little pieces of information would emerge as they grew from infancy. Besides knowing their design, they also knew of their unique talents they each possessed to carry out their purpose.

Besides that, the only other aspect they all shared was the fear of the Dark Sun. What was worse than the fear was not knowing what exactly the Dark Sun was. They didn't know whether it was an object, a living being, or a place. Whatever it was, like all the others, Cannon was occasionally haunted by it in his deepest nightmares. Even the minions that had no other purpose than to assist them feared it. Regardless of the unknown, Cannon pushed on with his plans.

Pham started to make a gagging sound. He leaned over the hole and retched. After a couple of releases of contents, he sat back on his haunches and wiped off his mouth. Then he covered up the hole with care as though he was a father swaddling his infant.

Without looking up at him, Pham said, "Come back five years' time and see my work."

"What did you do?"

"I changed the components of the fungi and made it better," Pham replied as he stood up. "Now I go, carry out my work to Shad'Dyn."

Cannon returned five years later. He saw the big picture of what was to come and smiled broadly. As long as he did his part, this catastrophic end was going to be a magnificent one to see.

1

Pocky was exhausted from the day and had no trouble falling asleep when she hit the pillow. Instead of being engulfed in a series of dreams, she involuntarily went somewhere else, into the deepest part of her mind. She was in a dream that wasn't a dream but was unsure of what else it could be or what to call it.

She floated in the middle of what she supposed was the known universe and gazed in awe at the celestial body that was so far away no units of measurement or time could quantify its distance. Yet it was the size of thousands of galaxies if they were clustered into one, making it look much closer than it was. Somehow, she knew this. She also knew its name was the Dark Sun. It wasn't a traditional star that looked white in space or yellow when seen under an atmosphere. The Dark Sun was as black as dark matter in space, but she could see its circular shape from the blue flares that bloomed from it.

It was breathtaking.

The celestial bodies on either side of the Dark Sun were tiny grains of sand in comparison. For reasons that eluded her, Pocky had a love for all of them that was as immeasurable as the distance between them. And she loved being able to see them in this dream that wasn't a dream.

A small blue glowing orb, no bigger than her head, with pulsing spikes spiraled up to her. Because the dream would fade from her memory when she awoke, it took a moment for her to recall what this entity was. Pocky smiled at the approaching orb, remembering that she regarded this entity as a friend. It liked to be called Ember, and in return, it preferred to call her Boss.

As the entity reached her, Ember spoke in a childlike and feminine, yet monotone and direct, voice. *"Hi, Boss."*

"Hey, Ember. How're you?"

"I could be better," Ember replied remorsefully.

"Oh? Something wrong?"

"Yes, a lot is wrong."

"Right," Pocky gently said, recalling that there was *something* wrong. "Uh, I'm sorry, I don't remember ..."

"No matter. You'll forget when you leave here anyway, so we don't have to go over it again."

"Humor me?" Pocky asked with a smile. Ember let out an annoyed sound that made her imagine it rolling its eyes—if it had any. "What?"

"You say that every time," Ember said with sharp exasperation. *"We have the same conversation every time you come here, almost verbatim. I'm sorry but I'm just not in the mood to go over it again."*

"Oh, I'm sorry. I just wanna help if I can."

"I know you do, but because you never remember, there's no point. And I'm ... I'm just cranky because I'm supposed to be dormant."

"Dormant?"

"Yes."

"Why are you supposed to be dormant?"

"It's part of my life cycle, how I grow and mature. When I'm awake like this, it stunts my growth."

"Oh? That sucks."

"Yes, indeed. I'm quite annoyed."

"How long have you been awake?"

"Nineteen years."

"Nineteen years?" Pocky echoed. "Well, what happened that made you wake up?"

"Something happened that made you kick me out of your first subconscious level to your secondary one. And before you ask, yes, you have a secondary one. You normally refer to it as your archives."

"Whoa, that's a lot to unpack."

"Seriously, let's not."

"First," Pocky began, ignoring Ember's protest. "How do I have a secondary subconscious level?"

Ember sighed before answering, its words rapid and annoyed. *"Short answer, you were born with one for the purpose of storing your archives. And before you ask, your archives, metaphorically speaking, is an infinite library that you can access for something you need to know. It cannot be stored in your first subconscious level or even your conscious level because the human mind doesn't have the capacity to hold that much information. Which is why you were born with a secondary subconscious level so that you can access information without harming yourself."*

Pocky raised her eyebrows. "Is the information really that much?"

"It is as vast as the universe you're seeing."

"Huh ... So all people have that capability?"

"Just a few like you."

"But how does that even work? Accessing my archives, I mean."

"Metaphorically speaking, you would come here and scroll through the aisles and books. Once you found what you needed, you would then transfer that information to your first subconscious level. That information would then become instinctual or intuitive for you to use. How and where you got it from is forgotten in order to preserve your mind."

"Why can't I at least remember that I have a secondary subconscious level?"

"Because the temptation to absorb knowledge is overpowering. To the point of collapsing your mind and becoming brain dead."

Pocky tilted her head, considering Ember's words. "Guess that's why I never remember you or that I even come here. Right?"

"Exactly."

"Okay, well since I'm here, how can I access my archives to help you?"

"That's part of the problem, Boss. Because you put me here, your archives had to shrink to the size of an atom, making it impossible for you to access. In fact, that's why you come here. You know something's wrong and come here for answers. What you find instead is me, and then this conversation ensues."

"So there's no room for both you and my archives to fit?"

"Unfortunately, no. I occupy it in its entirety. In fact, this place is a tight fit."

"Oh? I'm sorry."

"Not your fault. I'm dealing, as you would say."

Pocky replayed their conversation, getting more intrigued as she remembered some of their previous ones combined with the current one. "Well, you said I kicked you out of my first subconscious level. Why'd I do that?"

"Short answer, to protect me."

"Protect you from what?"

"Best you not know. But to be honest, I'm surprised that you even knew I was there in the first place."

"Why are you surprised?"

"I was dormant and as small as your archives are now. I should have been virtually impossible to see, but you did somehow."

"Okay ... and why is it best for me to not know?"

"Because the first and only time I told you, you lost your shit. As you would say. It was a traumatic event."

"Traumatic?"

"Yes."

"That was nineteen years ago, right?"

"Yes. The chain of events led to where we are now."

"So, something traumatic happened when I was four that awoke you and prompted me to send you here. Do I have that right?"

"Correct. And because I'm here, I can't sleep like I'm supposed to."

Now at the age of twenty-three, Pocky thought back to when she was four for what could have possibly instigated Ember's dilemma. She and her twin brother, Thomas, had been living in an orphanage before being bought by Cannon Hyashi. A lot of horrific memories surfaced from that time, but nothing stood out as a possible traumatic event.

"I can't think of an event that had caused this. Can you describe the moment it happened?"

"Since I was dormant, I only caught 0.02 of a second of it. Not enough to explain it, but perhaps I could metaphorically."

"Please," Pocky encouraged.

"Okay, think of it like you're on a ship treading along the ocean on a nice day. Your body is the ship, and your brain is the bridge. There's a lot of 'yous' on the bridge, one at each of their own appointed stations. You have a captain, a communications officer, and a medic monitoring your vitals and other bodily functions, including your 'hull.' Those are the only 'yous' that are relevant in this metaphor. You following me so far?"

Since Pocky was a medic on an Oceanic Search and Rescue Squad, she could easily picture this. "I am, keep going."

"The medic suddenly reports that there's a breach in the hull and you're taking on water. An alarm goes off. Shutters start covering the windows. The medic yells at the communications officer that they need to contact the Healer. The communications officer relays that the coms went down as soon as the breach was felt. The captain immediately sends me here. The captain was in a state of panic for my safety, but otherwise, the other 'yous' were calm and factual about the whole event. It was weird, as you would say. Does that help you understand?"

"Not as much as I'd hoped, but thanks for trying."

"Sure."

Pocky looked down, only to see more of the vast universe in her dream that wasn't a dream. "It sounds as though I was in a terrible accident or something. Like contacting the Healer obviously means that I needed a medic, but I was never—"

"Contacting the Healer wasn't referring to a medic. It's literally a person that is referred to as the Healer."

"What's the difference?"

"A healer is someone specialized beyond what you are capable of as a typical medic. In truth, I've been trying to figure out how to contact that person."

"What for?"

"Because you need the Healer. We both do."

"Wait, I still need the Healer?"

"Yes, very much so."

"Why? Are you harmful to me?"

"I'm not, but something else is."

"Something else?" Pocky said, then felt her stomach sour. Whether it was Ember's reference to "something else" or something entirely different that made her stomach turn, she wasn't sure. "What exactly is 'something else'?"

"Best you not know."

Now it was Pocky who was annoyed. But she suddenly understood from their previous conversations up to this point that she wasn't going to get any further.

Ember sympathized with her irritation and spoke more gently. *"Look, I'm working on it for both our sakes. It's taken time and a lot of patience and trial and error, but in the next coming days, I'm going to attempt to get the Healer's attention."*

Pocky didn't like the sound of that. "By doing what exactly?"

"Best you not know, and you won't remember anyway."

"I don't like attention being drawn to me, Ember," Pocky said sternly. "And I don't like drama either."

"Tough shit, as you would say."

Pocky started to feel as though her sinuses were filling up with fluid, and she shook her head, trying to focus. "Why were you in my first subconscious level anyway? I mean, what are you, and why are you in me?"

"I won't answer for two reasons. One, you won't remember anyway, and two, the first time I told you, again, you lost your shit."

"I did?" Pocky asked. Her hands flew to her head. A sudden ache started to throb behind her eyes, and her stomach turned as though she hadn't eaten for some time. "Are you sure you're not harmful to me? Because I feel really sick."

"Even though your archives are inaccessible, your second subconscious level doesn't know that and has been trying to push you out. When you wake, you'll be confused for a moment, and then you'll be okay."

"Oh? I—"

"Time to go."

"What? Wait—"

Pocky awoke with a startle. A pounding sound was coming from somewhere. It took her a moment to comprehend that she was in her temporary quarters onboard a ship called *Gaia*. She sat up and rotated her legs over the edge of the bunk. The cabin consisted of two bunks that were so close to each other that there was no way to move around another person.

The pounding sound came again from behind the door. "Wake the fuck up!" a booming voice shouted in their military dialect they called Origin.

Bren, her medic partner, groaned from the bunk next to her. Pocky quickly got up and answered the door. Sgt. Daniger, a middle-aged man temporarily in charge of them until they were handed off to their new team, stood just outside with his usual annoyed gaze. He wore the typical IMF uniform: a black collared short-sleeved button shirt with a gray elbow-length tee underneath, black cargo pants, and boots, along with an eight-pointed hat with a visor. Additionally, he also carried a thick leather belt that holstered his gun, a radio, and other pockets with useful items. The entire ensemble was as imposing as it should be.

Pocky stood at parade rest and kept her expression neutral. "Yes, sir."

"Shit and shine. Report to C1 for debriefing in twenty-five, then meet at the Reception Area. Clear?"

"Yes, sir."

Pocky closed the door after Daniger walked away. Warm excitement filled her chest, and she smiled so wide her cheeks hurt. For the first time in eight years, she was finally going to be reunited with her brother.

But that warmth was quickly replaced by trepidation. This reunion was not by chance or coincidence, but by a carefully constructed plan that had been half a year in the making. More than that, though, the idea had been hers. In order for the plan to work, it required Thomas to be physically present. She hoped, if everything went well, her brother would be none the wiser to his part. But if he did find out, she hoped even more that he would forgive her.

2

Lance awoke to an abrupt voice saying ... something. The small vehicle jolted, helping Lance center where he was. He rubbed his eyes.

"I'm sorry, what?" he asked the driver.

"We should be seeing Daria Harbor soon," the woman replied in a tired voice.

Lance gazed out the window, beaming with anticipation as adrenaline pumped through his body. The driver, Mickala, had picked him up from his family's farmstead late last night and had been driving since. At twenty-three years old, he was finally leaving the only home and way of life he'd ever known, and for good this time. Before turning fifteen, he told his parents that he didn't want to be a farmer, inherit the farm, or settle down. His father naturally didn't take it well. Lance was, after all, their only son, and the first son always carried on the farm and traditions, and he was denying all of it.

It wasn't Lance's intention to be hurtful, but ever since he could remember, he'd never felt he belonged and couldn't shake that. It took time, but his parents eventually came to terms with the fact that his place wasn't with them and that he needed to be free to explore other possibilities. Though he had their blessing, he was at a loss for what he wanted to do with his life. He had first traveled to Theton and spent almost four years there before returning to Shad'Dyn. Instead of going back to his family's farmstead, he explored his home country. But after two years of trying to find something that would inspire him, he returned home feeling even more at a loss.

Then, by chance, Lance saw an ad in his local town for a new CCO research project that was looking for agriculturists. The Conservational Council of Oxtaria had been created for the sole purpose of conducting environmental studies around the world. Lance had seen these ads almost his entire life but had never applied because he wasn't interested. Though CCO projects were something people vied over, he was trying to get away from agriculture, not further pursue a career in it. But something about this one had made him pause. It looked no different from the previous ads, and per usual, nothing was said about where it was going to be, the longevity of it, or even how many people were needed for it. Yet he found himself interested in where it could lead. He was certainly qualified for the position and thought it couldn't hurt to explore the possibility.

To his disbelief, three days after he had applied, Lance was notified that he'd been selected for an interview. Even though he assumed his chances were still slim, he was excited about the prospect. His interview took place the following day at his local town's law office. A CCO Rep had greeted him and introduced herself as Ruckers. The woman was older than him by maybe a decade and had stunning aqua irises that stood out exquisitely against her ebony skin. Her other curious feature was her lack of hair. He'd never seen a bald woman before but felt she looked amazing with it.

Ruckers thoroughly reviewed Lance's background, including his farm life and their operations. After an hour, Ruckers thanked him and then told him the two words Lance didn't think he would hear so soon.

"I'm sorry, what?" he'd said, glad they were still sitting.

"You're hired," Ruckers stated flatly. "You are more than qualified for the agriculture position. But before you sign your name away, I need to disclose a couple of facts about the project before you fully agree to be hired. Clear?"

"Yes, ma'am," he managed to say, silently thanking the Divine Universe for not letting his voice crack.

"So, this project involves exploring an uncharted location and researching the plant life within the area. The longevity of this one is slated for up to a year, maybe even longer. Can you commit to that timeframe?"

"Yes, ma'am. Absolutely."

"Good," Ruckers said with a nod. "You will be teamed with two other agriculturists, a cartographer, an engineer, and two IMF medics. Your role is to collect, catalog, and store plant samples. Any questions before I continue?"

This sounded far more exciting than picking fruit all day. Lance tried not to smile too broadly as he asked, "When do I start?"

"Getting to that," Ruckers replied with more warmth than she had throughout the whole time, perhaps from feeling his elation. But then she looked away and frowned. "As with any project, there is always a risk of injury or death. There's no telling what you'll find in an uncharted area. But as an agriculturist, I'm sure you're no stranger to animals and insects, yes?"

"Yes, ma'am." Lance nodded with confidence as he could see where she was going with this. Or so he thought.

"Unfortunately, there's also a human opposition we're dealing with too."

"What?" Had he heard her right? *Human* opposition?

"There's a radical group that has attempted to stop CCO projects. We call them the Protestors."

"And they are?" Lance asked, frowning.

"People that have funding and too much time on their hands."

"Are they protesting against environmental harm?"

"Unsure. They haven't taken a clear stance yet." Ruckers shook her head. "But the CCO goes to great lengths to ensure that the ecosystems are as unscathed as possible in its research. Regardless, we have to warn everyone that's being considered for hire."

"Well ... how far have these people gone to try to stop you?"

Ruckers sighed heavily. Lance could see in her eyes that it was a valid question but looked reluctant to answer, as though her reply would deter him from wanting to take the job. And for most people, her assumption was probably right. For him, however, his choice would depend on her answer. He was good at reading people and could usually tell if they were being honest or not. Either way, if she was authentic, his decision would be easy.

"There have been injuries, but thankfully no one has been seriously hurt. That doesn't mean that there won't be, though. Your team will be under military protection at all times, and they'll take every precaution possible for everyone's safety. But nothing in life is a guarantee. Now ..." Ruckers eyed him warily. "Given these facts, what's your answer?"

Lance didn't hesitate. He was all in. Regardless of all the "what-ifs" and risks, he felt solidly for the first time in his life that this was the path he was supposed to be on. Plus, an opportunity to explore an uncharted territory was too good to pass up. His mind raced with the possibilities of where they might be going.

Ruckers slid a packet toward him. Lance took it and read over it carefully as she continued. "Your assigned project number is L5229, and your designated team name is GPT-2. Your Team Coordinator is Naiko Mascai. She handles everything pertaining to your needs and will train you for your job. This packet will be sent to her. So if you need certain medications or have specific dietary needs, she'll make all necessary arrangements. She'll also go over all CCO procedures and policies, what your accommodations will be, and so on. She also acts as a liaison between your team and the CCO and keeps everyone updated with what's going on or if there are any changes. Questions about that?"

Lance shook his head as he began filling out the packet. Ruckers remained silent until he was finished.

"Alright, you are to meet with Naiko and your team three days from now at The Traven restaurant in Daria Harbor for a complimentary breakfast and orientation. I will arrange for your transportation to get there. And the ship you and your team will be traveling on is called *Gaia*. The exact location of where you'll be going will be disclosed at orientation. Questions?"

"No, ma'am."

"Good. You need only to bring a backpack of clothes, nothing else. Hygiene products and other supplies will be provided to you. You are allowed to bring a small box of personal items, such as pictures or whatever you deem valuable. And finally, for you and your team's safety, everything discussed here stays in this room. You can't even tell your family that you have been hired. Clear?"

"Oh?" Lance tried to swallow his surprise as Ruckers frowned at him. "Right, okay. What should I tell them, then?"

"I don't know." Ruckers shrugged as she looked over his packet. "Make something up."

Lance mulled that over, thinking that shouldn't be too hard to do. Several minutes later, Ruckers had everything she needed from him. They shook hands, and she wished him a safe journey. He thanked her graciously and parted ways from the office.

When Lance got home, he couldn't hide his smile from his parents. But he did what Ruckers had instructed and told them he was going to work at a shipyard in Theton. Though they didn't want him to leave, his happiness was important to them. It was only then that he wished he could have done the same for them.

"And there it is," Mickala abruptly said, pulling Lance out of his reverie.

Even though the morning was still illuminating the landscape with fog obscuring his view out the front window, the unmistakable lights of the port appeared upon the horizon. Daria Harbor supported both passenger charters and tankers with the shortest route to Theton. The Charter Channel, as it was famously called, bustled with thousands of charters every day. Lance smiled broadly at the thought of being on one of those charters soon.

As they got closer, the fog lightened some. When a massive ship came into view, docked on the south side of the port, Lance did a double take. He'd never seen one of that scale before. It looked to be ten stories high and much larger than the mega tankers lined behind it. Though the design was different, it still had the same pattern as a regular charter ship with white topside decks and a black hull. Four black smokestacks also gave him an idea of how long the ship must be. It was impressive and intimidating.

"Is that a charter?" he asked in awe.

"If it is, it's the largest one I've ever seen," Mickala replied.

Lance peeled his eyes away from the ship, checking his reflection in the rearview mirror. He had shortened his dirty-blonde hair to the length of his thumbnail and trimmed his beard to a low, rugged look. He couldn't stand being completely clean-shaven and felt a little stubble should be okay. He met his brown eyes and smiled. He hoped to make a good impression.

As Mickala turned left onto the main road, the tires sloshed through puddles. She turned right, then turned again into a large mostly empty parking lot. A huge building with a covered porch was the center of the lot. A sign off to the side of the stairs read The Traven. Mickala followed the curved perimeter and stopped in front of the building. Lance's excitement had him feeling like he could shoot into orbit.

"Good luck," she said with a smile.

"Thank you for driving me," Lance said as he opened the door.

He put on his backpack and climbed out. Though Ruckers had said he could bring a box of items he deemed valuable, Lance didn't want to carry anything but his backpack. Plus, this was a fresh start to his new life; he didn't want anything from his old carried with him.

Once Lance was on the sidewalk, Mickala drove off. As much as he wanted to savor the salty smell in the air and listen to the sound of the ocean, he was eager to get inside. As he climbed the shallow stairs to the wooden porch, he appreciated the restaurant's rustic brown boards, rocking chairs, and hanging plants. It was a place that invited you to sit and enjoy the view.

The smell of food and coffee greeted him as he pushed through the double doors. The Traven was an adequate size and fashioned nicely with wooden pub tables, tall stools, and giant windows that gave a great view of the port.

Nearby, a woman was talking with a tall man. The woman was an older lady with faded green eyes and white hair that was pulled back into a bun. Her eyelids were flat and her bronze complexion shone with her pleasant smile. Her CCO attire of a light brown long-sleeve swoop-neck shirt and black pleated dress pants was very professional.

The man looked to be around Lance's age and had rugged features, light brown eyes, a charismatic smile, and thin, dark brown hair that stopped just below his ears. The man's buttoned black leather jacket hugged his torso while his ash-washed jeans were wrinkled and loose. To Lance, the man could have passed for a commercial model.

The duo seemed to know each other, as their body language showed an ease between them. As Lance walked toward them, they finally noticed him. The man stayed back while the woman approached and gave him a welcoming smile.

"Hi," she said. "Are you here for the project?"

"Yes, ma'am. I'm Lance."

"Ah yes, wonderful," she said as she stuck out her hand. "I'm Naiko, your

Team Coordinator."

"It is very nice to meet you, ma'am," Lance said as he shook her hand.

Naiko turned to the man behind them. "Lance, this is Haize. He's the engineer on our team and a returning member," she said fondly.

Haize approached and stuck his hand out for a shake. Dimples appeared as he smiled wider.

"Nice to meet you, Lance," Haize said as they shook hands.

"Likewise."

Gesturing toward Naiko with a hand on her shoulder, Haize said, "Naiko is one of the best TCs with the CCO. We're definitely in good hands here."

Naiko blushed and waved her hand dismissively at the comment. Clicking sounds and a muffled voice erupted from within her pocket; she quickly pulled out a radio and answered it.

"Naiko here."

"The charter is docking, ma'am," a feminine voice said.

"Great! I'll be there in a minute. Call, out," Naiko said, then clapped twice in delight. Turning to face them, she said, "That's for Kaori. She's another one of our agriculturists. I have to go pick her up. You two should get some coffee and get to know each other. We shouldn't be long."

"Yes, ma'am," Haize said with a cheeky smile, watching as Naiko rushed out the doors. He then turned his attention to Lance. "Don't know about you, but I need some coffee."

"Same," Lance replied with a nod.

"I'll get the server. You pick a table."

Lance nodded again and then headed for the table that gave the best view. He let himself soak in the excitement and took a reassuring breath.

He felt his life was finally beginning.

3

Thomas gazed out the window of his hotel room, trying to ignore the wet smacking sounds coming from his "guest." Though daylight was just warming up the view of the port, the massive ship he would soon be on couldn't be missed. The nameplate embedded on the stern read *Gaia*. When Ruckers had told him the name of their ship, he'd assumed it was a regular charter boat that was two-tenths smaller in comparison. He'd never seen or heard of one that was even close to this size. *A genius engineer must have designed it,* he thought. They were truly at the peak of the industrial age.

Besides being in awe of the ship, the sight of it also made him want to shout out like a little kid. The ship didn't just represent a new beginning to his life, but a reunion that had been long overdue with his twin sister. They hadn't seen each other since they were fifteen when they went off on their separate career paths. While he went into agriculture, she joined the IMF. He assumed they would have been able to meet up along their journeys, but when he had time off, she didn't, and vice versa. Their schedules never seemed to work, even when they'd tried to plan. The separation had been hard on them both, but today that was going to change.

Thomas looked at his appointed bodyguard, Fally, who sat at the small square table as he took advantage of the food service they were given for breakfast. Though Thomas didn't feel he needed the protection, the hotel attendant insisted he be given a guard regardless of his protest. To his astonishment, though, Fally wasn't just any bodyguard; he was an IMF-grade bodyguard. At first, Thomas hadn't been sure why a soldier was even needed but then remembered Ruckers had mentioned that the team would be under military protection.

Fally was built like a draft horse and intimidating-looking in uniform. He had rounded features and light brown eyes and skin. With his hat off, he was clean-shaven all around. Though the man looked formidable, he turned out to be a really nice guy.

"May I ask you a question, Fally?" Thomas asked.

"It depends on what you're asking for, sir," Fally replied as he smeared jam on a piece of toast, "but go for it."

His response didn't surprise Thomas. Unless you were in the service, the IMF refrained from sharing information about their operations and culture with outsiders. Since information was passed around by word of mouth or local papers, very little was known about the military outside of the services they provided. What was common knowledge, though, was that the majority of IMF soldiers were orphans. And orphans were considered Theton's trash because they were from lower class provinces, so that didn't help the IMF be warm and open to the public.

Iarothia was the largest province in Theton. It bordered along Xozon from coast to coast. According to Pocky, the vast, flat, dry land enabled the IMF to build everything they needed to run an efficient military power. Everything they used was made by their own infrastructure, from weapons to ships, from clothing to medicine. Even entertainment, such as sports and music, was produced within their compounds. But his question had nothing to do with any of that.

"Would you happen to know of my sister?" Thomas asked as he sat across from the soldier. Though it probably was a long shot, with the two of them being in the service, he figured there might be a chance they knew each other.

"She in?" Fally asked, then took a bite from his toast.

"Uh, yeah, been in for eight years."

"What's her name?" he asked with a mouthful.

Thomas had always referred to his sister as "Sis." After going through the initiation trial, she earned what the IMF deemed a Given Name. Though she wasn't thrilled with how she'd earned it, the name fit her perfectly, and she embraced it with fondness. He did as well.

He smiled. "Pocky."

Fally tilted his head to the side, mulling the name over before answering. "I've heard it, but I don't directly know her. Why?"

After her first letter, Pocky stated that she was going into the medical field, but that info was nothing new. Being a medic had been her passion from the moment she could read. When she graduated at sixteen, she was assigned to the Oceanic Search and Rescue Company, or OSAR. At first, she was all too excited to talk about the training exercises she was undergoing and couldn't wait to go on real rescues. She also talked fondly of her squad and how they were quickly becoming a well-oiled machine.

Then, around a half year later, Pocky went dark and didn't speak again of anything that pertained to her military life. Bren, their best friend since they were eight—who also happened to be Pocky's med partner—had also gone quiet. Because both of them had gone silent at the same time, and given how the IMF operated, Thomas figured that maybe they couldn't disclose anything military related after their training was done. They still spoke of other things at least, and they sounded happy. Though he was curious as hell about the restricted side of their life, he never pressed either one of them.

Thomas was hoping to learn something about Pocky from an outside view, but it didn't matter because he would see her soon. She and Bren just happened to be his team's medics. When Ruckers had told him the news, Thomas had made a complete spectacle of himself by cheering, but he didn't care. He was reuniting with his family after eight long years of being apart. Nothing could compare to how happy he was then and still was.

"Just curious," Thomas replied nonchalantly, then stood. "I'm gonna shower."

"Sir? Aren't you gonna to eat?"

"Nope, I'm going to eat with my new team at The Traven. Have all you want, big guy."

"Fuck yes!" Fally exclaimed, pounding both fists on the table.

Laughing, Thomas headed for the bathroom. The anticipation of the day ahead filled him with the same gusto as his guest felt about his food. The team would be arriving soon, and Thomas wanted to be one of the first people there.

He couldn't wait to meet everyone. But he'd never been on a project before, and nervousness churned in his stomach. The hot shower helped settle him a bit.

After stepping out of the shower, Thomas wrapped his lower half with a towel and then wiped the mirror as he set about fixing his hair. Even wet, it fell past his shoulders in waves, and his crimped beard was almost just as long. He loved it that way, but it hadn't always been kept in this style. In fact, he was far different now than when Pocky and Bren had last seen him. His golden tan had darkened from years of being outdoors, and he'd gone from an awkward, lean frame to a tall, muscled build with well-defined abs he worked hard for. How different would Pocky be after all these years? Regardless, their eyes—their matching blue eyes—would still be the same.

When Thomas was done grooming, he stepped out of the bathroom and winced at the sudden cold air in the room. As he went for his leather backpack to retrieve his clothes, he eyed Fally curiously, who had finished eating and was busy cleaning up his mess. Was Fally's attention to detail something that had been instilled in him by the military, or had he always been that way?

Thomas dismissed his curiosity and pulled on a pair of loose blue jeans. He grabbed a short-sleeved white shirt next, leaving the top buttons undone. Once he had his boots on, he checked himself in the full-length mirror.

"Looking good there, sir."

"Thank you, Fally."

Thomas went for his backpack. Everything he owned was inside, and he preferred it that way. Since he was on the move a lot, he always traveled light. He slung the bag over one shoulder and found Fally already waiting by the door, one hand on the knob.

"You coming with me to The Traven?" Thomas asked.

"Yes, sir, I am," Fally replied with a grin.

Thomas smiled back. "Well, alright then. Let's go."

When Fally opened the door, Thomas's stomach instantly dropped. A tall, heavyset man blocked the door completely. He wore a tan pelt coat, white slacks, and shiny brown shoes. His black hair was slicked back with an expensive gel Thomas remembered all too well. In his hand was a brown paper bag.

Shit, fucking shit, Thomas thought.

"Hello, brother." The man—Stellan—beamed.

Thomas backed away, any response he could muster caught in his throat. *Oh, shit, no.*

Stellan frowned, his eyebrows furrowing. "Well, aren't you happy to see me?"

Thomas didn't realize how far he had backed into the room until he felt the table against his legs. He'd unknowingly dropped his backpack along the way. *Stellan, here?* Thomas's lungs tightened. Stellan was the only son the esteemed Hyashi family household had produced. His unwed father, Cannon Hyashi, compensated for the lack of children by buying Thomas and Pocky when they were four. Their four years of living there had been one long nightmare, and Stellan had been the worst part of it.

Stellan took a step inside the room. "Brother?"

Thomas swallowed, unable to answer. What was just as startling as Stellan's unannounced presence was his appearance. His brown skin looked ashen and waxy with dark liver spots. Stellan was even more hideous now than when they were kids. What was even worse was the stench that emanated from the guy, like he had rolled in something dead. Thomas put the back of his hand over his mouth and tried not to gag.

Fally stepped in front of Stellan, blocking his entrance. "Sir, you are not welcome here. You need to—"

Stellan's eyes widened. "Don't you dare speak to me, flea!" he roared. "You have no authority here, so fuck off!"

"And you have none over me! So make me, asshole!" Fally challenged.

The two men were almost chest to chest, seething with anger and heavy breaths. Though Fally could very much handle himself, Thomas suddenly feared for the man's safety.

"F-Fally, please! Step aside," he pleaded. "It's okay."

It took a second for Fally to comply, and he did so reluctantly, casting a few annoyed looks in Stellan's direction.

"Stellan," Thomas said, trying to infuse delight into his voice. "What brings you here?"

Stellan's upper lip twitched as he refocused on Thomas. "When I saw your name on the project, I thought how lovely it would be to see you and catch up."

"M-my name?" Thomas asked. "H-how did you know that I'm on the project?"

"I'm a board member with the CCO."

Of all the people to be a board member ...! Why would Stellan be one? The boy Thomas once knew had never been about making the world a better place like the CCO intended. Stellan liked hurting anything that moved and had, at times, forced Thomas to watch him do so. Memories of those moments flooded Thomas's mind, and he instantly felt sick, but he held it down. He had to get out of this situation somehow.

"That's, um ... neat," Thomas said with as much interest as he could.

"It is, isn't it? In another five years, I'll become an Executive Board Member," Stellan said proudly. "Wouldn't that be something?"

The CCO consisted of three execs who ruled over ten board members, as well as the project coordinators. Below them were the project development teams, the reps, and then the team coordinators, who came last. Thomas paled at the thought of Stellan gaining a seat, overruling all those people. There was no telling what havoc the man would unleash.

"We should dine so I can fill you in on everything," Stellan said. "Have you eaten at Shellers? The fourth floor has a gorgeous view of the port."

"Um, well ..." Thomas swallowed hard. "T-that's nice of you, but I've already eaten, uh, hotel food. Maybe when I get back? I have to get going for orientation. I'm already super late."

Stellan's eyes narrowed. "That's how it's going to be, little brother? I haven't seen you for fifteen years, and this is the reaction I get? You're not even at least a little bit thrilled to see me?"

Of course, Thomas wasn't thrilled! Stellan's reign of torment began the very moment they had entered the Hyashi household. The man's first "welcome to our family" gesture was spitting in Pocky's face. Thomas never had any affectionate feelings toward Stellan as a person, let alone as a brother.

Unfortunately, Thomas's grim expression and silence only made the situation worse. Stellan's face twisted with fury. Fally began to breathe heavier as the guy stepped farther in, holding up the paper bag.

"Alright. Let's do this another way. Get in the bathroom, shave your beard, and cut your hair. You'll find a pair of scissors and razors in here. I also brought gel in case you needed it, and clearly you do. *And* I brought proper clothes for you to wear as well. What you got on"—Stellan waved a hand toward him—"will not do."

"S-Stellan, please don't do this," Thomas whimpered.

"Don't do what? I'm only here to help you. Now, get going. I want to get on the ship before your team does."

"You're going?" Thomas asked, mortified at the thought.

"Yes, I am," Stellan said with a twisted grin.

"Why?"

"I already told you. I want to catch up, and what better way than to come along on the project with you?"

The lustful look on Stellan's face made Thomas want to retch. The man had always had perverted feelings toward him. Just thinking about it made Thomas's skin crawl. It was also the very reason why Stellan had spat in Pocky's face when they walked into the household for the first time. When Stellan tried to embrace Thomas, he had a bizarre look on his face. Pocky had quickly assessed Stellan's intentions and intervened to protect Thomas. He couldn't begin to imagine—didn't want to imagine—what his life would have been like without Pocky there to protect him. She, as well as the servants, had to continuously protect him from Stellan's constant desire to want to be alone with him.

His current situation was getting out of hand, though, and Pocky wasn't here to get him out of it this time. Thomas had to try and deter Stellan from going somehow.

"Stellan," he started with more firmness in his voice. "Please let me do this on my own. If you truly"—Thomas paused, trying to hold bile down as he spoke on—"love me as a brother, let me go on my own."

"If you want to see your cunt sister, you'll do as you're told!" Stellan shouted. "Or I will remove you from the project!"

"Alright!" Thomas yelped, then forced himself to take a calming breath. "Okay, alright, I'll do as you say."

He snatched the bag from Stellan and headed for the bathroom. He had hoped Stellan wouldn't use Pocky to push him to this point, but the man knew that she was Thomas's weakness.

"He still needs to attend orientation, sir," Fally said. "As a CCO board member, you should know how badly it would reflect on him to not show up."

"Naturally. We will be there," Stellan said in a calmer, more sophisticated voice than before.

Before Thomas fully closed the door, Fally shouted after him, "I will not leave you alone, sir!"

The vow in Fally's voice gave Thomas some comfort. Even though they were adults now, the thought of being alone with Stellan completely revulsed him. *What a fucking mess,* he thought as he tried to pull himself together.

Thomas opened the bag, frowning as he reached for the scissors. As he began to cut chunks of his hair off, he let the tears flow, but he wouldn't allow himself to cry aloud. How was Pocky going to react to Stellan being here? He had hoped the project and being with her again would be the beginning of a happier life. Now he wasn't sure what the future would hold with that monster around.

After finishing his hair, Thomas then began to carefully cut his beard away. As he trimmed, he met his eyes and was suddenly filled with an unexpected hope. His eyes were her eyes, and he drew strength from that. His hair would grow back, and so would his beard. What was important was that Pocky would fight for him, and so he needed to do the same.

4

Before sitting across from Lance, Haize removed his jacket and nodded at the waitress approaching their table. After the waitress set up their table with water and coffee, they began a casual conversation about their families as they flavored their coffees. Lance was surprised to learn that Haize had also grown up on a farmstead. With being an engineer, he had presumed Haize was from Theton. Specialized schools for such professions were all over Theton, whereas on Shad'Dyn, they were few and far between.

"Yeah, I've lived in Theton long enough that I've probably lost my accent," Haize joked. "But good on you for finally breaking free of traditions as well. I can completely relate."

"No doubt," Lance said, pleased they had something in common.

"So, how big is the fam?" Haize asked, hinting at a common inside joke.

"The usual. Parents, grandparents, dozens of aunts and uncles, and ..." Lance grinned, then they said the last words together. "And a shitload of cousins."

They laughed before Haize went on to talk about his passion for engineering. Unlike Lance's struggle, Haize knew exactly what he wanted to be very early in life. The guy spoke of particularly enjoying building motorized bikes. That was typical of an engineer though. They were tinkers and inventors in their trade. Masterminds, really, and the current times worked in their favor. The massive ship outside proved that.

"My father about lost his shit when I fiddled with one of the tractors that was giving him heartburn," Haize said, then sipped his coffee. "Until he realized I fixed the problem. After that, he really didn't want to let me go. But at fifteen, I was gone before the sun rose that day and didn't look back or go back unless I had to."

Lance nodded. Fifteen was the permitted age to leave home. Though it was more of a free choice than it was a legal matter, he had considered joining the IMF when he became of age. It was the only direction that had appealed to him at the time. Being a soldier felt more right than anything else ever had in his life. He didn't know why he felt strongly about that, especially since he knew very little about the IMF. Though they had a few bases within Shad'Dyn and way stations along the coast that supported OSARs, there was little interaction between them and the public. Regardless of that, he was ready to commit. To his disappointment, however, the only youngsters they took in were orphans. Unfortunately, that wasn't commonly known in Shad'Dyn.

Instead of going home, Lance took the opportunity to travel across Theton, hoping something else would inspire him. What he discovered opened his eyes about how boxed in his upbringing had been despite growing up in a vast, wide-open space. Though people visited Shad'Dyn, it was surprisingly a very small number compared to Theton's actual population. He had never been around so many people at once before, practically shoulder to shoulder no matter where he went. At times it had even been suffocating. From the provinces he journeyed through, he learned that the majority of people within each one knew very little outside of themselves besides their neighbors. And there were thousands of provinces. That made the disconnect between nations clearer.

Despite how crowded Theton was, he endured and searched in the hopes of finding himself. After almost four years, nothing stood out as a calling, and he returned to Shad'Dyn. But instead of going to the family farm, he continued traveling within his home country. Though he found nothing different from the way he'd grown up and didn't see the point of exploring further, he continued onward for another year before finally returning to the farmstead. Though being a farmer and inheriting the farmstead wasn't the worst life he could live, he still couldn't shake the sense that he was supposed to be doing something else or to be somewhere else. And the longing to be a soldier never fully went away either. Though the last few years had been a struggle, he was content with where his path was heading.

"I'm really looking forward to all of this," Lance thought out loud.

"Same here. I've been under training for the last few, so this'll be my first solo project. I'm super fucking excited to finally be on my own," Haize said with a cheeky smile.

Lance nodded. "So, what exactly is an engineer needed for on the team?"

Haize was all too happy to answer—and used his hands expressively. "The habitat we'll be living in has technology that will blow your mind, Lance! It was built with all kinds of equipment that, as an engineer, is even beyond my imagination. But as fancy as everything is, there still needs to be an engineer to fix or repair anything that breaks. And believe me, there's always something that does. Doesn't matter how advanced technology is; something always needs tending to."

"Technology like what?"

"Hang on, I'll get my workbook so you can see for yourself!" Haize went to his backpack and rummaged through it until he found the book he was referring to. Before sitting back down, he handed the flexible manuscript to Lance. The cover was worn from years of use. "This book covers every piece of equipment and habitat the CCO uses for projects. Look up Habitat Sub Unit Seventy-Two."

Lance found the section and was immediately amazed by what he saw. The first image was a transparent outline of the habitat from an outside view. It initially appeared as an ordinary one-floor apartment raised off the ground by pillars with a stairway that led to a covered porch placed in the center of the building. When he turned to the next page, the diagrams gave more details about the layout of each room. Haize's handwritten notes along the sides were in a language Lance was sure only an engineer could understand.

As Lance read farther into the chapter, he scrutinized the technology Haize was referring to. His mind was indeed blown away as he tried to understand the mechanics. The entire habitat was powered by solar panels, and every room was voice-activated for lights, desired temperature, and even music. The kitchen was equipped to make cooking easier, including a processor that would chop vegetables in mere seconds and an appliance that could rehydrate food. And that was only the beginning as he read on.

When Lance reached the end of the section, he looked up at Haize with amazement. "This is incredible."

Haize wiggled his brows. As Lance put the book down, he couldn't help but wonder why some of this technology wasn't used in everyday households. The solar panels and kitchen appliances would be especially useful.

"So, where did all this tech come from anyway?" he asked.

"It's military technology, believe it or not," Haize replied with a broad smile.

"Seriously?"

Haize nodded firmly. "I felt the same as you when I first learned of this. They're a hundred years ahead of the rest of us and got some of the brightest people working in my field. I hate to admit it, but it makes me look like an amateur. The CCO at least finds me useful though."

"Still, where do they find people with capabilities like that?" Lance asked.

"At any engineering school, there's an event in our final year to invent something that we then present to the IMF recruitment team to evaluate. They assess if our work is something they deem useful for them. For most of us, it's a make-or-break moment before our careers even start."

"I thought you had to be fifteen and an orphan to join?" Lance asked.

"That's true for the majority that join, but seeking talented people like engineers and scientists is part of what makes the IMF so efficient in what they do. To do what they do, they need people that go through specialized schools so that they can advance in technology."

"Huh," Lance considered. "Did you create something for them to see?"

"I certainly did," Haize said with a slow nod, his eyes heavy as he blinked.

"Mind if I ask what happened?"

"I didn't make the cut."

Haize didn't say anything further and had a faraway look as he held his coffee mug midair. Since the guy was an engineer and was good enough for an institution like the CCO, Lance got the sense that maybe it still wasn't the same as being selected to work for the IMF.

"Are you bitter?" Lance asked.

Haize lifted his head and shrugged. "Yeah, kind of. Well, I mean I have no ill will toward the IMF about it because obviously I wasn't creative enough to get their attention. It was my own doing, and I can't be upset with them for that. But I do get frustrated with myself sometimes when I look back and think of the 'what-ifs.' What would my life have been like if I had just been better, you know?"

Lance nodded. He knew that feeling.

Haize suddenly perked up as though he was done brooding and downed his last sip of coffee. "Anyway, *Gaia* is equipped with some of that tech, so you'll have a chance to get familiar with it along our way to wherever we're going."

"*Gaia* was modified by the military?"

With an amused smirk, Haize cleared his throat before saying, "Ruckers interviewed you, right?"

"Yeah."

"And she didn't tell you?"

"Enlighten me," Lance said with a shrug.

"*Gaia* may be the property of the CCO, but she's an IMF battle cruiser. I know you saw her on your way in. She can't be missed."

Lance raised his eyebrows and couldn't help the smile spreading across his face. "You're fucking kidding."

Haize didn't hold back his own cheeky grin. "Yes, sir, that big girl's our ride."

Before Lance could bombard the engineer with questions, the front doors of The Traven flew open. Naiko walked in with whom he presumed was Kaori, who looked relieved. She was pale with thin lips, a pointed nose, and an oval face. Freckles sprinkled across her cheeks and nose. Her bob haircut was light red, a stark contrast to her casual cream-colored linen pants and a loose light blue collared button shirt. She hefted her backpack—her only belongings, it seemed—higher on her back.

"Hi, we're finally here," Naiko said, then let out an annoyed sigh. "The ocean is choppy today. Took forever for the captain to dock her boat."

"She at least took the care to get us there safely though," Kaori said. She had a harsh accent that Lance hadn't heard before.

"You got a point," Naiko said, then directed the woman toward them. "Guys, this is Kaori. She's a specialist in not only agriculture but botany and horticulture as well. Neat, right?"

Lance's first impression of Kaori was how reserved she was. She was calm as though she was just strolling through a park and slowly taking in her surroundings.

"Welcome to Shad'Dyn, Kaori," Haize said with gleaming eyes and a wide grin.

"Just call me Kai. And thank you. I'm really thrilled to be here," she said nonchalantly and then turned to Lance with an open hand. He shook it, not surprised to feel remnants of old calluses. In their line of work, calluses and wounds were the norm.

"Very nice to meet you, ma'am," he said.

A light laugh escaped her as she said, "Really, just call me by my name. I don't like being that formal."

The front doors opened again as another woman entered The Traven. Her dark brown spiral curls floated around her as she twirled in a circle. Her tight blue jeans showed off her curves, and her pink tank top exposed her lower belly. She was carrying her bag with a single strap across her torso.

"Hello, are you here for the project?" Naiko asked.

The woman turned in surprise and then laughed. "I am! Hi! I'm Bayana," she said whimsically, as though they were on a holiday. "You can just call me Yana."

"Ooh, I like that," Kaori said quietly.

Naiko introduced herself and then the others. Instead of shaking their hands, they each got a hug from Yana. Lance laughed lightly; he liked her free-spirited nature. Kaori was the only one who didn't look thrilled about the hug, and Yana took immediate notice of this.

"Sorry." She laughed nervously. "I've had way too much coffee."

"No, you're fine," Kai assured her.

"Yana here is our cartographer and another first-timer," said Naiko.

Yana did a cute little bow as they welcomed her to the team.

"So, you're obviously from Shad'Dyn," Haize said to Yana, then turned to

Kaori. "And you're from Theton, but I can't quite place where exactly."

"I'm Alysian. It's a very small province in the northeastern corner next to the coast. We don't use Thetonian as a first language."

From his travels, Lance learned that most provinces didn't use Thetonian as a first language. Haize, despite having lived there since he was fifteen, acted as though this was the first time he had heard such a thing.

"Really? I'd love to hear more about it!"

"Maybe later," Kaori said, putting a hand to her throat. "I'm still feeling seasick and could use some water."

Since charters were small in design, every movement and motion of the ocean could be felt, making people easily seasick. Lance recalled all too well the endless barf sounds on the first day he had traveled to Theton and the six days thereafter. Though he did get nauseous, he gratefully never felt the full effect like some had. Now Kaori's demeanor made sense.

"Oh no, Kai, please sit. I'll go get some," Naiko said, then hurried off.

Everyone sat at the table, and Haize casually got a conversation going between himself and the ladies. While Yana was giggly and bouncy, Kaori remained reserved as she spoke. Lance sat back in his chair and considered his team, enjoying the banter. The setting easily gave him a picture of what the next year was going to be like, and he smiled at the image.

5

Before entering Conference 1—or C1, as it was usually called—for their debrief, Pocky and Bren carefully inspected their uniforms. The military expected them to always appear professional and sharp. All soldiers took that aspect very seriously to represent the pride in who and what they were.

Their uniforms were nearly identical with V-neck scrubs. However, instead of cargo pants, Pocky wore capris that stopped just below her knees, which were split at the sides. She also wore black running shoes; she loved to run on any occasion and found these much better than the typical heavy hiking boots.

After looking themselves over, Pocky and Bren then scrutinized each other. Pocky smoothed out the creases on Bren's muscular back. Her partner was well above average height for a man, even though everyone was tall to her. His black hair complemented his light brown skin, and he kept it cut in the usual low and tight way all military men were required to have. They were allowed to grow beards as long as it was maintained properly. Bren kept his no longer than his thumb.

They switched places, and after a quick review, Bren tugged the sleeve of her scrub shirt and then gently patted her shoulder. "You're good, Partner."

Pocky nodded her thanks, then wrangled her wavy dark brown hair back and adjusted her hat. She pulled on her fingerless gloves. She usually didn't wear them, and only Bren knew the real reason why she was using them today.

Finally, they double-checked their guns, ammo, and medical packs, then calibrated their med watches. The devices not only updated them on time but with their vital signs as well, and they were an essential tool when someone needed medical attention. Pocky's had been alerting her to false alarms for the last few days, and she hoped it would function properly today. Once their watches blinked green, they were ready.

Pocky hissed in a deep breath as her nerves suddenly exploded. Eight years of not seeing her brother had taken its toll. The circumstances of how they were brought together now were eating her up. Bren placed a hand on her shoulder. When she gazed up at him, his brown eyes and small smile reflected genuine kindness. He knew what this day meant to her but was unaware of how that came to be.

Except for higher ranks, all military personnel were required biyearly to participate in a project. The CCO and the IMF had worked out their relationship that way. For Bren, there had been nothing new to that routine when they had been assigned to this new project. But this one in particular was being used to lure someone that Pocky had hoped to never hear about again: Stellan Hyashi.

He was as vile as a human being could get, yet even she was surprised that the guy had managed to get the IMF's attention. She didn't know what he had done, but there had to be a terrible reason for her people to turn a CCO project into a trap for the man. Thomas, unfortunately, was the bait. That part had been her idea.

Pocky put a hand over her mouth and gagged.

"Whoa! Hey, Partner!" Bren gripped her by her upper arms. "Pocky? You good?"

Though Stellan wasn't expected for the next couple of days, the notion that she had even suggested for Thomas to be used as bait made her insides liquefy. Pocky grabbed onto Bren's shirt, trying not to fall over as her breathing quickened. The very idea of that fucker being near her brother made her want to break the ship in half. Stellan had made his intentions toward Thomas very clear from the moment they had entered the Hyashi household.

"Shit! Pocky? Don't fall apart on me before our brother gets here. I don't want to have to explain why I had to throw you in the clinic."

Bren's threat made Pocky swallow back whatever was trying to come up. She took a minute to gather herself up, and then they quickly straightened their uniforms again. Bren pulled out a small towel from his pack. She realized then that she was crying.

"Fuck, what's gotten you so shaken up?" Bren asked as he started wiping her face.

Because the operation to arrest Stellan was secretive, Pocky couldn't reveal her part or why she was falling apart because of it. In a way, she felt she was betraying Bren just as well. He wasn't just her med partner of the last seven years; they had been best friends ever since they were eight. They were so close that some even wondered why they weren't together as a couple. The military was already a family in itself, with everyone tied to each other like long-lost siblings—especially for the orphans who made up the majority of the service. For both of them, though, their friendship was more profound than a couple could ever be. Plus, he was already committed to *Gaia*'s Security Chief—or SC Viper, as she was usually referred to as. Though their relationship wasn't open knowledge among their colleagues, he was still dedicated to her regardless.

After wiping Pocky's face off, Bren put the towel over her nose and told her to blow. "Okay, we gotta get in there, or we'll be in a world of shit. You good?" he asked as he tossed the towel into the bathroom across from C1.

"Yeah, sorry. I just—"

Bren waved a hand dismissively. "S'ok. You alright without your sling?"

"Yeah, my shoulder feels better today," Pocky said, a half-truth. She felt she didn't need the sling because it didn't alleviate her discomfort, but some believed otherwise, including Bren. However, he at least didn't push her to wear it. The issue with her shoulder was unfortunately something that wasn't ever going away, and the damn sling would never change that.

"Good. Just don't let Geara see you without it."

Pocky nodded.

Geara was their Executive Officer—or XO—overseeing the Stellan operation. Because of that, he was also in charge of the entire ship for the duration of the project. Roughly a year ago, Pocky had been approached by the man after he had learned that she and Thomas had lived in the Hyashi household. At first, he just wanted insight into the guy. Apparently, Stellan had eluded their attempts to find him. Her assistance eventually led to where they currently were. *What a fucking mess.*

"Okay, ready, Partner?" Bren asked with hope in his voice. Pocky nodded and followed him inside C1.

As usual, the debrief was quick and simple. The officer reminded them to speak in Thetonian when around civilians and to represent the IMF to their fullest capacity. Though Thetonian was universal, it was Pocky's least favorite language to speak. It was slow, with some syllables being dragged out longer than words should be, and at times had a whine to it similar to a child pining for something they badly wanted. Origin was in her top ten favorites. The IMF's language was rapid so that soldiers could communicate quickly. It also had some letters that buzzed or vibrated off the tongue. She loved that sensation when she spoke it.

The officer also told them that their project was the only one going this round and that the IMF was using the space to train recruits. This was highly unusual, but Bren thankfully didn't question why. Though *Gaia* was a battle cruiser, the IMF allowed the CCO to utilize the ship, enabling the institution to conduct multiple projects concurrently. To anyone else, it would seem a waste of resources just to transport one team for a project. However, in Geara's attempt to capture Stellan, and to minimize potential casualties, he had canceled all projects except this one. They weren't even using CCO employees for staff positions. It was all being run by soldiers this time. Besides Pocky, the only ones who knew the real purpose of this operation were Geara's Spec Ops team.

After being dismissed, they made their way to what was called the Reception Area, which was located on the second level under the stern's well deck. They found Daniger standing by the gangway looking outward. Usually, the place was filled with soldiers awaiting to be escorted to their assigned teams that were either being hosted at The Traven or another restaurant the CCO typically booked.

"Good," Daniger said flatly without looking away. "Still waiting for the order to go, so relax."

"Yes, sir," Pocky and Bren said in unison.

Pocky stood at ease while Bren began pacing in a wide circle. His boots pounded into the dark wooden floor with every step. This was one of his signature ways to deal with nervous tension. Bren always got this way before meeting a new project team. Given the turbulent relations between the IMF and civilians and their personal history of rescue calls, Pocky understood his trepidation. Though Bren made his judgment of the civilians before even meeting them, Pocky liked giving them a chance first. She hoped Thomas's presence would ease Bren somewhat—and maybe even enjoy a project for once.

"You need to relax, Music Man."

"I will, once—"

Shooting pain flared in Pocky's right shoulder blade. She winced as she hefted off her med pack and began to rub her shoulder.

"Hey, you okay?" Bren asked as he walked up to her.

Knowing he would see through even the slightest fib, Pocky sighed. "I don't understand. It's been getting better, but—" She turned away and grimaced as another wave of sharp pain erupted.

"Where's your sling?" Bren demanded.

"I don't need it."

"Woman, don't make me put the damn thing on you!"

"I'll be good, I swear," Pocky said, but Bren raised an eyebrow, obviously unconvinced. "Look, I just want one damn day with Thomas without the drama. Okay? Please."

Bren glanced away and sighed. He knew firsthand just how protective her brother could get when it came to her well-being. After another moment, he said, "Alright, fine. Take a few painkillers at least and put the sling in your front pocket just in case."

"Yes, sir," she said with a forced smile.

Bren resumed his pacing as Pocky grabbed her canteen from a side pocket and downed two pills. A pungent stench suddenly filled the air, and she knew who was coming before he entered through the port side doorway. She sighed as Shox stepped in a moment later. He was filing his nails and looked to be chewing something. He was a tall man, but Bren still towered him by a head. He was also pale and lean without muscle, obviously doing the less than minimum requirement for exercise. For some reason that eluded her, though, the man stunk badly. It wasn't body odor, but it was a reek that reminded her of unclean toilets.

Shox was what the IMF called a Floater, which was someone who was without a team. Given the man's record of being kicked off every team he had been assigned to, Pocky was surprised that he wasn't the first person to be kicked out of the IMF period. But once you were in, they owned you for life. Even when someone retired or was too injured or old to carry out their duties, they remained in and were cared for until they passed on. Shox, however, was a special case. Because of his outrageous and unruly behavior, no one liked him, let alone knew what to do with him. The man was a prankster, not in the fun way but in the pushing everyone's buttons kind of way. He had already pulled one too many on her just within the last several days.

Pocky narrowed her eyes at Shox when he spotted her. He flashed a sinister grin.

"Hiya, Pocky," he called mockingly.

"Fuck you, Shox."

Daniger turned and snapped, "Where the fuck is your babysitter, you piece of shit?"

Shox shrugged. "Dunno. Taking a massive shit maybe."

Daniger pulled out his radio and barked orders for someone to get Shox. The man wasn't bothered by this in the least; he continued grinning at Pocky, then began laughing to himself.

"Hey, remember that time—"

Bren stepped up, halfway blocking her view. Pocky was more than happy to move back and let her partner handle the guy.

"Leave her alone, asshole."

Shox smiled even wider as though amused by the challenge. "Shit, man, I'm really surprised you're not banging that ass—"

Bren chased Shox for a few steps, ready to hit him, but Daniger intervened before that could happen. "Fucking cut it out!"

Another officer Pocky recognized—but didn't personally know—ran out from the port side corridor and began shouting at Shox. The soldier apparently was his appointed warden.

"Sorry, sir. I can't even use the head without this fucker ghosting me."

Daniger got in Shox's face. "I hear you do that again, I'll toss you in the brig!" he snapped. "Clear!"

"Yes, sir," Shox replied, tempering his smile. "I'll be a good boy. Promise."

Their sergeant looked at the other soldier. "Make him run fifty laps."

"Yes, sir," the soldier replied with a smile. He grabbed Shox by the shoulder and directed him toward the stairway.

"Oh no! The humanity!" Shox taunted as they climbed.

"Wait!" Daniger shouted. The babysitter immediately halted. "Make him do fifty laps and then put him in the brig. I don't want him seen by the civilians."

"Yes, sir."

After the men disappeared, Bren let out an exasperated sigh and looked at Daniger. "Sir, why the fuck is that asshole still here?"

Daniger motioned for Pocky to move away so that he could speak more privately to Bren. She complied and went to the starboard side of the Reception Area and looked out one of the square windows. Though they spoke in low voices, she could still hear every word.

"Listen, I'm not supposed to say, but a report went very high up to headquarters. That crap he pulled on Pocky was the last line crossed on his long list of fuckups, and they're working on a more suitable punishment."

"Good to hear something's being done about it," Bren said. "That guy is beyond redemption."

"Agreed," Daniger said. "But you didn't hear all this from me, clear?"

"Yes, sir," Bren said, then joined Pocky. "You okay?"

"Oh, I'm not gonna let that guy ruin my day," Pocky said. She meant it too. "I'm good."

Bren nodded with a small smile.

Silence engulfed them. Pocky tried not to look at her watch every five seconds while Bren resumed pacing. The painkillers thankfully kicked in and gave her some relief. After several minutes, Daniger's radio finally clicked. Their sergeant answered, then looked at them when the call ended.

"Time to go. Move out!"

Pocky smiled broadly as she carefully put on her med pack. She couldn't believe she was just minutes away from seeing her brother again. As they walked, every time her betrayal threatened to surface again, she would force it back down. She was under orders to keep the plan quiet anyway and couldn't warn or tell Thomas even if she wanted to. Orders were orders without question, but that didn't lessen the sting. But for one day, she would fight to keep it back and enjoy their long-awaited reunion.

6

After getting out of the shower a second time, Thomas dressed in his new clothes and shiny brown calfskin shoes. He applied the gel into his hair and styled it the way the Hyashi servants had taught him years ago. Looking at himself in the mirror, he instantly felt disgusted and wanted to punch his reflection. At first, he'd felt like a scared little boy when Stellan had shown up, but now anger mixed in with his fear. That asshole was just a CCO board member whose job was to solely approve funding for proposed projects and had no authority over anyone. Still, Stellan was dangerous. Dangerous in a way that Thomas and Pocky understood all too well. There was only one way that Stellan had found him, and the notion of that made his fear go up another notch.

Thomas had always felt the Divine Universe had given him an aptitude that went beyond what was typical for twins. As twins, he and Pocky had always had a special connection. They could gauge each other's thoughts and speak simultaneously; that was just their norm. However, when Pocky was within a certain distance from him, he could *feel* exactly where she was. Literally. Sensing her energy was like seeing a tiny flame on a candlestick moving around in the dark. Strangely, though, she did not possess the same ability or anything remotely like it. She wasn't bothered by that and was instead honored to be a twin of one who did. Though Thomas didn't think he was any more special than anyone else, he did feel a tremendous appreciation for having such an ability, like it was a way of protecting her.

Stellan, however, had a similar ability, but it wasn't for one specific person. Somehow, the man could detect the heartbeats of any living being regardless of barriers or materials between them. And Thomas knew for a fact that Stellan had found him this way. Why the Divine Universe had given them both such a gift was beyond him. A balance of wills or nature, he didn't know, but it left him wondering if the Divine Universe understood the difference between good and evil. For Stellan was the poster boy of pure evil.

Before Thomas exited the bathroom, he took a long breath. Throughout his time regrooming himself, he'd been able to hear Fally and Stellan speaking but unable to understand them. Though they were being snarky to one another, so far they had kept the volume down. Until now.

"Fuck you!" Fally shouted.

Thomas opened the bathroom door just slightly and asked, "What's going on? Fally?"

"We're good here, sir. But we do need to get going," Fally said, his voice loud but steady.

"Okay, I'm almost done." Thomas was going to shut the door all the way, but when Stellan spoke, he paused.

"So, I had also heard—"

"Know what I've heard, sir?" Fally interrupted sharply. "We're pretty close to getting the assholes that are responsible. And when we do, we each get to piss in their face. I'm especially looking forward to getting my turn."

Thomas had no clue as to what the soldier was referring to and wasn't sure if he wanted to know. His priority was to get to his sister. That was all that mattered right now. He stepped out and went for his backpack, then stuffed his clothes and boots inside.

"You look beautiful, brother," Stellan said with lust, licking his lips.

Fally let out a snort that was between amusement and disgust. Thomas grimaced and hurried to the door. His bodyguard somehow managed to get behind him before Stellan could, and Thomas was extremely grateful not to have that guy breathing down his neck. By the time they got outside onto the sidewalk, Fally and Stellan were spewing heated obscenities at each other. In the end, when silence fell upon them, Thomas wasn't sure who had won the battle of words.

When The Traven was in his sights, Thomas wanted to break into a run.

Perhaps sensing that he would, Stellan yelled for him to stop. He reluctantly did so and turned to face the man.

"Here's what we're going to do," Stellan said as he leaned in closer to Thomas. "I'm going inside with you. You will have five minutes to introduce yourself, then we're leaving for the ship."

"But I have to stay for orientation!" Thomas exclaimed. "I can't miss that."

Stellan hitched his upper lip and spoke through gritted teeth. "You have five minutes or nothing at all."

Knowing he was pushing Stellan's patience and not wanting to unleash what could happen if he pushed the man further, Thomas relented. "Okay, fine."

"I'll inform my XO that you're coming onboard," Fally said, "but I'm not leaving Thomas."

Stellan almost growled in reply. "Acceptable."

Again, Thomas felt tremendous relief that Fally was staying with him and hoped Stellan wouldn't embarrass him in front of his team. Even more so, he hoped Pocky would be inside. Sadly though, when he reached the top of the stairs to the restaurant, he didn't sense her presence. Her flame had gone out as the distance grew between them when they parted ways eight years ago, and he hadn't felt it since. *Will it still even work?* he wondered.

Thomas didn't realize he had stopped before the entrance until Stellan slammed the door open. His chin twitched nervously as he went through the doorway.

***

Lance was about to take a sip of his coffee when the front doors of The Traven opened with a bang so loud that it made everyone but him flinch. The two men who entered looked out of place. They were both well-groomed with dress suits and ties as though they were on a business trip. The taller one frowned, and he squinted as though annoyed by something. The other man looked worried and kept his eyes focused on the floor. Besides the hair and clothes, the two looked nothing alike.

A soldier not far behind them spoke quickly into his radio. Lance wasn't sure if the soldier was for the men who just walked in or for all of them. The guy stayed by the doorway as the suits stepped farther in. Naiko seemed to suddenly recognize them and quickly approached.

"Shit," Haize whispered. "That's Stellan Hyashi. Everybody stay quiet, I'm serious."

They did as the engineer instructed.

"Naiko Mascai, I presume?" the taller man asked.

"Yes, sir. This is an honor. I wasn't—"

"Yes indeed. I'm sure it is for you. This is my brother, Thomas," Stellan said with a proud smile. The second suit—Thomas—seemed appalled; his jaw dropped, making Lance anxious as to what the guy's predicament was.

"Oh!" Naiko said. "I didn't know Thomas was related to you."

"Do you know any other family with the last name Hyashi?" Stellan asked condescendingly.

Disgusted by Stellan's attitude, Lance looked to Haize in a way to ask if they needed to intervene. Even though he looked to be feeling the same, Haize gave a quick head shake, indicating not to. Lance reluctantly held himself back.

"I apologize, sir. Thank you for—"

"I'm letting him introduce himself to the team," Stellan interrupted. "Then we will be on our way."

"Uh, with all due respect, sir—"

"I don't give a shit what your fuss is, woman."

Naiko straightened her posture and spoke more firmly. "With all due respect, sir, he has to stay for orientation. As a CCO board member, you are not to interfere with—"

"Ma'am!" the soldier shouted. "An escort is on their way to get your team. You can conduct your orientation onboard. I promise Thomas will be there. Clear?"

"Uh ... okay." Naiko huffed. "If that's how it has to be."

Stellan glared at the soldier, seething with anger. He then turned to Thomas and spoke through gritted teeth. "You have five minutes."

Stellan stalked off toward the entrance. The soldier held the door open and then followed Stellan outside. No one seemed to breathe until the door was fully shut. Everyone looked at Thomas expectantly. He gave Naiko an apologetic smile as he walked up to her.

"I'm not like him, I swear," Thomas said. "I'm truly sorry for his actions."

Naiko exhaled a shaky breath and then put a hand up to her forehead. "It's alright. I just didn't know you were related to him."

"Oh, I'm not! My sister and I were, well, we were sort of adopted. But we dropped the surname when we left. It's a long story that I'd rather not get into."

"That explains why I didn't see the surname on your papers." Naiko shook her head dismissively and then put her hand out to him. "I'm Naiko Mascai, your Team Coordinator."

Thomas's face lit up as he shook her hand. "It is a pleasure to meet you, ma'am. I'm so happy to be here."

"It is very nice to meet you. An honor really."

"Please don't treat me like that," he said, frowning. "I'm no different from everyone else here. My sister and I are not aristocrats in any way. I promise I'm a hard worker and not afraid to get dirty. And I'll follow orders without any questions or hesitations."

"Well, I ..." Naiko gave him a real smile. "I'm very pleased to hear that. Let me introduce you to everyone else."

Everyone stood and met them halfway. Thomas shook everyone's hand as Naiko stated their names and titles. Lance liked the guy right off. Thomas had an innocent way about him and seemed as though he would be easy to get along with.

"I'm looking forward to working with you both," Thomas said to Lance and Kaori.

"We are as well," Kaori said with a smile. "You're ready to dive in, huh?"

"Oh, I'm beyond ready to get started. You have no idea how much I want to rip this monkey suit off and burn it!" Thomas laughed.

Everyone laughed with him, but the tension returned as the front door swung open with a bang. Again, everyone but Lance flinched.

"Thomas!" Stellan roared.

"Sorry!" Thomas shouted back, then quickly turned to Naiko. "Please, tell my sister I can't wait to see her."

"Oh?" Naiko said in surprise. "She must be one of our medics then."

"Yes, ma'am. Her name's Pocky. We're twins," Thomas said proudly.

"Oh! That's—" Naiko started.

"Thomas! Now!"

Thomas spoke as he began walking backward. "You guys are gonna love my sister. She's great!" He then turned and walked outside after Stellan.

When the door fully closed, everyone let out their version of an anxious sigh.

"Good grief," Haize said, rolling his eyes as he rubbed his forehead.

"Who was that jerk? The tall one I mean, not the hot guy," said Yana.

"That was one of the CCO board members," Naiko replied. "Stellan Hyashi."

"Oh shit." Yana's eyebrows lifted. "What a dick."

While the comment got a shocked reaction from Naiko, Haize laughed hysterically. Lance just shook his head at the absurdity of all of it.

"Okay, that's enough," Naiko said to Haize with a playful smack on his arm. When she turned her attention to Yana, she spoke sternly. "And you, tone down your vocabulary."

Yana immediately straightened herself. With wide eyes, she replied earnestly, "Yes, ma'am."

"Alright, before we leave, let me make a quick call," Naiko said as she pulled out her radio and then moved away.

Kaori excused herself to the ladies' room while the rest of them sat back down. Lance quietly sipped his water, mulling over what just happened. The whole event was bizarre, and he didn't know what to make of it, but then again, he had never been around an aristocrat before. If they all behaved that way, then he was glad that he hadn't met one.

When Kaori returned, Naiko was finished with her call. "My apologies, people, but we're gonna have to move our breakfast onboard the ship. Our escort is on their way. Let's go meet them."

Lance was fine with that idea. As everyone got up and gathered their bags, he pushed away the strange end to their time in The Traven, his excitement renewed as they headed for the giant ship that would become their home.

7

Pocky and the others were halfway to The Traven when Daniger's radio clicked three times in rapid succession. This indicated an urgent matter, and they stopped immediately for their sergeant to answer. Daniger moved away for more privacy. Pocky and Bren exchanged concerned looks as Daniger's voice rose with every word.

"Motherfucker!" the sergeant shouted after ending the call. He glared at them, dark anger in his eyes. "Follow me!"

As Daniger took off toward one of the warehouses, Pocky and Bren followed. Once they reached the door, he ordered them inside. The place was dark and without windows. They grabbed their flashlights from their packs, and as they caught their breaths, Daniger was once again on his radio.

Pocky looked at Bren with unease and mouthed, "What the fuck?"

He just shrugged, his eyes wide. She didn't want to speculate, but she hoped this had nothing to do with her brother or Stellan. And if it did, she would have coarse words with Geara regardless of his rank. She'd told the XO everything she remembered about Stellan, from his heinous tormenting of her to his perverted intentions toward Thomas. She had revealed everything except for his ability to feel heartbeats and recognize individuals just by their pulse. She wasn't willing to risk her career by making such a claim—mostly because it was too fantastical even for her, but also because she wouldn't know where to begin to explain such a phenomenon like that.

Pocky had hoped what she had given to Geara was enough and wouldn't hear any more of the matter. But then several months ago, the XO sought her help again, reaching for anything that could help capture Stellan. When she had nothing else to give, he'd stormed off. Perhaps feeling a sense of duty, she had run after the man. She had hated what she was about to do but did so anyway—and regretted it ever since. She thought back on that moment with mixed feelings.

"Sir!" Pocky had said with a quick breath. "I have an idea."

"To find Stellan?" he muttered and kept walking. Geara was a lightly tan man with flat eyelids and an oval face. He was either allowed to grow out his black hair a little or just hadn't bothered to have it properly cut; Pocky wasn't sure. His gray hairs had grown more abundant over the months, and though the stress of the job was obviously taking its toll on him, his stony expression always remained unreadable. If anything, the XO's voice carried more emotions than his facial features.

"No, but I know a guaranteed way to lure him out."

Geara slowed his pace, seeming to mull over her words. After a couple more steps, he stopped altogether and turned to her in disbelief. "Your brother?"

Pocky felt her face pale as she whispered, "Yes, sir."

Geara thought on this for a minute as logic overtook assumptions. "Yeah, but after all these years, would Stellan still feel that way toward him?"

"Yes, sir. I highly believe so." With another heavy sigh, Pocky licked her lips, then continued before she could think better of it. "Thomas moved to Shad'Dyn before starting school because of a close call. That fucker is obsessed. I'm positive it'll work."

Convinced, Geara set up a meeting with other superior ranks. Pocky was mandated to be there as well. She listened as the XO and the others came up with an idea to bait and ensnare Stellan in their trap. Since Thomas was an agriculturist and Stellan was a CCO board member, a project was going to make the perfect setting to draw the guy out. Many of their Spec Ops personnel were already working within the institution. To Pocky's surprise, one of them turned out to be Ruckers. Spec Ops were the kind of unit that infiltrated as though they were ordinary people. Even other soldiers couldn't tell them apart from civilians. They were that good. She had known Ruckers for years and had no clue.

After Geara and the others were done writing up the plans, the only thing they couldn't understand was Pocky's insistence that they actually had to use

Thomas as bait. When the XO had first pitched the idea to the higher ranks, they hadn't realized that she meant to literally use her brother. They had argued for almost an hour trying to persuade her that he didn't need to be involved, let alone be at the port. They said they just needed to use his name and that Thomas didn't even need to be privy to what they were doing, but she asserted that his physical presence would be vital for their trap to work. Trying to convince them of that without revealing how was incredibly challenging to the point of wishing she had just kept her mouth shut. But she had opened this door, and she needed to follow through.

"I know him," she'd said. "You can't lure Stellan with just Thomas's name on paper. The moment that asshole steps onto the ship, he'll know immediately if Thomas is really there or not."

Naturally, all of them looked at her in disbelief as to how that was possible.

"Okay, well, what if we get a decoy that looks like Thomas?" one officer asked.

Pocky slammed her fists down on the table, making everyone flinch. "Believe me," she said, her voice filled with fire, "I would much rather use a decoy and keep Thomas out of this, but I was brought here because I know Stellan better than any of you. And I'm telling you, he'll know! And all of this will be for nothing!"

To Pocky's surprise, Geara was the only one who was convinced. "I agree with her. Thomas needs to be physically there. It'll make it more authentic."

"Okay," one officer replied respectfully despite her skeptical tone. "Tell us your thoughts on how," she said to Pocky.

"Thomas doesn't need to be in sight. He just needs to be on the ship. That's all. I know that sounds batshit crazy, but you have to trust me. Without seeing him, or even being on the same floor, Stellan will know."

Geara vouched for her, and with reluctance, the other officers agreed. After everyone had left the room, Pocky broke down into an uncontrollable sob. The weight of what she'd done slammed onto her shoulders and hadn't lifted since.

Months later, the Spec Ops team set everything they needed for their trap. The Project Coordinator, who was also a spec operative, sent a fake affidavit to the board members of a later date the project team was supposed to meet, while

Ruckers made sure the team would have the real date. The project was now in motion.

Pocky swallowed hard as she took in the dimly lit warehouse, again praying that whatever was currently going on didn't involve her brother. She wanted to ask Daniger, but he slammed the side of his fist against the door and yelled another obscenity. Minutes went by and nothing happened until another call came over Daniger's radio.

After ending that call, Daniger looked at them with some relief. "Okay, your team is on their way. We're going to meet them. Clear?"

"Yes, sir," they replied in unison.

Pocky wanted to feel the same excitement as before, but she wouldn't until Thomas was in her sight. As soon as her team came into her view, she was going to make a run for it. Yes, she would get in trouble, but it had been eight years, and it was worth the consequences.

***

Thomas was grateful for Fally staying between him and Stellan. The soldier had a hand against his left shoulder, pushing him forward at a brisk pace. He didn't realize how much distance Fally had put between them and Stellan until Fally spoke again.

"We're gonna get you out of this, sir. Just trust us, okay?"

"Yes, sir," he replied, hitching a smile as nostalgia poked at his mind.

Thomas trusted the IMF immensely. He and Pocky had been dumped into a corrupt orphanage that sold children. That was how Cannon Hyashi had bought them. They lived in the household until she suddenly felt the urgency to run away shortly after they had turned eight. At first, he feared the consequences if they were caught. But she had insisted, and he couldn't refuse her plea. The Divine Universe was on their side for once, though, for what happened after turned out for the betterment of not just their lives, but also for one of their most cherished friends, Bren.

They had taken a steed from the manor's stable quite a distance before continuing on foot. They ran as fast as their little legs could take them. Thomas remembered how hard it was to keep up with Pocky; she ran as though someone's life depended on it. How very true that had turned out to be. By the time they had reached an abandoned industrial park, Thomas felt as though he was going to pass out, but she needed his help and encouraged him to follow. He didn't understand but trailed after her anyway. Somehow, she had heard the cries of someone stuck at the bottom of a two-story dumpster. That person turned out to be Bren.

Bren was an orphan from the same orphanage they had come from and had gotten away before being taken by a purchaser. He thought he was being clever by hiding in the dumpster, but then he couldn't get himself out. He was little back then and couldn't reach the first metal rung on the ladder designed for adults. Thankfully, they figured out a way to get him out, and Bren had cried in Pocky's arms for almost an hour. The poor kid had been stuck in there for two days and thought he was going to die alone. The three of them had forged a bond and formed a family from there.

After Pocky tended to Bren's wounds, they were at a loss for what to do next or where to go. They wandered into the nearest town, trying to think of something. Bren spotted a local law agency and suggested going in. Thomas agreed but came up with a plan in case that idea went south. Unbeknownst to them, the agency was actually an IMF station. From there, they were sheltered and protected in a different orphanage until they were fifteen.

As they got closer to *Gaia*, Thomas pushed away his memories and appreciated the giant ship. It was truly intimidating up close yet a marvel of what she represented for the future. *What's next? Flying vehicles?* he thought and almost laughed out loud at the absurdity of that notion.

Barking from up ahead made Thomas refocus on his current predicament. A cluster of soldiers from a canine team surrounded the gangway and were heavily geared with rifles. The sight of them gave him even more confidence in Fally's words. He dared a glance over his shoulder. Stellan was not far behind and surprisingly sported a casual expression. Thomas figured it was to keep up appearances in front of others. However, the military seemed to know what

Stellan was. But what outcome did they want from this situation? As long as they got him out of it, Thomas didn't care.

When they reached the gangway, Fally pushed past Thomas to clear the path. An officer gestured for Stellan to ascend the gangway first.

"Welcome to *Gaia*, sir. By right as a board member, please."

Stellan snubbed his nose at the soldier before replying, "Naturally."

"Ruckers is in the Reception Area waiting for you, sir."

Stellan headed up the gangway. Fally let Thomas go ahead after a long gap but kept a hand on his shoulder. Halfway up, movement caught his attention on the port. Two soldiers were running down where they had been. Maybe it was the escort Fally had mentioned earlier to Naiko?

Fally encouraged him to keep moving. Once inside, a crowd of soldiers moved behind them, blocking the entrance. He looked around for Ruckers, but he didn't see her anywhere. Instead of meeting the CCO Rep, he watched a group of soldiers approach Stellan.

Thinking he was supposed to join them, Thomas started over, but Fally quickly steered him toward the stairs instead. When they reached the foot of the stairs, Thomas looked back at Stellan, fearing how he would react to the sudden departure. So far, Stellan's attention was on the officer speaking with him.

Before Thomas disappeared to the next floor, Stellan glanced over and met his gaze. The man didn't react in a way that Thomas had expected. Instead of scowling or erupting in a tantrum, Stellan relaxed his brows and smiled. An electric chill skittered through Thomas's body. He knew then with certainty that the man was up to something.

Fuck.

8

Lance and his team were crossing the main road when their escort met them. An older man was followed by a woman who looked to be in her early twenties. She had a dark bronze complexion, and her straight black hair was pulled back into a tail. She pointed her rifle down as her light brown eyes scanned the area, and didn't stop to greet them as she moved past them to take up the rear. Despite holding his head high, the man looked troubled as he walked up to Naiko. She slowed her pace as he approached and then almost stopped.

"Don't stop, keep walking," the soldier said, waving them on.

"Yes, sir," Naiko replied, a hint of anxiety in her voice.

"I'm Executive Officer Geara," the man said as he fell in line with Naiko, "and this is *Gaia*'s Security Chief Viper. We're here to escort you to the ship."

"Oh! Well, thank you, sir. I wasn't expecting you to personally escort us, but I appreciate it," Naiko said, then turned and looked at them. Her pleasant expression looked forced. "Everyone, this is XO Geara. He oversees our security and military personnel on the ship. And, um, sir?" She slowed her stride as she looked back at Geara. When the XO didn't slow down with her, Naiko rushed to catch up to him. So did everyone else. "Sir! I'm sure you were informed that Hyashi is—"

"Yes, I'm fully aware of the situation, ma'am." Geara interrupted. "We're handling it. Hyashi won't further interfere with your team or the project. You have my word."

"Oh? Oh, good! I wasn't told that he was even coming, otherwise I would have made proper arrangements for his arrival."

"We're handling that too."

"Oh? Well, thank you again. But one of my team members is with Hyashi. Thomas—"

"We handled that too. He'll be waiting for you in the Starboard Café."

"Is he okay? He didn't seem to be comfortable in Hyashi's company."

"He's fine. Hyashi is just being a dick."

Yana let out a sharp laugh and said, "Ha! Told you!"

Naiko gave her an unamused look and sighed. Lance smiled, glad for the assurance that the whole event had been just an aristocrat being a jerk and nothing else.

Everyone remained quiet as they walked through an alleyway and onto the port. A looming tanker came into full view. Since civilians weren't allowed around this part of the port, Lance appreciated the chance to see the large ship up close. But when they turned toward *Gaia*, the sight of her was so incredible that he slowed a little, completely in awe of the giant ship. Seeing it from a distance outside the harbor didn't do the vessel justice. His admiration made him lag behind his team a bit. Haize slowed his stride until they were shouldered again.

"Impressive, right?" Haize said proudly.

"Yeah, it is."

"A floating city she is. Even has her own clinic."

Lance almost couldn't believe it. "What are those?" he asked, pointing to the three levels of spikes along the hull.

"*Gaia*'s a battle cruiser; those are her guns."

"Fucking for real?" Lance asked, turning toward Haize in amused disbelief.

"Yup, there's six hundred on each side. They can't move though, they shoot straight on."

"Damn, well that should deter any Protestors from getting up close."

"Right! I never had an encounter with them, but that in itself would make me turn around."

They shared a laugh before Haize continued telling Lance of *Gaia*'s other finer parts when Yana spoke up.

"Wait, where are—" she began.

"Sir?" Naiko called. "What's going on up there?"

Lance looked ahead. Down by the gangway and along the port, there was some sort of military activity in motion. A convoy of large black trucks was unloading a slew of soldiers. Some even had dogs with them. He was astounded to see that many uniforms. If Naiko hadn't asked Geara about it, he would have assumed the numbers were normal.

"We're training Freshers."

If Lance had to guess, he presumed "Freshers" was a reference to recruits.

"Oh? Yeah, that makes sense. Especially since we're the only team you're transporting."

"Wait, we're the only project going?" Haize asked.

"Not only that, but we're gonna be the only civilians onboard," Naiko replied.

Haize raised his eyebrows curiously. "What? Not even staffing onboard?"

"Nope," she replied with a pressed smile. "Crazy to think, right?"

"Gonna be boring," Haize said with a sigh, then looked at Kaori. "But we'll at least get our own cabins."

"Well, I for one will definitely appreciate that," Kaori said flatly. "I don't like crowded spaces."

"Well, with you being a nature girl, I'm not surprised," Haize said with a laugh. Kai gave him a snarky smile, then laughed with him. Lance didn't mind either scenario but appreciated having his own cabin for his first project.

A woman in uniform cheerfully ran toward them from across the port, grabbing everyone's attention. Two other soldiers were not far behind her. As she ran, she began shouting something he couldn't hear yet. Her enthusiasm was like daylight punching through an overcast day. He smiled, wondering what was so joyous.

Geara abruptly spoke sternly to all of them. "Do not mention Thomas or Hyashi. Clear?"

"Ah, okay. Is that Pocky running at us, then?" Naiko asked.

"Yes, she's expecting her brother to be here. They haven't seen each other in eight years, so this might get emotional."

"Oh great," Haize said under his breath. "Incoming cry fest."

Viper, who had moved slightly ahead of them, turned and glared at the engineer for a moment in disgust. Lance bit his upper lip, feeling embarrassed by his teammate's remark and tone. Haize's manners were a sudden contrast to his earlier conduct.

"Oh? That's a long time—"

"Not a word!" Geara shouted.

"Yes, sir," Naiko replied hurriedly.

As Pocky came closer into view, Lance's breath escaped involuntarily and his heart stopped. Her eyes grabbed him first. The blue hue shone against her brown eyebrows—which looked like they had been drawn by a master artist—and her wavy hair bounced jubilantly with every step. He smiled wider as she got closer, but then frowned when he finally understood what she was shouting.

"Brother!" Pocky shouted again in excitement. Her glee slowly faded as she realized her brother wasn't responding. Without stopping, she weaved from side to side, looking at all their faces. The pain on her face was heartbreaking. She slowed to a walk and then halted altogether. "Thomas?"

Geara raised a hand, waving her over. She put on her hat, then jogged to the XO. Instead of facing forward and walking beside him, she walked backward ahead of him with ease.

"Sir? Where's my brother?" Pocky asked between heavy breaths.

Before Geara could answer, the other two men caught up. One was heated red in the face and was clearly about to yell at Pocky when the XO intervened and told the man to head for the ship. Simultaneously, Viper ordered the other man to follow her and went off in the same direction.

Pocky looked puzzled by the XO's orders. "Sir? What's going on?"

Lance was surprised she had asked in Thetonian instead of in Origin.

"Thomas is already onboard the ship," Geara replied flatly.

Pocky turned to look at the ship and then back at him. "Why's he on the ship and not with our team?"

"There was a situation. It was handled."

Her eyes widened. "What situation? Is he okay? Was he hurt?"

"He's fine. I'll debrief you later." Geara said firmly, then scrutinized her. "Where's your sling?"

"I'm fine without—"

"That's not what I asked!" he barked.

"My pocket."

"Put the damn thing on!"

"Yes, sir." Pocky took off her pack and pulled the black article out, but then had a dilemma of holding the pack while dressing the sling.

"I can hold your pack for you." Lance offered.

"Much appreciated," Pocky said as she handed him her pack.

Lance watched as she slipped the sling on, wondering what had happened to cause her to need it. When she was ready, he offered to carry the pack for her.

"Thanks, but I can manage," she said with a small smile.

Lance handed the pack over. Pocky reached for the right shoulder strap with her left hand and then placed it in her right hand to hold. He frowned. Seeing that this routine wasn't new meant that whatever was wrong with her arm had been ongoing for a while. Or she was just that adaptable.

Pocky then turned to Geara and waved her left hand around the sling. "Satisfactory, sir?"

Instead of answering, he said, "Introduce yourself."

"Yes, sir." She turned toward their Team Coordinator with a smile. "Naiko Mascai?"

"That's me! Nice to meet you, Pocky," Naiko said.

As they shook hands, she replied, "Happy to serve, ma'am."

"Pocky is such a cute name. Mind telling how you got it?"

Pocky looked away and almost rolled her eyes. Lance couldn't tell whether it was the reference to her name being called cute, or if it was the question that bothered her.

"After my initiation trial, the group I was with teased me about my height. They said I was so small and cute that I could fit in their pocket. So, for a few days, I was called Pocket, but then it was shortened to Pocky."

"Oh? Well, I think it's adorable."

"Thank you, ma'am," Pocky said. "My partner goes by Bren. Just for civilians, though; we all call him Music Man, or just M. Just for you to know so that you don't get confused."

"Music Man, huh? That's original. Let me guess, he likes playing music?" Naiko said with a chuckle while snapping her fingers.

Pocky laughed. "Something like that."

Her laughter made an explosive excitement rush across Lance's chest. He was more captivated by her than the ship or any other ingenuities that pushed the limitations of the human mind. He wanted to hear more of her laugh, more of her voice.

"So, you're with an OSAR squad, huh?" Naiko asked.

Lance looked at Pocky's insignia embroidered above her right breast pocket, which read OSAR Squad AOT-86. Underneath those words was her rank as a First Class Medic and her name.

"Yes, ma'am," she replied proudly.

"Bet you got some great stories." Haize piped in with cheeky enthusiasm.

"I don't share stories," Pocky said, her words polite but stern.

Haize's demeanor instantly changed to a blend of disappointment and annoyance. Perhaps feeling an awkwardness brewing, Naiko said, "So, um, are you excited to see your brother again? I heard it's been a while."

"Yes, ma'am, very excited." Pocky perked up. "You're gonna love him. He's great."

The fact that she and Thomas had used the same words to describe each other amused Lance. It wasn't often he'd met twins. Though they were vastly different height-wise, he could see the similarity in her beautiful eyes. He tried not to stare, but it was hard not to.

Pocky then went on to greet Yana. Their cartographer seemed anxious as they exchanged words, as though she wanted to voice something else but refrained. Haize was next, and while he kept it polite, he wasn't as warm as before.

"So, what's up with your arm?" Haize asked dryly, as though he had to be the one to ask.

"No," Pocky replied flatly. She moved away and faced forward.

Clearly her arm wasn't open for discussion. Lance could understand why Pocky wouldn't want to air out her business in front of a bunch of strangers. He would feel the same in her position. Though he was curious, he was more interested in knowing who she was.

Pocky abruptly turned and stepped in line ahead of him, again walking backward. Lance swallowed nervously. Her smile was radiant. He smiled back and hoped it wasn't goofy looking.

"And you are?"

"Lance, agriculturist. Nice to meet you."

Pocky's eyes lit up as she spoke. "Oh! Are you the one that grew up on a farm?"

Her eyes were so mesmerizing that he almost forgot she had asked a question. It was only after he realized a few seconds had passed that he exclaimed, "I did! Yeah, I did."

Pocky bit her lower lip, as though trying to hold back excitement. "That is so cool. I hope you don't mind if I ask you a million questions."

"Certainly, but have you not met an agriculturist who grew up on one?"

"You would think, right? But the ones I've met are usually from Theton, straight out of school. There's definitely a huge difference."

"Huh, yeah. Very true."

"I would have loved growing up on a farm, so I appreciate you indulging me."

"Sure. I can even take you there if you'd like," Lance said, then immediately hoped he wasn't being too forward.

Pocky beamed. "I would love that."

Lance smiled at her, again hoping he didn't look awkward as he did. She was the most stunning woman he'd ever seen. Perhaps sensing his awe, Pocky blushed and looked away. He couldn't help but grin wider at how cute that was.

She then went on to Kaori. When the woman greeted her, Pocky tilted her head curiously and then spoke in another language that matched Kai's accent, which immediately made the woman jump in delight.

"Oh my gosh! You know how to speak Alysian?" Kaori asked.

Instead of answering in Thetonian, Pocky went on speaking in Kai's native tongue, and the two engaged in a happy conversation. Lance was even more intrigued as Pocky spoke fluently. Her voice was beautiful even when annunciating the harsh words.

Something Kai said excited Pocky, and she spoke more quickly. Kai matched her energy, but her retort had Pocky slowly frowning, and her golden complexion paled. She stopped walking, which caused a chain reaction for all of them to stop. Something was obviously very wrong.

9

Pocky's gaze narrowed at Geara as shock and anger washed over her. Her throat tightened. The very scenario that was never supposed to happen was happening.

"Pocky?" Geara asked, eyes wide as he looked at Kaori and then back to her.

Because she didn't want her team to know about her business, Pocky went against protocol and replied in Origin. Her lips felt like concrete as she spoke. "Stellan ... is here."

"Shit," Geara said sharply, looking away.

While Pocky was speaking with Kaori, the woman revealed that despite Thomas's quick appearance, it had been nice to meet him. Excited, Pocky had asked Kai how he looked. The reply she got was not what she had expected.

"Oh! He's so handsome! He looked so nice in his suit and tie," Kaori had said.

Stellan was here earlier than Geara had planned, and even worse, he had already intercepted Thomas. The suit and tie were a dead giveaway. Her brother hated suits and ties and had vowed to never wear them again after their stay at the Hyashi household. He was an outdoorsy guy and preferred clothing that he didn't mind getting dirty and sweaty in.

Pocky was numb. Her worst fear had become real.

She stepped up closer to the XO. "Stellan got to Thomas before he got to The Traven?"

Geara waved at her team in a quick motion for them to continue on, but Pocky was so focused on the man that she wasn't sure if they obeyed as the XO tried to explain. "I had a soldier with him. He was between Thomas and Stellan the whole time. He—"

"When did Stellan get to him?" Pocky interrupted, her voice rising with every word.

"Before they left for The Traven. But my guy handled it and got Thomas safely onto the ship."

Pocky curled her upper lip. "And Stellan? Did you arrest him?"

"We did," Geara replied with a nod. "He's in the brig and secured. Your brother is safe and waiting—"

"Why is Stellan here early? How did he find out the real day we were boarding?" Pocky snapped. Knowing Stellan's ability, she didn't need to ask how that asshole had found Thomas.

Geara's voice rose slightly, a sign of his growing impatience. "I don't know yet. But I can assure you—"

"You need to get Thomas and these civilians away from here."

"I just told you Stellan is secured. He can't harm anyone in there."

"With all due respect, sir, you don't know him."

"I know him a lot better than you think I do."

"Then why did you even need my help?" Pocky waved her hand dismissively. "Doesn't fucking matter anyway. You still need to get my brother and the civilians away from here."

"No," Geara replied through gritted teeth.

"At least delay—"

"I said no!"

"Why?" Pocky asked, throwing her left hand out sharply.

"We are mandated to transport your team on time regardless of the situation."

"Un-fucking-believable. I'll get him off the ship myself then," Pocky muttered, turning to leave.

Geara grabbed her left shoulder strap, spun her around, and got in her face. "Pocky, I'm giving you a direct order," he said, voice low. "You are locked into this project, but if you obstruct, I'll remove you and have you walk back to base. Clear?"

Following orders was important, but Thomas's safety was more important. "Sir, please remove my brother," she said.

"No. Don't push me again."

"If Stellan is here before you planned it, only means he has a better one," Pocky snapped. "I did my part, I'm clean. But if anything happens to my brother because of your fuckup, you'll lose all my respect."

That phrase, the loss of respect, was rarely spoken from one soldier to another. It was a cut that went deep into the heart, regardless of rank. Though it was just a threat, Pocky could still see the hurt in Geara's eyes.

He let go of her strap and then did a double take to his right. "This isn't a fucking show! Move!" He then looked back at her. "Go with your team. Now!"

"Yes, sir," she replied in the same tone.

Pocky jogged off past her new team, the sting of embarrassment hot in her chest. She didn't stop until she was far ahead of them. She couldn't bear the looks on their faces.

"Pocky?" Naiko's voice was suddenly next to her. She turned her head to look at the woman but didn't stop moving. "You okay?"

Stellan almost got my brother, and that's my fault.

"No," Pocky replied uninvitingly, hoping Naiko wouldn't push.

"What can I—"

"Ma'am, I'm gonna say this as respectfully as I can. Stay out of my business."

Not wanting the TC to have a chance to retort, Pocky decided to run on ahead again. As she went, her anger threatened to turn into sorrow. Her eyes and throat burned. It took a lot for her to push it down. She walked the last couple of steps to Bren, who was standing by the gangway, and caught her breath. Her partner nodded in a way that told her he had been informed. She stood at parade rest next to him and swallowed a painful gulp. He broke protocol and placed a sympathetic hand on her shoulder.

Pocky steeled herself, thinking of Thomas. This was not how she pictured their reunion. She thought they would have a few days to catch up without the worry and stress of Stellan being nearby. Now she was anxious as hell about what that guy was up to, and that would be on her shoulders until he played his hand or whenever Geara removed him from the ship. She trusted the XO, but she should have known better and stayed out of it when Geara approached her a second time. And most importantly, she should have kept Thomas out of it.

Viper stepped up to her and began to explain how they extracted Thomas and what Stellan's current status was. To Pocky's disbelief, he was surprisingly being cooperative despite his situation.

"So," Viper continued, voice still confident and proud, "once the recruits get onboard, the convoy will take Stellan to the nearest base." The SC paused and then placed a compassionate hand on Pocky's arm. Off duty, they were close friends, and the woman knew very well what Stellan was to her and Thomas. "Until then, you have my utmost assurances your brother and team are safe."

Pocky just nodded in response, then fell within herself and lost time. She didn't realize their team had caught up until Bren tapped her lightly with his elbow. She watched as Geara introduced Naiko to Bren. The noise from the dogs and soldiers made it hard to hear their exchange of words. The XO then motioned for the woman to start up the gangway.

As their Team Coordinator stepped on, Yana called out, "Wait a damn minute!" Naiko looked back at her in surprise. "I've been trying to ask, but why are we down here? The charter boats are back that way!" Yana shouted, pointing in the other direction.

"This is the ship we're taking," Naiko said. "This is *Gaia*."

Yana's expression paled. "Well, I had thought ... I mean, we're a small team. Why do we have to go on this big-ass, stupid boat?"

A chuckle threatened to burst free from Pocky's throat, and she held it in as Naiko tried to reason with Yana. She wasn't the first person to protest going onto *Gaia*, and Pocky was certain Naiko had handled this kind of objection before. However, their TC wasn't winning this round.

"Oh no, oh no! I'm not doing this!" Yana said as she tried to backtrack.

Kaori hurried after her, gently setting her hands on Yana's upper arms. "It's okay. I've got you, and I can get you through this. You need to trust me though, okay?"

Yana's voice and body both trembled as she said, "I, um, I can't do this."

"Yes, you can. And I'll help. Okay?" Kai said firmly. After a few seconds of thought, Yana grimaced and nodded. "Okay, good. Now close your eyes and take my hand." Yana did exactly what Kaori instructed and held tightly with both hands. "Great, now start singing your favorite song."

As Kaori led Yana up to the gangway, she began to wail an unfamiliar song. Pocky winced at the sound; the poor woman couldn't carry a tune. Some of the nearby soldiers laughed but were quickly shut down by an officer. Naiko followed close behind them as they went farther up the gangway.

Geara instructed Lance to go next. Pocky glanced at him, and when he caught her gaze, her stomach fluttered. The compassion in his eyes made her heart melt. He had a pleasant demeanor, yet a strong presence about him. When he smiled, Pocky was surprised to find herself blushing again and had to look away. She then scolded herself for how childish her reaction was and straightened herself up.

"Get going, *Martar'le*," Haize teased, giving Pocky a wink.

She blushed again and almost laughed. *Martar'le* was an Origin reference to a great male lover. She was surprised Haize knew the word, but he probably didn't know it was commonly used by her female colleagues when they got a good lay in. Lance glared at Haize with narrowed, amused eyes, then stepped onto the gangway. Haize followed with Geara behind him. Pocky didn't look at the XO but followed him. Halfway across, she paused and looked down at the waters below. She was glad that Yana had her eyes closed. Even though the gangway and ship were steady as a rock, the sea below said otherwise.

"Pocky!" Geara yelled. "You got one crashing!"

Pocky sprinted the rest of the way to *Gaia* and into the Reception Area. Yana sat on the built-in wooden bench along the right-side wall. Lance was trying to get her pack off while Kaori held her up. Yana was pale and looked as though she was about to faint.

Pocky already knew what was happening. She crouched down on one knee in front of Yana and opened her pack, then moved her sling backward to dive into her bag. She pulled out her med stick and then a small capsule encased in a clear wrap.

Pocky looked up into Yana's eyes and put the back of her fingers against the woman's forehead for a moment. Yana felt clammy to the touch.

"Hey Yana, you did great on the hard part, gettin' here. Proud of you," Pocky said as she unwrapped the capsule. "Take this and let it dissolve on your tongue. It's gonna help relax you, okay?"

Yana slowly nodded but otherwise didn't move. Her lids were nearly closed.

Pocky ended up putting the capsule into her mouth for her, then gripped Yana's hand and got her med stick ready. "So, this is gonna go around your wrist and give me your vitals. Ready?"

Again, Yana only made the slightest motion that she understood. Pocky put the med stick on the flat side of the woman's wrist and let it snap around in place. Yana tried to jerk her hand away, but it was a reaction Pocky was all too familiar with. She held firm, keeping the woman's hand in hers.

"You're okay. It's supposed to do that," Pocky said, then tapped her watch against the med stick, linking them. It would take a few minutes for the vitals to appear. "So, where you from, Yana?"

"Orphanage down in Hiem'Trig," she replied, voice low and slurred.

"Respect. Was it nice?" Pocky asked.

"I thought so."

"Were you sad to leave it?"

"Nope. I'm one of those weird people that was glad to grow up in one, thankful to have no ties. I literally had no tears when I left."

Pocky huffed out a laugh. "What did you do after you left?"

"Went to school for cartography and then traveled abroad. Well, just within Shad'Dyn, anyway."

"What was—" Pocky began to say, but then her watch beeped and flashed green, indicating that it was ready to report. She tapped the corner and read the numbers, smiling at the results. "Okay, your heart rate is slightly up, but the rest of your vitals look good. I'm gonna take this off now. It'll feel like an adhesive pad coming off."

As Pocky gently peeled the device off, Yana asked, "So—ouch!—that thingy really told you my vitals?"

"Yeah, pretty cool, right?" Pocky replied as she tossed the device back in her bag.

Yana raised her eyebrows. "Apparently."

"So, do you always get anxious when on a ship?" Pocky asked. "Or is it just this one?"

"This one," Yana replied tiredly. "Well, actually, I don't know. Never been on a boat before."

"Nothing wrong with that either way. Most people do, even soldiers."

"Really?"

"Uh-huh. But we'll work on getting you used to the ship at your own pace, okay?"

"Really?"

"Yup, first we'll—"

"Holy crap!" Yana interrupted, eyes wide as she moved her jaw around. "This shit is good."

Pocky laughed as she sat back on her haunches and folded her arms on top of her knees. "It just takes a minute, but yeah. Feeling better?"

"Greatly better! Thanks."

"Certainly," she replied with a smile.

Pocky turned in search of her XO, only to see everyone had scattered around the room. Kaori and Haize were beside the stairs while Naiko and Geara were in the far corner. Lance and Bren were not far in their own space, and Bren was grinning. Grinning! *Unusual*, Pocky mused. The fact that he was so relaxed around Lance just made Pocky more intrigued by the agriculturalist.

"Hey," Yana said, getting Pocky's attention. "So, what was all that drama about?"

"No," she replied, then shoved to her feet. "You should visit the clinic soon. Either I or Naiko can take you, okay?"

"Uh—"

"Hey!" Geara shouted next to her, almost making her flinch. "You done with this bullshit?"

"Yes, sir," Pocky replied coldly.

"Pocky," Naiko said as she joined them. "I'm giving you and Thomas twenty minutes before the rest of us catch up, sounds good?"

"Much appreciated, ma'am."

"He's waiting for you in the Starboard Café on level one," Geara said.

"That's our designated area," Naiko added. "We'll have orientation within an hour and a half in the café. I think that should give everyone enough time to eat and settle a little. Okay?"

"Yes, ma'am. Thank you, ma'am."

"Go," Geara commanded.

Pocky didn't hesitate and headed up the stairs. As she ran, she tried to push away all her fears and anger. For the next twenty minutes, she would just pretend that only she and Thomas existed in the entire world.

10

Thomas sat on top of one of the four large tables in the Starboard Café. It was on the bow side at the end of the corridor across from a few cabins. Its brown walls, low lights, and chalkboard sign listing the daily specials gave off a cozy vibe. For the moment, it was his sanctuary as he waited for Pocky.

Iza, a soldier tending the café, handed him a canteen. She had long straight blonde hair pulled back into a tie, and her complexion almost matched her almond eyes. As he drank, Thomas tried not to think of Stellan and that smile he had as he walked up the stairs. After Fally had secured Thomas in the café, he'd promised the XO or the SC would explain what was going on and not to worry about that asshole coming near him and his sister. Even though Thomas trusted the IMF and their capabilities, he wasn't sure why separating him from Stellan seemed important but was patient for all of it to be clarified.

Again, Thomas thought of that smile Stellan gave him. It chilled him to the bone. He wished he could shake it off, but ever since he and Pocky had escaped the Hyashi household, he'd been scared shitless of running into Stellan. A close call before he'd started school only intensified that fear. Since then, he'd been constantly looking over his shoulder. Thomas was tired of being in a constant state of alert—and on the run—because of it.

Throughout his time in Shad'Dyn, Thomas was always on the move for two reasons. The first was practical, as part of his job was helping farmers with whatever problems they were having, which turned out to be mostly that weird fungus that was going around. The other reason was unconsciously aligned with the first. His four years in the Hyashi household had left its mark on him, but that close encounter with Stellan had dug a wound even deeper into his core than he'd initially thought.

When Thomas was fifteen, he was a weak, malnourished-looking boy who no longer had the orphanage to protect him. He was also without Bren and Pocky for the first time in his life, and knowing exactly what Stellan wanted to do with him sent explosions of pure fear reverberating throughout his body. And it wasn't just Stellan's sexual desire for him that had molded Thomas into who he was then and now, but he also felt his very life depended on him constantly staying on the move.

After the close call, Thomas didn't even bother to report his dismissal to the school and moved to Shad'Dyn immediately. But his resolve didn't stop there. Just in case Stellan somehow found him again, he was determined to become physically stronger. Instead of traveling by vehicle, he ran. Pocky had always loved to run. He, on the other hand, had grown to hate it because of why he had to do it. He had also learned to fight from anyone willing to teach him, and the opportunities had turned out to be bountiful in Shad'Dyn. In this country, farmers didn't use their local law agency to handle their disputes, even though nothing had ever escalated beyond harsh words. Still, all boys growing up on these farmsteads were taught to fight in case they had to. This worked in Thomas's favor; he refused to go down if Stellan's entourage managed to grab him.

Given all that, Thomas wasn't fully aware of his motives at first: running, fighting, and bulking up. He convinced himself that he loved it. It would be nearly two years before he realized the real damage Stellan had caused. The likelihood of that guy finding him was nearly impossible. Shad'Dyn was so vast that he was smaller than a flea in a haystack. Yet even with that realization, it still wasn't enough for him to feel safe. When he had gazed at *Gaia* through his window at the hotel earlier, he truly felt this project was going to be a new beginning. One where he would be free of the fear, and free from himself. Now that he was stuck on the ship with Stellan, his very nightmare coming to fruition, he had little hope that he would ever know what being free from that man would be like.

"Thomas," Iza began gently. "Your team and your sister will be here soon.

Would you like me to get you some new clothes? You don't look like you like those."

Thomas unexpectedly found himself laughing awkwardly. "Uh, yeah, I really don't, do I? Please, that would be nice." Though he had two sets of clothes in his backpack, fresh clothes for a fresh start sounded appealing.

"Okay, I'll be back in a bit."

"Thank you, ma'am."

Iza disappeared through the entryway. Fally backed away to let her pass, then resumed his position. As much as he wanted to ask the soldier questions, Thomas decided to shelf it and try to be a friend instead.

"You okay, Fally? I know Stellan rattled you. I'm sorry for his behave—"

"Don't you ever apologize for that fucking asshole. Not ever," Fally said, his glare heated.

Why was there such hatred in his tone? The two men shouldn't have known each other, yet he got the sense that this was personal to Fally.

"Fally? What did he do?"

"Not my place to say, sir. Told you the XO will fill you in."

Thomas didn't like the sound of that, but a familiar sensation made him put all other thoughts aside. He nearly dropped his container as he leaped from the table. As though a beacon had been switched on, he felt the flame of his sister nearby. She was on her way to him and moving fast. His eyes watered as she got closer.

"There she is! She's coming, sir," Fally said with a big grin.

Fally quickly moved out of the way as Pocky charged into the café. Her face, not much different from when they were kids, still glowed even though her expression was strained with emotions. With arms wide open, she slammed into Thomas and hugged him tightly. He tried to wrap his arms around her but couldn't get a proper hold with her backpack on. She quickly shrugged it off, and they held each other in a long embrace. Holding her almost felt like a dream. Her scent, a mixture of soap and a flowery shampoo, told him just how real this was. With his cheek on top of her head, he realized just how much taller he was now and found that amusing.

"Don't make fun of my height," she said.

Thomas laughed as they pulled away. They took a moment to look at each other, taking in their now grown-up faces.

"Who said you could be taller than me?" Pocky asked, narrowing her eyes with an accusatory smile.

"Wasn't trying to be," Thomas said, laughing. Pocky gave him her signature "I forgive you" expression and then laughed with him.

They sat down and held hands. The material of her fingerless gloves was thick, but he still felt her warmth through the fabric. Her eyes darted around his face, as though wanting to absorb his features. Thomas did the same but then became serious as he took in the rest of her appearance. The uniform suited her, and he couldn't have been more proud.

"You look good, Sis."

Even though she blushed, Pocky didn't turn away. "You as well." She abruptly beamed and got excited. "Tell me everything! I wanna hear all about the animals and—"

"Oh, there's plenty of time to hear all my boring stuff. You first! What's it like being a medic? I mean, I know you're probably limited with what you can say, but—"

Pocky frowned and shifted uncomfortably, making Thomas pause. "Something wrong?" he asked.

"Well, um ... I know it isn't fair, but I don't like talking about my job. The pressure and stress of people's lives in my hands is ... too much to share. No matter how hard I try, people die sometimes. Kids are the hardest." She said the last words slowly, then looked away, pressing her lips together.

Thomas swallowed. All this time he assumed she had kept quiet because that was how the IMF worked, when in fact it wasn't that at all. Incidents happened all the time with charters and tankers. It was why the OSAR existed. Whether it was mechanical failure, running aground, capsizing, or something else entirely, OSAR was there for any rescue. Given that he never once thought of possible casualties, visualizing it now was like a reality slap in the face.

"I'm so sorry," he said. "I never once considered—"

"S'ok," Pocky asserted quickly. "There's a lot that I'd love to tell you though. I love being on the ocean and working with my squad. They're good people and have been like a family. I'd rather tell you about them than the job, but we don't have much time. Naiko was kind enough to give us a little breather before our team joins us. She wants to give our orientation within the next hour. Do you want to wait for them, or would you like me to show you your cabin?"

Thomas desperately needed another shower. "Cabin. I want to get this shit out of my hair," he said, running a hand through his hair with disgust. Pocky laughed for a moment, which made him smile. "What?"

"Your voice is so deep now. It's gonna take some time for me to get used to that."

"We have a lot to catch up on, don't we?"

"That's an understatement," Pocky said with a grin, then grimaced slightly and rubbed her right shoulder.

Thomas frowned at her movements. He wanted to ask, but Pocky ushered them into the corridor. She then asked which cabin he wanted. All the nameplates started with S1, followed by a dash and a number. He had no preference, so he picked S1-4, which was directly across from the café.

Pocky opened the door, and Thomas followed in after. It was a modest room with two beds, a dresser, and a small round table with two chairs. Another doorway against the far wall had to be the bathroom.

Before Thomas could appreciate his new living quarters, a disembodied feminine voice coming from somewhere in the room spoke. "New occupants detected. Please state how many are staying in this room."

"One," Pocky answered.

"Thank you. Please, state the name occupying this room."

Pocky gestured for him to say his name.

"Uh, Thomas."

"Thank you. Please state your room preferences."

"Uh—"

"*Gaia*, please set everything to basic for now," Pocky said. "We'll set up preferences later."

"Yes, ma'am."

She looked at Thomas and blushed as though embarrassed. "I know it's weird at first, but you'll get the hang of it in no time."

"What is that?" Thomas asked with amazement.

"It'll all be explained during orientation. But *Gaia* can also explain if you ask. Especially when you're ready to shower."

"Like how?" Thomas asked, shaking his head. This was beyond anything he'd ever imagined for a ship.

"*Gaia*, tell me how the shower works," Pocky said.

"Please, state the desired water temperature."

"Ninety-nine degrees."

"Water temperature set. Step into the shower. Water will automatically turn on."

Thomas smiled in wonder. "That's fucking amazing."

"It certainly is. Military technology is pretty cool these days, right?"

Before he could reply, a soft knock came from the door. Since Thomas was closer, he answered it. Iza grinned up at him and offered him the clothes folded in her hands.

"Hi, Thomas. Here are your—Pocky!" Iza exclaimed as she moved into the room.

"Hi, Iza. Good to see you again," Pocky said.

Thomas took the clothes and put them on the bed as the women started bantering in their dialect. Pocky had always been good at picking up other lingos, speaking them as though she always had. Thomas paused for a moment, wondering if that was an ability like his or if it was natural as he'd always assumed.

"Iza, we don't have long," Pocky finally said.

"Okay, I'm going." Iza turned to Thomas. "The SC wanted me to tell you the XO will be on his way in a bit to explain everything."

"I appreciate that. Thank you," Thomas replied, then watched Iza leave the cabin. He turned to Pocky with apprehension, unsure whether she knew the precarious situation he had been in or of Stellan being onboard the ship. Her expression was a mixture of dread and guilt he knew all too well. However, that still didn't indicate whether she knew or not. He approached her, hoping he could calmly explain and reassure her. "Hey, Sis, look, um, this is going to be a shock to hear, but Stellan—"

"Thomas, I'm so sorry," Pocky said frantically. "I can explain. I mean, I-I can't right now. But please give me a chance to explain later. Please." Her face grew pale.

"What are you talking about?" Thomas asked.

Instead of answering, her mouth opened and closed. Then a small squeak escaped from deep within her throat. Thomas put his hands on her upper arms. She flinched her right shoulder and hissed, making Thomas let go immediately.

"Shit! I'm sorry. Did I hurt you?" Thomas asked. *Did I grab too tightly?*

With a horrified look, Pocky embraced him. "No! Not at all. You could never hurt me. But I ... need to shower too. I'm ... sweaty. We'll talk after orientation though. I promise, okay?"

"Okay ... okay," he said soothingly, stroking the back of her head.

Pocky held him even tighter. Thomas knew she was deflecting. As much as he wanted to press, he didn't want to cause her any more distress. There was certainly something going on behind the scenes with Stellan, and maybe she had some involvement with that. Whether it was that or something else, he knew she needed time, and he was willing to wait. They had all the time in the world now.

11

While the twins took their allotted time, Naiko gave the team a brief tutorial on how their cabins worked and how to navigate desired settings. Usually, this was provided during their orientation, but she figured it would be best to have everyone up to speed to help them settle in their cabins better. Everyone except Yana had chosen rooms that offered an ocean view.

After adjusting the lights and setting the room temperature, Lance messed around with the music options. He grinned; he never thought he would ever experience technology such as this.

Feeling pleased with his cabin, Lance headed to the café to see if anything was happening yet. When he closed his door, a small window screen lit up underneath the cabin plate, indicating who occupied the room and if they were inside or not. A red screen denoted the room was vacant, while a green screen indicated the occupant was inside. As he walked along toward the café, he took notice of the screens on the other doors as he passed them. Everyone's screens were green, except for Thomas's, which indicated the man was elsewhere.

Nobody was in the café when Lance arrived, which he was fine with. He reviewed the chalkboard menu; they'd already eaten, but he considered the beverages that would hopefully have a kick to them. Travel lag was starting to creep up on him, and he wanted to stay sharp for the meeting.

"Oh," an unexpected voice said nonchalantly. "Hey, Lance."

Surprised by her voice, he turned to find Pocky stepping up next to him. "Uh-hi!"

She gave him a slight smile as she ran her fingers through her beautiful hair. Her wavy strands were like ocean waves; they went wherever they wanted.

Back by the gangway, as Naiko was being introduced to Pocky's med partner, Bren, Lance wondered if she had a partner in another way—a romantic partner. He inhaled deeply as he remembered how cute she was when she blushed. Unbidden, he'd imagined himself and her together intimately, then scolded himself, surprised his mind had even gone there. *Get a grip! You just met the woman.*

Lance smiled nervously but then frowned when he noticed her eyes were slightly red, like she'd been crying. "Hey, um, sorry," he said, shaking his head. "Are you okay?"

"Yes and no," Pocky replied as she set her med pack and hat down on the closest table. She then pulled out her sling from her back pocket and began to put it on.

Everyone was perplexed by the heated exchange between Pocky and Geara, especially after they switched to their military dialect. However, Thomas and Stellan's names came up quite a few times. Between her anger and Thomas's unease around Stellan when they had entered The Traven, Lance couldn't even begin to guess what their conversation was alluding to, other than it couldn't be good. Thomas had to be in some kind of precarious situation, but what?

Though Lance wanted to offer some sort of comfort, he didn't know Pocky well enough for it to be appropriate. He instead opened with what he hoped was just kindness without it being mistaken for nosiness.

"Is Thomas okay?"

As she struggled with the sling, Pocky looked up at him. "Yeah, he is." She stopped and let out a frustrated sigh. "Um, I know we just met, but would you mind helping me with this damn thing?"

"Yeah, sure." Lance approached her, pressing his lips together as he tried to focus solely on the sling and not her lovely scent or the fact that his hands brushed along her shoulders. He frowned, realizing what the problem was. "Uh, you have it inside out and the strap is twisted. You need to take it all off—I mean, just the sling!"

Lance felt like an idiot, but Pocky laughed, which eased his embarrassment.

"Right, I took it off so quickly before, I didn't think," Pocky said as she removed the sling. As she righted the article, she muttered to herself, "I don't even need this damn thing, but everybody has such a fucking heart attack if I don't."

Lance laughed lightly, which made her look up at him and laugh too.

"Sorry," she said, "I'm not usually this flustered."

"No, it's understandable. I get it."

Pocky blushed. *Damn, you're cute when you do that*, he wanted to say. Instead, he tried not to smile awkwardly as he watched her tentatively put the sling back on.

Pocky smiled shyly when she was done. "Much appreciated."

"Sure, happy to help," Lance said with a nod. "By the way, you were amazing with Yana."

"Always happy to serve. She's a nice girl. How's she doing?"

He shrugged. "Whatever you gave her didn't last long, and she felt dizzy. She couldn't get into her cabin fast enough. Obviously, she took one that doesn't have an ocean view."

Pocky nodded slowly, then paled.

Lance's first instinct was again to ask if she was okay but felt the question was redundant. "Are you hungry?" he asked instead. "Iza is still in the kitchen. She's our attendee, by the way."

"Yeah, I know her. I ... just need some water," Pocky said but looked as though she wanted to say something else. She started toward the counter, then turned back to him. "Look, I'm sorry for the scene earlier. It wasn't proper in front of all of you."

"S'ok. I mean, I'm not going to pretend that any of us know what's going on. But it's none of our business, so don't worry about anyone's curiosity or judgment. As long as you and Thomas are okay, that's all that matters."

Pocky nodded, somehow getting paler as her shoulders slumped forward. Again, Lance wanted to do or say something that would be uplifting, but it wasn't his place. Bren walked in with heavy steps, grabbing his attention. The big guy smiled at first but frowned and moved past Lance.

"Partner?" Bren asked as he stopped in front of Pocky. "What's doing?"

Pocky put her free hand over her face and started breathing heavily. "It's crashing in," she said, her voice cracking. "Stellan's here. He almost got Thomas and that's my fault."

Bren set his hands on her shoulders as he asked, "How the fuck is that your fault?"

Pocky began speaking in their dialect. Even though Lance couldn't understand a word, he could tell Bren was trying to reason with her. Feeling the two needed a moment to themselves, Lance began to leave, but Haize walked in before he got to the doorway. The engineer's expression went from delight to annoyance when he saw what was going on.

"For fuck's sake. What's the drama now, girlfriend?" Haize asked with a groan.

Lance stilled himself. Haize was obviously trying to provoke one or both of them. He wasn't sure what the man's reasons were or why his demeanor had changed. Since he didn't know either man well, it was hard to gauge if the situation would settle or get worse. Lance looked at Bren, who glared at Haize. This was definitely going to get worse.

"*Girlfriend*? Don't fucking call her that, you piece of shit," Bren roared.

"Hey, ease up, big man, it's just a name," Haize said condescendingly. "No big deal."

"Yeah, just a name." Bren's eyes narrowed. "I know all about yours and your reputation."

"Wait, what?" Haize asked, eyebrows raising. "What reputation? My engineering rep?"

"The other one, you moron. You're not getting in between my partner's legs," Bren said, his hands balling into fists, "so don't fucking try to charm your way in. You feel me?"

Pocky locked eyes with Lance and shrugged. Haize was stunned speechless, his mouth opening and closing wordlessly.

"In fact," Bren continued as he cracked his knuckles, "since there's only three women on our team, you keep your hands off all of them or you'll have my hands on you. Clear?"

Haize held his hands out to his sides. "What the fuck are you insinuating?"

"Your fucking reputation of 'I'm gonna fuck anything with a vag on my team' is not happening."

"Are you shitting me? Any woman I'm with is consensual, always."

"Don't fucking care, not happening while I'm on this team."

"Hey, if they wanna be with me, I ain't stopping them, but if you wanna deck me before that happens, go for it now, asshole!"

Bren stepped forward and cocked his fist back, ready to swing.

Lance stepped between them. "Okay, guys, take a breath!"

Bren's heated eyes went from Haize to Lance.

"Come on, man," Lance said gently yet firmly. "Take a step back." Though he thoroughly believed the guy could break him in half, he wasn't intimidated. He had never been afraid to get hit and had been a few times when he had to intervene, like he was now. Thankfully, Bren backed off, and his posture relaxed.

"What's going on here?" Naiko asked as she walked into the café, Kaori and Yana just behind her.

"Just getting acquainted, ma'am," Lance replied.

Naiko crossed her arms. "Didn't sound that way from the corridor."

"It's nothing," Haize quickly said. "Just boys being boys."

The TC rolled her eyes. "Whatever. I'm ready to start the meeting." She paused and looked around. "Where's Thomas?"

"He went to the stern's well deck," Iza said from behind the counter. Lance did a double take, wondering when and how long she had been standing there.

"Haize and I will go get him," Lance said. Though he could have gone alone, he felt Haize still needed to cool off a bit. Plus, he didn't quite trust Bren and Haize in the same room and didn't want the women to deal with it if they went at it again.

"Great idea!" Naiko said. "Be back in five, though, please. We still have a tour to do afterward."

"Yes, ma'am," Lance said, then gestured for the engineer to follow him.

Haize followed without question, and they walked in silence until they reached the double doors that led to the well deck.

"Hey, I'm sorry you had to come in between that. That guy is a—"

Lance turned toward Haize. He wasn't in the mood to lecture but would if he had to. "I'd rather not end up in the clinic before the day ends. Bren may be hot-tempered, but you provoked him. I don't know what you were trying to accomplish, but the only one you're impressing is yourself."

Haize sighed tiredly. "Hey, I can't help it if I get more action than he does. And his partner is too frigid for my taste. Wasn't gonna go for her anyway."

Did Haize's attitude stem from Pocky's earlier rebuff of his invitation to share stories? He presumed the engineer was one of those guys who wasn't rejected often. The man's past of being turned down by the IMF probably didn't help his ego either. Lance supposed he could've been way off since he'd only just met Haize, but he wasn't usually far off the mark.

Perhaps sensing Lance wasn't thrilled with his retort, Haize continued, "Look, we just got here and already two out of the three women on our team are stirring up drama. I'm too travel lagged to deal with their bullshit."

"Is that how you see it?" Lance asked flatly.

"Don't you?" Haize countered.

"Not in the least. Try not to be abrasive toward them, though, okay? It's only the first day of a whole year ahead of us. It's not a good start for us as a team."

"I tried to backtrack until that asshole said I had a rep!"

"Yeah, so? Do you really want to earn another? Because that's where you're heading."

Haize's expression went from irritation to thoughtfulness, but he shook his head as though not wanting to consider it.

"Yeah, okay," he said, rolling his eyes. "I'll be the bigger man and play nice."

Lance took that as it was without criticism. People never changed that drastically, but he trusted it was a start at least. He'd probably still have to intervene at times and was fine with that if he had to. Being a peacemaker had inadvertently been his role among his cousins as well. He was used to it.

"Alright, good enough. Let's get Thomas and get back," Lance said, then opened the doors.

12

Thomas leaned against the hull railing, curiously watching a fleet of IMF ships farther out to sea. After Pocky left, he had taken every piece of clothing off and tossed the much-hated clothes—and the shiny shoes—out the window. He showered and got that stupid gel out of his hair, then changed into the white cotton T-shirt and dark green cargo pants Iza had given him. Once he had his boots on, he was ready to explore his new home. The café was the first place he wanted to go. Since he hadn't eaten yet, he was starving. Iza was nice enough to give him a snack before heading to where he was now.

Lance and Haize stepped out onto the deck from the starboard corridor entrance. Thomas turned and smiled at their approach.

"Oh, hi guys. What's doing?"

They both regarded him for a moment, and Thomas realized he must've looked quite different from earlier. His hair now fell to his jawline and resembled his sister's.

"You look better," Lance said.

"Thanks."

"Glad to have you back with us," Haize said with a small smile.

"Same."

"We came to get you," Lance said. "Naiko's ready to give our orientation."

"Oh good," Thomas said. "I know we're supposed to be collecting plant samples, but do you think it involves that fungal problem too?"

"The what?" Haize asked sharply.

"The fungal problem farmers are struggling with. Haven't heard of it?"

"Uh, no, and I doubt that's what you agriculture nerds are going to be doing.

Most projects I've been on have you guys treading through the wilderness and hogging up the medics."

"Oh," Thomas said with disappointment but then smiled. "Well, I'm with my sister again. That's all that matters."

"Speaking of *your* sister—" Haize began.

"Haize." Lance shot the engineer an exasperated look. "Don't."

Haize put up his hands as though in surrender, and with an eye roll, turned away.

Thomas looked at Lance, perplexed. "What about my sister?"

Lance sighed. "She's obviously upset about something, but I'm not going to speculate as to what."

Thomas understood why Lance didn't want to comment on something he knew nothing about. He was fairly certain Pocky was aware of his situation earlier with Stellan. That or just aware that the man was present on the ship. Either way, she was rightfully unsettled. Stellan popping up out of nowhere had to be unnerving for her, just as it was for him. The XO would hopefully let him know what was going on soon.

"We need to get going," Lance said. "They're waiting for us."

Thomas followed the two men into the corridor. As they walked along, Lance slowed his pace until he was shouldered with him, then slowed down even more. He understood what the guy was doing and followed suit, letting distance grow between them and Haize.

"What's up? This about my sister?" Thomas asked.

"Uh, no. She's a lovely woman though. I like her a lot already. Hope that's okay for me to say."

"Yeah, of course. So, what's doing?"

"Wanted to ask you about that fungal problem. You know of it?"

"Oh yeah, spent the last eight years going from one farmstead to another trying to understand it," Thomas said. "Fucking shit is impossible to kill. Right?"

"Yeah, it is," Lance said, frowning. "I'm surprised that you know of it though. I thought it was just a localized problem in my area."

"Unfortunately, no. In fact, it's got me concerned for the future of the world's food supply on an epic scale."

Lance halted, making Thomas do the same. "Seriously?"

"Yeah, it's that bad. I'm hoping the project involves finding a way to eradicate it, or at least find ways to stop it from doing further damage."

"Wait, you think somehow the three of us can?"

"With you and Kaori, I'm hoping we can."

"How so?" Lance asked.

"I've been studying it extensively but with outdated equipment and no access to proper labs. With the IMF's technology, I'm hoping to get a better understanding of it. I can't wait to get inside the lab we're going to be training in. I have a ton of fungal samples in my pack to look at."

"Yeah, but that doesn't answer my question. I'm just a simple farmer. How can I contribute?"

"Honestly, I could use an extra set of eyes," Thomas said. "I've been alone at this and could use the help. You may see something I can't. And with Kaori's background and expertise, I feel confident that maybe the three of us can get further along."

Lance nodded and started walking again. Thomas followed.

"So, how did you come across it?" Lance asked, his voice still uneasy.

"The Vic'Dorns farmstead. They were the first to kindly take me in and were willing to educate me, but they were also hoping for a fresh look at an ongoing problem. I didn't know what to make of it either, but that's how it started. You?"

"About a year ago, my father and I went hunting in a corner of our land that at one time had been heavily wooded," Lance said. "We hadn't been there for a few years, but when we got there, it was ..." He paused, then met Thomas's gaze. "It was decimated. Like it had never existed. Even the creek was gone."

"You're not the first to say that, and why I'm concerned," Thomas said. "This fungus isn't just invasive. To the naked eye, it consumes everything, but I have found that it goes even deeper than that. It also consumes the nutrients in the ground, which can prevent new growth for years. Sure, growth will eventually come back, but if farmers have nothing to feed their livestock until then, then they die. What's just as bad is the wildlife encroaching on farmsteads because they have nothing to sustain them either. This fungus is affecting everyone and everything."

"Fuck," Lance muttered.

They walked the rest of the way to the café in silence. Thomas felt he'd unloaded enough on Lance about the fungus situation for now. Explaining just how bad it had gotten for some farmers might be too much at once. Unfortunately, some families had lost their entire farmsteads.

Before reaching the Starboard Café, Thomas spotted a man in uniform standing at ease before the entryway. The way the guy was looking at them—or more so at him—made Thomas anxious. Haize nodded to the soldier as he entered the café, and Lance did the same. He then blocked Thomas from going inside. He stepped back, unsure of the guy's intentions.

"Easy," the man said, holding out his hand. "I'm Executive Officer Geara."

Thomas shook the XO's hand and tried not to show how nervous he was greeting a high-ranking officer. "Nice to meet you, sir."

"Likewise. I have served alongside your sister for almost a year now, and it's been an honor. She's an extraordinary woman, and I regard her fondly."

"Well, that's amazing to hear, sir. I'm honored to meet you, then," Thomas replied.

"After orientation, I want to sit down with you both and explain what happened earlier and what we're doing with Hyashi, okay?"

"I would very much appreciate that."

"Also, the medics are supposed to stand at parade rest during your orientation, so try not to distract your sister," Geara said, then moved to let him inside.

Thomas wasn't sure if the XO was serious or joking. He bet on the former and tried to be respectful of that as he walked in. Everyone was grouped at different tables, chatting quietly.

Before Thomas saw Pocky, Bren stood up with a big grin and opened his arms wide. "Brother!"

Thomas lost his voice for a moment, almost unable to believe the boy he'd last seen was twice as big now. "Holy shit, Bren?" he asked, eyes wide as he approached his old friend. They embraced for a long minute before parting. "I fucking can't believe how big you got."

"You should talk, skinny boy," Bren said with a laugh.

Thomas laughed with him. "It's good to see you."

"Same. We'll catch up after all this. Okay?"

"Yeah, absolutely. I—"

"Medics!" Geara shouted. "Assume assigned positions against the wall!" Bren and Pocky moved between two tables, then lined up against the far wall as they were told. "At ease!"

In unison, Bren and Pocky widened their stances and put their hands behind their backs. They gazed forward, expressions neutral. Thomas admired both of them for a moment. He was so proud of them. It seemed so surreal that they were all together again. Then he frowned when he noticed his sister's arm was in a sling. He hadn't noticed it at first because it camouflaged well against her uniform.

Shit, he thought, remembering how she had reacted earlier when he grabbed her arm. *Why is she trying to hide an injury from me?* he thought and then realized why she kept it from him.

When it came to Pocky, Thomas, of course, felt an overpowering need to protect his sister. He was her brother, so why wouldn't he? However, his younger self would have come unglued, and she knew that, hence why she kept it quiet. But they were adults now, and he wanted her to see how much he'd matured. Especially since Pocky could be wearing the sling for many reasons. It could have been from exercising or something else that wasn't nefarious.

"Thomas? Could you please sit?" Naiko asked politely.

Thomas shook his head. "Oh, yeah, sorry."

He thought Naiko would start, but then Geara ordered Pocky to step forward. "As with our agreement with CCO regulations, explain your weapons, medic."

"Yes, sir." Pocky pulled her gun from the holster. Since she was left-handed, Thomas bet that she was probably thankful the sling was on her right. She pointed the gun up and away so that everyone had a side view. It almost seemed too big in her hand. "This is an XR-17 class handgun with interchangeable capabilities. Currently armed with rubber bullets. If you're hit by one, it won't kill you."

"But it hurts like a bitch," Bren added.

"Sounds like you know from experience," Haize mused.

"We do," Bren and Pocky replied in unison.

Thomas grimaced and tried not to picture the two of them in agony. Geara then ordered Pocky to resume her place and gave the floor to Naiko. Thomas turned to face their TC and listened tentatively as she went into the details about the project. To his disappointment, the project didn't involve the fungus like he had hoped. For the next year, they were going to remote areas along an island chain to collect plant samples while Yana would graph the uncharted areas. Though it wasn't what he had expected, it still sounded like exciting work.

"*Gaia* is being prepped for tug as well as in the beginning stages of being warmed up," Naiko said. "We'll be on our way by early tomorrow morning. Finally, this is our designated café, where you will eat all your meals. If you haven't met Iza yet, she is our personal attendee. If you need clothes, linens, hygiene products, or food, she's the one to see." Their TC paused and took a breath, then smiled. "That's it for now. How about a fifteen-minute break, then I'll give the tour. Sound good?"

Everyone agreed. Thomas tried not to rush as he stood and looked at Pocky. She leaned against the wall with her left arm crossed over the sling as she spoke with Bren. He approached and tried not to seem anxious. Bren turned his attention to him and gave a small smile.

"I gotta use the head," he said, then walked away.

Thomas silently thanked Bren for the privacy as he turned back to Pocky. Her expression didn't change as she gulped. Getting her to open up had never been easy, but given his adolescent behavior, Thomas understood. He hoped to change that.

"Hey," Thomas said carefully, then touched her arm lightly. "Are you okay?" She shook her head slowly but didn't look away. "What happened?"

"No," she replied flatly.

Pocky's retort didn't surprise him, but it also didn't unbalance him like it would have when they were younger. As much as he was concerned, he didn't want to force the issue and push her further away.

"I—"

Yana plopped on top of the table next to them and sported a big smile as though the scene was entertaining. "Don't bother, Thomas. She says 'no' to anyone that asks."

"Yana, do you mind?" Thomas asked, glaring at her.

"Actually, I do. I'm really curious."

"Yana," Lance said from across the room with a warning in his tone. "Leave them be."

Yana rolled her eyes and groaned as she moved away.

Thomas turned back to Pocky. "I won't press. I just want to be sure you're okay."

She blinked tiredly and spoke softly. "I'm alive and well in front of you."

"But I—"

"You two, sit!" Geara commanded, gesturing toward them. He then instructed the rest of the team to wait outside.

They both sat as everyone else shuffled out. As soon as they were all gone, Geara sat down across from them. Thomas braced himself for whatever the XO was about to disclose.

13

Pocky's leg bounced nervously as Geara revealed how they had planned to lure and capture Stellan, her part in it, and how it all led to where they were now. Her stomach threatened to turn. She fully accepted whatever Thomas's judgment would be of her; she just prayed he wouldn't reject her. She anxiously watched her brother, waiting for his reaction. The only fact the XO left out was why they sought Stellan's detainment, which she was still glad not to know. When Geara concluded, she had expected the worst, but Thomas's unreadable expression didn't change as he spoke.

"How did he find out the real day we were boarding?"

"I'm working on that. I have confidence we'll know soon. For now, I can only apologize. It was a scenario that none of us foresaw, but here we are." Geara paused, his eyebrows furrowing as though trying to be careful with what he would say next. "I want to add that your sister's insistence on using you to get Stellan here was not what she wanted—"

"She was right to," Thomas interrupted. "Stellan would have known immediately that I wasn't on the ship if you hadn't used me. I didn't even need to be visible. He would have known."

Geara squinted, like he was trying to rationalize how that was possible. Pocky couldn't even begin to speculate on what was churning in the XO's head. Whether it was the fantastical notion that Stellan perhaps had some sort of unnatural intuition, or something else, it didn't matter. She wasn't going to step in and offer an explanation. All she understood was that the man could sense heartbeats and could even remember their "signature pulsations," as he had called it. He'd repeatedly found them whenever they hid from that fucker while under the Hyashi roof. It was downright frightening that someone like him had an ability like that.

"Tell me how—"

"Oh no," Thomas said, shaking his head. "If Pocky didn't tell you how Stellan would know, then I'm certainly not going down that fucking rabbit hole either. What's important is that your plan worked."

"That was her argument. She insisted that it wouldn't work without you at the heart of the operation, and she was convincing enough for us to go with it, but I want to assure you—"

"I don't need your assurances. I already know she would never directly or intentionally compromise me over to Stellan. It's okay that I was used." Thomas turned to Pocky, his gaze softening. "It's okay, Sis. It really is."

Pocky looked away, unable to hold her emotions. She wiped away her tears, and Thomas rubbed her back gently. She wanted to hug him but couldn't in front of the XO.

"As I was going to say," Geara started, no longer exuding patience, "I can assure you that you can trust me—"

"If we're done here, I'd like a moment with my sister," Thomas said firmly.

Geara's face turned red, no doubt furious at being interrupted a fourth time. Thomas was pushing his limits, and Pocky knew it.

"My sister may be under your thumb," Thomas continued, "but I'm not."

Geara tilted his head. "I understand you're angry with me but—"

"Fucking right I am! My sister gave you an idea, and you approved it. Stellan almost got his hands on me. That is *your* fuckup, not hers. If you would've told me, I would've helped. Instead, I was blindsided because of *your* decisions. And you may have thought I didn't need to know because you had a solid plan, but Stellan showing up early only means he has a better one." Thomas shook his head and sighed. "Heed my warning, sir, be diligent with him in your custody. Good fucking luck with that."

Silence bloomed for a long moment before Geara nodded, then stood. Before exiting, he said, "We're transporting him out of here soon. I'll keep you informed."

After Geara left the café, they heard him shout to their team to make room. Naiko popped her head in as though making sure they survived the man's wrath. "You good?" she asked.

"Can we get a minute alone?" Thomas called back to her.

"Sure, just a minute though," Naiko said with mild reluctance, then backed into the corridor.

"Brother, I'm so sorry. I'm so sorry. I—" Pocky began in a panic, but Thomas gently put his hands on her upper arms and hushed her.

"Don't beat yourself up," he said softly. "I'm not mad at you. You did what you felt was your patriotic duty. You're a good soldier. Plus, it was a chance to get that asshole for whatever he had done. You were right to use me."

"No, I shouldn't have spoken up. It felt dirty. *I* feel dirty."

Thomas closed his eyes and grimaced as though the words hurt him. When he opened his eyes, Pocky not only knew but felt what he was about to say.

"I need you to let go of that," he said. "I'm here right in front of you, unscathed. The circumstances brought us together. For me, this is a new beginning, and we're going to have a whole year together, and I just want to enjoy that. Fuck Stellan, and fuck Geara."

Pocky smiled lightly but sobered quickly. "Geara is a good guy. Believe me, this whole debacle will lie heavy on him for a while."

"Well ..." Thomas let out a slow breath. "I truly hope he's careful. Who knows what hand Stellan is playing. I'm trusting Geara and whatever people he's got to keep Stellan locked up, but I'll feel better once that asshole is off the ship."

"Same," Pocky said, smiling a little.

Naiko cleared her throat from the entryway, then spoke almost musically. "We need to get going, please."

"Yes, ma'am," they said in unison, then laughed.

As they stood, Thomas pulled Pocky into a hug. She exhaled as though she'd been holding her breath ever since Geara had approached her. She was beyond elated that her brother didn't turn her away, but then scolded herself for even thinking that he would. Their bond went deep. But still, this had involved

Stellan. Thinking of lines that shouldn't be crossed, Stellan stood alone on that list. She shook her head dismissively. The air between them was settled, and that was more than she had hoped for. Her mind didn't just feel it; her body did as well, practically singing with relief.

Pocky hefted her pack on and struggled with the right strap. Suddenly, the air escaped her lungs with the sensation that it wasn't coming back, and her body flushed with heat. As the alarm on her med watch went off, she put out her hand against the surface of the table to prevent herself from collapsing to the floor. Her vision went dark as someone gripped her arm and side.

What's happening?

"Fucking damn it, as you would say," a voice snapped.

All she could see was darkness, and it took Pocky a moment to recognize the voice. "Ember? What's wrong?"

"I'm trying to get the Healer's attention, and it's not as easy as I thought it would be. I need to increase—"

"Wait, you're trying to get whose attention and why?"

"Doesn't matter. What you're experiencing isn't more than five seconds. So, you'll be spared the drama. Now get out!"

"Wait, what?"

Pocky's vision came back. Her watch's alarm beeped again. She turned it off with a frustrated sigh, then drew her head back so that she could see the numbers more clearly. While trying to understand what she was reading, she realized someone had their hands on her and was saying something. Her first instinct was to launch into defensive maneuvers the IMF had taught her, but she looked at the person first.

Thomas.

She smiled at him, then frowned when she saw his concerned expression.

"Sis?"

"Yeah?" she replied before looking back at her watch. The readings puzzled her.

"Are you—"

"Partner? What's going on with your watch?" Bren asked as he walked into the café. Naiko trailed behind him.

"It's malfunctioning again," Pocky said with frustration. "It says I spiked a fever."

"No, you were about to faint. You *were* fainting," Thomas said, then looked to Bren. "Bren, she was fainting. That wasn't a malfunction."

"Really?" Pocky replied casually. Thomas gazed back at her as though there was something to be concerned about.

"You need to take this more seriously," Thomas said.

Pocky sighed. When it came to her well-being, Thomas always became unhinged. She'd be lying to herself if she thought she missed this side of him.

"Brother," she started firmly, reaching out with her left hand. "It's been a stressful morning. I honestly thought you would turn me away because that's what I thought I deserved. I probably just got a little lightheaded when I stood. Please don't make it a big deal."

Thomas's chin twitched as he looked at Bren, as though needing their friend to reassure him, which he did with a firm nod.

"Okay," Thomas said, his voice wavering as he looked at Pocky again.

Bren grabbed her hand and gently rotated her wrist to look at her watch. He tapped its surface a few times, scrunching his lips to one side as he read. Pocky was certain he was looking through the history log of her vitals.

"You're gonna have to go to the clinic to have it checked out," Bren said as he let go of her hand. "It's saying you've been spiking fevers. The intervals are too short though. It has to be a malfunction." He placed the back of his fingers against her forehead. "Your temp seems fine to me, and you look okay."

Pocky let out a frustrated sigh. "I was hoping not to, but you're right. Yana needs to go too anyway." She looked at Naiko. "I'll take her after breakfast tomorrow, if that's okay with you, ma'am?"

"Oh! That'll be a great opportunity for the both of you to get to know each other," Naiko said. "A little one-on-one time, right?"

"Yes, ma'am," Pocky said with a forced smile, hoping it would hide her annoyance. Most TCs were chipper and all about bonding as a team, which Pocky normally didn't object to, but Naiko seemed to be one of those people who took it to another level. She couldn't get out of her presence fast enough.

"And thank you, I do appreciate that," Naiko continued.

"Happy to serve, ma'am."

Naiko then looked as though she was about to step on nails. "So, you're really good to go?"

Pocky glanced at her brother. He leaned against the opposite table, arms folded across his chest and eyebrows furrowed. He was surprisingly keeping himself together.

She gave their TC another forced smile. "Yes, ma'am."

"Good, let's get going with the tour then."

14

Lance was chatting with Bren and Naiko when an alarm went off in the café. Bren and Naiko hurried inside, and though Lance was concerned, he was confident Bren could handle whatever the issue was and would call for help if it was needed.

Haize and Kaori were farther away from the door but perked up at the alarm.

"That's a med watch going off," Haize said to Kaori. "Probably Pocky's vitals."

"Their watches read their vitals?" Kai asked.

"Constantly, and it goes off if something's wrong."

Lance frowned and looked back at the café door.

"Really?" Kai asked. "Is she okay?"

"Oh, I'm sure we would've heard some sort of drama by now if there was a real issue. Sometimes the watches malfunction. No biggie to fix it," Haize said with a shrug.

Kaori nodded nonchalantly, then looked around. She frowned when she noticed one of their team members was missing. "Where's Yana?"

"She opted out of the tour, wanting to stay in her room," Lance said.

"That's probably for the best," Kaori said with an affirming expression.

Lance agreed. There would be time to acclimate the woman to the ship at her own pace.

Everyone from the café moved into the corridor. Pocky sported a huge smile, making her glow. Her cheeks reddened when she met Lance's gaze, and he tried to rein in his own smile, but it was hard. She seemed fine despite the alarm; however, Thomas looked worried. Lance was all too familiar with that brotherly concern, which he'd seen often from his cousins back on the farmstead.

"You okay there, girlfriend?" Haize hollered, throwing a smirk in Bren's direction. The big guy glared back.

"Yeah, I'm good," Pocky said. "False alarm."

"Thought so. Need me to calibrate it?"

Pocky shook her head. "Nah. Going to the clinic tomorrow to have it checked."

Before Haize could respond further, Naiko called out, "If we could get moving, that'd be great!"

Everyone followed Naiko. Their TC didn't waste time pointing out the two obvious exits to the well decks before leading them to the midship stairwell that gave access to every floor. However, civilians weren't allowed to go any farther down than the first level they were already on. The canine handlers at the bottom of the steps made the idea of trying very undesirable. Naiko led them to D Deck, or the main deck, next.

When they stepped out onto the covered deck, Lance wasn't expecting to see so many soldiers strewn about. Most were clumped in groups and acted casually as though they were on break. A few with dogs looked to be on patrol.

Though his civilian team looked misplaced among the uniforms, Lance didn't feel out of place among the soldiers. No matter where he had been, he never felt that way, but this was different. It had a familiar feel to it that he couldn't quite pinpoint, especially since he had never been around so many soldiers at once. Even as they approached the gangway, he felt the same, like an itch in the farthest reaches of his mind. He shook his head, trying not to analyze it.

A soldier from one of the groups shouted a string of words in Origin and pointed at Bren. Everyone erupted in cheers and then started chanting his Given Name. With a big grin, Bren spread his arms wide and spoke back in a booming voice, which got the soldiers even more amped up. He joined the group, even sharing a smoke with them. *He must be popular*, Lance thought.

A soldier came up behind Naiko and tapped her on the shoulder. "Ma'am, I'm Sergeant Calski. You wanted to speak with me?"

"Oh yes, good!" Naiko said, then looked at the team. "Stay put, I'll be back in a minute." The TC walked away with Calski, her voice fading as they moved toward the bow. "So I have a team member that's anxious being on the ship, and so I was wondering ..."

Lance noticed Pocky was watching Naiko with a lot of interest until the woman disappeared. She leaped with excitement, startling Thomas as she shouted, "Woo!" She dropped her pack off and placed it against the hull. To everyone's surprise, she then took her sling off too and tossed it out to sea. Lance laughed.

"Uh, Sis, don't you need that?" Thomas asked.

Instead of answering, Pocky stretched her arm out as she walked backward toward Bren and shook her head with a smile. She then turned around and joined the group. She hugged a few soldiers before leaning against the hull railing and falling easily into whatever conversation was going on. When the smoke was passed to her, she gladly accepted and took a puff before handing it back.

"My sister smokes?" Thomas said, mostly to himself, but it made Lance realize he'd been staring and felt heat rise in his cheeks.

"They all do that," Haize said. "It's a bonding thing, sharing a smoke. Don't take it as a habit."

"Oh, okay," Thomas replied with acceptance but still with disapproval in his voice.

"Are they a couple?" Haize asked. "Your sister and Bren, I mean."

Thomas laughed sharply. "No way. Bren is like our older brother, even though we're the same age. They may be glued at the hip, but they'll never be more than that."

"How'd you all meet?" Kaori asked with an inviting smile.

Thomas frowned. "We were eight ..." He paused, then shook his head. "You know, that's a story I'd rather not get into."

Haize rolled his eyes and sighed. "The two of you are the most tight-lipped people I've ever met. You need—"

"It's not exactly a warm fucking fuzzy story to share," Thomas snapped.

Kai put her hand on Thomas's shoulder. "And you don't have to. I'm sorry,

I was just curious." She then turned to Haize and said, "So, you've been on the ship before. What treasures does the main deck hold?"

Haize perked up. "Well, we got the restaurant up toward the bow there. It's off-limits to everyone except guests, which is unfortunate because it holds some of the finest liquor I've ever tasted."

Kai raised her eyebrows. "And how would you know that?"

Haize's smile turned mischievous as he replied. "If you're adventurous, I'll show you later."

"We'll see," Kaori countered, tilting her head from side to side as if seriously mulling over the invitation.

Haize went on to explain the gym across from them. Lance looked through one of the large windows as he listened. Several soldiers were inside using machines and equipment he had never seen before.

"We all have access to the gym no matter the time of day," Haize said. "By the way, just a heads-up. The main deck here is a track for them to run, so don't be startled if you hear pounding feet before dawn."

Lance liked hearing that. He loved to run and exercise and would gladly utilize the facility. Maybe Bren could even show him how the equipment worked. Or even better, Pocky could show him. He smiled at that notion.

"And finally, we got the Rec Hall down on the end. It's mainly used by the IMF, but all are welcome. In fact, I don't doubt they're using it for a Blitz party tonight."

"A what?" Kaori asked.

Again, Haize grinned mischievously. "Oh, you're in for a treat, Kai. Soldiers know how to party. They may walk around with a stick up their ass during the day, but they let loose at night. They play—"

"It's a mash-up of music." Thomas piped in, getting an interested look from Lance. "Bren told me about it. They play a mixture of heavy metal and rapid digital music with slow trance-like intervals."

"Is it live music?" Lance asked.

"According to Bren, sometimes it is but also recordings too."

"It's pretty wild shit and they go nuts for it," Haize added.

Kai sighed, looking disinterested in the topic as she gazed outward, but Haize took her demeanor another way.

"What? You don't approve?" he asked with a smug expression.

"Huh? Oh, no, I don't care about that," Kai replied, half shrugging. "Just eager to see our lab. You know where it is?"

Haize pointed a finger upward. "C Deck. Naiko'll take us there next."

Thomas perked up and started talking to Kaori about the fungus. Lance listened in; the dialogue between the two was similar to the one he had with the man earlier. When they were done, Haize let out an amused grunt.

"What?" Thomas glared at the engineer.

"Nothing," Haize said. "I'm sure you nerds will have a great time doing your thing."

Though Lance felt he had nowhere near his colleagues' expertise, he didn't mind the reference. Thomas rolled his eyes but kept quiet otherwise.

"So, team," Bren said as he joined them, "Pocky and I are playing music tonight in the hall. You're all welcome to come."

The comment got a few reactions at once, but the medic solely focused on Thomas.

"Seriously? You have a band now?" he asked with a huge smile.

"Not exactly. *Gaia* is already equipped with instruments. Shitty ones, but good enough. And it wasn't hard to find some fellow soldiers to play keys and drums. It's gonna be heavy shit though."

"The heavier the better," Thomas said, then offered his hand. Bren clasped his grip, and then they laughed as they quickly pulled back and snapped their fingers.

"Is that why they call you Music Man?" asked Kaori.

"Something like that," Bren replied with an amused shrug.

"Bullshit," Thomas said and then looked at Kai with excited, wide eyes. "Bren's got the uncanny ability to be able to play anything just by strumming a few cords or keys."

"Really?" Kaori asked.

"Nah, what's amazing was teaching Pocky how to play bass," Bren said to

Thomas, then laughed deep within his throat.

"Yeah, she said you taught her a few notes. Is she decent?"

"Passable, and she doesn't kid herself thinking she's more than that. But she enjoys it and that's what matters. Helps keep her mind off things."

Thomas frowned. "Like what?"

"Missing you mostly."

Thomas nodded solemnly.

"So, Bren, what do you play?" Kaori asked.

"I do vocals and electric guitar."

Lance raised his eyebrows. He had attended a lot of concerts while he traveled through Theton. Regardless of the variety of entertainment that was strewn between thousands of cultures, music was the most in-demand by the public. Though he had never heard of "heavy" music, he was interested to hear how it would sound and to watch them play.

Naiko returned shortly before a few soldiers walked up next to Bren. They were eager to meet Pocky's twin, and their TC couldn't refuse the opportunity. Besides their hair and eyes, the two were vastly different. The first two soldiers didn't waste the chance to poke fun at the height difference before the last one shooed them away. The man was as tall and broad as Bren but had a darker complexion, and his features were dappled with black freckles.

"This is Buki," Bren said.

Buki clasped Thomas's hand with both of his and spoke in a deep accent that Lance hadn't heard before. "It's nice to meet you, Brother. More handsome than I expected. Your sister, my best friend. She saved my life once, yeah."

"Really? How so?" Thomas asked.

Bren looked at the soldier curiously as though he didn't know either. Buki glared back at the medic.

"Remember Project Fall on Our Asses?" Buki raised his eyebrows, making Bren burst into laughter. "First time on a project with these two fuckers," Buki said to Thomas. "'Go on a hike,' Pocky say. 'It'll be great,' she say. Brother, I don't like the woods. Grew up city boy."

"Newsflash, Buki. We all grew up in the city," Bren said.

"You know what I mean, asshole. Anyway, we walk for hours, don't like it, and suddenly I feel something on the tip of my dick."

Bren cackled. "He starts ripping everything off, wailing like a girl, 'Get it off, get it off!'"

Buki made a guttural sound in the back of his throat. "Damn bug was trying to crawl up my pee hole like it was looking for something. Pocky got it off me."

"Well, I would have," Bren said, chuckling, "but I had to hold you down so that she could."

"I know you jealous."

"Totally," Bren said with seriousness, then laughed again.

Lance laughed alongside them. He and his cousins had run into similar incidents many times over the years.

Buki's expression grew somber. "But seriously, Pocky would put her body in between anyone to stop them from being hurt. She brave, you should know that. We, family, respect that, respect her. You should know that too, yeah."

Thomas nodded. The man looked between being proud and worried by Buki's words. For Lance, a warm excitement spread across his chest. The soldier's story was just a small slice of Pocky's world, and he wanted to know more.

"And, Brother, how the hell does she know so many damn languages?" Buki asked. "Even my captain calls to her, 'Pocky! Come the fuck over here and tell me what the hell these people are saying!'"

"Uh"—Thomas shrugged awkwardly—"she just reads a lot, I guess."

Buki looked at Bren. "Like we have time for that bullshit." They both laughed, but then the man grew somber again and spoke with dread in his voice. "By the way, M. Trooper is working in the clinic, yeah."

Bren closed his eyes and sighed through his nose. "Fuck."

"Yeah, didn't think you knew."

"I didn't. I'll deal with it later. Thanks."

After Buki parted ways, the medic's expression grew even more withdrawn.

"Bren? You okay?" Thomas asked.

"Yeah."

"So ..." Kaori began cautiously. "Great story. Bet you and Pocky have a ton of those."

"Sometimes," Bren replied with a shrug. "Being a medic isn't always glamorous, and Pocky doesn't share. Neither do I most times."

"Why so?" Kaori asked.

Bren shrugged again. "Trying to rescue people over the open ocean is not easy. It's a dangerous job even on a good day. And no offense, but you civies aren't exactly nice when you need us."

"What, you expect someone that's bleeding out to be civil?" Haize drawled.

"That's a given, asshole. I'm talking of the ones that don't have a scratch on them that get in our way. We've been spit on, yelled at, beaten, sometimes worse. I was even stabbed once."

"What?" Thomas gasped. "Why?"

"Trying to save a little boy, and the father didn't think I was moving fast enough. Thankfully we had two trainees with us, otherwise Pocky would have had a difficult choice to make."

"What the fuck?" Thomas shook his head in disbelief.

"Where at?" Lance asked.

Bren took his index finger and drew a slight line down between his sternum and left pectoral muscle as he spoke. "Almost got my heart. Came up behind me. No one saw him coming because everyone was so focused on the boy. Pocky was trying to help me when it happened and punished herself for not seeing it coming. Had to be evac'd. It's a miracle I survived. Well, I thought so, anyway. Felt like the knife went deep, but when I got to the infirmary, they said it wasn't as deep as they expected. Good thing it wasn't."

"Shit," Thomas whispered, his face grimacing.

Lance couldn't imagine nearly losing a loved one like that, nor could he fathom a father attacking a medic for trying to save his child.

"Was she able to save the boy?" Kaori asked with hesitation.

"No," Bren murmured. "Kids are the hardest to save because of their small bodies. Babies especially. That's why we don't like to talk. It was a bad fucking day for everyone."

"Is it like that every time?" Kai asked.

"Just about." Bren looked at Thomas. "Didn't mean to kill the mood, but I did need to rip the bandage off. Buki's story isn't the only one you're gonna hear. Good ones like that are far and few between." He sighed. "And Pocky would lose her shit if she knew I was saying this much."

Thomas looked down at his boots. "She never said anything in her letters. About herself or you."

"She didn't want you to worry."

Thomas's expression warred between worry, confusion, and hurt. Lance couldn't even guess how the man was processing all that for the first time. It was difficult even for him to picture any of it.

"Um, Bren?" Naiko spoke up. "If you don't mind me asking, what's wrong with her arm? Will it affect her job?"

Bren's expression hardened. Lance wasn't sure if anyone else caught it, but Naiko asked the question in a way that their medic had to answer, like bending his arm. Lance understood why she had done it but still didn't care for the tactic. She most likely just wanted everyone to know so that the question didn't linger on everyone's minds. Though he wanted to know, this wasn't how he would have preferred it.

Bren gritted his teeth. "It's not her arm. Her shoulder blade was broken in two places a long time ago. The last rescue call we were on aggravated it, but she was cleared for duty. If you want the report that says so, I'll hand deliver it."

Before Naiko could reply, Thomas asked, "How the hell did that happen?"

"And that's the exact fucking reason why she keeps her mouth shut, 'cause it always leads to the next question," Bren snapped. His fists tightened at his side. "I'm warning you right now, leave it be."

"But—"

"I'm telling you, she'll shut down if you do. I'll tell you about it later, but not now."

Thomas put his hands up. "Okay, alright."

Bren turned sharply to Naiko. "Ma'am, do you mind if Pocky and I go? We need to practice."

"Practice?" Naiko asked.

After the medic explained what had been discussed earlier about the two of them playing in the Rec Hall, and clearly reading the man's agitation she had caused, Naiko allowed them to go. Bren grabbed Pocky's pack and stalked off. Before disappearing into the crowd, the big guy tapped Pocky on the shoulder and then gestured for her to follow him. She looked back at Thomas and smiled before following her partner.

Whatever had caused Pocky's injury was clearly just as hurtful for Bren. Something about that made the farthest reaches of Lance's mind itch, and he didn't like it.

Before moving on in their tour, Lance asked to be alone for a moment, wanting to reel in his troubled mind. Naiko thankfully allowed it. Thomas asked if he could join him, and he welcomed the company. They stood over the hull railing in comfortable silence until they were ready to move on.

15

Thomas tried not to let Bren's words overtake his mind and revert to his old ways as Naiko led them to C Deck. At first, she spoke with nervous excitement but gradually got a sense of herself again.

This level of the ship was divided into two parts with a passageway leading to the port side stairwell. The bow side consisted of the guest area, which, just like the restaurant, was off-limits to the IMF and civilians. According to their TC, the stern side was considered the best asset of the entire ship. They learned why that was. Besides the lab where he, Kaori, and Lance were going to be trained, there was also a greenhouse with curved glass windows that gave an amazing view of the Charter Channel and the IMF fleet. The plants grown inside weren't just for training but were also a food resource for the ship. He was humbled by that.

What was just as incredible was the library across the corridor. Thomas never dreamed he would be on a giant ship that housed such a place and gave a nod to whoever thought of the idea. Its brown furnishings and low lights reminded him of the one in the nicer orphanage they were homed in. And what made the place even more unique was its four private reading sections with floor-to-ceiling windows. He and his team sat in the last section, which had a wraparound couch, and marveled at the view of the harbor. The convoy that had lined alongside *Gaia* was now gone. He hoped that meant Stellan was long gone too, but until Thomas had confirmation, he wouldn't feel completely at ease.

Time got away as the five of them chatted and became more comfortable with each other. After a brief announcement spoken in both Origin and Thetonian, they watched as *Gaia* was slowly pulled away from the port and tugged out to sea. From this height, watching Daria Harbor grow smaller was beyond incredible, and Thomas couldn't believe how fortunate he was to be able to experience such an event. He exchanged a look with Lance, who seemed to feel either the same or something similar.

As they settled back down onto the couch, Naiko moved away when her radio went off. While they'd been sitting there, music from the floor below had been steady but not loud enough to know what Bren and Pocky were playing. Thomas wanted to take apart every word Bren had spoken, replay it, analyze it, all to get a detailed picture of what his sister's life had been like. But the day and travel lag were beginning to etch their way into his mind. While he really wanted to eat dinner and crash for the night, he also wanted to see his sister and Bren play at least one song. He was determined to stay up for that.

"Thomas?" Naiko said.

He jerked awake and shook his head slightly. "Ma'am?"

"The SC is on her way up here. She says it's urgent to speak with you. Mind waiting for her by the entrance?"

"Yeah, sure," he said, then stood.

Thomas moved slowly at first, not feeling the urgency until he remembered Geara would keep him updated on Stellan's status. The SC should be privy to that as well; Thomas picked up his pace. He didn't have long to wait, as shortly after he got to the library's entrance, a woman with enough gear to be her own army walked in. The expression on her face didn't give him confidence that everything was going well.

"Thomas?"

"Yes, ma'am."

"Security Chief Viper. Nice to meet you," she said and extended her hand.

The name gave Thomas pause; was this the same woman Bren had mentioned in his letters? Because of the situation, he decided not to ask and shook her hand.

"Pleased to meet you, ma'am. So, what's up?"

"I've come to update you on Stellan."

"Figured."

"He's still on the ship," she said flatly, then quickly added, "still in the brig."

Thomas looked behind him. Why were they being tugged if Stellan was still onboard? He looked back at Viper and tried to remain calm despite the way his heart hammered in his chest. He had dreaded this, that Stellan would somehow find a way to stay onboard.

"Why?" Thomas snapped. "Why is he still here?"

"We have our reasons, but Geara wanted you to know. I assure you, you and your sister are safe—"

"No, we're not!" he spat. "That asshole was *smiling* as I climbed up the stairs. He has a plan, and you need to get ahead of it!"

Viper's jaw slackened, then straightened. "Look, I can't say anything further, and I'm only telling you this because my XO ordered me to," she said. "I can assure you that we're ahead of it. I promise to keep you updated as we go."

Thomas spread his arms wide. "My sister and I don't really have a fucking choice, do we?"

Viper's gaze flicked down, then sharply back up at Thomas. "I'm sorry." She looked past him, and Thomas turned to see his team moving toward them. "I'll keep you updated on the situation," she said, then exited.

"Everything okay, Thomas?" Naiko asked gently as the team caught up to him.

"Not really," he muttered. "Stellan's still onboard the ship, but she wouldn't tell me why."

"Ah, yeah, Geara informed me of the situation but didn't disclose what he had done. I won—"

"Wait, he told you I was used to bring Stellan here?"

Naiko's eyes widened. "Used you? No, just that they had a warrant to arrest him."

Thomas sighed. He couldn't believe he so easily revealed his part in Geara's plan to get Stellan. Naiko, thankfully, took it as something else.

"Well, you did say he was your adoptive brother at one point, so I guess Geara figured Stellan would want a family reunion," she said.

"My sister and I weren't adopted. We were purchased," Thomas replied, surprised he was being candid about it in front of the others. Maybe it was because he wanted other people to know Stellan wasn't the upstanding aristocrat who enjoyed funding CCO projects.

"Excuse me?" Naiko's eyebrows rose. "What do you mean by purchased?"

"Just that. Back then, orphanages brokered children for pervs until the IMF intervened."

Thomas let the comment linger in the air as he thought back to the day he, Pocky, and Bren went into the IMF station. It was a day that didn't just change their lives but also all the others who were unwilling participants in the trade. He smiled slightly to himself; it was a good feeling to know they'd helped save so many kids.

Naiko made a disgusted sound, and Thomas realized he should've followed up on his statement. He hadn't meant for the others to draw their own conclusions as to his and Pocky's fate. Of all of them, he met Lance's gaze, whose angered expression made Thomas quick to ease their minds.

"We weren't bought for that purpose," he said. "But our four years there were a long fucking nightmare regardless. The IMF rehomed us, and that's how Pocky and I met Bren. But Stellan is a sick, perverted person and was grossly cruel—"

"Thomas, please," Naiko interrupted, almost gagging on her words. "I love people and getting to know them, but you don't have to say anything further. I get it. We all get it."

Thomas nodded, feeling regret for his admission. Lance clasped his shoulder, his expression full of compassion yet holding a certain steadiness that helped Thomas feel a little unburdened. A familiarity suddenly hit him. It was as though the two of them had shared a moment like this before, but they'd never met, so how was that possible? Thomas shrugged it off; maybe he'd just met someone similar to Lance before.

Lance led the way out of the library, and the entire team followed. Thomas went through the motions, his mind growing foggy. Travel lag was hitting him hard now that the adrenaline from his conversation with Viper had worn off.

"What are we doing now?" Thomas asked no one in particular.

"Dinner," Naiko replied quietly.

"Yeah, if any of us can eat after that," Haize countered.

Thomas shook his head, wishing he'd just kept his mouth shut. Lance shouldered with him. Again, that familiarity came back, but it strangely felt more nostalgic this time. He shook his head again. He was too travel lagged to contemplate it.

***

Lance felt a little recharged after they ate. Yana had joined them but declined to go topside with them, as did Naiko, who retired for the night. He felt for her. The woman hadn't seemed to recover from Thomas's words, and he couldn't blame her. Though Thomas had been quick to point out that he and Pocky hadn't been subjected to sexual intentions by the Hyashi family, the implication that something like that had even gone on was disturbing on an epic level. Because Yana had grown up in an orphanage, even though it was within Shad'Dyn, they had all mutually decided not to share this with her.

While they ate, D Deck was audibly filling up with people; the music growing louder. After they were done cleaning up their mess, Iza offered an alternate way to the Rec Hall. They went behind the counter and followed her through the kitchen and up a stairway that led to the restaurant.

"This is how we sneak in and sample the liquor," Haize said to Kai, wiggling his brows. Laughing, she rolled her eyes.

They followed Iza through a connecting bathroom to the gym, then into another connecting bathroom that led to the Rec Hall. Iza happened to have the keys to the locked doorways that partitioned the bathrooms. By going this way, they avoided shoving their way into the Rec Hall from the main deck.

Once they were inside, Lance was glad they'd gone this route. The place was packed. There was no way they could have gained entry otherwise and gotten there just in time.

The crowd went insane as Bren roared into his mic and began playing. It was hard to see the big guy and Pocky, but it was better than not seeing them at all.

The others cheered wildly with the mass of soldiers. Even in his enthusiasm for the music, Lance kept his eyes on Pocky. She bounced to the beat as her fingers moved over the strings, a wide grin spreading across her face. Though there was an obvious degree of pride in being a soldier and a medic, Lance got the sense that at this moment she was letting go of that persona and was being her raw self.

As Lance watched her, a new sensation filled his veins. Pocky was beautiful and talented, and he badly wanted to know more about her. Then, for a sudden split second, he remembered who he really was, who she really was, and why they were really there. But it was gone from his memory in a flash.

Lance shook his head, feeling there had been a lapse in time. He summed up the delay as just being tired. It had been a more eventful day than he had expected. Though he could crash into a blissful sleep at this very moment, he wasn't going anywhere and enjoyed the performance as the night went on.

16

Pocky lost count of how many songs they had played but knew it was late. She was tired and her fingers were starting to ache. When they finished the current song, she signaled to Bren that she was done. Her partner nodded, then asked the crowd if they were ready for more. The mob went ballistic and started chanting his Given Name. She laughed at how righteous that was. She regarded her best friend for a moment. He was a brilliant medic, better than five of them put together, but he was really at home when it came to music.

Pocky traded the bass for her med pack, said good night to the other band members, and then made her way to the stage's back door. The private passageway led to a small lounge and the gym's entrance. She went through the door and navigated her way through several sections of bathrooms, showers, and locker rooms. Once in the gym's main space, she dodged the various equipment strewn around and into the bathroom shared between the gym and the restaurant. Unbeknownst to everyone else, Iza kept the connecting door that led to the restaurant unlocked just for her and Bren. She appreciated the quick access back to their café.

When Pocky reached the stairway that led to the café's kitchen, a sharp electric pain erupted around her right shoulder blade, blinding her to the point of almost passing out. The pain was more acute than ever before. She went down on one knee and nearly puked. The alarm on her watch went off, making her ears ring. She shut it off and didn't bother to read the numbers. She staggered to her feet and forced herself to keep going.

Getting to the café felt like an eternity, and climbing over the counter was equivalent to the steepest mountain Pocky had ever hiked. She hefted off her pack on the closest table and took a minute to catch her breath. She was sweating and trembling. She grabbed one of her water containers and downed the entire contents along with some painkillers. During practice, she had taken her scrub shirt off and was thankful for that decision as she carefully pulled the tight gray undershirt off. Now down to her bra, she undid the right strap. She then sat on top of the table and went into her pack.

After rummaging a bit, Pocky pulled out four stiff packs the size of her hand. Breaking the packs in the middle would activate an intense coolant substance. She broke the first pack and waited for it to cool. Unfortunately, there was nothing else she could do until the painkillers kicked in. She hoped numbing the area would help until then.

When it was ready, Pocky placed the pack on her shoulder and almost cried out. The cold was so overwhelming that she wished she'd grabbed a bite stick. She held steady. Several agonizing minutes later, the ice pack had lost its coolant, and unfortunately, it wasn't enough. Before using another, though, she had to warm her fingers up. Unable to feel them, she put her hand between her thighs and folded her right arm against her chest. Her leg bounced nervously as she tried to relax.

A squeak from a boot made Pocky sigh in disbelief. Obviously, someone had entered the café and was surprised to see her. *Fucking great.*

"Pocky?" Lance asked.

She sighed again, feeling embarrassed. This couldn't be any more awkward than it already was, sitting there in her bra with a hand close to her crotch. She heard him moving closer, then sucked in a breath when his fingertips brushed her good shoulder.

"I'm sorry," he said quickly, pulling his hand away. "I didn't mean to—"

"No, you're fine," Pocky said, not wanting him to feel bad for something she surprisingly didn't mind him doing.

"What happened?"

The kindness in his voice made Pocky look up at him. The compassion in his eyes was captivating. She blinked a few times, lost in them. He spoke again, pleading for her to answer. It suddenly occurred to her that with the position she was in, she probably looked as though she had just been assaulted.

"My shoulder ... I don't know why," she said. "I'm icing it, but I'm waiting for my hand to warm up before doing another." She held up her left hand on the last word.

Lance relaxed a bit, and then to her surprise, he took her cold hand in both of his and hissed with a grimace. "Shit, your fingers are freezing." He blew hot air onto her hand, then rubbed her fingers, warming her near-frozen digits.

She involuntarily smiled, then shyly pressed her lips together.

His eyes darted to her shoulder, then to her unused ice packs, then back to her. "Uh, if you're comfortable with it, I could hold the next pack?"

Pocky found herself nodding before thinking. "You wouldn't mind?"

"No," Lance replied almost in a whisper. He gave her another reassuring smile. "Where do you want me to place it?"

"Right in the middle of my shoulder blade, please."

Lance placed her hand respectfully down in her lap and looked over her shoulder. Pocky held in a breath as his scent hit her. She wasn't sure if it was something he used for his hair, his beard, or his laundry soap, but whatever it was, she wanted to inhale it and hold it in her olfactory system forever. Biting her lower lip, she moved her eyes to his neckline, to his tan skin, and to the way his neck muscles flexed as he swallowed. She wanted to touch him with her hands, with her lips. But when he spoke, she lost her voice for a moment. She had momentarily forgotten that he was viewing the two scars the size of her thumb nails on her shoulder blade.

"Bullets?"

When Pocky didn't answer, Lance pulled away and frowned at her. Again, the compassion in his eyes was brilliant. She nodded her answer slowly, then shook her head, hoping he would understand that she didn't want to talk about it. Thankfully, he did. That awful event still haunted her. She couldn't even talk about it with Bren.

"Okay," Lance said, then grabbed an unused ice pack.

Pocky instructed him on how to activate it but encouraged him to use a towel to prevent his hand and fingers from going cold like hers. She had been in so much pain that she hadn't thought of that. Lance did everything exactly as she had said. The moment the ice pack hit her skin, she tried hard to hold in her discomfort. She didn't even realize she had grabbed the front of his shirt until he gently took her hand in his. She focused on the feeling of his skin, liking how that felt.

As the ice pack lost its coolant, Pocky realized that Lance had moved so close that her forehead was pressed against his sternum and her other arm had wrapped around his back, her once numb hand tangled into his shirt. The softness of the material and his scent mixed in with her senses. She was suddenly caught between the residual pain and the desire to explore his body. Her mind tempered her body before giving him the wrong signal. She didn't want to give him the impression that she was the kind of woman who would make sexual advances to someone she had just met because she wasn't like that in the least.

"Okay, that's good enough," Pocky said as she let go of him, her whole face heating.

Lance pulled the ice pack off. The painkillers were finally kicking in. Pocky exhaled a long breath. She covered her face with her hands and felt her tears that had streamed like a raging waterfall. She went into her pack for a towel, then cleaned herself up. Afterward, she re-strapped the right side of her bra, grabbed her scrub shirt, and buttoned it up.

When she felt brave enough, she turned to him. "Thank you for helping me … again."

Lance nodded instead of replying. Pocky thought perhaps that the usual phrases of "Are you okay?" or something similar didn't sit right with the man. That, or something else was going through his mind.

"Of course," he said finally. "Does … this happen often?"

"Actually, no. I was fine until I almost got here. I don't know what got it agitated."

"Playing bass, you think?"

"Shouldn't, but I don't know," Pocky replied with a tired sigh. She then got up and started cleaning up the mess.

"Speaking of that, you were beautiful up there."

Pocky slowed her motions and was thankful she had her back to him so he couldn't see her blush. "Thank you. So ... you made it, huh?"

"Except for Yana and Naiko, we did."

"Nice. Whatcha think?"

"Never heard music like that before, but I liked it. Thomas enjoyed it too, but he didn't stay long. He was tired."

"No doubt the day had taken a lot out of him. Plus, he traveled from Sirk'Tans. Wherever the hell that is."

"Damn, that's three days by vehicle ..." Lance said, his words trailing off.

"Something wrong?" Pocky asked as she finished tidying up.

"No. Just thinking of something Thomas had said to me earlier."

Pocky turned to face him. "About what?"

Lance told her about the brief conversation the two had about a fungus problem farmers were having and her brother's concern. As he spoke, he sat down on the bench, folding up one leg. Pocky straddled the bench beside him and listened to his family's predicament back on their farmstead. She couldn't imagine finding a whole portion of property destroyed like that.

"I know firsthand what kind of damage that fungus can do," Lance said. "I hate that it's more widespread than I knew. I understand why Thomas's worried. That shit is hard to kill."

"But you were able to, right?"

Lance turned his head away. "Sort of."

He shifted his position a little and lightly scratched under his chin. Seeing he'd become uncomfortable, Pocky reached out and placed a reassuring hand on his forearm. He gazed back at her with wide eyes.

"Sorry," Pocky said, pulling away. "My hand still cold?"

Lance grabbed her hand and held it in his. "No."

Pocky blushed again when he didn't let go. Not quite ready to acknowledge that they were having a moment, she tried to press on with the topic. "I, um, know we just met today, but I promise to be respectful when you're ready to share. If you ever *want* to share," she said.

Lance pressed his lips together, his eyes downcast. When he finally did speak, his voice was quiet. "That fungus can't be killed. My father and I tried everything. Home remedies, fire, drowning it, none of it worked. We even tried chemicals, stuff that had never been used on our soil. Nothing worked. But then I had a moment that I still don't understand, and it was strange. Still spooks me a little, and it's also ... embarrassing."

Not wanting to give words of encouragement or assurances, Pocky squeezed his hand gently instead. It was her way of saying that she was listening and that he could continue if he wanted.

"We had a few trees that were being consumed by the fungus and were almost stumps. I was alone, writing notes on my maps, logging where the infected areas were. Then, next thing I know, I'm pissing on one of the stumps. That's not like me. It wasn't just the lapse of how I went from where I was to there, but if I needed to relieve myself, I would have gone into the woods nearby. But what happened next gets even weirder.

"Where my urine had landed, the fungus started to dissolve. It was dying. I could see the bark again. At first, I was elated and wished I understood the chemistry of how that was possible. Then—" Lance paused and sighed tiredly. "Well, the first person I tell, of course, is my father. Long story short, he tried, my mother, extended family, our neighbors." He paused again, shaking his head. "No one's worked except mine. And I'm still struggling to understand that."

Pocky now understood his trepidation. It was one thing to discover that your urine worked effectively on something that couldn't be killed, but another when it was only yours that did. That had to be disconcerting. Plus, his explanation about how something had seemed to take over his mind and body was something she could relate to, and surprisingly, she found herself talking about it.

"Had a rescue call like that once in my first year of duty," Pocky began. "A fishing town called Nyrathia sent a distress call for aid, saying that they were being attacked. Our Strat Units are trained for that kind of thing, but they couldn't get there fast enough, but we could. We didn't know what we were getting into, though. We thought it was just another minor conflict, but ... it was far from being that. It was ... an all-out war. We didn't know till months after that neighboring provinces were killing each other to take over the town." She paused, paling at her own words. She had never spoken of that time, not even to Bren. Her eyes dropped to her lap. "When we got there, it was horrifying. Our captain was even stunned by what we were seeing and didn't want us getting off our ship, thinking that these people would kill us before we could help anyone.

"We were ordered to stay inside and get some sleep if we could. The booms of gunfire were constant and rapid though. It was constantly going, and going, and going, and loud as fuck. We'd been trained to get over that type of noise of course, but this was different because we could hear people dying in the distance. Those kinds of screams are ..." Pocky rubbed her forehead. "Anyway, I remember somehow falling asleep, and then the next thing I know, I've got boots on the ground, running in the night and into a war zone, not knowing why I'm doing it. But there were people that needed my help. I knew that for certain, and I had a drive to get to them. But I was also disobeying an order. I just left my team without a word, without even telling M."

Pocky looked Lance in the eyes. His expression was troubled, but his eyes were compassionate. She looked away and pressed her knuckles against her forehead. "It was twenty-one days of hell and how my shoulder got fucked up. And how I got these." She held up her free hand, palm out.

Lance let go of her other hand and then took the one she was holding out. Pocky moved her palms together so he could see that both were badly scarred. His jaw dropped.

Lance took her hands into his and looked up at her with wide eyes. "Fuck, I ... I'm so sorry. You didn't have to tell me that."

"I didn't show you this for sympathy," Pocky murmured. "I just wanted you to know that I can relate to that feeling."

"It was like someone switching you on autopilot, right?"

"Yeah, exactly."

Silence fell between them as their eyes locked. Lance's expression seemed to be between wanting more and exhaustion. As much as she wanted the same, she was running on fumes and decided it was time to part ways for both their sakes.

She smiled shyly. "We need sleep."

Lance let go of her hands. "Sorry, hope I wasn't being inappropriate by that."

"I'm not committed to anyone, so you're not," Pocky said casually.

The sudden hope in his eyes made her bite her lower lip. She was attracted to him, and Lance seemed to be attracted to her. For her though, this was a first. It was almost ridiculous to think, but she hadn't met anyone who made her feel like this, especially with how many good-looking men she was constantly around, Bren being one of them. But she had been so career-driven since getting into the military that being with someone had never been a thought. She laughed quietly to herself.

"What?" Lance asked, a delighted but confused smile lighting up his face.

"It's just been an interesting day," Pocky replied with a wide grin.

"Yeah, it has," Lance said, smiling back. "And I'm not with anyone either."

Of course, Pocky wanted to be friends with Lance, and she got the sense that he did too, but the possibility of having something deeper to explore made her stomach flutter.

They said their good nights and parted ways. Before drifting off to sleep, Pocky thought of the way Lance had held her hand, the light in his eyes, and his scent. She couldn't wait for morning.

17

The first morning hours couldn't have gone better in Thomas's opinion. After breakfast, his team went their own ways. Pocky took Yana to the clinic; Bren headed to the gym; and Thomas, Kaori, and Lance followed Naiko to the lab to begin their training. With nothing to do or a place to go, Haize was the only one who hung back.

Their lab completely entranced Thomas. It was equipped with instruments he had never seen before. Kaori, coming from a highly recognized school where she received diplomas in both botany and horticulture, was excited to show him how most of the devices worked. However, some of the tools at their disposal were new to even her.

The machine that mesmerized them both was the projector that took slide samples and pulled the sample up into a 3-D image above the lighted surface. With just a touch of their fingers on the surface, they could rotate, enlarge, and magnify the image. The slides on hand were of leaves from common trees around Shad'Dyn. Thomas could examine them down to their square cells, far beyond what he could see under a normal microscope. He couldn't wait to see what secrets his fungus samples held. With this technology, he felt confident he would learn more about the invasive species.

When the three of them returned to the café for lunch, Haize was chatting with Iza. The engineer looked happy enough for the company but didn't seem to be his usual chipper self.

"Hey, guys. Where's Naiko?" Haize asked dryly.

"She was called away for a meeting," Lance said. "What's up with you?

Feeling okay?"

"Something's weird going on," Haize replied.

"How so?"

"Well, as an engineer, and from being on this ship before, I'm acutely aware of how *Gaia* sounds and feels when she's being warmed up, and it's not happening."

"Like, at all?"

"Nope. She's stone cold, and that's unusual after being tugged."

Everyone looked to Iza as though the woman would know. She spread her hands apart, eyebrows raised. "Like I would know. I'm just a Floater."

"What's a Floater?" Lance queried, much to Thomas's relief that someone would ask.

"It means I don't have a team," Iza said. "Anyway, I'll go prep your lunch."

Thomas wanted to ask why Iza didn't have a team, but she busied herself with gathering a fresh pot of coffee and supplies for them before heading into the kitchen.

After settling at a table with their mugs, Haize asked, "How was training?"

Kaori and Lance responded casually, each giving their take on it. Thomas tried to interject what he could, but the question of why *Gaia* was cold lingered on his mind. He hoped Stellan wasn't part of the reason, or *the* reason.

Bren walked in a few minutes later, a teasing grin on his face as he set his med pack down. "What's up, my people? And Haize ..."

Haize raised his mug with an unamused smile. "Fun."

Bren fixed himself some coffee, then sat across from Thomas. They exchanged another old greeting by bumping the back of their fists twice, laughing at the nostalgia of it all. Despite his worries, Thomas felt better in Bren's presence and couldn't wait to catch up.

"So, how'd your training go?" Bren asked after they sobered up.

"It was—"

Yana appeared in the doorway and squealed like a kid when she spotted Thomas. Dumbfounded, everyone watched as she made her way to him and sat. She bounced up and down with excitement, her breasts following the motions.

Thomas buried his face in his hands with embarrassment.

"Oh my shit, Thomas!" Yana slapped his upper arm. "I have the best news ever!"

"Uh, Yana?" Bren said slowly. "What did the clinic give you?"

"Something chewy," she replied, still focused on Thomas. "Did you know your sister's a war hero?"

Thomas stared at Yana as she began to elaborate. When Bren tried to stop her, she didn't listen.

"No, no, no! Fucking stop!" Bren slammed his fist on the table, and a loud snap reverberated through the café. Since the table was metal, Thomas was worried Bren had broken a bone, but it got Yana's attention. "Where'd you hear that?" Bren snapped.

"Trooper at the clinic," Yana said casually. "Why? Was he lying?"

Bren placed his palms against his eyes. "Fuck!"

Yana ignored Bren's reaction and tried to begin again. Seeing whatever she had to say was upsetting the man, Thomas tried stopping her from speaking further, but she ignored him too.

"Yana!" Lance shouted, shoving to his feet. Everyone looked up at him. Everything around them seemed to go silent, even their heartbeats. Yana looked away as he spoke to her. "Whatever you know, it's no one's business."

"But it's a beautiful story of her saving people," she mumbled. "Thomas should know."

"Read the room," Lance said sternly. Yana slowly looked at Thomas, then to Bren, and finally back at Lance. She shrugged, still not understanding. He sighed. "It may be a beautiful story to you, but for Bren and Pocky, it may not be. Get it?"

Yana slightly shook her head, still not seeming to understand. Thomas got the sense that the woman hadn't seen much of the ugly side of life. Some events just needed to stay unspoken and unshared. Of course, he was curious, but he also didn't care for everyone else to know either. Lance got that, and Thomas was thankful for his efforts.

"Okay, fine, but I've got a burning question that I gotta ask her," Yana said.

Bren pressed his fists against the table, voice tight. "Yana, I'm *begging* you, don't bring this up around Pocky. Don't say a word to her. Please."

"But I wanna ask—"

Bren shook his head rapidly. "It took almost a year for her to be right again, but she's still not over it. And I almost lost my partner. I'm not over it!"

Thomas's heart felt like it skipped a beat. "Wait? What?"

As though realizing what he'd said, Bren gritted his teeth, then dropped his face into his hands and rubbed his eyes. He was about to break; that was clear enough to Thomas. The big guy abruptly got up and left the café. Thomas knew he should go after Bren but was in a daze until Lance tapped him on the shoulder.

"Go." Lance nodded toward the entryway.

Snapping out of it, Thomas jumped up and went into the corridor, catching a glimpse of Bren just as he went through the doors that led to the bow's well deck. Thomas ran after him.

Outside, Bren leaned over the railing and vomited. Thomas scanned the area, grateful that they were alone. He helped lower Bren to the deck when he was finished spitting out the remnants of what was most likely their breakfast. Then Thomas sat sideways next to him, legs crossed.

Bren sobbed quietly, tears pouring down his face. His breaths were uneven and ragged. It pained Thomas to see him like this. In fact, he hadn't seen Bren like this since they found him in that dumpster as kids.

Thomas tried not to let his mind race as he waited for Bren to gather himself.

"We were on a rescue call," Bren began hoarsely. "There was a fishing village under attack by several neighboring provinces. We were still Freshers. Our captain docked us alongside an old port, hoping no one would notice us."

Thomas swallowed hard, worry gnawing at his gut.

"Brother, it was an all-out war," Bren said. "Gunfire, rockets, explosions, people screaming, people dying. It was horrifying, and we couldn't do a damn thing about it, but we couldn't just leave either. None of us could sleep, but I eventually passed out from sheer exhaustion. I don't know how long I was asleep when one of the officers woke me up. Pocky was missing, and no one could find her. We didn't know if she had stepped out onto the deck and was kidnapped or if she had gone out on her own."

Bren's eyes were filled with grief as he continued, "She was gone for twenty-one days." He covered his face with his hands. "I was fucking scared out of my mind," he said, voice wavering. "I thought she was dead, and felt responsible for that. I was racked with guilt and clueless about how I would tell you. How would I tell my brother that I lost our sister?"

Thomas could easily picture Bren stricken with grief, maybe even losing his sanity from worry. With that many days, it had to have been hell. Ever since they had met, Bren had been protective of them both, but more so of Pocky.

Thomas leaned against the hull as his friend broke down sobbing. *No, my brother. Our brother,* he corrected himself. That was something Bren had always been. They were a family forged with the determination to be self-reliant despite the terrible odds they'd been given as kids. But Thomas had never referred to Bren as the brother he was to them and suddenly felt guilty for not acknowledging that. He was going to change that from here on.

Thomas waited patiently for the rest of the story, trying to resist the urge to fill in the blanks. Obviously, Pocky wasn't dead and supposedly had rescued people. But twenty-one days without Bren? Without backup? The hairs on the back of Thomas's neck stood up. He took in a deep breath and exhaled slowly.

Bren stared blankly down onto the deck as he cradled his hand to his chest. Thomas didn't doubt it was probably painfully throbbing by now.

"Brother?" Thomas asked.

Bren jerked his head up, his jaw slack. Thomas had never called him that before. Again, guilt pierced his heart, ashamed that he hadn't yet. He waited a moment, letting them both relish the meaning. He hated to spoil it, but he needed to know how Pocky came out of that situation. Bren knew very well how Thomas used to come unglued if Pocky had even gotten a paper cut, but he wanted Bren to see he'd matured.

"Please tell me how she got out of that," Thomas said softly.

Dark circles had made their home under Bren's red-rimmed eyes. He blinked tiredly before he said, "A Strat Unit found her and the handful of people that were with her." He blew out a breath through his lips. "She was a fucking mess and taken to the nearest infirmary with the rest. She smelled of … death and smoke. She was malnourished and shaken. The worst, though, was that she'd been shot twice in the shoulder. Thankfully, they were low-caliber bullets, or it would've been much worse. But still, her shoulder blade shattered, and without immediate and proper medical attention, it didn't heal right. She's got some nerve damage and arthritis from it now but won't admit that it bothers her."

"The sling?"

Bren nodded slowly. "She doesn't like it and thinks she doesn't need it. She'll claim it's just a little sore or downplays her discomfort, but I know better. I try not to push her to wear it. I think it reminds her too much of that time." He swallowed. "It took almost a year for her to be right again."

"Nightmares?" Thomas asked cautiously.

"And then some," Bren murmured, then looked away, obviously not wanting to elaborate.

Taking the cue, Thomas asked, "Did she ever say why she left the ship?"

Bren looked back at Thomas and sighed. "To this day, no one knows how or why she disappeared."

"What?" he asked. Dread filled his veins, and he took a deep breath, trying to temper his sudden anxiousness. How was that even possible? Wouldn't the IMF know?

"When she was lucid enough to give her account, she couldn't speak of it. Any of it. From start to finish. The only bits the IMF officials eventually came to know of her side were from the survivors they found her with. But whenever she's approached about it, she shuts down, and it takes a while to get her out of it."

"And that's why you want Yana to stay quiet?"

Bren nodded. "Yeah."

Thomas looked away, thinking of the person Yana had spoken to. He looked back at Bren. "Who's Trooper and how does he know any of it?"

"He was one of the survivors. Orphaned under the circumstances and joined when he came of age."

"Well, if he works in the clinic and you knew she was going there—"

"I told y'all I was going to the gym. Before I did, I went to the clinic and got some medics that know our history to keep that guy away from her. Luckily, they were able to after she parted from Yana to get her watch fixed, but I watched him try. He's always so thrilled to have a reunion, but whenever she sees him, she turns away. She won't tell me why, but she doesn't have to. Anyway, I know it's unrealistic, hoping they won't run into each other, but I didn't factor in Yana."

They were silent for a moment. They were just sixteen when this had happened, and Thomas remembered exactly when it did. *It had to be right before their letters abruptly changed*, he thought grimly. It was also the time when Pocky suddenly started pleading with him to meet. As much as he wanted to see her too, at the time, she was on the west side of Theton. *I'm never going back to Theton*, he had told her. But if he had known, he would have dropped everything.

Guilt overwhelmed Thomas again, and a few tears slid down his cheeks. He brushed them away. There was one last question lingering in his mind that needed an answer.

"Bren, did she ever confide in you? You don't have to give me details. I would just feel better knowing if she did."

Bren pressed his lips together, then winced as he rubbed his fist. "For months, I didn't know she was locking herself to our bunk with handcuffs. I confronted her, not even thinking that it had anything to do with that fucking event. She told me then that she was scared she'd run off again just like she had that night. She told me her actions weren't her own. Like someone else had taken over and made her run off. She went on about how she would never disobey an order, that she would never leave me—leave without a word or leave period. She didn't want to go into that hell, knowing that there was nothing she could do but get herself killed. Brother, I didn't know what to make of that, but I believe her. I know to her core that she wouldn't have left like that. That isn't her. And ... that's all I know of it. That's all she would tell."

A chill worked its way down Thomas's spine as a long-forgotten memory surfaced.

"Brother?" Bren asked, voice low.

"She did that before," Thomas spat out.

"What? When?"

"Before we found you when we were eight. Or more like when she found you."

"What do you mean?"

Thomas ran his fingers through his hair and turned away as the memory of how she found Bren came back at him like a thunderous wave. He'd thought they discussed leaving and formulated a plan to escape the Hyashi household, but that wasn't how it went at all. To comprehend the bizarre chain of events, his mind had rationalized something else entirely.

"Brother?" Bren said, gripping Thomas's forearm.

Viper burst through the doors, her expression a mixture of anger and trepidation. "Thomas! I need you to come with me right now!"

Thomas looked at Bren, who nodded for him to go. He shoved to his feet and went to Viper. She opened one side as Lance opened and held the other. The man had Bren's med pack over one shoulder. He nodded thanks to him and followed the SC inside.

"Is Pocky okay?" Thomas asked.

"No—I mean, this has nothing to do with her."

Shit.

18

Lance walked onto the well deck and headed for Bren. The day was bright and warm with a light wind. He welcomed the scent of the salty ocean and relished the sounds of the water below.

Movement to his left drew his attention. *Gaia* was now surrounded by the IMF fleet that he had seen in the distance when their ship was still docked. The ships were now close enough for him to tell them apart.

The fleet consisted of two types of vessels. The larger ones were the IMF's warships and were a third of the size of *Gaia*. Most varied in color from gray to navy blue. Some were toned with two colors in diagonal stripes. Each warship had three sets of cannons on the front and middle with smaller guns along the sides. The smaller vessels with red tops and black hulls were known as transport ferries. While in the library yesterday, Haize explained *Gaia* had a docking port on the starboard side that allowed the transport ferries or other similar vessels to dock. Though the subject had intrigued Lance, it put others to sleep.

Lance watched for a moment as a ferry navigated between two warships, then focused on Bren. The big guy was lost in thought. He already knew what little Pocky had told him of the event Yana was desperately trying to tell Thomas about. He didn't like that he had to intervene, but it was nobody's business unless their medics wanted to share. After leaving with Viper to find Thomas, he wasn't sure if Yana would still talk, but he hoped not.

Rubbing the bottom of his hand, Bren got up and nodded to Lance. He gestured toward Bren's hand. "Your hand okay?"

"Hurt like a bitch at first but feels okay now. Sore, but okay."

Lance tilted his head. "Really? Could have sworn I heard something snap, thought you broke something."

"Fucking felt like I had in the moment, but I guess not. Trust me, I would know."

"Hmm." Lance gave a slight nod. "Well, glad nothing did then."

"Same."

As Lance handed Bren his med pack, one of the warships named *The Mesmir* caught his attention. It was parallel to *Gaia* on the starboard side and close enough for him to see the soldiers—who looked like tiny ants—busy with their duties. Lance leaned over the hull railing and watched. Bren rummaged in his pack before joining him. He leaned against the hull with his back facing the ocean and pressed a cold pack to his hand.

They stood in silence for some time before Bren chucked the cold pack back into his bag. As the medic flexed his fingers slowly back and forth, Lance gave him a light pat on the shoulder and stepped across to the other side to view Daria Harbor. From this distance, the port appeared small.

Haize had mentioned *Gaia* being cold, unready to sail. Lance walked backward toward the bow until he got a look at the first smoke stack. If *Gaia*'s mechanics were similar to regular charters, then it should have boilers that would pump the pistons to turn, which would make the propellers rotate. There wasn't even a hint of smoke brewing. Bren joined him.

"Huh, well that's unusual," he said. "I wonder what's doing."

Lance shrugged, figuring it was most likely an engineering issue. "So, you okay?" he asked instead.

Bren glanced away. Looking between being embarrassed and angry with himself, he replied, "Yeah, sorry for the drama."

"Don't be, it was valid."

"Yeah, but—"

"Music Man!"

They looked up to see several soldiers leaning over the main deck's hull railing and chanting Bren's Given Name. The medic smiled and waved his unhurt hand at them.

"Hey!" one woman shouted and then laughed. "Pocky's up here on Fresher detail. You better come rescue them."

"Hell no!" Bren shouted back with a laugh. "They get what they deserve. Which side is she on?"

"Starboard."

"Thanks." Bren looked at Lance and gestured toward the door.

At first, Lance thought they were heading for the main deck, but Bren stopped before the entrance and pulled out a smoke from his pocket. Thinking the medic still needed a minute, Lance leaned against the opposite wall, folded his arms, and waited patiently. He had nowhere to be anyway. To his surprise, after Bren lit the smoke and took a drag from it, he offered for Lance to take a puff. It wouldn't be his first time. He didn't care for it as a habit but remembered what Haize had said. Regardless of whether Bren was offering it for a bonding moment or just sharing, he wouldn't pass on the opportunity.

"Keep it between your fingertips and thumb, not between the fingers," Bren said as he passed it over.

Lance figured as much from what he had observed yesterday. He inhaled a small amount and then blew out a small O-shaped ring. Bren laughed, then took it back. He was glad to see the medic more relaxed.

"So, what's Pocky up to?" Lance asked as Bren took another drag.

Bren nodded and then blew out smoke while he spoke. "Freshers is our slang for recruits. They're most likely doing something formal in the Rec Hall, so volunteers inspect their uniforms. Pocky likes doing it while the rest of us don't. She takes it very seriously." Bren laughed. After taking one last drag, he pressed the smoke into the bulkhead, which had obviously been done several times before. He gave Lance a tight-lipped smile. "Thanks, by the way. For not prying."

"No one's business," Lance said with a nod. Unless Bren wanted to share, he would listen, but he wasn't going to inquire.

Bren looked down. With his lips still pressed together, he shook his head as though mulling something over. "Really wish that guy wasn't onboard."

Lance tilted his head in consideration, thinking Bren's comment could have been taken as an invitation but was unsure. Hoping he wasn't reading into that incorrectly, he decided to keep his retort simple and let the medic lead from there. Plus, he had no idea who the big guy was referring to.

"Who?"

"Trooper, down in the clinic."

Bren then told Lance who that was, which led to his side of what happened after Pocky had disappeared. He was surprised Bren was comfortable telling him the details but didn't dare to interrupt. The medic then took it further and divulged more of what happened after Pocky returned: nightmares, flashbacks, and handcuffing herself to their bunk. It was chilling.

Lance's throat grew dry, much the same way when he had listened to her. It was appalling that something like that had gone on in the world. With the lack of word spreading on even a topic like that, he was certain that the majority of people didn't know like him. It made him sick to think that at sixteen he was brooding about what he wanted to do with his life, while on the other side of the world, Pocky was risking her own to help people.

"She always turns away from Trooper when he approaches, but he just smiles. I think he gets it but still feels grateful to her no matter how things are now. I just worry that she'll shut down."

Lance nodded. He understood Bren's concern but knew they had to be practical. "It's bound to happen whether you want it to or not. The ship may be big, but the chances of them running into each other are likely."

"Yeah," Bren replied with a faraway gaze. He sighed and gestured toward the door. "Come on, let's go see her."

Lance followed Bren through the doorway and then to a spiral set of stairs before the first cabin. When they reached the main deck, they were met by a swarm of soldiers walking about. The Freshers stood out more with their formal attire, while the rest were in their regular uniforms. Lance now easily recognized the patrols that went about as well. They always had dogs by their sides and traveled in two pairs.

They were about to turn onto the starboard side when an uproar suddenly erupted behind them.

"Medic!" several soldiers screamed from the port side.

Bren shouted, "Lance, with me!"

Lance hurried after Bren to the port side. Soldiers scrambled out of their way. The ones who had called for a medic led them farther down. Ahead, the crowd was tightly packed and unmoving. Bren yelled for them to make a hole. When the mob parted, they were met by four soldiers with big grins, holding big buckets. Despite knowing what was about to happen, they were too late to backtrack from the onslaught of freezing cold water. Cheers erupted so loudly that it was deafening, but Lance found himself laughing at the obvious prank. The last hour was so intense that this needed to happen.

"You fucking assholes!" Bren bellowed with a laugh. He looked at Lance with worry, then relaxed when he realized he wasn't upset in the least. "Come on," he said with another laugh.

Lance followed Bren to the starboard side, which seemed more crowded. Farther down by the midship stairwell, he could just make out Pocky and Haize. The engineer leaned against the hull as she inspected a Fresher. Lance couldn't help but smile; Pocky's grin turned her from beautiful to radiant. She appeared to be enjoying something Haize was saying.

When they walked up, Haize was the first to spot them. He raised his eyebrows, laughing. "What the hell happened to you guys?"

Pocky glanced over and did a double take. "Were you pranked?"

"We certainly were," Bren said as he flicked water from his fingertips.

She looked at Lance and bit her lower lip. "I'm so sorry."

"Don't be," Lance laughed. "It was needed."

Pocky tried to hold in her laugh, and it was so cute that Lance wanted to see more of it. He wanted to hold her hand again too. Pocky turned back to the Fresher she was inspecting, but not before Lance caught a glimpse of her reddened cheeks. He watched in fascination as her hands diligently skimmed over the young girl's buttons, patches, pins, and even the white braided rope that hung off the right shoulder. She then took the girl's hat and brushed back the few strands of hair that had poked through.

"You need to grow out your bangs so that you can keep 'em under your hat easier," Pocky said.

"Don't like bangs in my eyes," the girl replied quietly.

"Longer bangs or get yelled at. Pick the lesser of two headaches," Pocky said. Her voice left no room for argument.

Bren dove into his med pack and withdrew two small towels, then handed one to Lance.

"Thanks," Lance said as he started to dry his hair and face.

After dismissing the girl, Pocky tagged another soldier to take over, then went for her med pack and grabbed one of her water canteens. Turning to lean against the hull, she drank as she watched him and Bren attempt to dry themselves. She offered Lance her other water canteen when she was done with hers. He gladly accepted it and purposely brushed his hand against hers. She let out a tickled laugh, which made Bren raise a curious brow to her.

"What's wrong with you?"

"Nothing," she said quickly, with height in her voice.

Pocky moved away and kept her back toward them as she crossed her arms on top of the rail. Lance assumed it was to hide another blush. Bren squinted at him, amusement glittering in his eyes. Lance shrugged, and Bren went back to drying himself. With the weather being pleasant and in lighter attire than Bren's uniform, Lance would be dry soon enough.

Giving up on the towel, Bren said, "Right, well, this ain't gonna be enough for me. I'm gonna go change. I'll be back in a bit."

"Okay," Lance said. After Bren went through the doorway into the stairwell, Pocky turned and leaned against the hull and checked her watch, making him remember why she'd gone to the clinic in the first place. "They fix your watch?"

Pocky half rolled her eyes and shook her head. "No, they looked it over and said nothing's wrong with it, but the logs say I've had thirteen fever spikes within the last three days. You'd think I'd know if I had, right?"

"Huh," Lance said, frowning.

"Sure it isn't hot flashes, girlfriend?" Haize asked with his signature cheeky smirk.

"Oh, fuck you," Pocky said with a laugh, making them chuckle with her. Lance loved her laugh; it was contagious.

"Seriously though," Haize said, sobering up. "Next time it goes off, let me look at it, okay?"

With a smile, Pocky nodded.

She resumed inspecting Freshers while Haize engaged Lance in a conversation about the warships. He followed along as Haize used *The Mesmir* as an example, pointing to the ship's obvious features. As the deck became more crowded, though, Lance became distracted by what was going on around them. He couldn't soak in everything enough. As the engineer spoke on, some soldiers began chanting a cadence that got them all going like a wave rolling over. Pocky followed suit and pumped her fist in sync with the others. Lance realized when the deck was starting to disperse that the chant was like a call for the Freshers to go into the Rec Hall. Pocky and the other soldiers finished inspecting the remaining few, then watched as everyone piled into the hall. A booming voice erupted, shushing everyone inside before continuing to speak.

Now it was just the three of them, a few patrols, and some other soldiers hanging back from the assembly.

Haize started to ask a question when Bren returned with Yana and Kaori in tow. Yana, of course, pressed herself flat against the bulkhead as she moved out of the stairwell. Bren didn't appear happy as he leaned against the wall with folded arms. Lance wasn't sure if it was Yana or something else that was bothering him now.

"Look who decided to try and come out," Kaori said cheerfully.

Pocky smiled. "Good to see you up here, Yana."

With her eyes tightly closed, Yana replied through a burst of tight breaths. "Yeah, well, it's with the understanding that I get to ask you a question."

"Lucky me," Pocky said, eyebrows raised.

Bren looked away in disgust. Had he promised Yana the opportunity to ask her burning question from earlier, so long as she went out on deck? Maybe he thought Yana wouldn't go through with it.

"Mine first though, okay?" Pocky said.

"Okay, but hurry," Yana replied, her voice wavering.

"Did the clinic give you something to help your anxiety?"

"Um, yeah, they gave me some sort of chewy thing. They told me not to swallow it and to spit it out when it lost its flavor."

Pocky closed her eyes with a heavy sigh as Bren and Haize burst into laughter. Lance held back his own amusement.

"M, don't fucking start," she said sternly. "I've had enough dick jokes."

"We could change it up with vag jokes," Bren countered, hardly being able to say the words between laughing.

"Oh, my man! Please do!" Haize hollered with wide eyes.

"Please don't," Pocky snapped, but Bren was too delighted not to and looked to Haize.

"What happens when you blow a bubble into—"

Pocky growled and quickly put on her pack. "Okay, I'm leaving."

"Wait!" Yana yelled. "My question!"

Pocky sighed again, folded her arms, and turned to Yana. "Right. What is it?"

"Well, it involves a beautiful story of you rescuing people. It was amazing!"

That tempered Bren's mood. Haize and Lance's, too.

"I don't have beautiful stories of rescuing people," Pocky said flatly. "I don't rescue people anyway. My squad does. I just mend them if they're hurt."

"Yeah, but this one involves Trooper. I ran into him at the clinic."

Pocky looked away, her mouth slightly opened, and then spoke more to herself. "He's onboard?"

"I meant to tell you," Bren said apologetically. "Sorry."

Lance watched her intensely, bracing for her reaction.

Her expression was unreadable as she spoke to Yana. "I don't like drama, so you better not be leading me into a rabbit hole of shit."

"Uh, I don't think it will."

"Okay," Pocky dragged out the word with annoyance yet patience in her voice.

"Well, how'd you find them? I mean, he said they hid in a root cellar under the house. The only access was a small floor door, and someone put a rug and a dining table over it. So, how'd you know they were there?"

Pocky blinked. Her brows furrowed as her eyes moved back and forth. Her mind was obviously searching for an answer. She looked back up at Yana a long moment later. "That's ... actually a good question."

Haize was about to say something when a flash of light and smoke erupted from *The Mesmir*. The sound and shockwave reached them a second later with such force that it knocked everyone down onto the deck. Lance temporarily lost his hearing and felt his upper arm burning.

19

After leaving the fresh air behind, Thomas followed Viper to the fourth level of the ship, then through several passageways. This level was vastly different from his team's designated floor. The walls were dark gray, and the yellow lights made it look more like a dismal dungeon. Heavily armed soldiers scrambled from one place to the next. All around them, soldiers yelled and dogs barked wildly. Whatever this was about, Thomas knew it had something to do with Stellan.

Viper led him into a small room barely larger than a closet. There was only enough space for a small desk and a low table lamp. Geara sat behind the desk, his expression strained from exhaustion and something else Thomas couldn't place. The SC closed the door and stood beside him.

"Thomas, you and Pocky were right," Geara said, voice hoarse. "Stellan does have a better plan, and he's squeezing our balls."

He closed his hands into fists. "What did he do?"

Geara gestured for Viper to take over. Her expression hardened, but her eyes betrayed her unease. "After you left the Reception Area, my second officer and team confronted Stellan," she said. "He willingly surrendered after I explained that he was under arrest for the crimes he had committed against us. We brought him here to the brig for holding until we were ready to move him. However, he threatened that if he were to be removed, the Charter Channel would be attacked. We took that threat earnestly and kept him here."

Frowning, Thomas glanced at Geara. "And you truly believe he can?"

The XO nodded. "I do."

"He then threatened our ship if we didn't keep her cold and tugged out to sea," Viper added.

"Okay, and how would he even do that from here?" Thomas asked, unsure why they took the man's word as truth. Though Stellan was dangerous, even those threats seemed out of his league.

"I should tell you what got us here in the first place and why we are taking this seriously."

"Okay," Thomas replied, already feeling sick in the pit of his stomach.

"Roughly two years ago, a training exercise involving six new OSARs was attacked by an unseen enemy," Geara said. "All ships exploded from under their hulls. At least that much was reported over the radio. A few survivors couldn't confirm much else, and because they were over the deep ocean, physical evidence couldn't confirm much either. Before I was brought on, the investigation concluded that sabotage was the most likely cause."

"How could someone sabotage that many boats?" Thomas asked.

"Explosives that were snuck on and detonated on a timer," he replied. "But then Hyashi claimed responsibility. He said it wasn't explosive devices but something we didn't even have the imagination for, whatever the fuck that meant. After he orchestrated another attack, we took him at his word. I was brought on and have been searching for him since."

Fally's words from yesterday echoed in Thomas's mind. *We're pretty close to getting the assholes that are responsible. And when we do, we each get to piss in their face. I'm especially looking forward to getting my turn.* Thomas suppressed a shiver.

"We still have no idea how he coordinated the attacks and what technology was used to bring our ships down." The XO rubbed the back of one hand. "Stellan knew we set him up and wanted to be captured for some reason. And even though we have him, I'm unsure of how he could still arrange an attack from here, but I'm taking his word that he can. I swear if I had known, I wouldn't ..." Geara shook his head.

Thomas admitted to himself that all this was beyond surprising, but tried not to show it. When he had said Stellan had a better plan, even he hadn't imagined it would be on this scale. This was something more of what Cannon would do. When Stellan was a boy, he was shortsighted and only sought what pleased him at the moment. Cannon, however, was a mastermind, so the apple seemed to have fallen very far from the tree. Perhaps, as Stellan grew older, he'd become more like his father. It was hard to fathom, but Thomas was sure it was true. The last time he had seen Cannon, the man was almost ninety years old, so he had to be dead by now.

Dread washed over Thomas. "Why am I here?"

Geara sucked in a sharp breath. "He has a new demand."

A chill shot through Thomas's chest. "He wants to see me, right?"

Geara looked down and pressed his lips together as he nodded. He was clearly angry that Stellan had figured out a way to control the situation and was forcing them to bend to his will. Having the responsibility for everyone's safety had to be an epic burden. And now, Thomas shared that burden too. It was clear what had to be done.

What was more frightening to him was how far that asshole was gonna take this—and how much Thomas was willing to give in. *Did Stellan do all this just so he could have his way with me?* He tried to swallow. With his second worst fear on the brink of coming true—the first one being losing his sister—he honestly wasn't sure if he could give in to the man's desires. But how many would die because he wasn't willing to let it go that far? *What is his end game?*

"Take me to him." Thomas barely forced the words out. "But I'm not ... I can't promise anything more than seeing him."

Geara shoved to his feet. "I have deployed every Strat Unit on float monitoring our ships. I know you warned me, but I'm trying to get ahead of this. I'll keep him behind bars and not let it go further than a conversation, I swear. We won't let him touch you. I'm ready to put a bullet in him if he even suggests wanting something more and deal with whatever consequences stem from that. Viper and I will be there with you. We won't leave you alone. Okay?"

"Yes, sir," Thomas replied with a heavy breath.

The three of them left the closet, Geara leading the way. Thomas couldn't believe this was happening. Why couldn't this be just some nightmare he could wake up from?

Thomas used his ability and located Pocky on the main deck. Was their team with her? He imagined them enjoying a conversation about something pleasant, perhaps even with spirited banter. He could see it all and smiled a little, letting that possibility comfort him.

As they moved toward the stern side of the ship, barking grew louder. Thomas figured this had to be where the kennels were set up. A curious thought occurred to him. *Did the IMF have a brig onboard, or had they changed a kennel room into one?*

When they stepped through the next doorway, his question was confirmed. The narrow passageway was lined with kennels on either side. The kennels were separated into small sections by a floor-to-ceiling chain-link fence. The rancid smell of dogs, urine, and shit was overwhelming, but a smile crept over Thomas for a moment, hoping Stellan was enjoying his accommodations. That unfortunately didn't seem to be the case as the guy came into view.

Stellan was already smiling and standing when they approached; he'd probably sensed Thomas's heartbeat and knew he was coming. Farther down, a soldier sat quietly with his back turned. What had he done to be sent here? Thomas realized then that he was purposely trying not to look at Stellan. But when Stellan spoke, Thomas's eyes flicked in his direction.

"Hello, boy," Stellan sneered.

Thomas stiffened. The way Stellan spoke reminded him of Cannon. The Hyashi patriarch had always referred to Thomas as "boy," mockingly. He was perplexed by this. This was not how Stellan had behaved in the hotel.

Thomas raised his eyebrows. "Stellan?"

"Very much," the man replied flatly, losing the smile.

"You, uh, wanted to see me?" Thomas asked slowly.

Stellan smiled momentarily again, then grew cold. "Yes, I'm sure you think this is all about you when, in fact, it isn't at all. So don't flatter yourself."

"Uh ..." Thomas stammered, unsure how to proceed.

"However," Stellan continued, his lips morphing into a sinister grin as he spoke, "I still want to pound my dick into your ass and hear you wail in pain."

Thomas backed into the kennel door behind him, eyes wide. Geara put an arm across him as though protecting him from physical harm.

"Fucking asshole, we're done!" Geara shouted, then turned Thomas toward the exit. "Go!"

"I'm not finished!" Stellan roared.

"You are!" Geara turned toward Stellan. "I don't know why I even let myself think you could do anything in here. Make all the threats you want; I don't fucking believe you."

"Well then"—Stellan spread his hands apart—"allow me to demonstrate."

They all froze, waiting for whatever this demonstration was. Thomas counted to twenty-six and was almost embarrassed for the guy until a booming explosion vibrated through the ship. An ear-piercing alarm followed. His eyes widened and his jaw dropped as Stellan smirked. *Shit, what did he do?*

Geara yelled something to Viper that made her run off. Thomas immediately searched for Pocky while the XO screamed at Stellan. She was still on the starboard side of the main deck. At first, she was still, then got up, staggered, and moved away. She was alive, and Thomas thanked the Divine Universe for that. He wished he could sense if Bren was okay too.

"Give me what I want, or I'll have my army pluck every fucking ship until there isn't any left," Stellan said flatly.

"What do you want!?" Geara spat.

"I'm not done with Thomas," he replied in a sophisticated tone, as though the chaos around them was nothing.

Thomas pushed the XO's arm away and stepped up. "I'm here, I'm listening."

Stellan's eyes narrowed. "As I said before, I'm not here for you."

When Stellan didn't elaborate, Thomas shook his head, not understanding what his game was. "Then what?"

"Not what. Who." Stellan's eyes gleamed.

Thomas lost his breath as fear engulfed him. His body grew cold with the awful realization of who Stellan was implying. "Not my sister," he said. "Not her."

The asshole let out a deep, throaty laugh. "Oh yes, her."

"Why?"

"Oh, now that's coming later, but I don't mind sharing that my father bought the two of you for a reason. I'm sure you probably thought it was because I wanted a brother when really it was all about my father having her. Did you know he died a few years after you ran off?"

Thomas didn't answer.

"No matter," Stellan continued. "Because he's now inside me. Just like he's inside your sister."

Thomas's throat tightened.

"What the fuck do you mean by that?" Geara asked, a mixture of horror and anger in his voice.

Stellan stared at Thomas. "Remember your first night at our house? My father made her drink that juice?" He grinned viciously. "It had his urine and cum in it. My father is inside your sister, boy."

Thomas felt his body go numb. His vision blurred, and he was going down, but Geara held him up.

"You motherfucker!" the XO screamed.

"I hope you agonize hard about what makes her stand out above you, brother. But first things first. Geara—" Stellan paused and started fussing with his suit. "I want to be moved to a guest cabin and be treated as the guest that I am. And a warning, if you remove the boy and his cunt sister, I'll know. And I will unleash my wrath. *Clear?* As your people would say."

Thomas felt feverish and was on the verge of retching. Geara quickly ushered him to the nearest toilet. The unclean bowl and stench made the vomiting even worse. Afterward, he was pulled along through the passageways in a daze. Between the alarms blaring, soldiers shouting, and dogs barking, it was hard to walk upright. He went through every piece of their fifteen years together and tried to think of anything that made Pocky stand out. The only time that significantly came to mind was right before they escaped the Hyashi household that led them to Bren.

Now that Thomas recalled what actually happened, he picked it apart. He smiled briefly, remembering how long Pocky's hair had been, and then frowned as he played out the event. Dawn was just peeking over the horizon, and most of the residents were still sleeping. He was leading Pocky to the kitchen when she suddenly seized his hand. Her eyes were closed, and her head bobbed in short jerks, then went still. He put his other hand to her face, unsure what was wrong.

"Sis?"

Pocky opened her eyes and met his. "We need to leave, or he'll die. We need to leave right now."

From there, it was a blur as Pocky took off, and it was clear that if Thomas didn't keep up, he would be left behind. He followed her into the stairway that led to the stables and quietly descended. He figured she intended to take a horse, but getting one with a servant in the way was going to be difficult, or so he thought. The servant in charge of morning chores took advantage of their presence and had them take a horse out to pasture. They obliged and took one together but didn't return for another.

Neither one of them had ridden a horse before, but Thomas caught on instinctively. However, because their muscles weren't used to that kind of exercise, Thomas encouraged the steed to move slow at first before picking up speed. Pocky clung to him even tighter as she directed him to the industrial park. They got there just before dark. Though he was hungry and thirsty, and certain she had to be too, she dismounted and didn't stop running until they reached the dumpster. To his disbelief, he heard Bren's helpless cries. He couldn't comprehend how she could have known and thus remembered it differently. He couldn't fathom, back then, that it could be an ability.

But is it really that far-fetched from my own? he wondered.

At some point, Geara was replaced by another soldier, and Thomas was led to the midship stairwell and then was left to himself. Before going up the stairs, he sat on a step, trying to steady his breathing as he replayed the past. That day, Pocky somehow knew Bren was in trouble, and his brother admitted before Viper grabbed him that it may have happened again. Was this an ability similar to his own, and was that why Stellan was after her?

He looked up. She was just up the flight of stairs. He didn't just need his eyes on her; he needed answers.

20

Pocky was in a dream that wasn't a dream but was unsure what else to call it. She floated in what she presumed was the middle of the known universe, and gazed upon the Dark Sun. She smiled, but then felt something was very wrong. She shouldn't be here yet. It was the middle of the day, and she'd been doing something but couldn't remember what.

"Boss," a wavering voice said from somewhere.

It took a moment for Pocky to remember her friend. She frowned, unsure why she couldn't see the entity yet.

"Ember? Where are you?"

"I'm all around you. I usually show up as an orb so that you have a reference. But I can't right now."

"Why? What's wrong?"

"I can't see through your eyes, so I don't know, but you are here earlier than usual," Ember replied sadly. *"But something else is wrong."*

"What? Are you okay?"

"I'm not. I've tried getting the Healer's attention by making your body react in a way that should have drawn him to you, but I can't. I can't seem to get the right chemical reaction to even cause a fever. I tried decreasing the sensitivity to the nerves around your shoulder blade to where even your breathing would cause pain, but that didn't work either. I'm sorry, I won't do either again."

It took several moments for Pocky to recall some previous conversations they had had about the Healer and Ember's efforts to find him. *Him?* That was something she didn't know before.

"Who's the Healer?"

"Doesn't matter. You'll wake up within the next 0.02 of a second and won't remember the name. You can't help me," Ember said.

"But I'm trying to understand. Why do you need the Healer?"

"It's been a while since I told you that both you and I need him. I need him because I am physically present within your body, smaller than an atom, but I'm supposed to be dormant. My life cycle requires a host for me to be able to do that, and I've been awake too long. You need the Healer for a different reason."

"For what?" Pocky asked, growing frustrated when Ember didn't elaborate.

Instead, a conversation ensued that shadowed so many previous ones about a breach, her spotting Ember, and shoving it into this place. Something had happened when she was four that caused this chain reaction, but Pocky couldn't recall anything traumatic at that age. Nothing physically, anyway. Or perhaps the moment was so traumatic that she couldn't remember. She needed to ask Thomas—maybe he would know—but was unsure how she would remember to even do that, but then thought of an idea.

"Ember, you said I come here looking for answers from my archives and that when I find what I'm looking for, it gets transferred to my first subconscious level, and then the information becomes instinctual or intuitive, right?"

"Correct."

"Well, is it possible to force a question for me to ask my brother? Can you send a question to my first subconscious level?"

There was a long pause, and then Ember's voice brightened. *"That actually might be possible. I need to think on this and see how I can. Now you need to go."*

"Wait—"

Pocky's vision blurred as she opened her eyes. At first, she couldn't move. Something terrible had happened and was still happening. As her sight cleared, she saw Lance struggling with Haize. The engineer was thrashing; why? Then she watched in horror as smoke smoldered along his left arm and face.

Her hearing returned to a roar of people shouting, feet pounding, the shrill of the emergency alarm, and Yana screaming. The shutters that enclosed the main deck came down in loud clicks. Red lights flicked on as darkness engulfed them.

Lance helped Haize to his feet. He was looking at someone else when he yelled, "Get them inside, I'll get Pocky!"

The man's words were a good thing to hear. Pocky assumed she wasn't hurt enough to need immediate medical attention, and that meant she could help others who were. Pushing herself up felt like an eternity as Lance moved to her, but she was sure it was probably only a few seconds. He helped her to her feet, and she gagged at the smell of burning flesh. A wave of dizziness made her lose her balance. She leaned heavily into him, and he grunted as he compensated to keep her from falling.

"Sorry," she said, her voice wavering.

"S'ok, we're almost there," Lance replied between heavy breaths.

Once inside, Pocky spotted Kaori sitting against the right wall, tightly holding Yana, who was still screaming. The woman was bleeding from her lower lip pretty badly.

"Kaori!" Pocky cried. She crouched down and removed her pack, ready to tend to the injury.

"I just bit my lip, I'm okay," Kai said calmly.

That was fine, but Pocky was still going to aid the woman—until Bren bellowed at her. For a split second, she felt a sharp sting in her heart as her partner spoke.

"Pocky! Lance, third-degree burn, left upper arm! Move!"

Pocky moved toward Lance. He sat cross-legged next to Haize, who was in far worse shape. As they were trained to do, Bren tended to the most critical person first. Lance held his left elbow with his right wrist, his hand slightly trembling. A burn bigger than Pocky's hand cut diagonally across his bicep. His right hand and the left side of his face and shirt were speckled with ash and smaller burns. He grimaced.

As Pocky reached into her pack, she spoke quickly. "Pain level, one to five?"

"Four."

"Do you want a bite stick?"

Lance shook his head. Pocky exchanged her fingerless gloves for rubber ones, then grabbed a capsule and tore the wrapping off.

"Open your mouth," she said. When he did, she placed the capsule on his tongue. "Let it dissolve. It'll help take the edge off, okay?"

He nodded.

Pocky grabbed her med stick and placed it around Lance's left wrist, then synced the band to her med watch and began pulling out everything she would need to mend his wounds. Though the IMF was advanced when it came to treating burns, it was still going to hurt like a bitch.

Next to them, Haize squeezed his eyes shut and tilted his chin up, tears streaming down his cheeks. He whimpered deep in his throat as Bren began the treatment process. Pocky hated that Lance would be experiencing the same within a minute. Why had this even happened? *How* had this happened? What was that explosion?

She pushed those thoughts away as her watch's alarm went off, flashing yellow. She paused to read the numbers and let out a relieved breath.

"Okay, naturally, your body is upset that something happened, but I'm not concerned with your vitals yet," Pocky said.

She tried keeping her expression neutral as she looked him over. She tilted his head right, and he allowed her to examine closer. He had several tiny burns along his neck and face, but those looked to be mostly mild. She then looked over his chest and other arm. His right hand had a few second-degree burns, but that was it. The burn on his left upper arm was the worst.

"Okay, gonna explain what I'm doing. First—"

"Please don't," Lance said through gritted teeth.

Pocky nodded. She couldn't blame him for not wanting details. She shook a small canister, then sprayed over the burn. The application would numb the surrounding area, but unfortunately, there was no way to numb underneath the burn. She paused as an announcement that spoke both in Thetonian and Origin came over the speakers.

"All personnel, stay where you are until cleared by an officer."

Pocky and Bren exchanged looks of acknowledgment, then continued to tend to their patients.

"Don't be alarmed if you taste garlic for a couple of hours," she said.

Lance nodded tiredly. Pocky took a mini silver tube and squeezed the contents over the burn. Using a tongue depressor, she spread the jelly-like substance. The solution was a bacterium that would eat the burned tissue. Depending on the size of the area, this process could take up to several hours. Afterward, a liquid-netted sheet would be placed over the burn. Over the course of a few days, the sheet would eventually become new muscle and skin. However, this specialized sheet would have to be applied by a medic from the clinic. Pocky had never personally experienced a burn but had been told that the bacteria was the worst part to endure. Some patients said it felt like someone ripping raw skin off very slowly. Lance hissed a few times as she finished spreading the jelly.

"Sorry," Pocky said, grimacing apologetically.

"Tell me about you," Lance said with a labored breath. "Distract me."

"I'll be done in five minutes, then I'll tell you anything you want to know."

"You're beautiful," he said shakily.

Pocky wasn't surprised by Lance's honesty. Most people were when traumatic events happened; it gave them pause to examine what was truly important in life.

She grabbed one of her canteens, then helped him drink before tending to his right hand. She guessed that a hot object had impacted his arm and he'd used his right hand to pull it off. She spread the bacterium substance over the burns, then placed his hand gently on his lap.

Before tending to the smaller burns along his face and neck, she took one of her towels and doused it with a different solution to clean his face and neck. His complexion had paled, and he was trying to control a grimace. The usual compassion in his eyes was replaced with exhaustion, and they started to water. Sorrow and anger threatened to overwhelm Pocky, but she pushed on.

As she'd been working, soldiers pounded past them, shouting as they went. The alarm continued to blare as some soldiers moved onto the main deck while others climbed the stairs to the next floor. Some had dogs with them. All of it was a dull roar as she worked.

"Okay, almost done," she said. "Once we get the all clear, I'll take you to the clinic. Okay?" she said, meeting his eyes.

He nodded tiredly.

When Pocky was finished and satisfied that nothing else needed to be done, she turned to Bren and Haize. Her partner, of course, was beyond finished. His mess was cleaned up, and he'd moved on. Even after all these years, it still blew her mind how fast he worked. Haize had either passed out or just looked to be. Either way, she wasn't going to disturb him. Bren had cut most of the engineer's shirt off and tended to three burns along Haize's arm, one on his neck, and three on his face. *Damn, Bren's good,* she thought proudly.

She turned and found him tending to the women. Still cradled in Kaori's arms, Yana had stopped screaming but was still crying. Bren had placed a special bandage that was made for soft tissue on Kai's broken lip. Kai gave Pocky a tired yet uncertain smile. She gave her a nod in return.

Lance was definitely feeling the full effects of the bacterial substance now. He'd shut his eyes and raised his chin, and he breathed through gritted teeth. Pocky hated seeing him go through the pain, so she distracted herself by cleaning up her mess. As she did, a soldier went through the doorway carrying a limp dog. The smell of burnt dog hair and flesh made her gag and cough.

After Pocky caught her breath and continued to clean up, her mind tried to rationalize what had happened. Obviously, a nearby warship exploded, but was it an accident or deliberate? The only thing she was certain of was that many of her fellow soldiers were dead or were dying. And where was Thomas in all this chaos? Pocky had pushed that question as far from her mind as possible, but now that the team was taken care of, it fully surfaced. Kaori had said that Viper was looking for him. Pocky assumed the SC had found him, but where would she have taken him? And for what?

Lance put his left hand along her cheek. Pocky stilled and realized that she didn't want to look at him because she didn't trust her emotions, but tears had already started and she hadn't noticed. Lance wiped one away with his thumb. Pocky clasped his hand with hers and held it while she buried her face in her other hand. Bren came up behind her and placed a hand on her shoulder. His concern shone through his expression.

"Partner?"

Knowing what he was asking, Pocky replied, "Thomas."

Bren nodded but didn't offer false comfort that their brother was probably fine. He knew her well enough that she didn't care for such comments.

"Naiko is here," he said. "Yana is in shock, but otherwise, they all look okay."

Pocky nodded. Crossing her legs, she leaned against the wall between Lance and the doorway while Bren sat on the second step of the stairwell next to Haize. Pocky shuddered and buried her face into her other hand, trying not to let her mind recall another time of people burning and massive explosions. She was determined not to let those horrific memories resurface. Time went by at a snail's pace when she heard someone coming up the stairs but didn't look up until the person spoke.

"Sis?"

A massive weight lifted off her shoulders. Thomas crouched down next to her. Thinking he was leaning in for them to embrace, she reached up to him, but he gripped her upper arms and pushed her against the wall instead. Her eyes widened as he spoke.

"How did you know where Bren was?" he demanded.

Pocky shook her head. "What?" Why was he asking this now?

"When we were eight, you knew where he was. You knew he was in trouble. How?"

"I-I don't—"

"Brother," Bren snapped, suddenly next to them. "This isn't the time—"

Thomas turned toward Bren but didn't let her go. His voice echoed within the stairwell. "It is the time! We didn't just happen upon that fucking industrial park and certainly didn't just happen to pass the one dumpster you were in. She knew exactly where you were." He grabbed the front of Bren's scrub shirt. "It took us all day to get to you. She knew that morning that you were in trouble."

"Okay, so she knew. Divine Universe premonitions or some shit," Bren said, his voice heated. "Why the fuck does that matter right now?"

"Because *he* wants her, and I can't think of any reasons why!" Thomas cried.

Bren blinked a few times, then shook his head. "Stellan?"

Thomas nodded rapidly.

"Brother, that asshole is just trying to get under your skin, and what better way than to make threats that he knows will?" Bren said. "He's just fucking with you."

Pocky pushed up on her knees and reached for him. Thomas gazed at her in a desperate panic. "I agree," she said. "He's just using the opportunity to get in your head. Don't fall into it."

Thomas gathered Pocky into his arms, his voice breaking as he said, "I just got you back. I can't lose you."

Pocky wanted to reassure him that he wouldn't, but she knew better than to make promises she couldn't keep. All she could do was hold him.

A thought suddenly came to her. No, not a thought, but a question. A question for him, but she was unsure what the words even were. It was as though the words were blurry but still there nevertheless, and they hung in the forefront of her mind for the rest of the day like an itch she couldn't scratch.

21

Eleven days after the explosion that sank *The Mesmir*, the mood around *Gaia* was starting to return to what it had been before the incident.

"Incident" only loosely described what had happened. Geara hadn't disclosed whether the incident was deliberate or an accident. Most were leaning toward it being an accident because nothing suspicious was going on when *The Mesmir* exploded. Either way, the XO was keeping the matter tight within his circle.

Even without knowing all the facts, there was one undeniable truth: hundreds were dead or missing. That was the hardest part for all the soldiers. On *Gaia*, only fifty-eight people were injured in total. Lance and Haize were included in that number.

Lance's team was steadily getting into a routine. *Gaia* was still cold and tethered to two warships on either side of her. Besides Yana, no one was complaining about their extended stay. To keep her mind off things and out of everyone's hair, Kaori had steered Yana into ocean topography. Though the woman didn't care much for the open seas, she found the underwater landscape fascinating. Haize was granted clearance to aid the engineer teams below, significantly improving the man's mood. Bren and Pocky spent their time assisting in the clinic. Though *Gaia* was the largest among the fleet and was well-staffed, they still welcomed the help. Lance, Kaori, and Thomas continued their training with Naiko.

To help get everyone out of their funk, their medics played music almost every night. Per usual, when Pocky was done, Bren would switch on recordings, giving her a chance to enjoy the music. To Lance's surprise, she loved dancing and was actually really good at it. It was fun to watch her move to the music. He had grown close to everyone on his team, but he especially had gotten closer to her and Bren since the incident.

For Pocky, they were taking intimacy slow but getting to know each other quickly. She couldn't get enough of his stories of farm life and his travels. In return, she tried to be as open as possible. She was mostly comfortable talking about her squad and past projects. He took anything he could get and never pressed her on rescues or her upbringing.

With Bren, there was a mutual, unspoken sense of familiarity, as though they had known each other their whole lives and were just catching up after being apart. The man had even started referring to him as Cap and told him to consider it an honorary Given Name, just as Thomas inherited Brother from everyone. Whether it was short for captain or something else, Bren didn't explain, and Lance didn't feel the need to ask.

Before Lance and his team finished breakfast, Pocky was called away for an urgent meeting. Lance dreaded that it would have something to do with Stellan but kept that to himself. He was certain, though, that Thomas and Bren were feeling the same.

After finishing their meal, it was routine for their medics to recheck their patients. Since Pocky had left early, Bren checked both Lance and Haize and tended to their burns. Lance was amazed at how well their wounds were healing. The one on his upper arm still itched, but otherwise, it no longer bothered him. The tiny ones along his face and neck were hardly even noticeable now. Haize's were healing even better than Lance's. The engineer even teased Pocky that he'd gotten the better medic, which she in no way disputed and was proud of her talented partner.

After they were done cleaning up their mess, they all thanked Iza for the meal. Lance smiled as the soldier took Yana for another adventure to the bow's well deck. Iza didn't just serve them meals and coffee; she'd become an essential extension of their team. Along with Pocky, Iza was happy to help Yana overcome her fears and even made a conscious effort to get to know them personally.

After they parted ways, Lance, Kaori, and Thomas followed Naiko up to the lab. When they reached C Deck, they found a sergeant Lance recognized as Marker guarding the doorway that led to the guest cabins along with three other soldiers. Marker was tall and lean with a long face and bulging eyes. His black hair and beard pushed the limits of the IMF's requirements, which made him more distinguishable among the others with their low and tight crew cuts. His brown complexion was tinted with a sunburn. Marker was in charge of a Strat Unit that had transferred onto *Gaia* the day after the explosion. Since that day, Lance had come to know quite a few soldiers and unsurprisingly felt comfortable among them.

"May I have an hour to myself?" Lance asked Naiko, not really feeling up for more lab training.

"Sure," Naiko said. "Just an hour, though. We have work to do."

"Yes, ma'am," he replied.

Unlike his two fellow teammates, who were enthralled with their work, Lance wasn't so enthused. And besides, something else weighed heavily on his mind, but he couldn't figure out what exactly. Maybe he was just restless from being cooped up; he'd rather be doing the actual work. And while that was true, it still didn't fully satisfy whatever seemed to be bothering him.

As his team moved on, Lance approached Marker and forced a small smile.

"Hey, Cap, another fun day of training?" the sergeant asked with a yawn.

"Yeah," Lance said. "Been up for a while?"

"Since midnight. I'm on for a little bit longer, then going for a break."

That was another matter Geara had yet to disclose. For some reason, security had increased around the guest cabin entryways, making everyone speculate as to why. Some thought that perhaps a high-ranking officer or general was secretly hidden away. Lance didn't care to indulge the theories.

"See you in the gym later?" Lance asked.

"Might be called for a double, but maybe."

"Brutal."

"If I am, share a smoke afterward?"

"Yeah, sure. Later."

"Later."

Lance headed into the corridor. At first, he wasn't sure if he wanted to stroll through the greenhouse or the library but ultimately decided on the latter. He was fairly certain the place would be empty at this time of day, which worked in his favor. He needed a quiet place to unravel whatever was bugging him.

He went to the last private section. Whether alone or together, it had fast become a favored place for his team to hang out. When he reached the section, he found Pocky sitting alone—much to his delight. She wore her typical uniform but no longer wore the fingerless gloves. Now that Thomas knew of her scars, she didn't feel the need to wear them. She still hadn't shared how she'd gotten the scars, and no one dared to ask.

Lance frowned as he observed Pocky. Usually, if he found her here, she was reading a book or looking out the window. Instead, she was sitting cross-legged with her hands linked, resting her chin on top. She looked deep in thought and hadn't noticed him.

"Hey," Lance said, trying not to reveal his concern.

Pocky gazed up in surprise, her expression instantly brightening. She was beautiful, and he couldn't help but be in a better mood just by the sight of her.

"Hey," she said quietly but didn't get up like she usually would have. Her smile began to fade.

Something was definitely up, and Lance wondered if it had something to do with her meeting.

"I'm sorry, I didn't mean to interrupt," he said. "I didn't know you were in here."

"Oh no, you aren't. I'm happy to see you. But I am struggling with … something." Pocky glanced away and let out a heavy sigh.

Lance sat next to her and took her hand in his, lacing their fingers together. She turned to face him but stayed cross-legged. Was now a time to push, or a time to let her lead the conversation? She smiled earnestly as though waiting for him to speak first. He took that as it was.

"Is it something I can help with?"

"Maybe. Talking it out might help, but you first."

Lance's eyebrows furrowed. "What?"

"I can tell something's been bothering you. You hide it well, and I didn't want to pry. Figured you would open up when you wanted to." Pocky gave a small shrug. "You give me that respect, and I want to return the same. If you don't want to share, I understand, but I wanted you to know that I'm aware that something's on your mind."

Lance looked down. Just like that, he knew exactly what was bothering him and why. He trusted Pocky, but that still didn't make it easy to open up about something embedded deep within his heart.

"I've ... felt lost my entire life," he said slowly. "Like I was born into the wrong family, the wrong life, or something. My family are good people, and I struggled to come to terms with why I always felt I didn't belong there. That I didn't belong to them. Like I was supposed to be somewhere else, but no clue as to where. I went to Theton when I was fifteen. To join the IMF."

Lance paused for a moment as he watched Pocky's reaction. Her brows popped up slightly, and her jaw dropped before she reined it in.

Even though he'd never shared this, the more he spoke and the simple feeling of Pocky's hand in his, made it easier to continue.

"IMF requirements may be common knowledge in Theton, but not in Shad'Dyn. I understood why I couldn't join and didn't feel bitter about it, but it was the only path that felt right to me. After that, I was even more lost. It's why I traveled. I was looking for something, for my place in the world. Eventually, I returned home. Feeling defeated to the point of almost losing my sanity. I know it sounds stupid that I couldn't just accept my life for what it was. To be a farmer. Inherit the farmstead. Settle down. Make babies. Continue the cycle. But that isn't me, and it ate away at me."

As much as it hurt, and as raw as this wound on his heart was, sharing with Pocky felt right. Her expression was warm and inviting.

"When I saw the ad for this project, I actually felt a sense of direction for once, and I'm beyond grateful for the opportunity," he said. "Sometimes I can't believe I've gotten this far. I feel my place is with you and our team. That feels absolutely solid down in my bones, but ..."

"But?" Pocky prompted.

He shook his head. "There's still something else that's not quite right. I didn't realize until now that this project still doesn't feel like my purpose or where I should be." Lance placed his free hand over his forehead. He sighed heavily. "I'm so sick of feeling like I'm supposed to be doing something important and not a fucking clue as to what."

Pocky pulled his hand away from his face and held it in hers. She didn't need to say any words to offer a resolution or to fix it. Just listening was enough, and she knew that, but he could still see that she wanted to, just as he wanted to for her. Given what her life had been like, he suddenly felt selfish for unburdening on her.

"Sorry," Lance said with a heavy exhale.

"Don't be. I want to know you deeper than what I see on the surface. And you're not alone with how you feel."

Lance tilted his head. "What do you mean?"

"Well, not me personally," Pocky said respectfully. "But think of what you've learned about our teammates."

Lance looked down at his lap. She was right. Though Haize wanted to be an engineer and was one, the man still badly wanted to be in uniform. Being a soldier had been just as important to Haize as being an engineer.

Yana, who never could attach herself to anyone, wandered all over Shad'Dyn as though looking for someone or something to hold onto. That fact had been shared privately between them.

And Kaori was not truly an Alysian. She'd been dumped on their doorstep and was raised as one. Her sense of longing to find her real family had motivated her to travel in the hopes of finding them.

"Huh," Lance said, gazing back up at her. He smiled more for the sense of feeling a camaraderie with his team rather than the epiphany. He looked at her lovingly and gently squeezed his hold. "Thank you for pointing that out and ... thank you for listening."

Pocky smiled, but her radiant expression faded into a frown. He hadn't forgotten that something was on her mind too, and sharing wasn't easy for her, but Lance hoped she would open up. Not because he had shared but because she wanted to. For her, it wasn't about trust. It was more about the hurt when talking about hard issues.

"So, what's going on with you?" Lance asked gently.

Pocky swallowed nervously. "Well, it's two things that aren't related to each other. The first has been going on ever since the explosion, and I'm not sure how to explain it."

"Okay."

With an exhale, Pocky asked, "You ever have those moments where there's a word on the tip of your tongue? You know it, but can't say it."

"Yeah."

"Well, for some reason every time I see my brother or M, I have this strange need to ask them something, but I don't know what. It's just like that feeling. I know it, but I don't. Does that make sense?"

"Yeah, completely. Lost for words."

"Right. And that sensation hasn't gone away. It's getting annoying."

Lance squeezed her hand. "That has to be frustrating, I'm sorry."

Pocky nodded. "S'ok, just wish it would go away, or reveal itself so I can ask and get it over with. But that's it for that part."

"Are you comfortable talking about the other?" Lance asked when she didn't continue.

Pocky took both her hands away and rubbed her forehead with her fingertips. The stress of whatever this one was about was beyond evident.

"Thomas can't know this," she said slowly, "or he'll lose his shit."

"Of course. Whatever is said between us, stays between us."

Looking up at Lance, Pocky pressed her lips together. "Stellan is demanding to see me," she said quietly, "and for some reason, Geara is making me."

"What the fuck!" Lance said sharply in alarm.

Over the last several days, he had come to know Stellan through Thomas. That asshole had really gotten into Thomas's head, and he only felt comfortable talking with Lance about it. Though it was hard for Lance to hear of their time at the Hyashi household, he still listened. And not because it was a way of getting to know Pocky better, but because he strongly felt indebted to all his teammates if they needed him. Now that he knew who Stellan truly was, it made him sick to think that Geara would even entertain the idea of bringing them together.

He shoved to his feet. "Absolutely fucking not."

Pocky stood up too, closing her eyes as she took a deep breath as though bracing for pushback. "I can't just disobey an—"

The library doors slammed open. Pocky put a hand on her gun and moved in front of Lance. It was an understandable reaction, but Lance didn't like the idea of her protecting him. He felt that way not just with her but with their entire team. He'd been that way with his cousins too. The drive to protect the people around him was innately in his blood.

A stench filled the air, making them back away a little. Pocky winced, then gagged. It was a poignant odor that Lance couldn't place at first, but it made alarms go off within the back of his mind as though he should know it.

"Shit," Pocky whispered. "It's that asshole."

"Who?" Lance whispered back.

"Shox."

"Is that his—"

"Yeah, he reeks badly. I fucking hate him."

"Really? Why?" Lance asked. The IMF treated each other as a family with the utmost respect for each other. If Pocky felt that way, there had to be very good reasons as to why.

"He mocks the IMF and plays nasty pranks. He did a number on me not that long ago." Pocky's eyes narrowed. "Come on, let's try to slip past him." She grabbed her med pack and kept it only on her good shoulder. She moved, then paused, her brows furrowing.

"Pocky?" Lance said, still in a whisper.

She met his eyes. "It's strange that he's even in here. He's supposed to be in the—" Pocky shook her head. "Never mind. Just don't engage. Just let me deal with him, okay?"

"If it gets out of hand though, I will," Lance replied firmly.

Pocky nodded and led him out of the section, closer to that terrible smell.

22

Shox had just come up to the first section when he saw them. *At least he's not armed,* Pocky thought. Floaters weren't supposed to be anyway, but nevertheless, confirming that put her more at ease.

Shox's smile was strange, creepy even, and his uniform was in disarray. Even his hat was skewed mockingly to one side. Anger heated Pocky's face. It was bad enough that the guy represented everything the IMF wasn't, but she was equally embarrassed for a civilian to witness this.

And why is this asshole even up here? Pocky thought Daniger had made it clear Shox had to stay in the brig. She didn't have time to think on that though. She was worried the guy would provoke Lance by teasing her. Hopefully she could get them outside before he could try.

"Pocky," Shox said in a delighted, childish way. "Just the girl I've been looking for."

Fucking great. They stopped just before the next section, and Shox did the same, effectively blocking them in.

"Fuck off, Shox," she snapped. "I don't have time for your bullshit."

"Oh, but I wanted to see you." He spread his hands apart, as if that proved his innocence somehow, but Pocky knew better. "No bullshit," he added. "I promise."

"If it'll get us out of here faster, get on with it," Pocky said with an annoyed sigh.

"It's something personal. Can we talk alone?"

Pocky stepped slightly in front of Lance, knowing he wouldn't allow that. She dropped her med pack into her right hand. "No."

Shox's weird smile faded into a frown. "Well, I, uh, really need to speak with you though. It's important."

"Whatever it is, it isn't important to me," she snapped. "Nothing you say would ever be."

"Oh, come on, Pocky," he pleaded. "Look, you're putting me on the spot here. I need to confess to you."

"No, you don't. This is just another one of your pranks, and I'm not falling for it. Move away, now."

Shox bared his teeth as he took a step closer. His eyes darkened. Pocky had never seen this side of the guy before. To Shox, everything was laughable, and he always had an upbeat persona. Thinking maybe it was part of his prank, she shrugged with annoyance and wished Bren or someone else was here to deal with him.

Lance took a step forward. "She's not asking again," he said, voice hard.

Shox put his hands to his sides again, then stepped away, indicating they could pass. They moved forward in unison, but before they even got near him, he said, with all the seriousness in the world, "I'm in love with you."

Pocky and Lance both stopped dead in their tracks. Lance looked at her in disbelief. Pocky tried to hold down a chuckle but couldn't. She shook her head.

"See," she said with a nod, "I *knew* it was a prank."

"It's the truth!" Shox shouted.

"Fuck your truth, Shox. Unlike you, we have a job to get to."

Pocky attempted to move again, but Shox stepped in their path, blocking their way. Lance was about to unblock their way, but Pocky quickly dropped her pack and leaned against him, preventing him from intervening.

"Ahh." Shox drew out the word, and his weird grin returned. "Now I see how it is. Didn't think you preferred civilian dick."

Pocky felt Lance's body tense, and she leaned her shoulders more into his chest. This was getting out of hand.

"He's as much a man as my brothers-in-arms," she said. "And it isn't any of your business."

Shox frowned and took a step back. "I'm being serious, Pocky," he said, his voice turning strangely robotic. "I really do love you. In fact, I'm madly in love with you, and I wanna be with you. I know I've played a prank on you, but I realize now it's because of my feelings for you, and I didn't know how to express them. I'm sorry. But I'm hoping you'll look past that and give me a chance. Give us a chance."

Pocky pressed her lips together, trying not to laugh again, but she felt a rumble brewing within Lance as he tried not to laugh either. The asshole was so full of shit that it was embarrassing. She quickly composed herself.

"Are you done?" she asked.

Shox looked at her, confused. Again, Pocky wanted to laugh. Shox really thought his confession was sincere.

"Didn't my words move you?" he asked.

"They moved my bowels. Now I need to use the head," Pocky said dryly.

Lance chuckled lightly.

Shox's face flushed red. "Oh, you think this is funny, farm boy?"

Oh shit. Pocky stilled as Lance moved around her. Now knowing how he felt about his upbringing, she knew the name hit a sore spot. Having lived in the Hyashi household, she could relate and wouldn't care to be called an aristocratic brat or something similar. Shox crossed a line.

"Do not call me that again," Lance said firmly.

"Or what?" Shox sneered. "Think you can fight me? The IMF taught me how to fight clean. You got nothing on me."

"And I grew up with cousins that taught me how to fight dirty. You got nothing in comparison."

Shox eyed Lance suspiciously, then turned his attention back to her. "Pocky? Please?"

"Oh, no. I'm staying out of this pile of shit you got yourself into," she said.

Pocky realized then why she had tried to keep Lance back from this. Every soldier was heavily trained for hand-to-hand combat. She knew how efficient they were, and she'd been worried Shox would have the upper hand if it came to physical blows. Pocky fully respected Lance, and he would have made a great soldier, but she didn't know how he handled a fight. Without him knowing it, he'd become the leader of their team, often showing his want and need to protect them.

But fighting was a different element entirely, and she feared to see him falter, especially up against another soldier. She couldn't bear to see the man she had grown fond of beaten. Even more so, she couldn't bear to see him defeated. Specifically by a worthless shithead like Shox.

With the confidence in Lance's voice, though, she wondered why she had been worried about this. She knew deep within her heart that her man was more than capable of handling someone like Shox. *My man?* she thought with a smile, liking the sound of that.

"Look, I'm being for real here," Shox said. "This isn't a prank. I truly do love you and I want you to be with me."

Pocky sighed and turned to Lance. "Yeah, true love. Just weeks ago, he sends his babysitter to me in a panic because he was masturbating in the shower, slipped, and fell on his dick. I go rushing to his cabin thinking he needed medical attention. I find him on his bunk, buck naked, holding his boner. Before I can ask what's going on, he says I need to suck it to make it better."

Shox cackled. "Oh, that was the best! The look on your face was priceless!"

Pocky sighed and looked at Lance. "Does that say 'true love' to you?"

Shox continued laughing as he said, "I just wanted to see if you spit or swallowed."

That was Lance's breaking point. Shox was laughing so hard that he didn't see Lance coming. He shoved Shox hard enough to send him crashing to the floor. Pocky could see Lance had restrained himself from using his fist. Shox scrambled to get up, his face turning beet red.

"Fucking asshole!" Shox roared as he charged Lance.

Pocky stepped away, grabbed her med pack, and watched. Lance was like a tree, unmoving, no matter how much force Shox threw into every charge. The guy truly shamed the IMF. Lance made Shox look like a toddler having a tantrum. Every punch Shox threw, Lance swatted it away without much effort, then shoved the asshole farther and farther. After a few bouts, she realized he was herding Shox out of the library. She followed not too closely behind.

Once in the corridor, Lance continued to move Shox toward the midship entrance and deflected the onslaught. At one point, Pocky almost burst into laughter as he grabbed Shox by the wrist and hit him with his own fist, causing a bloody lip. Halfway to the entrance, Shox stopped and leaned against the wall, gasping for breath. He wiped the blood away with his hand.

"Told you I fight dirty," Lance said flatly.

Shox smiled. "Well, I do have one dirty move I think you'll like. It's a final kind of move. Wanna see?"

Lance shrugged. Shox smiled wider and then kicked up his chin. Pocky wasn't sure if the gesture was part of the final move or was the actual move. Whatever it was, it was pathetic. Shox frowned as though something was supposed to happen. He lifted his chin again. When nothing happened, Shox paled.

Lance was no longer interested in what the guy was trying to do. "Break's over, keep moving."

"Who are you?" Shox said, his eyes wide.

"Someone you don't fuck with!" Lance stalked toward him.

Shox didn't argue and started quickly moving away.

Before they passed the lab, Thomas poked his head out. When he saw Lance, he stepped all the way out. "Lance? What's going on?"

"This asshole was inappropriate to your sister," Lance said with heat biting every word. "I'm not having it."

Thomas moved toward Pocky. Again, that strange, annoying question lingered in her mind, but it was still out of focus. She had no idea what it could be.

"Sis? You okay?" Thomas asked.

"Yeah," Pocky said casually, as though nothing was wrong at all.

Kaori and Naiko came out after and asked her what was going on. Pocky explained the situation. A moment later, they heard Lance shove Shox through the door, and Pocky realized why he'd steered the asshole that way. Lance wanted to hand him off to one of the guards. The sergeant in charge would definitely be happy to do that. If it was still Marker, he would want a report of her side of it, so she began to excuse herself.

"Sis, wait," Thomas said, grabbing her arm gently. "Can I talk to you privately?"

Without having to ask, Kai and Naiko went back inside the lab. Pocky tried to ignore the blurry question swirling in her head.

"What's up?" she asked.

Thomas's expression turned apologetic. "I'm ... well, I just feel like we've barely had any time to catch up. I know you've got your duties, I've got training, and ... you and Lance seemed to be hitting it off, and I don't want to get in the way of that, but ... but I really want to catch up."

Pocky looked down, feeling guilty even though she wasn't purposely avoiding him. Most of the time, when they tried being alone, they were interrupted by one thing or another.

"How about after lunch?" she asked, already forming an idea of the perfect place to go.

"Yeah, that'll work. Where you wanna hang?"

Pocky beamed mischievously. "The one place no one will find us."

Thomas grinned. "Okay."

They embraced for a long moment. Again, guilt gripped her. She couldn't tell Thomas about Stellan and his demand to meet with her. That asshole really did a number on him, and she wasn't sure what this new development would do. For her, the thought of being in the same room as Stellan made her want to retch, but the XO wasn't asking. It was an order. For now, she pushed her unease away.

Bren and Lance joined them. Lance still looked bothered, but Bren sported an amused grin.

"Oh, my shit, Partner," he said with a laugh. "You should have seen Shox groveling to Marker for mercy." Bren's tone turned mocking as he said, "'Please don't take me back to the brig, I swear I'll stay in my cabin! Please, please, please!'"

"Did Marker oblige?" Pocky asked, hoping the sergeant didn't give in.

"Going back down to the doggy cage," Bren replied with a laugh.

"Good," Pocky said. "Why was he even let out?"

"Believe it or not, Stellan sexually assaulted him."

Pocky jutted her face forward with wide eyes in disbelief. "Fucking what?" she and Thomas said in unison, which amused them despite the revelation. Speaking the same words, in the same tone, simultaneously, was becoming more frequent. She'd missed that.

Bren winced. "Yeah, apparently the guards were taking them both to the head, then Stellan turned on Shox and shoved his tongue down his throat. Took a hard minute for the guards to separate them. Because of that, the warden granted Shox to be placed back in his bunk." He shook his head in disgust. "Stellan is a sick fuck. Can't imagine how you two dealt with that."

"Yeah, he was always beating on his dick around the house. Cannon was—"

"Sis, let's not, okay?" Thomas interjected with a high-pitched voice.

"Sorry," Pocky said and pressed her lips together.

"Anyway," Bren continued, popping his eyes wide on the word. "That was right after the explosion. He's been isolated in his cabin since, so—"

"Ah, excuse me?" Naiko interrupted musically. They all turned to her attention. "I need my agriculturists, please."

"Yes, ma'am." Lance and Thomas said almost in unison.

"We gotta go too, Partner," Bren said. "Came here to get ya. Sergeant Holiday needs us back in the clinic."

Pocky hugged her brother again, then watched him walk into the lab. She then embraced Lance and held him tightly. They kept their hands linked even when they pulled away. Lance's expression remained hard, so Pocky gestured to Bren to give them a moment. He obliged.

"You okay?" she asked.

Lance frowned. "Did I overstep?"

"Not in the least. In fact, I should have just let you deal with it from the start."

"I wasn't going to stand for his behavior, but I wasn't trying to be disrespectful to you."

"You weren't," Pocky said with a reassuring smile.

Lance let out an anxious breath. "Okay. I just wanted to be sure. See you for lunch?"

"Yeah."

Lance smiled brightly, then kissed the back of her hand.

After parting ways, Pocky joined Bren. Her partner knew something more than friendship was going on between her and Lance, and he smiled as though he approved.

"All good, Partner?"

Again, that blurry question hung on the forefront of her mind, just out of reach to make sense. *No*, Pocky wanted to say, but she didn't. Instead, she said, "Yeah, let's go."

23

After lunch, Lance and Bren headed to the gym. Besides watching Bren and Pocky practice their music in the Rec Hall, going to the gym had also become a favored part of his day. Plus, it was a nice release of tension after being in the lab. Training in the greenhouse wasn't so bad, but he loathed the lab immensely. Trying to identify leaves and what plant group they belonged to was tedious work. It was fast competing with which one was more fun: fruit picking or staring at slides all day. Since *Gaia* still wasn't moving and had no timeframe for when they would, Naiko only trained them for half the day.

Between the boring lab work and his confrontation with Shox, he needed to let out his aggression on a punching bag. Bren happily agreed and led him to the section that had a few available.

Pocky usually worked out with them while Thomas would stay for an hour before going back to the lab with Kaori. However, today, the twins opted to sneak into the restaurant instead. The two hadn't had much of a chance to reconnect thanks to everything going on. The restaurant was the perfect place for them to go to be unbothered and uninterrupted.

After settling their stuff down by one of the punching bags, Bren pulled out a roll of tape from his pack. As he started taping Lance's right hand, he said, "Thanks for dealing with that asshole, by the way. I've wanted to knock the shit out of Shox ever since Pocky told me what he did."

"I definitely wanted to. It was hard not to let loose."

"No doubt. But still, I'm thankful you intervened before he pulled another one on her."

Lance nodded, then furrowed his brows. "Why'd Pocky call it a prank though? She's not minimizing it, is she?"

"Nah—well, I mean—sort of," Bren said flatly, finishing Lance's hand. "That good?"

Lance flexed his hand. "Yeah." Bren then started on his left. "Well … I just wanted to ask. Most shit seems to roll off her, but … that kind of thing is different."

"Shit like that doesn't bother her—I mean, yeah, it annoyed her, but that's all it was to her. She's been through too much and seen too much for something like that to unbalance her."

Lance had come to know how very true that was. Pocky wasn't easily rattled and didn't hide how she felt. What everyone saw was exactly that. She was a no-nonsense person who had no time for trivial bullshit or drama. She was direct and to the point, but playful when she felt it was appropriate. He could always tell what mood she was in just by her body language or expression. She could light up any moment just by her smile.

"For me though," Bren continued, working on Lance's left hand. "I wanted to throw that motherfucker over the boat."

"No doubt," Lance said, repeating Bren's words with a small smile.

They were silent while Lance taped Bren's hands. When the medic was good to go, he was ready to let his aggression out, pretending the bag was Shox's face. Bren held the bag steady while Lance got into an easy rhythm. He was careful not to agitate his wound. Bren was good at making sure of that too.

After throwing a couple of punches, Bren grinned. Lance paused. "What's got you smiling?"

"You and my partner," Bren said with approval in his voice, but also a hint of something else.

"She's fucking amazing. Never met a woman like her. Does it surprise you that I'm interested?"

"Surprised by you? No. Surprised by her? Totally. Can't tell you how many guys have tried, and she shuts them down."

Lance already knew this of her, and in return, she knew his history—or lack of it. He started punching the bag again and spoke in between hits. "Well, since you're her other brother, you approve of me?"

"Oh, you would've already known if I didn't." Bren laughed. "So, you can officially call her your woman if you want."

Lance smiled at that and then concentrated on his aim. When he noticed the bag was giving a little, he paused again and looked at Bren. His gaze was unfocused, like he was deep in thought.

"Speaking of our women," Lance started cautiously, "you catch up with Viper yet?"

As her role dictated, Viper had been busy with the Stellan crap and then the chaos that ensued after the explosion. They rarely saw her, and when they did, it was usually to talk with Thomas or Naiko. Bren always attempted to converse with her, but she'd say she didn't have time, leaving the man worried. Lance could understand Bren's concern; Viper seemed more stressed every time they saw her.

Bren met his eyes, then moved away. Lance didn't follow until he saw the medic heading toward their stuff. Bren grabbed his canteen and took a long pull from it; Lance grabbed his own and did the same. Just like with Pocky, he never pushed and waited patiently for his friend to either talk or move on to something else. This time Bren chose to talk.

"I haven't been able to snag her for one fucking second. But something's got her spooked. And yeah, that has me on edge."

Lance clasped Bren's shoulder. Besides listening, there was nothing else he could do. Bren then went into a rant and vented his frustration through words and the punching bag. Relationships weren't easy in the outside world, but being in the military added an extra element to contend with. Between the man's duties from being on an OSAR squad and Viper stationed on *Gaia*, their relationship was already strained, but they made it work. However, with everything going on, Bren felt helpless and unsure of what to do or how to help her. Because of his rank and them being unmarried, there was technically nothing the man could do.

After Bren vented, they moved on from the punching bag to free weights. Lance thought about his relationship with Pocky and where it could lead.

They'd be together for a year for the project, but what would come after that? No doubt she'd go back to her squad, while he may go on to another project …

The idea of being separated bothered him greatly, but Lance wasn't ready to think that far ahead, so he dismissed his thoughts.

They spent the next hour chatting about how Lance's older cousins taught him to fight, and he even showed Bren some of the mechanics. His friend was surprised to hear that Lance had been in several fights before—mostly to stop them or to defend someone. He didn't mean for it to sound like he was bragging, but he seemed to score even more points with the big guy.

When they were finished and ready to hit the showers, the gym doors slammed open. Heavily geared soldiers drew their weapons as they entered the gym, shouting in Origin. Almost in unison, everyone stopped what they were doing and scrambled to stand at parade rest. Lance had been around the soldiers long enough to recognize this was a Strat Unit. They moved with quick precision as they fanned out. Viper stepped in after them and bellowed something in Origin.

Lance didn't think twice and stood at parade rest out of respect. Since the clothes Iza had given him were no different from everyone else's, he blended in well.

"Am I good?" Lance whispered to Bren.

"Yeah," the medic replied, voice low.

The gym, larger than it appeared from the outside, was currently accommodating almost fifty soldiers. It took time, but the unit checked every face in the room. They were obviously looking for a particular person or persons. Viper stepped up to Lance and Bren but didn't directly look at them as the unit finished their search. The SC looked as though she hadn't slept in days. Dark circles sat under her eyes, and her bronze skin was ashen. Lance didn't doubt this would escalate Bren's concern for his woman.

A soldier yelled to Viper from across the room. She yelled back, then the soldiers moved inside the locker room. They most likely were searching the showers and bathrooms too. The SC yelled to everyone else, and they went back to whatever they were doing.

"Viper?" Bren said with a warning in his tone. "Who are you looking for?"

"It's not Stellan," she replied quickly.

"Then who?" he pressed.

"Follow me."

Lance didn't think he was invited until Bren gestured for him to follow. They waited outside the locker room until a few soldiers came up, giving the all clear. Viper ordered everyone to get out, not caring if they were in mid-shower, mid-dressing, or mid-shitting. After the soldiers walked out, she checked that the place was empty. Afterward, she ordered a few from the unit to guard the entrance and the others to keep searching, then she led Bren and Lance inside. He still wasn't sure why Bren brought him along, thinking the two needed to be alone, until they came to the open arched doorway of the last shower room.

"You mind making sure no one comes near, Cap?"

"Yeah, sure," Lance said, then leaned against the wall next to the entrance, folding his arms.

Bren took Viper inside the shower room. The room wasn't that big and echoed, so Lance could hear everything, but they spoke in their dialect. It was as private as it could get for the two of them. At first, there seemed to be a heated exchange before there was a long pause. What happened next made Lance understand why Viper needed absolute privacy. She let her guard down and broke into a sob. Although he was still speaking in Origin, Bren's words and voice were soothing, his deep voice loving yet stern. Lance wished he could understand the language.

A sharp pain pierced Lance above his right eye, and the smell of iron overtook his nose. He was about to call Bren but was shocked still by what he heard next and was unable to speak. As though the Divine Universe granted him a single wish, he somehow could understand every word spoken between the two.

"Viper, please, you gotta talk to me or you're gonna burst. Please don't make me relieve you of duty. Hate me all you want for it, but I will. Whatever's going on isn't worth your well-being."

"Fuck," she breathed. "Stellan. He's holding us hostage. That's why *Gaia's* cold. He somehow blew up *The Mesmir* and has threatened to blow up not just the rest of us, but the Charter Channel and the port. And before you ask how that's possible, Geara and I have been racking our brains on it and have come up with shit. There were no other ships in sight or on radar when *The Mesmir* exploded. We dared to even think of sabotage from within, but every soldier and ship has been checked, rechecked, and triple-checked. Even the dogs haven't detected any hidden explosives. We don't know how he's doing it, but we're taking him seriously."

"What in the hell? Why's he even doing this? I mean, what's the point? Did he say?"

Viper hesitated, then said, "He wants Pocky."

"What?" Bren said sharply. Lance tensed as he listened on. "Why?"

"Won't say. Just keeps saying that this is all about her and has been stringing this out like he's in no hurry. He made us move him to a guest cabin, and we've been waiting on him like we're fucking servants. And then last night he said he would be meeting with her soon. It was weird how he said it. As though it was going to happen without arrangements, without our consent or even hers. We gave her a heads-up this morning but tried not to alarm her. M ..." Viper's voice wavered. "I'm scared. I'm actually fucking scared. I'm scared for her and for us."

"Fuck," Bren whispered. "So what Thomas said was true? I thought that asshole was just fucking with him. What the hell does Stellan want her for?"

"Wish I knew, and now I got another fucking problem on my hands."

"What now?" Bren asked with a heavy sigh.

"Shox, two soldiers, and a medic that were taking him to the brig are missing. They never reported in and haven't been seen since leaving C Deck."

"Shit." Bren shuffled a few steps away.

"We're searching everywhere. Like I really need this bullshit."

"The twins, they're in—"

"Already checked, and I don't care why they're in the restaurant. They're safe."

After another exasperated huff, Bren spoke carefully. "Is there something I can do?"

"I would get in trouble just by telling you—"

"Woman, I'm talking about *you*," Bren interrupted harshly. "What can I do for *you*? I don't know what to do about the rest of it, but what can I do for you right now?"

There was a long pause before Viper replied. "I don't know. I ..."

Lance moved away until their voices were distant and unintelligible. Besides being able to understand them, that conversation had his head spinning. He suddenly felt an urgency to check on the twins, but Viper had said they were safe, so he waited for Bren to be finished.

How could he possibly—and suddenly—understand them? During his travels in Theton, he had been able to pick up a few words in several different languages, but not an entire dialect in a second. Lance massaged his scalp. The more he thought about it, the more of a headache brewed. The danger they were all in didn't help that either.

A few minutes later, Viper passed him and regrouped with the unit that came with her. Bren walked up to him a moment later and did a double take.

"Hey, you okay?" Bren asked.

"No. Do you have painkillers?"

"I do," Bren said and then retrieved his pack. A short moment later, Lance swallowed two pills. "Fuck," the medic muttered, "I don't need to worry about you too."

"I'm fine, just a headache," Lance quickly replied. He wasn't sure if he should share his bizarre sudden ability but then decided to hold off for the time being. "Your woman okay?"

Bren let out a frustrated huff, then revealed the conversation, which Lance was grateful for.

"Maybe Thomas's right about Pocky's premonitions making her desirable to that fucker," Bren muttered.

"I don't think so."

The day after the explosion, the four of them had extensively discussed Pocky's "premonitions," as they were dubbed. Because Lance had heard their conversation in the stairway, they brought him into the discussion. Pocky disclosed that she had no memory of what initiated both occurrences. With Bren, she went from walking through the Hyashi household hallway to holding onto Thomas as they rode their stolen horse. For Trooper and his group, she went from a dead sleep to running into a besieged town. What she recalled with absolute certainty was knowing exactly where to find them and that she wasn't going to stop until she did. How all that was possible eluded her. She wasn't even sure what made Bren and Trooper stand out among the many.

"Why not?" Bren asked Lance.

"Because if you just found out about Trooper, how would Stellan know of that event?"

"True, but maybe he doesn't know those in particular, just that she's capable of doing so."

"Yeah, but her insight seems random. I don't see how that would make her valuable to him unless he somehow knows a way to harness her ability."

"Her *ability*?" Bren raised one eyebrow.

Lance shrugged. "What else would you call it?"

"True." Bren gazed down, then swallowed. As he continued, his voice wavered. "Premonitions, ability ... whatever it is, she saved me. Because of that, I wanted to save people in return, to make something of my life so that I could. Underneath, it was really to return the favor to her in that way. We were dealt shitty hands, but I admit to feeling the Divine Universe wove some good out of a bad situation. And not just for the three of us, but for all those who were inadvertently in the orphanage trade. Because the IMF did something about it, I wanted to serve and pay back my debt to them, even though there isn't one. And that all started when she saved me."

Bren looked away as a tear ran down his cheek. He quickly wiped it away. Lance put a hand on the big guy's shoulder.

"Look, we'll figure this out," Lance said. "There's obviously more to this than we're seeing. It may not even be about premonitions or abilities. Let's shower, then get the twins. I don't want either of them out of our sight until we're out of this shit, okay?"

"Yes, sir."

24

The restaurant was smaller than Thomas had expected, but Pocky explained that *Gaia* had a low capacity to house guests, so accommodations for them were minimal. The place was windowless and had parallel double wooden doors for the starboard and port side entrances. The floor, walls, furnishings, and bar all had that sleek black wooden finish to them. The lights were low, giving the place a romantic atmosphere. The restaurant certainly appealed to who it was meant for—aristocrats—but for him and his sister, the place was a temporary playground.

Thomas couldn't remember the last time when he and Pocky had this much fun. Even the days leading up to their separation hadn't been this good. They messed around with the sound system, which only played what aristocrats listened to—which was pure crap, in their opinion. For almost an hour, they made fun of the music by replacing the words with something tasteless or vulgar. They also mimicked how they assumed the nobles would dance to the awful beats. Pocky laughed so hard she got a stomach cramp. Their only interruption was when Viper came in with a Strat Unit searching for someone. Aside from that, for the first time since they parted ways, Thomas felt connected with his sister again.

When they were ready to do something else, they went through the stock behind the bar. They lightly sampled and judged the liquor, then impersonated how an aristocrat would react to the different tastes.

"Oh my, this will not do," Pocky said in a low, mocking voice. "It stings my palate."

"Agreed. Shall we try something more fruity?" Thomas replied.

Their banter quickly became a game of who could mock better. Thomas felt he won, as Pocky couldn't keep up from laughing.

After composing herself and going back into her real voice, she said, "Fuck this crap. Let's have a real drink."

While Pocky retrieved their next beverage, Thomas grabbed two chairs from one of several stacks against the wall. All the tables were spread apart from each other and bolted down to a central iron bar and base. He set up the chairs on the corner of a table so that they could face each other. Pocky returned a short moment later with one bottle in hand. They got comfortable and shared the brew. He almost spat out his first sip; the liquid was dark and extremely bitter.

Pocky laughed at his reaction. His display of yuck face from when they were kids hadn't changed much and still amused her. "Yeah, it's why I like this kind," she said. "It doesn't motivate me to drink the whole thing."

"Uh-huh. So, is it a bonding thing like smoking?"

"Nah, just when I want to be numb. Especially on bad days."

"Do you ... talk to anyone about bad days?" Thomas asked carefully.

Pocky looked away, then slightly popped her brows as though shrugging. "Don't see the point of it. Most soldiers like to shock people with their stories; I don't. Even talking with M doesn't ease me in any way. I discovered very early that talking about it doesn't take away the people I tried to save. I still see them. I still see their faces."

"What? What do you mean by that?"

"Ghosts, I guess. They just pop in randomly in my view. I've gotten good at not reacting to them."

"Dead people?"

"Sometimes," Pocky said with a sigh. "Trooper is a good example of one that isn't. M tries to steer him away from me because he thinks the kid will remind me of that awful time. When really, I remember every second of it every damn day. I avoid him because no matter how many years it's been, I still see blood on his face. I know it isn't really there, but I see it regardless." She took a long pull from the bottle. "That irritates me because I really like the kid." She paused for a moment, her eyes distant. "Can we talk about something else?"

Thomas nodded, feeling guilty for even asking. A chill settled across his skin, but he tried not to fixate on her words and instead said, "Right, so, you and Lance—"

"Oh no, we're not talking about me this time. It's well past your turn to spill."

He smiled at her, thinking she was due for her turn. "I'm an open book."

Pocky grinned back. "You and Kaori seemed to be getting chummy. Noticed you two go back to work a lot after lunch. Never seen agriculturists train this much," she said as though hinting at something.

"Yeah, she's cool to work with, but we're not training."

"Oh?" Pocky said with a sudden blush that puzzled him.

"Actually, training's over, which is why I think Lance is getting frustrated."

"Yeah, he's definitely not as engrossed as you two are."

Thomas nodded. "Yeah, what Naiko has us doing is redundant at this point, but I think she's just doing it to keep us busy."

"So ... What are you and Kai working on then, not that it's my business, but ..."

"Uh, well, we're collaborating on a few fungus samples I have."

"Oh." Pocky pressed her lips together.

"What did you think we were doing?"

"Um, you know. What two people do when they like each other," she said with raised eyebrows and an amused grin.

Now it was Thomas who blushed. "Uh, no. I like her, but I'm not interested in her that way."

Pocky tempered her grin and spoke cautiously. "Has there ever been someone who did interest you?"

"No, don't see the reason to bother," Thomas replied. She let out a small huff of a laugh, making him curious. "What?"

"As different as we are, I forget sometimes how similar we are too. I never was interested in anyone either until now ... But anyway, still on you. Is this fungus the same one Lance was telling me about?"

"Yeah, it's so fascinating, but it's scary too."

"How so?"

"With the technology the IMF has, we've been able to have a closer look. It's incredible. Beforehand, all I knew about it was its ability to consume plant life and its hardiness to survive. I mean, I still haven't figured out how to kill it. Anyway, Kai and I have been studying it. It's weird, Sis. All this time, I thought it was a fungus. It certainly looks like one, and maybe it even was one at some point, but the components don't match anything that's been cataloged."

Pocky sported a contented patient smile.

"Sorry," he said. "I can bore you with something else."

"Whatever. Knowing you is knowing you, no matter what you tell me. I may not understand but still want to hear it."

Thomas nodded, then went into some more details about the fungus but quickly steered his storyline from where it all started, which was his journey across the ocean to Shad'Dyn.

After a while, Pocky wanted to walk and talk more wherever their legs took them, but Thomas wanted to address something first.

"Before we go, I need to ask you something."

"Yeah, sure."

"Or it's more like, are you ever going to ask me your question?"

Pocky's eyebrows raised. "What do you mean?"

"Sis, I can always tell when something's on your mind. And for the last couple of days, I can tell you have a question, and I've been waiting patiently for you to ask." Thomas paused, watching her eyes widen and jaw drop. "If you're asking if I approve of Lance, then—"

"No," she quickly interrupted. "Remember when we were kids and tried to do that mind-reading game?"

"Uh, vaguely," he said. "Why?"

Pocky moved her chair closer. "Let's try it now."

"What? Did that even work?"

"Sort of. I mean, you wouldn't get the exact words right, but close enough."

"Okay, and why are we doing this instead of just asking like a normal person would?"

Pocky chuckled at that. "Because I do have a question, but I don't know what it is."

"Uh—"

"Just humor me, okay? Just try. If it doesn't work, whatever."

"Alright," he said. "How'd we start? I don't remember."

"Um, I think we just stare into each other's eyes," she said with a laugh.

Thomas laughed with her. "Okay."

The first couple of times they tried didn't work because they ended up laughing. But finally, they got serious and more focused. Seconds went by. Thomas didn't think it would work until he suddenly did see her words. The words were fluid, though, and kept changing, but had the same meaning.

"Did something happen to me? Four, something happened to me? What happened at four, to me?"

They changed again. *"Healer, Healer, I need the Healer. Communications down. Breach, invaded. Foreign, invaded. He's inside me, I can't fight him. Healer needed. Foreign, contained. Healer needed."*

Thomas shuddered. The sharp tang of iron filled his nose. He suddenly remembered who they were, who the Healer was, and why they were here. He also knew what she meant by foreign and invaded, and why she needed the Healer, why she needed Bren. Adrenaline pumped in his veins with urgency.

"Brother!?" Pocky said with alarm, reaching for him. "What's wrong?"

Thomas grabbed her upper arms. "We need Bren! Now!"

"We ... we? Uh, okay," she replied quickly.

As Pocky put on her pack, a commotion came from the kitchen. Figuring it was Iza, they waited for her to walk through the door. But when it opened, a terrible stench emanated.

"Shit," Pocky cursed under her breath, then raised her voice. "Fuck off—"

Thomas watched as a soldier appeared, raised a gun, and fired two shots. The impact of the bullets hit Pocky in the stomach. With a short, guttural cry, she went down. Before he could react, pain exploded in his left temple. Everything instantly went dark.

***

Thomas's head pounded in time with his heart. He forced his eyes open, only to find a horrifying scene.

He was lying on his right side, several feet away from Pocky. With her back to him, she was on her knees with her arms stretched out away from her body, tied to the table legs. His eyes grew wide as he realized she was topless; blood ran down her back in red rivers. Her head hung low, and he hoped that meant she was unconscious.

Thomas's vision blurred for a moment as he tried to move his arms, but nothing budged. Abruptly, electricity shot across his forehead and eyes, forcing him to be still. A sudden stench made him gag.

A soldier appeared, somewhat blocking his view. *Thank the Divine Universe, someone found us!*

Thomas's relief turned to horror as the soldier grabbed Pocky by her hair and forced her head back. He gritted his teeth and forced himself to stay still.

The soldier—or someone impersonating one—yelled into her ear, wanting her to wake up. After a spew of words, the guy got quiet and let go of Pocky's head. He unbuckled his belt and whipped it out quickly from the loops. Thomas jerked involuntarily as the asshole began hitting his sister across her back. His blood pumped faster as he tried to move—again, to no avail. Every smack of the belt across Pocky's skin made Thomas gasp for air. He wanted to scream for help but knew that would do no good until he had control over his body. It was excruciating to wait.

"Wake up, you fucking cunt!" the soldier yelled.

For some reason Pocky wasn't waking up, defying the man without even knowing it. Though Thomas didn't want her to wake up to this nightmare, the fact that she was still unconscious concerned him. The guy then whipped her one last time, so brutally that it sounded like a bone breaking. Thomas bit his lip, trying to fight back his anger.

The soldier then threw down the belt like a toddler having a tantrum and moved out of view. Thomas almost let out a pained whimper as he viewed his sister's back. The man hit her hard enough to break skin and capillaries.

With fierce determination, Thomas tried moving again. He had to get to

Pocky. Somehow, he was free; why hadn't their captor tied his hands? Either way, Thomas was glad for the oversight.

He reached behind his head and felt a chair leg. Gripping it with both hands, he quickly formed a plan and hoped he was strong enough to incapacitate their assailant long enough to get help.

Thomas watched patiently as the soldier returned and crouched behind Pocky. The guy moved his hands to her front side and spoke with eerie joy as he unbuckled her belt.

"Oh, I got something that will definitely wake you up, and you'll be in a shitload of pain when you do."

Whether he had the strength or not, Thomas wasn't going to allow his sister to be violated.

He threw the chair over himself onto the asshole's back. The man crashed to the floor and rolled onto his left side. The look of shock on his face pleased Thomas, but he almost came unglued as he recognized the guy for who he really was. It was Shox, a minion that aided the Abnormals. This particular one, though, thought of himself as one of the big players. The guy even thought he had an ability when in fact he had none at all.

Thomas tightened his grip on the now broken chair leg. "Didn't think I could fight motherfucker?"

Shox's eyes widened. He tried crawling away, but Thomas swung the chair leg over the minion's body. He wasn't sure where Shox was going until he saw the med pack on the floor. It wasn't Pocky's, so the guy had obtained one somehow. He paused for a moment to catch his breath.

A mistake.

Thomas's entire body started trembling. Shox took the opportunity and dove into the pack as though something in it could help him. He turned and rested on his elbows, breathing heavily. Something was in his hand. Thomas commanded his body to move, but he couldn't budge.

"Come on, asshole," Shox taunted with a sinister grin. "I'm gonna rape your cunt sister in every hole she's got."

Anger rushed through Thomas's veins. His body shook, whether from shock or rage, he didn't know. He didn't care. Thomas raised the chair leg above his head, ready to deliver a final blow. As he came down, Shox lunged and stabbed him in his calf muscle.

Thomas screamed. Shox had stabbed him with a needle, and whatever was in it burned.

With a quick swing, Thomas cracked the chair leg across Shox's face and hit him two more times before stopping. The chair leg slipped from his grip as he calmly reached down and pulled the syringe out with a grunt. The barrel was still half full, and Thomas hoped that was a good thing. He put the syringe down harder than he had intended on the closest table. *Or was it the floor?* The room swam around him, and his head felt foggy and heavy. There was something he needed to do. Something important, but he couldn't remember what it was.

Thomas then heard a familiar voice coming up behind him and turned.

"Stellan?" he slurred. The man was in the same suit that he was wearing at the hotel and looked awful. "You look like shit."

"So good to see you, brother."

"Fuck. You," Thomas replied drunkenly.

"Oh now, don't be that way. I love you and want to be with you."

"Thought you just wanted my sister now. And why is that anyway?" Thomas asked, his brain and mouth both getting more sluggish. "What do you want with her?"

Stellan didn't answer and just stared into space.

"I hate your face," Thomas muttered.

"Oh, come now, don't be—"

"Why do you want her?!" Thomas yelled. "You pissed and shit in her food. You doused her with cold water when we were sleeping. You were cruel to her, and now you want her?"

Stellan still didn't answer and continued to stare.

"Okay, I don't have time for your bullshit. I need to do something. Something important," Thomas said tiredly. His mind was so muddled that his vision was beginning to blur.

"Your sister, you mean?"

"Yes, my sister. She's ... she's in trouble. I need to help her."

"Your sister's dead, brother," Stellan said as though it was funny.

"What?" Thomas whimpered.

"I can't feel her heartbeat. So, she must be. Two bullets in the stomach would surely do it, don't you think?"

"But it had to be rubber bullets. Shox was doing something to her. He couldn't do anything if she was ..."

"Your mind is letting you think it was rubber bullets, but she has to be dead. You saw blood exploding from her stomach. I'm telling you the truth, brother. Her heartbeat is finished."

"You—" Thomas began and then broke down in tears. "You fucking asshole!"

He gripped something cold in his hand. A gun. He didn't know whose it was or where it came from, but Thomas was glad to have it. He started laughing.

"Yes, brother," Stellan hissed, his voice distorted. "Use this on me and be rid of me forever. It's what you've always wanted. Do it."

Thomas pointed the gun and tried to aim for Stellan's face. His vision was too blurry to see clearly from tears. To his surprise, though, when he pulled the trigger, the bullet went straight to the man's right eye. Stellan went down instantly and seemed to disappear as he fell. Thomas dropped the gun but didn't hear it hit the floor. All of that should have alarmed him, but he didn't care. He didn't care about anything anymore. His sister was dead, so nothing mattered.

Thomas staggered off. He may not have cared about anything anymore, but he didn't want to be wherever he was either.

Before passing through the double doors to the port side, Thomas heard banging from the other end, but didn't care what it was.

25

Finally, Lance and Bren were cleaned up and getting dressed. As he put on a pair of black cargo pants and a white cotton tee, Bren finished tying his boots.

Lance was anxious to get going. The thought of the twins being alone didn't sit well with him as the minutes passed. As he finished tying his laces, a burst of light erupted behind his eyes, momentarily blinding him. The smell of iron filled his nose again. His body swayed, and he reached out to steady himself against the wall.

"Whoa, Cap? What's doing?" Bren asked. "Still got—"

Lance's vision cleared. He sucked in a breath, then sprinted off. "The twins!" he yelled over his shoulder. "Hurry!"

He didn't understand how he knew, but Thomas and Pocky were in trouble. The certainty of that drove him forward as he weaved around soldiers and equipment. A familiar face stood out just ahead.

"Marker, with me!" Lance called.

He burst out of the gym and ran to the restaurant. He tried pushing through the double wooden doors, but they were locked. Lance kicked the spot between the doors with everything he had.

"Here, Cap, let me help!" Marker shouted.

Lance moved over half a step, and on their third kick, the doors burst open. They hurried inside, his eyes landing immediately on Pocky. His body shook with rage at the sight of her. She was topless, tied up, bloodied, and beaten.

"Marker, find Thomas!" Lance shouted, already making his way to Pocky.

As he crouched next to Pocky, Lance saw a bloodied knife next to her. He picked it up and used it to cut her right arm free, trying not to think of what else it had been used for. Once he cut through the rope, he gently swung her arm over his shoulder and then moved in front of her to keep her from falling. He then tried to cut the other tie but couldn't without letting her go.

Beyond belief, Pocky was awake and seemed to know what he was trying to do. She gripped the back of his shirt tight, giving him the freedom to cut the second rope. After freeing her arm, he dropped the knife and embraced her carefully.

Pocky held onto him, her voice faint but clear. "I'm okay, I'm okay."

Lance put a hand on the back of her head and instantly pulled it back with how wet it felt. Blood covered almost his entire hand. As he began to shake, Pocky's arms fell, and her body sagged against his. The room around him disappeared, and he began to scream.

"Bren!"

As though Lance had summoned the man out of thin air, Bren skidded to a stop next to them. "I'm here, I'm here! Put her down!"

Lance did as he was told and placed Pocky down gently. He moved to her left side as Bren kneeled on her right. He ripped open his med pack and dove in for what he needed.

"Partner, can you hear me?" Bren asked as he pulled out a towel, a clear bottle, and several thin antiseptic packets. He asked again as he snapped gloves on, then took the towel and placed it under her head.

Lance took off his shirt and used it to cover her chest. He swallowed hard. Blood was all over her face and neck. Her hair was matted over her forehead and eyes. He wanted to move her hair away but trusted Bren wouldn't want him to do that yet.

"Shit, she doesn't have her med watch on," the medic said, then went into his pack again. "Cap, get those fucking ropes off her wrists please."

Lance got the rope off her right wrist in time for Bren to slap his med stick on, then synced his watch. While waiting for numbers, Bren started an IV line to a vein along the backside of her right hand, then attached a small fluid pouch.

Bren bent down close to her ear. "Pocky? Can you hear me?" When she didn't respond, he grabbed her left hand. "Partner, squeeze my hand ... shit."

He let go and examined her entire head and neck. He pulled away and started putting on new gloves. "So far she's got one head wound that I can see," he said to Lance. "Bleeding has ceased. Looks deep. I need to stitch it."

After Bren pulled out his suture kit, he moved Pocky's hair away and was careful not to agitate the wound. He broke open an antiseptic pack and cleaned her forehead, making it clear where the wound was. A long gash traveled from her hairline to the middle of her forehead.

Bren's watch started flashing yellow rapidly.

"What does that mean?" Lance asked.

Bren didn't answer right away as he looked over the numbers. "Blood pressure down from blood loss, but thankfully not enough to where she'll need a blood transfusion. Her heart will replenish."

"What can I do to help?"

"Let me see your hands, palms up," Bren said, grabbing the small bottle he'd pulled out earlier. Lance complied and held out his hands. The medic cleaned his hands with the solution, then passed him a towel to dry them. He gave Lance a few small envelopes. "Use these to clean the lacerations on her hands and wrists."

Lance got on it as he ripped open the first packet and pulled out a thin wet antiseptic cloth. He began to clean the wounds on her left hand, only pausing as he watched Bren start to suture. His friend's movements were fast and flawless. Bren put Lance's mother to shame, who was, of course, their on-site medic for both humans and animals. When he was done, Bren then grabbed a small black canister from his pack. He shook it a few times before spraying a silver substance over the suture.

Shouting from across the room grabbed Lance's attention. That, or he just now registered the commotion. Marker's voice intertwined with Viper's and a few others, along with radio clicks. Lance prayed to the Divine Universe that Thomas was okay. He refocused on Bren, not wanting to think what state the man was in.

"Now I need to check the rest of her," Bren said as he put his suture tools back in their case. "Thank you for covering her up by the way." Lance nodded, then looked away as their medic lifted his shirt off Pocky's chest. "Shit, the assailant fired two rubbers into her stomach. Her right side is gonna be tender for a few days from the impact. Bruising is already appearing. I'm guessing she fought hard before the head wound knocked her out." He paused, taking in a deep breath. "Okay, I need to check her backside. I'm gonna need your help to turn her though. I know you wanna give her some civility—"

"Just tell me what to do," Lance blurted out.

Bren instructed him on how to cradle Pocky's head so he could turn her properly without straining her head and neck. Lance followed instructions and was ready. After securing her arm across her chest, he understood why the medic put the IV in her hand and not the crook of her arm. Bren placed a hand on her hip and grabbed a chunk of fabric while his other hand lifted at her shoulder. Once she was on her side, Bren paled. His eyes darted all over her back. Lance swallowed hard as he remembered what he had seen.

"Bren?"

"Motherfucker," Bren muttered, then reached into his pack.

Lance tried to control his temper as he spoke. "How bad?"

Bren's jaw flexed. "The assailant hit her with something, probably a belt."

Lance remained quiet as Bren pulled out several gauze and antiseptic pads and began cleaning Pocky's back. Lance felt cold with rage, hoping she hadn't been awake for that but knew most likely she had been. He grabbed her left hand, hating that she had endured this and whoever had done it.

"You still with me, Cap?"

"I am," Lance replied flatly as he observed his friend.

Bren continued working efficiently, but his stiff posture and tight face made it clear he was pushing through his own rage.

Pocky inhaled sharply. Her body jerked. Lance looked to Bren, wide-eyed.

"She's okay," the medic said calmly. "Just a reaction, and a sign that she might wake up soon."

"Is that even a good thing?"

Bren didn't reply right away as he began wiping her back with another pad. "Yes and no. Are you thinking along the lines of how she's gonna react to this when she wakes up?"

"Well, yeah."

Bren shook his head slowly. "Yeah, um, it wouldn't surprise me if she brushes this off."

Lance's eyes widened, and he shook his head. "I … I can't believe that. This is nowhere near what Shox had done. This is … too brutal to brush off."

Bren met his eyes before refocusing on Pocky's back. "I agree but I—honestly … I don't know how she's gonna be. Just saying, it wouldn't surprise me if she shrugged it off." He paused, reaching for another gauze pad. "That fucking war. In a lot of ways, it made her numb. Wish you could've met her before that happened. After we were rehomed, she was so cute and bubbly, always engaging us in some new game. We could be kids for the first time in our lives. She may not even be aware of it, but that war changed her. I wish I could've been with her or stopped her from leaving the ship. The details I got from Trooper were … awful."

Lance raised his eyebrows. "Trooper told you?"

Bren glanced at Lance. "I made him tell me. I mean, he's always bragging about it but only the nicer side of the story. I made him tell me the ugly bits. There were things she had to do to survive and to keep them alive. Stuff she didn't even want me to know." He paused, dropping the pad and grabbing another. "She and the others had to hide among dead bodies sometimes. The scars on her palms are from her cutting them and using the blood to smear on her face and the others, so they could pretend to be dead. And that's just a small part of it. There were things she was forced to do."

There was a long silence before Lance concluded what Bren was alluding to. "She had to kill people, right?"

"Yeah," Bren said, narrowing his eyes and scrunching his lips. "When she came back—I mean when she was somewhat like herself again—she was differ-ent. It's hard to explain."

"You don't need to," Lance murmured.

"I kind of do," Bren said sharply, meeting his eyes again. "If the two of you are going to be involved, then you need to come to terms with how she's gonna be when she wakes up. Whether she shuts down or acts as though nothing happened, I won't be surprised by either one, but she's certainly not going to be in a corner crying her eyes out or weeping in your arms. And I know you're thinking that *should* be the likely outcome because I had once thought the same back then."

Lance looked away. Pocky's words after he had untied her suddenly came back to him, making his stomach sour. "She said she was okay," he whispered.

"What?"

"Before you got here, she said she was okay."

"Yeah," Bren muttered. He exhaled harshly after finishing. The pile of bloody gauze and pads made Lance clench his jaw. Bren put on a new pair of gloves, then reached into his pack. He pulled out three large, thin packets that were half the length of his forearm. "Alright, she might react to these too. They feel cold at first."

"What are they?"

"Sheets layered with a substance that helps soothe minor stuff like first-degree burns, abrasions, bruises, that kind of thing."

Lance nodded. Starting from Pocky's lower back, Bren placed the medicated sheets from side to side until all three were used. He put a towel on the floor before settling Pocky back down. He checked her vitals again, then the fluid pouch.

Bren began cleaning up the area with a biohazard bag. Silence engulfed them for a moment before he asked, "You okay?"

Lance didn't answer until Bren met his eyes. "No. You?"

Bren didn't reply as Viper approached and crouched down. She had Pocky's med pack in one hand and a black shirt in the other. She placed the pack next to Bren's, then handed Lance the shirt. He thanked her for it and pulled it on. Viper looked down at Pocky with a hardened expression.

"Her watch is broken," Viper said. "I put that and her gun inside—"

"Thomas, is he okay?" Bren asked.

"Report first, medic," Viper said in a way of reminding Bren that they were soldiers to each other, and not as a couple at this moment.

"Yes, ma'am," Bren replied respectfully. He began clinically, but his voice grew angrier as he spoke. "Likely started with two rubber shots to her stomach. Defensive wounds on her hands and fingers suggest she fought at first. Laceration on her forehead—I'm presuming it knocked her unconscious. The assailant then ... tied her up, stripped her topside, and proceeded to inflict lashes along her mid and lower back with a belt or something similar. Her pants are snapped, but her belt's unbuckled, indicating possible attempted sexual assault. Please tell me you have the fucking asshole in custody."

"We do."

"Who did this?" Bren asked, pressing his lips in anger. "Viper, you better fucking tell me."

Viper spoke as though she hadn't noticed his use of her name instead of rank. "Before I say, you need to know someone beat the shit out of him. We're thinking it had to be Thomas."

"Is he okay?" Lance snapped, irritated that hadn't been answered yet.

Viper sighed. "We don't know. We don't know where he is."

"What do you mean you don't know where he is?" Bren asked rapidly with wide eyes.

"We'll find him," she said reassuringly.

Bren grimaced. "Fucking damn it!"

Lance found himself caught between wanting to stay and wanting to look for Thomas. Viper suddenly pointed her finger at him, catching him off guard.

"You need to explain yourself," she said.

"What?" Lance asked in surprise.

"How did you know the twins were in trouble? Marker said you demanded for him to follow. Glad that you did, but how did you know?"

"I ... uh ... don't know. I just suddenly knew something was wrong," Lance said. "That ... Thomas needed help." The memory of the sudden distress call or message, or whatever it had been, had almost faded, but he kept that part to himself.

"Seriously?" Bren asked with wide eyes.

"Yeah."

"And you have no other explanation of how you just knew?" Viper pressed, looking more clinical than skeptical.

"No, I really don't."

"Well, whatever the cause, I'm glad you did. When Marker got here, he found the assailant, but Thomas is nowhere here." Viper paused and looked Pocky over again. "Did you find any needle punctures?"

"Not anywhere on her upper body. Why?"

"Found a syringe half full of Lythic."

"Shit," Bren said and then looked over Pocky's body. "I'll check the rest of her."

"What's Lythic?" Lance asked.

Bren looked up at him. "We use small amounts to relax patients who are in a heightened state of panic, but too much can cause hallucinations."

"The syringe had a bit of blood on it," Viper said. "I'm thinking it might have been used on Thomas but also thought it may have been used on Pocky too."

Lance glanced away. He should have felt regret for not checking on Thomas but didn't. Or couldn't. And he knew the man would have rather for him to go to his sister first anyway.

"Who's the assailant?" Bren asked.

Viper crossed her jaw, obviously uneased with answering. "Steel your actions and know we got him. No interference. Clear?"

Bren hesitated, then said, "Yes, ma'am."

"It was Shox."

Bren closed his eyes, his light brown skin reddening with anger. Lance felt the same heated rage but understood that he had only come to know Pocky within the last few weeks, while she and Bren were in every way family. Bren grabbed a piece of a broken chair that was near him and flung it across the room. It shattered when it hit the wall. Viper put a sympathetic hand on his shoulder.

"Hold your emotions until this is over, medic," Viper said firmly yet gently.

"Yes, ma'am. Sorry, ma'am." Bren flexed his jaw and wiped sweat from his forehead.

Viper considered Pocky as she spoke. "I was hoping she would be awake.

Think she'll be able to talk when she does?"

"I certainly hope so." Bren let out a heavy breath. "The head wound might make her disoriented, but maybe."

"Okay, are you moving her?"

Bren looked at his watch. "Gonna give her about another five to wake up. If not, we'll move her to her cabin."

"Okay," Viper said with a nod. "I'm having Marker move Shox to the brig. Spec Ops is here. I'll be staying for a bit longer, talking with them before I report to Geara."

"Did you find that asshole's escort?"

"Not yet."

"How did that shithead even know the twins were in here?"

"I don't know, but it seems that he was hiding in one of the ovens in the kitchen. Maybe he heard them."

Bren sighed heavily again. Viper put a hand on his shoulder before standing. As she walked away, Bren said a loving remark in their dialect, making Lance smile a little. She looked back at Bren, returned the words, then walked away.

Lance continued holding Pocky's hand while Bren cleaned more of her face. As Marker and a few other soldiers began moving Shox, the asshole began shouting. The name the man tossed out had them both looking up with alarm. Shox's face was bloodied and swollen but still sported a twisted grin.

"Brengavion!" Shox repeated. Lance was among the few who knew Bren's full name. Shox shouldn't have been one of them. "Yeah, I know who you really are, motherfucker! Stellan isn't the only one that wants your pet cunt, but he's gonna get her first. He's gonna get his way with her, and cut her open from the pussy—"

Viper punched Shox in the gut, cutting him off. Marker and the others dragged him outside.

"That fucking asshole," Bren spat through gritted teeth. "I hope a dog bites his dick off."

Lance paled as Shox's words registered. "What the fuck was he talking—" he began, but then felt his hand being squeezed. Realizing Pocky was beginning to stir, he let go of his temper and smiled. "Bren, she's waking up!"

The medic moved close to her face. "Partner? Can you—"

Pocky inhaled a sharp gasp as she placed her hands over her head. Her face grimaced in pain as she began screaming, "He's inside me, I can't fight him!"

26

"Boss?"

Pocky wearily opened her eyes. It was dark all around her, yet somehow it was disorienting. She was tired and cold. She couldn't remember what had happened before waking in this place, but a residual sensation of Lance holding her was still there. His scent and warmth lingered, and she took comfort from that. Short images flashed through her mind. She had been gasping for breath when Shox tried to subdue her, and the mental imagery she got was of her not winning that fight. The next memory wasn't recalled with a visual component but with the sense of Lance trying to help her.

"Boss?" a childlike feminine voice repeated.

It took a moment for Pocky to recall who was speaking but still couldn't see anything. "Ember?"

"Are you okay?"

"No. I'm—"

"Oh my shit! As you would say. The Healer is tending to you. I can feel him using a little of his ability to heal you," Ember said with excitement.

"Who?"

"Doesn't matter. Look, Boss, I need to hurry to get his attention. You're not gonna like what I'm about to do. I'm so sorry."

"What—"

Suddenly, Pocky felt as though she was being thrown somewhere else, and what she saw was horrifying. It was Stellan's consciousness. For less than a split second, she observed his sick mind. Cannon was somehow infused with him. She saw what he wanted and beyond that. She saw his army and where they were. She saw how they were attacking the IMF ships and his plans for world destruction. Then she saw what Cannon wanted from her and began screaming.

"He's inside me, I can't fight him!"

***

Bren's surroundings faded from view until only he and Pocky existed with nothing but light around them. Time slowed down to milliseconds as her words brought him into crystal clear focus. In 0.01 of a second, he felt an instant change within himself as he became aware of who he truly was. However, this time he wouldn't forget like so many times before when it would barely surface, only to fade.

He put one knee between her legs and hovered above her. He removed her hands from her head, then placed his left hand under her neck. His energy seeped through her pores and into her body.

"Partner, look at me," Bren commanded.

Pocky's features and body relaxed under his hold. She opened her eyes and spoke as though in a haze. "I need the Healer."

Bren was the Healer Pocky was referring to, but he was much more than just that. By Oxtarian standards, he was an Outworlder, or a celestial being that was created by the Divine Universe. However, the Divine Universe was more like a custodian or a branch of itself that was charged with overseeing this world and the universe it resided in. Before gaining more details of what any of that meant, he wanted to better understand himself first. He reached into his archives and carefully extracted more information.

A great sense of elation came over Bren as he remembered more of who he was. As a healer, he could heal not only himself but others. It was how he survived so many close calls, like that one instance where he had been stabbed. The knife really had gone deep into his chest, just clipping his heart, but his ability saved him.

His ability was also why he could gain information faster from his archives than others could. Knowledge had to be transferred to their conscious levels delicately. For others, it could cause sharp pain behind the eyes, headaches, and even nose bleeds. For Bren, though, his ability healed him during the process. Still, he had to be careful with how much information could be extracted. He was still living as a normal human being who had a limited capacity of what could be retained.

This also explained how Bren learned how to play instruments so quickly. Any Outworlder could do the same if they wanted, but hand coordination was something that had to be practiced along with the knowledge. He had a natural advantage of such repetition.

The knowledge of how his ability worked came to him next. As a healer, every cell in his body could produce a transparent substance that could be transformed into anything the body needed to heal, like bone or muscle tissue. With a simple touch, he could see what the body needed, then transfer the substance by contact. He had done so thousands of times throughout his life and career without even knowing it. This truth clarified so much about himself. It explained why he was good at his job and why he loved it so much. Being a medic was natural for him.

0.02 of a second.

Satisfied with remembering who he was, Bren searched his archives for where he was. This particular world and its universe was referred to as the Bubbled Reality because it had to obey the restricted laws of nature and physics, starting with being birthed by a pairing of two individuals. What he found further startled him. For some reason, the Custodian had contained this particular universe, but the answers as to why were inaccessible to him. Which meant that the answer was too vast and complex for his human mind to comprehend.

Why am I here?

0.03 of a second.

Bren dove again and searched for those answers. He smiled. The Custodian had created him and his team for the sole purpose to prevent or stop catastrophic events in this reality. He was unsure who those particular people were and what their current assignment was. He further explored his archives to learn who was on his team first.

Bren grinned as he remembered the first person. Lance was their leader, their captain, or their commander. Regardless of titles, he always referred to the man as Cap. He instantly sensed that the two of them were also as close as brothers could get and always bonded easily whenever they met in these short lifetimes. That explained why he had felt not only an immediate ease with the guy but also how he could be so open, even with personal stuff.

Bren then remembered the rest of his team. Haize was their engineer, who would invent and build whatever equipment they needed for the assignment. Kaori and Thomas were their scientists, their problem solvers. Yana was their information gatherer and specialist. Lance, Iza, and Viper were their protectors, their warriors. *Viper? My woman,* he thought with trepidation as he wondered if they were together outside of this reality. That info was not needed for the time being, but he trusted they were.

The last member that came to mind was Pocky. She was always his medical partner in one way or another and was just as close to her as he was with Lance.

For 0.01 of a second, Bren indulged the dynamics of his team, careful not to remember specific lives outside of this one. He got the sense that he and Haize had always butted heads, sometimes to the point of hating each other, but stood by each other when they had to. Yana was goofy but brilliant at gathering information. However, she was equivalent to being an annoying little sister and grated on everyone's nerves at times. They would all get exasperated with Thomas and Kaori, especially when they were in sticky situations. Iza was the quiet one and easily irritated. Viper was prickly and hard on herself.

Overall, they were individually flawed, but as a team, they made it work. Lance was an excellent leader that kept them in line and kept the peace between them.

And Pocky. Pocky was the glue that held them together. Bren got the sense that in their darkest times, she was a light that shielded them. Especially for Lance, who literally felt the fate of the world on his shoulders. If the man lost her, he would lose his sense of direction and will. *Pocky!* Bren thought with sudden desperation.

0.04 of a second.

Bren couldn't spare any more time. He knew everything he needed to know about himself and his colleagues for the time being. He wanted to check the status of their assignment as well, but Pocky needed him, so he focused on her.

Keeping his left hand under her neck, he placed his other hand over her eyes and scanned her entire body. The areas of concern lit up like hot spots. Her current wounds were the brightest, and he sent his energy to them to increase the healing process. Though his ability wasn't an instant fix, it was still faster than leaving the body to heal on its own.

Pocky's shoulder blade had a faded pink aura, which indicated what Bren already knew. The broken areas never healed right, and the nerve damage messed up her neuroreceptors. There were times when she didn't feel pain at all, but when she did, it was overwhelming. He healed that too. Besides some minor injuries and aches, she seemed to be okay. Until he saw it.

Bren hyper-focused deep within her brain. To his shock, there was a tiny mass of something engulfed in a thick layer of tissue. Pocky's voice echoed around him. *'He's inside me, I can't fight him.'* Those words were what brought him forth, but that didn't mean he knew what that meant yet. He relaxed and dove into his archives again, hoping to find an answer. An instinctive warning reminded him that he needed to be careful not to absorb too much knowledge at once.

0.05 of a second.

An ugly truth surfaced. Bren could hardly control his temper as he relearned who Pocky was referring to. The man was known to them as Pestilence, a highly capable Abnormal. Abnormals were something the Divine Universe didn't create and were randomly birthed within the Bubbled Reality. Just as with most Outworlders, Abnormals had capabilities they used against the world they happened to be born into. Pestilence could produce parasites. After injecting the organisms into a victim, the man could completely control any living being. The parasites could even extend the life of those he governed until the body became too decayed to operate. The parasites were also linked to all others who were infected and could communicate in real time. Which made it tricky to find and kill the asshole entirely.

The thought of how his partner obtained the parasites made Bren want to roar with rage, but he channeled it as he started killing the parasites. There were hundreds of thousands of them, and he destroyed every single one in the most painful way he could inflict. Once he knew Pocky was clean, he inhaled a deep breath. A puzzling factor came to his mind as he exhaled.

Pocky didn't exhibit any signs or behaviors that parasites were within her. She was as normal as she always had been. Not only that, whenever any of them were in trouble, they could send each other subtle messages to whomever was closest to them. Like he had with her when he became stuck in the dumpster. Those weren't premonitions or even an ability. The Custodian enabled them as a team to be able to communicate if they were in a precarious situation, even when they didn't remember one another. Pocky should have been able to send a message the moment the parasites had entered her body. But she didn't. *Why?* Bren thought, shaking his head.

What was also puzzling was that the parasites were safely cocooned by a mass of tissue. That was something none of them could do. *Strange.*

Then there was also the question of how long the organisms had even been there and when she'd been attacked. Bren curled his upper lip as he concluded that it had to be before she had rescued him.

0.06 of a second.

As Bren gathered himself up, Shox's voice suddenly echoed around him. *"Stellan is not the only one that wants your pet cunt."* He paled as he remembered who Shox really was and what the fucker had almost done. *But why would Stellan or any of the others want her?* Unlike Lance and himself, Pocky didn't have an ability. The rest of their team didn't either. She should have been practically an unknown person to Abnormals and their minions. Yet the assertion said otherwise. If Stellan hadn't stated the same to Thomas, he would have thought the guy was just messing with him. *Or maybe they both were,* Bren thought further, but his instincts were screaming that they weren't. That they truly were after Pocky for some reason.

0.07 of a second.

Bren dove again into his archives for further information about Stellan and

Shox. A cold dread hit him hard. Stellan was Pestilence's son, and there was no doubt that asshole had his daddy's parasites within him. Shox was a minion who was full of himself; he even thought he had an ability like the big players.

Another cold dread washed over Bren. Shox had been in the brig with Stellan. Whether that was planned or a coincidence, he didn't know. But Stellan had attacked Shox by shoving his tongue down the guy's throat, a classic move to infect someone with Pestilence's parasites. Had Shox infected Pocky in the same way while she had been tied up? That notion made him want to retch, but that still didn't explain either one's implication. *Why are they going after her?*

Bren broke into a sweat and smelled iron in his nose. He didn't have much time left. With obtaining this much information, along with healing his partner and himself, he would certainly pass out soon. But he needed more information so he could report to Lance with what was going on. He tried to concentrate as he searched his archives one last time for anything that would make Pocky—and not someone like himself or Lance—desirable to the Abnormals.

He started with Pestilence's behavior and researched what the man's motives might be. What he found perplexed him even more. The guy usually collaborated with one or more Abnormals and supported whatever they were doing. Focusing solely on an Outworlder was highly unusual. This was beyond his understanding. He really needed to bring Lance in on this. This was too big for him alone.

Bren prepared himself to release Pocky and positioned to roll away when he returned to real time. Before he could, he suddenly felt his consciousness being linked with her archives but didn't understand how. That was not something he, nor the others, could do either.

"*Hi,*" a childlike voice abruptly said.

Bren couldn't see who was talking. However, no one should be talking to him at all in this place. "Uh—"

"*Healer, this is important for you to know. I have a lot to explain and not a lot of time. Try refraining from interrupting. Clear? As you would say.*"

"Uh, okay," Bren said, shaking his head.

"*My name's Ember, I am an entity living inside Pocky, but I'm supposed to be dormant and unbeknownst to my host. However, when Pocky was four, a foreign parasite invaded her body. I contained them. Somehow, she became aware of me and sent me here. Because of that, she couldn't send a distress message, and I'm sorry for that. Now that you killed the parasites, I can be dormant again, and I thank you for that."*

"Uh, okay, but what are you, and why are you in her in the first place? Are you a parasite too?"

"Not exactly, and no time to explain that either. But consider me a good entity. But, and I'm sorry for this too, Pocky is damaged because she put me here. Unfortunately, you will not be able to heal her."

Bren swallowed hard as dread engulfed his heart. The thought of Pocky being hurt beyond what he could fix would devastate everyone who cared about her. Besides himself, Thomas and Lance were the top two people on that list. He became livid with the entity and the possible outcome of what it had done.

"What damage—"

"And one more sorry." Ember interrupted.

"Shit, what?" Bren said with an exasperated sigh.

"To get your attention, I had to let the containment of the parasites down for 0.01 of a second. Pocky unfortunately linked with Pestilence during that time."

"Are you fucking kidding me?"

"It was the only way to get you here. I'm sorry. Now you need to go, Healer."

Bren tried to argue but felt himself unlink from Pocky's archives, and he came rushing back to the surface of real time. Again, time moved at its normal pace as he rolled away onto his side. He heard Lance's faded voice shout his name. Before he fully lost consciousness, Bren's last thought was, *What was his partner harboring and why?*

27

Pocky opened her eyes just as Lance leaned across her body. The compassion and concern in his expression took her breath away, just as it always did. But that concerned look wasn't geared toward her, and she wasn't sure why he was worried until she followed his gaze. Bren was passed out next to her.

Pocky put a hand on Lance's arm, drawing his attention. "He's okay. He just needs a minute," she said, unsure how she knew that. "Can you help me up, please?"

Lance searched her face, then placed his hands under her arms. Pocky grabbed onto his shoulders to help him lift her into a sitting position. She winced through the motions, her abs aching. When she was fully upright, something fell away from her chest.

"Here," Lance said, quickly grabbing the lost item. "Put this on." His face turned red as he helped her into the shirt.

Pocky was very aware that she was exposed but wasn't bothered by it because they were trained early on to get over themselves. Even though she was attracted to him, she also didn't care in her current state. She felt it was sweet, though, with how careful he was being.

"Thanks," she said. "Now can you help me stand up?"

Again, the compassion in his eyes warmed her heart. "Are you—I mean, are you okay? Are you sure you should stand?"

"Yeah, I feel … fine …" Pocky's eyebrows furrowed. She touched her head wound, then her abs. She didn't remember being shot in the stomach but knew very well how it felt to be hit by rubber bullets. She didn't recall her other injuries either but knew they were there. And yet, she felt no pain. Her injuries suggested she'd been attacked, but she couldn't remember anything about it or even what she'd been doing beforehand. Her mind was clear and focused, but perhaps her head wound had caused temporary amnesia. "I don't even have a headache."

Pocky dismissed her thoughts. She needed to speak with Geara right away. She detached the IV line and didn't bother to look for gauze to tape over the entry wound. Lance tried to protest her actions, but she cut him off. "Please help me up. I need Geara. I need to talk to him. It's urgent."

"Uh-okay," Lance replied, apprehension clear in his voice.

Just as before, Lance placed his hands under her arms and lifted. Pocky grabbed onto his upper arms, trying to steady herself as she put her weight on her legs. She wobbled for a moment, but he held her up. Once her legs felt solid, she embraced him tightly. He was careful of her back as he held her.

As quickly as she'd hugged him, she pushed away. Alarm bells went off in her head, urging her to speak with Geara *now.*

"Pocky?" Lance asked, his hands lightly gripping her elbows.

"I'm sorry, I need Geara." Pocky looked around and found Viper, who was speaking into her radio. "Ma'am!" The SC turned in surprise. "I need to speak to Geara. Could you call him, please?"

Instead of carrying out her request, Viper rushed up to them. "Pocky, do you remember what happened?"

"Not a thing. Please, I need Geara—"

"If you don't remember anything, why do you need him?" Viper interrupted. Pocky wasn't sure how to reply to that. "If it's that important, you can tell me."

"Viper, please," Pocky pleaded, purposely using her friend's name. "There isn't time to explain it to you both. It's life and death. I need Geara!"

Viper replied in a slow and gentle way. "Listen, you just had a very traumatic—"

Pocky didn't have time to be reasonable and took drastic measures. She snatched the radio from Viper's hand and moved a few steps away. She pressed the talk button with three rapid clicks.

"Pocky!" Viper shouted as she followed. Even though Pocky was still a little unsteady, she managed to stay ahead. Other soldiers in the room watched uneasily. "What the fuck are you doing?"

Pocky exited through what had once been the restaurant's doors and moved toward the stern. "Go for Geara," a voice said over the radio. In her peripheral vision, Pocky spotted Viper and Lance following her.

"Geara!" Pocky yelled into the radio. "Meet me on the starboard side main deck. Hurry!"

"Pocky?" he asked.

"Hurry!"

"On my way."

Pocky dropped the radio and walked along the bulkhead, using her right hand to keep herself from falling—not because of her head wound. High winds forced her against the bulkhead. *A storm must be coming,* she thought.

"Pocky? Where ... What are you doing?" Viper asked, more with concern than authority.

Pocky realized then that the woman was being extremely lenient with her. Perhaps it was sympathy for whatever took her down? Then she remembered Thomas. A sickening thought then crossed her mind that if she had been attacked, then he had been too. But she couldn't think about that. What she needed to relay to Geara was far more important than even her brother's life, a notion she would later hate herself for.

Pocky kept going until she reached a small cabinet with a keypad on it. Inside were emergency items for higher ranks to use, such as radios, batteries, a med kit, small handheld lights, and so on. She glanced at the lock, then at Viper. Both she and Lance looked confused.

"Open this," Pocky demanded.

"What do you need from it?"

Pocky wasn't patient enough to convince Viper to unlock the cabinet. She looked back at the small door, then placed her hand on the handle, focusing. She smiled as she remembered the voice activation code. "*Gaia*, open cabinet CM-109, code four three eight five."

The keypad flashed green, then the cabinet snapped and clicked. Pocky pulled the door open and grabbed the binoculars inside. She headed for the hull.

"What the fuck? How'd you know that?" Viper asked.

"It's in the manual," Pocky said as she moved past her.

Without using the binoculars, she glanced northwest toward the Charter Channel. The sky was darkening as a storm was definitely heading their way. Regardless, it didn't take long for her to spot what she was looking for.

"There you are, you fucking asshole," she whispered as she scanned the surface of the ocean toward the southwest. She moved toward the stern until the warship beside them wasn't in the way. Voices echoed around her, but she tuned them out until she saw what she had feared she would: unnatural movement in the water. "Geara!"

To Pocky's shock, Geara was suddenly in front of her, holding onto her upper arms. "I'm here. What's—"

"Here! Take these and look." Pocky shoved the binoculars into his chest. Despite looking perplexed, Geara took the binoculars. Pocky turned his face toward the Charter Channel. "Look seventy-eight degrees northwest toward the Charter Channel. You'll see two stationary charters."

Before looking into the binoculars, Geara looked at her with disbelief. "You can see that from here?"

"Yes. Now, please look," Pocky said with impatience.

Geara scanned the horizon for a few seconds before looking back at Pocky, again with disbelief. "I see them, but I still can't—"

"That's not important." Pocky grabbed him by his arms. "Those are Cannon's boats. Or Stellan's. They're monitoring us."

"What?" Geara shook his head. "How do you know that?"

"No time. Here, look this way," Pocky said, then pointed toward the southwest area past their fleet.

"What am I looking for? Another ship?" Geara asked as he put the binoculars up to his eyes.

"Yes, but they're underwater. Stellan calls them submersibles."

Geara gaped at her. "Are you fucking serious? How can you see—"

"There are six coming our way. They're going to attack us!" Pocky shouted. Her head began to swim.

"How do you know that?"

"No time! Just—"

"If they're out there, our radar—"

"They're using stealth technology. You—"

"How the hell do you know any of that?" Geara yelled with stunned disbelief.

"No time to explain!" Pocky paused, feeling lightheaded. Her words slurred as she spoke on. "You need to order the warships to open fire in a one hundred twenty-degree radius starting from the south line toward the southwest. You need to hurry—"

Pocky's vision went dark, but she was conscious enough to comprehend Lance was carrying her. She could tell by his scent. There didn't seem to be a hurry in his step, and she took comfort that was a good thing. They exchanged a few words before her world went dark again. She vaguely heard Thomas's voice; he seemed surprised by something. Though she wanted to move and speak, her body wouldn't respond. A deep sleep engulfed her like a warm blanket, and the sound of a storm rang in her ears.

***

Knowing Pocky was about to pass out, Lance reached for her before she collapsed. He gathered her into his arms and didn't wait for someone to tell him what to do as he made his way back to Bren. Geara and Viper barked into their radios as he walked away.

After Geara had appeared in front of Pocky, they spoke in Origin. Though he could now understand the language, the wind was so severe that he didn't catch most of their conversation. He wasn't sure what was going on or why Pocky had reacted so strangely, but an overwhelming need to get his team together somewhere safe overtook Lance. Since they were on a ship, though, he wasn't sure exactly where that could be.

"Lance!" Viper shouted after him. He glanced over his shoulder. "Get M, tell him to get you to C2! I'll get the rest of your team! Clear!?"

"Yes, ma'am!" Lance shouted. With Pocky's head injury, he didn't want to rush, even though his mind screamed at him to go faster.

"You smell good," Pocky murmured. "I like that."

Lance smiled. She was talking; that had to be a good sign. He wanted her to talk more. "Oh yeah? What else do you like?" he asked, not so much inferring to himself, but her retort amused him.

"Of you? Everything ..." She barely finished the last word.

Her body went lax. Lance frowned. After what had happened to her, and her frantic desire to speak with Geara, she had obviously pushed herself past her limits. Whatever she had to tell the man, she was willing to risk further harm to herself. Still though, how did she go from barely being able to move to full-blown awareness and swift reactions after Bren had merely touched her? And why was it all somehow familiar? Lance's head was beginning to hurt, and he gave up on trying to rationalize the moment.

Bren rushed through the opening that was once the restaurant doors just before Lance got there. Though Pocky had reassured him that Bren was okay, Lance was still relieved—elated, even—to see the medic on his feet again.

Carrying both his and Pocky's med packs, Bren smiled briefly when he spotted the two of them, then frowned. "Cap? What happened? Why are you out here?"

Lance explained everything Bren had missed, along with Viper's orders.

"Okay, we need to get Thomas first," Bren said. "Apparently, the other doors were unlocked, and he went right through. They found him on the port side toward the bow. He was shot in the temple by a rubber and thinks Pocky's dead."

Lance didn't like the sound of that, but he said, "Lead the way."

"Yes, sir."

They passed the restaurant, then rounded onto the bow area. Thomas sat against the hull with his head turned away. Two soldiers dutifully stood guard. As Bren and Lance moved closer, he could see a slight bloody bruise on Thomas's temple. His eyes were listless and lifeless, far from the excitement they held from the very beginning of all this. But Thomas *did* believe his sister was dead; of course he looked crushed beyond measure. Lance was thankful that wasn't true.

"We got him, you two can go," Bren ordered as he crouched down by Thomas. The two guards complied and walked away as Bren opened Pocky's pack. "Brother, I gotta look at your wound, okay?"

"I don't care," Thomas said, voice hoarse.

"Hey, our sister's okay. Pocky's alive."

Thomas glared at Bren. "Don't lie to me!" he cried. "I saw her shot in the stomach."

"Those were rubbers," Bren said gently. "She's okay. Lance has her, look."

"What?" Thomas's head snapped up, and his eyes went wide as he shoved to his feet and stumbled toward Lance. He set one hand against Pocky's cheek. "Sis?" His expression brightened into the elation only a brother could have, and his eyes watered as he took her head in his hands.

"Easy on her." Bren set a hand on Thomas's bicep. "She received a nasty head wound. Careful."

Thomas eyed the wound with concern, then looked up at Lance. His lips and chin twitched nervously. "Give her to me, please."

Lance hesitated for a moment but complied. Bren nodded when the exchange was done and was about to speak when every ship around them blared with alarms in rapid succession to each other. *Gaia*'s alarm then joined in the chorus.

"What's going on?" Thomas shouted to no one in particular, but no one answered.

Lance took a few steps forward and looked in the direction Pocky had shown Geara. He didn't see any ships or anything that would indicate a threat was approaching, but the warships were preparing for something as their side cannons moved.

The three warships farthest out fired a series of missiles. Booms reached *Gaia* a moment later, and they all crouched against the hull. The storm's wind quickly ushered a mixture of hot air and shockwaves over them. *Gaia*'s shutters began enclosing the main deck.

"Holy shit!" Thomas yelled above the noise. "What are they firing at?"

Lance didn't answer as he went to Bren. Their medic was ashen with shock. "Bren? Bren!" he said desperately, shaking the man's shoulders. Bren blinked, and his lower jaw began to tremble. "Bren! Focus on me!" A clash of emotions swept over his features as their eyes met. "Get us to C2! Now!"

Bren forced himself past his fear and moved toward the bulkhead. Lance grabbed Pocky's med pack and let Thomas get between himself and Bren. He put a hand on Thomas's shoulder in case he had to shove them down and cover them with his body. As they followed Bren to the stairwell, the barrage of missiles continued to an ear-piercing level even with the shutters down. Once they were inside, the sound became slightly muffled.

They continued to the second-level passageway, then Bren steered them into a narrow corridor. He led them toward the bow, then into a room with a nameplate that read Conference 2. The room lit up with low lights, revealing a large, rectangular, unfurnished space with a thin blue carpet.

Thomas took Pocky up against the wall and laid her down. Bren assisted him while Lance stayed by the door, looking down the corridor. Soldiers and medics were already crossing between the stairwell and other doors.

"Hold the fuck still," Bren said to Thomas.

Lance looked over and saw Bren trying to tend to Thomas's wound, then he focused on the corridor again. Personnel ran around, their voices competing with the noise outside. Lance didn't know where their teammates were, but he hoped they were on their way.

A hand settled on Lance's shoulder, and he turned to see Bren behind him. "Hey, I need to run to the clinic and restock our packs," the medic said. "Won't take me long."

"You gonna be okay going alone?" Lance asked, trying not to indicate his concern from earlier, but the medic knew anyway.

"Yeah, I just had a moment back there. I'm okay," Bren said. Lance handed Pocky's pack to him. Before leaving, Bren reached into her pack and retrieved her gun. He then offered it to Lance. "I know you know how to use this."

"Point and pull."

"Take it. Protect her. Those fuckers out there want her for some reason."

"I know," Lance said as he took the holster. He recalled Shox's disconcerting claim, yet Bren's tone seemed to hint at something more. There wasn't time to ask. "Stay focused and hurry back. Okay?"

"Yes, sir."

Lance watched Bren until he disappeared into a sea of uniforms. He quickly strapped the holster on, double-checked the ammo clip, and resumed his watch for his team.

The corridor continued to fill up, but there was still no sign of his other teammates. It made him torn between wanting to stay and wanting to search, but protecting his woman was a top priority. *My woman.*

A spark of light exploded behind his eyes like before, nearly bringing him to his knees. He braced himself against the doorframe. His entire body broke into a sweat, and he smelled iron in his nose. Trembling, he turned toward Pocky and wondered why he was just now becoming aware of who he truly was.

28

Thomas was thankful the onslaught of artillery wasn't as bad in the conference room as it had been outside. With his head throbbing, each boom intensified his discomfort. However, after Bren tended to his wound, he felt better with every passing minute.

He sat cross-legged by Pocky's side and held her hand. He almost couldn't believe she was alive. The image of blood exploding from her stomach held firmly in his mind. He lifted the hem of her shirt slightly, revealing two bruises on her midsection. With a relieved sigh, Thomas pulled her shirt back down and relaxed. Obviously his memory was clouded, but his mind wouldn't let go of what he thought he'd seen. Seeing the truth greatly helped to let that go.

Thomas regarded his sister, wondering how she was going to pull through this. He furrowed his brow as he realized her shirt wasn't her own. It was a better fit for a large man than her small frame. He glanced at Lance, who stood just inside the doorway and watched the hallway intently. He was armed now. If Thomas hadn't already met Lance, he would have assumed the guy was a soldier. Besides the "ready-for-action" posture, the clothes, and the gun, Lance certainly looked like one.

He looked down at Pocky again. A sudden realization hit him. The shirt she was wearing belonged to Lance.

The image of her tied up and topless with blood running down her back made him instantly sick to his stomach.

"Lance!" Thomas yelled, then gagged. Lance was by his side in seconds. "I'm gonna be sick," Thomas said as bile crept up his throat.

"There's a bathroom directly across from here," Lance said. "Go."

The next few minutes went by in a blur. Somehow Thomas managed to get into the bathroom without hurling but ended up vomiting in the sink instead of the toilet. He felt the burning sensation from the acid was just. He was angry with himself enough to want to throw himself over the boat. Whether his sister had been alive or dead, he shouldn't have left her that way for someone else to find. He should have stayed with her.

After cleaning himself up, he staggered back into the room and found a corner to cower in. With a knee propping up an elbow, he buried his face into the crook of his arm. *Some brother I am.*

"Hey," Lance said sharply.

Thomas glanced up. Lance was crouched in front of him, a mixture of bafflement and anger in his eyes. Sweat glistened across his forehead.

"What are you doing?" he asked.

"I just need a min—"

"No, you can have a minute sitting by your sister," Lance said sternly. "The first person she needs to see is you."

Thomas looked away. His throat tightened, making the burning sensation even worse. His voice trembled as he said, "I'm not worthy of being her brother."

"Whatever the fuck reason why you feel that way, do you really think that's gonna be her first thought when she wakes up?"

Thomas hated that Lance had a point, but it didn't change how he felt. "I-I don't remember much," he stuttered, "but I remember her being tied up, and I did nothing about it. That makes me unworthy."

"What did you do?" Lance countered.

Stunned, Thomas tried to recall, but not much came back. He closed his eyes and took in a deep breath through his nose, trying to recollect the event and before that. "It's spotty," he mumbled. "I remember us talking. I was telling her what Kaori and I were doing in the lab. Then it jumps. I remember her being shot, then waking up to find her tied up. That asshole was hurting her. Then he was about to ..." He paused, unable to finish his sentence. "I hit him with a chair to stop him. It gets blurry from there because he injected me with something. Then it fades again. I woke up where you found me, thinking ... thinking my sister was dead."

"But she isn't, and you stopped that fucker before he could hurt her more," Lance said. "That makes you very worthy."

"No." Thomas pushed to his feet. Lance stood too. "I left her tied up for you or someone else to find. That doesn't sit right with me, and it shouldn't with you either."

Lance's expression softened. "You were shot and drugged, give yourself some latitude. Bren and I were quick on the scene. We took care of her—respectfully."

Though being shot and injected *had* impaired him, Thomas wasn't about to use that excuse for just leaving Pocky hanging there. However, he had no energy to argue further. "Thank you," Thomas said, "for being there for her."

Lance nodded. "Now it's you that needs to be there."

While Lance took up his position by the door again, Thomas moved back to Pocky and held her hand. As though his hold was a signal for her to wake up, she began to stir. She opened her eyes slowly. The relief in her expression made him acknowledge Lance had been right. She knew they both had been hurt, and she needed to see that he was okay. He would have wanted the same had their roles been reversed.

"Thomas," she said with a weak smile. "You're okay."

"I am," Thomas replied, his voice wavering.

Pocky reached up, and he pulled her into a gentle hug, trying to be careful of her back. He was thankful to have a moment to themselves. Between being attacked and the uncertainty of whatever was going on outside, it gave him a new perspective on who he needed to be versus who he intended to be. He may have kicked the shit out of Shox, but he still froze at a critical moment that could have been more costly than just being injected with a substance. Even though he had bulked up and learned to fight, he was still a scared little kid.

Thomas held Pocky tighter. *That's going to change.*

***

Before Lance straightened Thomas out, he dove deep into his archives to get the status of his team's assignment. They were way off course, and the more he tried to unravel it, the more the answers disturbed him.

The fungus was an unnatural anomaly that threatened a worldwide famine, and his team had been sent to counter the problem. To ensure their assembly, a Pre-Team, as they were called, would birth, raise, educate, and protect them. But most importantly, the Pre-Team would help them become self-aware so they could carry out their assignment. This should have happened as early as five years of age, but it didn't. What was even more disconcerting was that they were never supposed to be separated in this way, spread across two continents. *What the fuck happened?*

The only conclusion Lance came to was that the Pre-Team must have been compromised and forced to split up. Some must have hidden his team in orphanages while the others had to go as far as Shad'Dyn. He wanted to punch the wall. *What could have caused that?*

The Pre-Teams usually consisted of up to thirty people. Eighteen of those would couple, then protect the women in their vulnerable states. Whether the Pre-Team was attacked, or if it was something else, they obviously did everything they could to ensure his team's survival.

Lance thanked them for trying, even if he didn't know what end came to them. He also understood now more than ever why he had always felt misplaced and why he wandered across the two nations. He was unconsciously looking for his team, just as some of them were doing the same.

Putting all that aside, Lance concentrated on his team and their current situation. Their assignment would have to wait until they were out of this mess. He needed Bren to be able to do that. Together, they could help everyone awaken to who they really were as carefully as possible.

Lance glanced over at the twins and smiled slightly. He was relieved to see Pocky awake. As much as he wanted to embrace her, the twins deserved to have a moment to themselves. Plus, he was in so much pain he didn't want to move. He broke into more of a sweat, and the smell of iron thickened. His brain and eyes felt like they were going to explode, making his headache—already brewing from the intense noise—worsen. He tried to relax, confident Bren would return soon and heal him.

Lance gazed at Pocky with worry. She was inadvertently another problem on his plate. He seriously needed to converse with Bren on this. Now that he'd accessed his archives, Lance recognized Shox as a minion, and his words echoed in Lance's head. *"Stellan is not the only one that wants your pet cunt."* He still didn't understand the meaning but was shaken by the implications. Pocky, of course, was personally special to him and a valued team member, but there wasn't anything about her that would make her desirable to the Abnormals. As much as Lance tried to rationalize why, he couldn't come up with anything. Between the frustration and the pain, he wanted to burst with rage.

"Lance!"

Lance looked down the corridor. Kaori moved flat against the wall as soldiers rushed by. As she approached closer, her expression was full of confusion and fright—and rightly so. Though Lance couldn't show it, he was relieved to see her. When she reached him, Kai embraced him tightly. He grunted, trying to hold in his discomfort as he hugged her back.

When she pulled away, she searched his face. "Are you okay?"

"I'm fine, but Pocky needs you," he said gruffly. "She was hurt."

Thankfully Kai hurried inside toward Pocky. *Gaia*'s alarms thankfully shut off right after, giving Lance some relief. Yana's familiar screams got his attention. Marker had her slung over his shoulder, and Naiko trailed not far behind them, looking dazed.

"I want off the ship! Get me off the fucking ship!" Yana demanded as she kicked violently. She managed to kick Marker in the balls a few times as they approached Lance's position, but the man somehow pushed through the pain.

"Put her down," Lance commanded.

Marker complied, then turned Yana in Lance's direction. The moment she saw him, she rushed forward and slammed into him as though he were a life preserver. Lance grunted, grimacing at the strength of her embrace. When he pushed her away, she began spewing words.

"Shut it!" Lance hated shouting, but he was in too much pain to deal with her properly. Yana immediately clammed up, looking at him with wide, terrified eyes. "Look, I know you're scared and want to get off this boat, but you need to dial it back," he said. "Go sit with your team and be quiet. I fucking mean it."

Yana squeezed her eyes shut before opening them again. "Okay," she whimpered, then moved inside.

Naiko went around Marker as he stopped at the door. Before going inside, Lance grabbed her on the shoulder, making her do a double take of his appearance.

"Lance?" Her eyes widened. "Are you a soldier?"

"I'll explain later, okay?"

With a nod, Naiko went inside the room. Lance turned his attention to Marker. The sergeant studied him curiously. He dove into his archives and found that he knew Marker—which explained why he seemed so familiar—but that didn't mean the soldier remembered him.

"Recognize me?" Lance asked with raised eyebrows.

"I do," Marker said flatly. "Knew who you were the moment I met you. There are a lot of us that do. You're very respected here, sir."

That explained why so many accepted him even though he was a civilian. Lance nodded, wishing the circumstances were different.

"You look like shit," Marker continued. "Where's Bren?"

"Restocking their med packs. I awoke after he left."

"Damn. Hate it when that happens."

"Yeah," Lance replied hoarsely.

"So, what's going on with your team?"

"I don't know," he said, sighing. "I don't know how we got separated, or even how we're all together now. But we're way behind on our assignment, and for some reason, Abnormals are going after Pocky."

"I caught onto that from Shox's bullshit." Marker paused, shaking his head. "Should have known who that fucker was just by his stench."

"Smells like he's been in a toilet for a week after someone took a shit, right?" Lance said rhetorically, recalling the smell when he had entered the restaurant and the library before that.

"Exactly."

Lance had dived into his archives for a general profile of Shox after recognizing the minion. He gritted his teeth at what surfaced. Most Abnormals and their minions reveled in torturing anything that breathed, but that one enjoyed raping his victims. The thought of that minion having his hands on Pocky—on *his* woman—twisted Lance's insides. His fists tightened, desperately wanting to hit something. He couldn't stomach that Pocky had come close to experiencing that kind of trauma.

"Sir," Marker began hesitantly. "Once I realized who that shithead really was, I interrogated him. Didn't take much to make him talk. You're not gonna like what I got."

"Okay," Lance exhaled slowly, bracing himself for the worst.

"He told me Cannon Hyashi is Pestilence."

Lance's whole body grew cold. The weight of what that meant was like the entire ocean falling onto his shoulders. The twins had been bought by Cannon, meaning they had been under Pestilence's grip, meaning they were both most likely infected with his parasites. The image of Pocky suddenly reaching for her head came back to him. Her words echoed within his mind. *"He's inside me, I can't fight him!"*

Rage exploded in Lance's veins.

The only glimmer of hope he had was Bren must have awakened and healed Pocky when that happened. Their medic must have used a lot of his energy for something that big; it was the only explanation for why he passed out after healing her. Knowing Bren the way that he did, he knew the man would have taken subtle measures to check Thomas too. But he wouldn't feel at ease until he heard it from Bren himself. Until then, he tried not to come unglued.

"Go on," he said to Marker.

"Cannon is dead, but he infected Stellan and hundreds of others. And Shox was infected by Stellan, but there aren't enough parasites for Pestilence to completely control him, which is why I was able to get a lot out of him. I'm thinking Stellan must have used his ability to find Pocky, then relayed that to Shox."

Lance's upper lip twitched. It explained why Shox had come to the library and later found her in the restaurant. His fists tightened again, thinking of what would have happened if he had decided to go to the greenhouse instead of the library. He really—*really*—wanted to hit something.

"Sir," Marker continued. "Why the hell do they want her? I mean, respectfully, she's just as ordinary as the rest of us compared to you and Bren, and others like you."

"Wish I fucking knew."

Marker's expression softened, then got serious. "Look, my team and I already completed our assignment, and we've been hanging around supporting others. If you're here, that means something big is gonna happen, and we'll gladly back you up from here if you want it."

"I'd very much appreciate that. We're gonna need you."

"Certainly. Unfortunately, your team isn't the only one we've come across that's lost."

"Fucking wondrous."

"Yeah, that's got a lot of us stumped," Marker replied with a sigh. "Besides you, anyone else awake?"

"Pretty sure Bren is."

"It's a start," Marker said. "Alright, I'll gather my team and meet back here."

Lance nodded, but his stomach churned. Marker gave him a salute, then hurried away. Iza and Haize approached not long after. The sight of Iza made Lance wonder how his team had come together now after all this time, but the answer to that had to wait. She tried to stop and chat, but he motioned for her not to. Whatever she wanted to say needed to wait until he was healed. Haize tried to stop as well, but Lance waved him on too. He then realized his nose was bleeding and they were just showing their concern.

Now that his team was together, Lance moved completely into the corridor. He rested his shoulder against the wall, trying to steady his breathing. Though he was just guessing that it could have been roughly thirty minutes since the bombardment of artillery began, it still seemed like an eternity.

Bren, hurry.

29

Several agonizing minutes later, Lance spotted Bren hauling ass toward him. Lance struggled to stay upright, but the pounding of Bren's feet gave him enough strength not to lose consciousness. He heard the med packs drop, and then the medic's hands were on him.

"I got you, Cap, hang on."

Lance felt one hand placed behind his neck while the other covered his eyes. He didn't have to pull up memories to know this had been done many times before. Bren's energy entered through his pores, the coolness of the substance providing near-instant relief. The pressure behind his eyes ceased.

As a slice of strength returned to Lance, he grabbed onto Bren. The thought that Pestilence may have injected his parasites into Pocky made his nerves go unhinged. Countless scenarios for how that could have happened flashed in his mind. He tried to speak. He had to know if Pocky was clean and if Thomas was okay, but no words came out.

"Don't fight me," Bren said harshly. "I'm almost done."

"The twins ... Pestilence ..." Lance stammered.

"Pocky was infected, but I neutralized it. Thomas is clean. Now fucking hold still."

With a grunt, Lance let his hands drop to his sides. His entire body relaxed, and his headache began to dissipate.

"Okay, now take a deep breath, then exhale slowly," Bren said as he moved one hand to Lance's shoulder to help hold him up. Lance complied and went through the motions. "Good, do that a few more times."

As he did, Lance felt more and more of himself with each breath. With a final exhale, he opened his eyes and gazed up at Bren. The expression on the man's face wasn't just relief but also an acknowledgment of their deep friendship that had been forged over thousands of lifetimes. They embraced as brothers who hadn't seen each other in ages.

When they pulled away, Bren's smile faded with an anxious sigh. "I'm so glad you're awake, Cap. I hope you've got a better idea of what the hell is going on. How did we get separated?"

"I don't know yet," Lance said, then reached for Pocky's med pack. He hoisted it on and buckled the snaps. Bren followed suit with his own. "I'll figure it out later. For now, I want you to focus on Pocky. She's—"

"Cap, there's some kind of entity inside her," Bren blurted out.

"What?" Lance asked. "What ... what do you mean, an entity?"

Bren told him about his encounter with the entity and how it contained the parasites. "I've searched my archives," Bren said. "I don't know what the hell that thing is or why it's inside her."

Lance did a quick search of his own, then shook his head. "I got nothing either."

The medic huffed. "The damn thing's so small, I didn't even see it when I scanned her body."

"Really? Smaller than the parasites?"

"Yeah, it's definitely physically in her, but I couldn't see it."

"Shit," Lance muttered, mulling that over. He looked back up at Bren. "Is it harmful?"

"Don't think so," Bren replied. "Could it be why the Abnormals are going after her?"

"Possibly. Depending on what's appealing about it to them."

"Uh, and Cap ..." Bren's expression tightened.

Lance couldn't take any more bad news, but that was clearly where this was going.

"Pocky sent the entity to her archives to protect it from the parasites. Because of that, it says she's ... damaged."

Rage exploded in Lance's body so hot and fast that he didn't even think as he tried to punch the metallic wall. Bren blocked the blow and held tight to Lance's fist.

"Cap," he said. "I'll fix it. I'll find a way."

Lance yanked his hand away, then covered his eyes as he leaned against the wall. His rage heated every word. "I can't ... I've been without her for too long. Now that I know that, it hurts. And that asshole hurt her. I should've been there."

"You couldn't have known."

"Fuck," Lance muttered, then looked up at Bren. A mixture of concern and sympathy was in the man's eyes. "What damage? Did it say?"

"Didn't have time to ask, but I'll figure it out. I promise, I swear."

Lance nodded. He was no less angry about it, but he had to trust Bren could do his job and do it well. He always had.

An explosion from the port side reverberated through the ship, causing *Gaia* to tilt drastically toward the starboard side. *Gaia*'s alarms abruptly blared. Lance and Bren covered their ears as they were violently smacked against the wall and thrown to the floor.

Gaia's metal frame groaned, and crashes echoed within the rooms and decks around them. The lights above them quickly changed to red. A new alarm blared as another explosion went off. Screams from inside the room had them both scrambling to their feet. As they did, *Gaia* righted itself for a moment, then severely listed to the port side, making Lance and Bren slam hard against the wall by the door.

The warship *Gaia* was tied to must have exploded and was now sinking—and taking them with it. Lance desperately tried to push Bren past the door, hoping to keep the guy from falling in but wasn't quick enough as the ship listed at a critical level, making them both hang onto the doorframe to keep themselves from falling into the room.

A mechanical, feminine voice suddenly came over the speaker. "Collision, collision. Brace for impact. Collision, collision. Brace for impact."

"Fuck!" Bren shouted.

"Hang on!"

Lance tried to keep his hold on the doorframe but lost his grip when the impact jolted the ship. He slid painfully down on his left side until his feet hit the wall that was now a tilted floor. Thankfully, no one was in the way when he landed. He breathed a sigh of relief when he realized *Gaia* didn't tilt any farther, but he wasn't counting on it staying that way. He looked up and smiled. Bren had somehow managed to keep his grip and was pulling himself up into the corridor.

As Lance caught his breath, he took in the scene around him, seeing if everyone was okay. Yana jumped in front of him, trying to climb up his body, screaming the whole way. He yanked her off and held her away. Thomas grabbed her and pulled her into a bear hug.

"Keep her so I can figure this out!" Lance yelled.

Thomas nodded and then glanced behind himself, looking down. Lance followed his direction and found Pocky lying on her side, propping herself up on an elbow. With everything tinged red, it was hard to read her expression, but she caught his eye and gave him a thumbs-up. He knew she wasn't okay and badly wanted to be by her side, but for the time being he couldn't. He looked behind him. Haize was trying to deal with Naiko, who was just as emotional about their situation as Yana was, and Kaori and Iza looked dazed but otherwise appeared to be okay.

"Lance!" Bren yelled from above. "If *Gaia* tilts any farther, you'll be trapped! Start throwing me bodies!"

"Thomas, Haize!" Lance called. "You first, then help Bren with the women!"

"Thomas!" Pocky yelled, turning both their attention toward her. She was now standing. "Give me Yana and go!"

Thomas didn't argue but didn't look happy either. He passed Yana to Pocky, then stepped up to Lance.

"I'm gonna toss you up. Try to climb and grab for Bren's hand, okay?"

"Got it."

Lance linked his hands together and braced for Thomas's weight. In the same motion he would use to lift someone onto a horse, he boosted Thomas up. The man was heavy but tall enough to catch Bren's hand on the first try. Another soldier appeared on the other side of the door and helped pull Thomas up.

Once Lance saw they were ready for the next, he ordered Haize to step up and repeated the process. Afterward, he looked to Pocky. He wanted her to go next, but she pushed Yana toward him.

"She needs to go next!"

Lance bit back his irritation, but Pocky was right. Yana was a mess. Tears and sweat ran down her face, and she was trembling terribly. He grabbed her by the forearms and spoke with a stern yet gentle voice. "Yana, please listen to me." When she didn't comply, he put a hand underneath her chin, forcing her to look up at him. "Yana, look in my eyes. Recognize me."

After a few gasps in her breathing, she blinked and then relaxed in his hold. "Sir?"

"Don't remember too much," Lance added. "I'm getting you out of here, but I need you to calm down enough so that I can, okay?"

"Yes, sir."

Thankfully, Yana followed his instructions and managed not to kick him in the face. He turned to Pocky and motioned for her to go next. To his dismay, she took a step back and pointed to Iza, Kaori, and Naiko behind him. He cursed under his breath and rotated to his right side.

"Let's go!" Lance demanded.

Besides making Naiko lose her shoes, Lance got her and Kaori to Bren with no issues, but when Iza stepped up, she hesitated. He didn't expect that from the warrior he knew so well and didn't understand her trepidation.

"Iza, come on," Lance said, putting out his hand. As she took his hand, tears began streaming down her face. He didn't understand until she spoke.

"I'm self-aware," she whispered. "I've been awake a long time."

"Shit," Lance murmured, pulling her into a hug. She must have recognized that he was too. "How long?" he whispered in her ear.

"Since I was six," Iza said, then broke down.

"Fuck," Lance said as he held her tighter. Being aware of who they were without their team was a nightmare scenario for all of them. He couldn't imagine how alone and scared she must have felt all these years, not knowing where they were or how to find them.

"Hurry up!" Bren shouted.

Lance pulled away and almost felt himself lose it. The whole situation was an epic clusterfuck. "Iza, I'm sorry. I'm so sorry."

"Ruckers found me when the IMF was cleaning up the orphanages. She's one of us. She branched off from her team to help me, and we've been searching for you and the others since."

Lance's heart sank deep into his stomach. He owed a lot of gratitude to Ruckers for her efforts. "We're together now," he said, looking Iza in the eyes. "Not all of us are awake yet, but Bren is. When everything settles down, we'll talk, okay?"

"Yes, sir. Thank you, sir."

"Now let me get you up there."

More tears flowed as Iza nodded and followed instructions. After tossing her up, Lance faced Pocky again. As she approached, her expression made his chest hurt even more than it already did. She looked tired, cold even. Though Bren had healed her, it would still take time for her to fully recover from what she had been through. He held out his hands. Pocky took them and smiled warmly. He pulled her in close and caressed her cheek. She closed her eyes for a moment as she leaned into his touch. She then gazed up, and their eyes locked. He hoped she remembered him.

"Please, recognize me," he murmured.

Pocky smiled wider. "I remember."

Lance embraced her gently and sighed in relief. As he felt her hands cross along his back, he wanted to be with her intimately, to feel her bare skin against his, to reconnect after so long. Bren shouted at them to hurry. Reluctantly, Lance pulled away, knowing the man was right. Now was not the time. But Pocky pressed her lips to his, and despite the alarms and red lights, it went from a simple kiss to an open-mouth frenzy. She tasted sweet with just a hint of iron, and Lance couldn't get enough.

"Hey! Save it for later!" Bren shouted.

Pocky pulled back, covered her mouth, and tried not to laugh. Lance imagined her blushing but couldn't tell in the red glow of the room. He bit his lower lip, loving that so much, then forced himself to get serious.

"Come on before we really piss him off."

"Okay," she said with a nod.

Lance lifted Pocky up, then tossed her. Bren easily grabbed her and pulled her up. Lance unsnapped her med pack and tossed it up once she was clear. He then calculated how he was going to get himself up and quickly formed a plan. He moved as far back as he could up the wall and was ready for a starting run.

Bren, seeing what Lance was about to do, encouraged him. "I got you, Cap. Come on!"

Lance was about to go when an eruption of screams came from above. He looked up at Bren expectantly. The man's attention was averted with whatever was going on.

Bren looked down at him with frantic eyes and yelled, "Cap, hurry!"

Lance broke into a run, hoping there would be enough momentum for him to at least get two footholds up the floor. Between the carpet and his boots, he was confident of the possibility. He leaped up and got three footholds in, enabling him to grab Bren's hand in time. The medic and Marker lifted him through the doorway—and into the horrifying scene unfolding in the corridor.

30

Thomas held Yana in a tight hug. *Gaia*'s awkward tilt made it hard to stand and hold her properly. She was understandably shaken and sobbing. The ceiling lights were down, making the corridor almost completely dark. Small lights along the wall gave enough visibility to see everyone's silhouettes at least. The red light spewing from the conference room helped some but not much. Between the alarms, the barrage of missiles, and all the shouting from ahead, he was amazed that his headache hadn't returned. Ever since Bren had cleaned his head wound, he felt tremendously better and could see why Pocky boasted about their brother's ability of being one of the best medics she ever knew.

With great relief, Thomas watched his sister being pulled up, but his relief was soon broken by a familiar voice shouting his name.

Trying to keep his balance, Thomas halfway turned. Stellan had somehow gotten loose and had both hands around Kaori's neck, cutting off her air. "Bren!" Thomas hollered as he pushed Yana away and fully turned.

Stellan wasn't threatening to hold Kai hostage; he was actually killing her, and Thomas couldn't wait for someone else to intervene.

"Stellan, let her go!" Thomas shouted.

"My father wants your cunt sister!" Stellan yelled. "Trade!"

"Cannon? I thought he was dead?"

"This woman is fading fast, brother. Need to trade quickly."

Thomas felt sick for what he was about to do, but he had to. He couldn't let Kai die. "Stellan, I-I know who you really want is me. And you can have me, okay? But let her go first."

Stellan's expression and grip softened. Kai sucked in a shuddering breath.

Stellan blinked in disbelief, then straightened himself. "I want you, but my father wants your sister. I must get her for him."

Thomas figured Stellan must have lied about Cannon's death, but there wasn't time to contemplate as to why. "Cannon isn't here, Stellan. You don't need to do what he tells you."

"He's inside me! He's ... hurting me." Stellan said almost tiredly, then snapped. "So give me the cunt or I'll kill this one!"

"Look, you can have me!" Thomas paused, frantically taking off his shirt even as disgust rolled through him. "See, you can have me! We can go to a room right now, and you can take me however way you want."

Stellan was stunned silent for a moment as he gazed at Thomas's body. "You are absolutely gorgeous, brother."

"Uh, I ..." Thomas swallowed hard. "I worked out, just for you."

"I want to taste you," Stellan said as though in a trance, then abruptly turned angry. "I wanted you for so long, but that cunt kept getting in the way! I thought you wanted me, but you don't! So don't lie to me!"

"No, no! I do! I do want you," Thomas said as he approached closer. He tried to hold it in, but Stellan's stench made him cough.

"Don't lie to me! I'll kill her!" Stellan shouted, his grip tightening on Kai's throat. She clawed at his arms, but it was no use.

"I'm not lying! And you're right, my sister did get in the way, and it ... it confused me. But I ... I really did want you from the moment I saw you. I want us together. Right now." Thomas hoped he sounded sincere, and he raised his arms as though ready for an embrace. "Let her go, Stellan, and you can have me."

Stellan seemed to calculate the possibility, and in that moment, Thomas could see Kaori was finished. Her hands fell to her sides. Her eyes were half closed and lifeless. She was either dead or about to be. Thomas's body trembled with a mix of rage and sorrow. A tear escaped down his cheek, which seemed to turn Stellan on. Stellan let go of Kai, and the monster's arms embraced him tightly.

There's still time to save her. There must be time, Thomas thought as Stellan greedily caressed his naked back. He tensed, disgusted as Stellan moaned in victory. Tears flowed as his teeth started chattering uncontrollably.

Stellan pulled away and gazed at him with lust in his eyes. He opened his mouth and moved in toward him, obviously going for an open-mouth kiss. Thomas braced himself.

The sharp point of a knife burst into Stellan's throat, but no blood came. Thomas recoiled, then fell back into someone. He couldn't take his eyes off the monster. The man stood motionless, confused, and then slowly pulled the knife out of his throat. Stellan then examined the long knife curiously as though it was the first time he'd seen one. He shook with rage as he looked at Thomas again.

"I will kill—"

A shot exploded in the corridor. Stellan jerked forward as a bullet pierced the back of his head, but just as with the knife, he didn't go down. He didn't scream in pain or even fall. He wasn't dead but in every way should be.

Thomas heard someone screaming but didn't realize it was him.

***

Lance struggled to get out from under Thomas, who began screaming. Thankfully someone pulled him away, allowing him to scramble to his feet. Trying to keep his balance, he cursed, wishing *Gaia* was upright. He unholstered his gun and watched the Abnormal examine himself.

Stellan wiggled his fingers and moved his arms. A strange grin spread across his face, then he turned to see who had shot him. Even in the low light, Lance easily recognized the shooter was Viper. He could only imagine how alarmed and confused she must be as to how Stellan was still standing. However, he knew this was no longer Stellan and was now Pestilence.

"Thank you," Cannon's distorted voice said to Viper. "My son's body has been dead yet his consciousness remained. That shot definitely finished him. Now it's just me in here."

For a moment, Viper lowered her gun slightly. Her expression was one of disbelief at what she was seeing. She snapped out of it and quickly raised her gun again.

"You could do that," Cannon said as Viper moved to pull the trigger, "but it won't put me down."

For a long moment, Viper seemed to struggle to comprehend how that was possible. Lance signaled for her to put the gun away. If the headshot hadn't stopped him, then another wouldn't either. Thankfully she saw his gesture and complied.

"Good girl. Now, I want the twin cunt. Give her to me and the carnage outside stops. Once we're safely away from all of you, all this stops. And I will disband my army," Cannon said. "I'll even hand it over to you. The ships, the personnel, all yours, on the sole condition that you allow me and her to disappear."

Everything clicked into place in Lance's mind. Cannon had somehow managed to build an army with an untold number of people infected with his parasites. He'd already demonstrated he was capable of sinking their ships. The team that should have taken out the Abnormal obviously didn't make it to prevent all this. Anger flared within him.

"Pestilence!" he roared.

The Abnormal rotated inhumanly, an eerie, toothy grin spreading across his face. "Ah, are you the one that's really in charge here?"

"I am."

"Then heed my request, soldier, and no one else dies."

"Why do you want her so fucking badly?"

Cannon tilted his head slightly, causing a neck bone to snap. "Do I know you? You seem familiar."

"Answer me!" Lance shouted.

The Abnormal's grotesque smile remained. "Why should I? You can detain me, but I can leave this body at any time and do this all over again with someone else. And since you know my real name, then you know that I can make good on that promise. I will find her again, and my army will destroy all of you as I do."

That unfortunately was true. Pestilence could very much come after Pocky through whoever else the man occupied. Lance played into the taunt, hoping to make the Abnormal think he was second-guessing himself.

"You get it now?" Cannon continued. "There's no place you can hide her. Oh, and you should know, if you don't already, that if I'm going after her, so are the others. I can protect her from them better than you can. Can't promise I'll be humane, though." The Abnormal laughed, a deep, throaty tone echoed as though thousands of others joined in the chorus. He reached for his groin and started groping himself. "Oh, she is a special girl. Somehow, she contained my parasites from penetrating her mind, but I almost penetrated her in another way through Shox. Got a feel of her breast before I was inter—"

At lightning speed, Lance lifted his gun and fired at Pestilence's hand, then two more at his crotch. Cannon screamed and almost doubled over but quickly regained himself. The impact of the bullets only seemed to irritate him, not causing pain so much. The Abnormal's toothy grin slowly stretched farther, breaking the corners of his mouth.

"You—"

"That's as close as you're ever going to get to her," Lance growled. "Doesn't matter what you or the others have. None of you will find her. And I don't need you to tell me why you want her. We have Shox, and I have my own genius ways of making him talk. You're done."

Lance walked up closer to Pestilence, building his energy up. He gestured to Viper, hoping she would understand an old signal of what he wanted her to do. That was, if she was self-aware.

"I control Shox," Pestilence sneered, "and I can keep his mouth shut."

That unfortunately was true too. Lance softened his expression, letting Pestilence assume whatever he wanted in that. The ruse worked. Cannon laughed triumphantly but abruptly stopped as Viper grabbed his arms from behind, just as Lance wanted her to do. He placed his hands on either side of Pestilence's head and sent his energy into his pores.

"What? You think you can harm me?" Cannon said condescendingly, then frowned. His eyes widened in panic. "What? Wait … what are you doing?"

"You know what I'm doing," Lance said flatly.

Lance's ability was the opposite of Bren's healing and only worked on Abnormals. By sending out his energy, he could enter their bodies and neutralize their existence. Even though Cannon's parasites were linked telepathically, he could only kill the ones that were physically present. It took less than a second for him to find the parasites and begin killing them. They popped like fireworks.

"Wait!" Cannon shouted as he tried moving away, but Lance and Viper held him tight. "How ... how are you doing this?" Lance didn't answer. Pestilence tried to kick in desperation as he grasped what was happening to him. "Wait! A new trade! I mean, I'll tell you why we want her! Please stop, and I'll tell you!"

Lance paused his onslaught. "Quickly," he ordered.

"I swear I'll stop my army, just let me talk to her, and I'll never harm another person. I just need to speak with her, then you can lock me up forever."

"You answer my question first. Why do you want her?" Lance demanded, trusting the Abnormal was too desperate to wait for a possible meeting.

"She has answers that we want."

"Like?" Lance asked with impatience.

"She knows why we exist, why we're here."

Lance scrutinized Cannon as he spoke. "As in you and the other Abnormals?"

"Yes."

"And how the hell would she know that?"

"She has something within her. Something very rare. Something we instinctively know has the answers to all things we desire," Pestilence said, then grinned weirdly. "We can smell it. We're drawn to her like flies to shit. We were drawn to another before her, but now we're drawn to her."

Lance swallowed, thinking of the entity Bren had mentioned. He kept his composure but was losing his tolerance for all this. His team was in bad shape, and the bombardment outside hadn't ceased. "Is that all?" he asked.

Cannon frowned, seeming to grasp that Lance didn't bargain. "Wait! I must know!" he cried. "Let me speak with her. She has the answers to everything! She knows what the Divine Universe really is. She knows if there's more than one reality. She even knows what the Dark Sun is. Everything!"

Lance almost couldn't hide his grin. "What do you want to know about the Dark Sun?"

"Well … what is it? And why does my kind fear it? That cunt knows those answers!"

At that moment, *Gaia* steadily returned to an upright position. Relieved applause echoed down the corridor. Some of the lights flickered on behind Lance, revealing how truly scared Cannon was. The desperation in the guy's expression was pleasing to see. The Abnormal never eased the suffering of the ones he invaded and only knew compassion for himself. And what Pestilence did to Pocky and thousands of others made Lance want to rip the guy in half. He relished the sensation of Cannon's parasites dying as he continued his assault on the remaining infestation.

Cannon screamed in true pain. "Who are you!?"

Lance was happy to answer. "I am the destroyer of all that is evil. I silence my foes that end lives and lay ruin to the worlds they are unwelcome in. I am unmerciful and relentless in ending all that is unnatural and abnormal. I am the darkness you and your kind fear. I am the Dark Sun."

31

It was late in the evening, and Lance's team was still a hot mess. Yana and Thomas were traumatized, with Yana ready to abandon ship and swim back to land and Thomas catatonic. Kaori was stable but was still unconscious. The rest of his team was shaken and bruised, but otherwise alright.

Lightning cracked in the distance as the storm continued to rage. Lance leaned against the wall next to Pocky's cabin door, waiting patiently for her to emerge. Iza was inside with her, while he and two soldiers from Marker's team guarded the door. He was grateful they were giving him space and talking among themselves. He wasn't in the mood to chat. Viper had long since left to assess the damage and wounded. Unable to stand around and do nothing, Haize went with her.

As he waited, Lance replayed the event after being pulled up into the corridor. He was genuinely proud of Thomas. He didn't hesitate or wait for someone to intervene when Stellan grabbed Kaori. Lance hated that Stellan had gotten his hands on Thomas and wished he could've spared him from that trauma.

Voices inside the café escalated for a moment, grabbing Lance's attention. Yana and Naiko were in there. Their Team Coordinator—who wasn't part of his original team and just an ordinary human—was diligently trying to calm their cartographer down. Though Yana was now aware of herself, that didn't mean she was less prone to having a natural reaction to a scary situation. He was grateful for Naiko's efforts, even though she was just as rattled.

Two soldiers from another team were guarding Kaori's cabin just down the hall. Bren was inside with her, dutifully looking after their friend. Though he was a healer, he couldn't bring someone back from death. Thankfully though, he was able to do so the old-fashioned human way; otherwise, they would have lost her for good in this life.

For Lance, losing a member of his team was equivalent to losing a piece of his heart. It was like that for all of them. Even though they returned to the same reality they were created from, living a lifetime without someone you deemed family was agonizing. Waiting on the other side was just as painful.

Thomas was inside his cabin as well. Of all of them, he was in the worst shape. He had pushed himself past his worst fear to save Kai's life but was in severe shock from doing so. The whole damn day had pushed the man well past his limits of sanity. By the time Lance regrouped with his team after Stellan was boxed up, Thomas was screaming and wouldn't stop. Pocky didn't know what to do, and any attempt to comfort him only made it worse. Thomas eventually passed out, which gave them the opportunity to transport him to his quarters.

Lance stood up when the door behind him opened. Iza stepped out, Pocky right behind her. Though she was still a bit pale, she looked more refreshed after her shower. Her hair was still slightly damp and already scrunching in its usual waves, and her head wound had a new silver line over it.

"Iza, would you please relieve Naiko so she can take a break?" Lance asked. "Yana's wearing her down."

"Yes, sir."

As Iza left, Lance regarded Pocky. For some reason, she stood at parade rest and waited expectantly, as though he'd give her orders too. He ignored the posture.

"I know you want to get back to Thomas," he said, "but could we talk first?"

"Yes, sir," Pocky replied with a serious expression.

Lance gestured for the other soldiers to leave. Before he could speak, she tilted her head and regarded him thoughtfully. He paused, letting her speak first.

"Respectfully, sir, you do understand me, correct?" she said in Origin.

Lance's eyebrows furrowed. If she was self-aware, she should have automatically known that he could. She also referred to him as "sir" even though they were alone. This indicated that she wasn't self-aware as he had assumed. She had said she remembered him, though. Had he mistaken her answer? Had she mistaken his question and thought he was referring to her head injury and potential memory loss?

That put him in a precarious position. Now that he was self-aware, he was very much the soldier he always was and wasn't even going to try to pretend to be a civilian. But that didn't mean he was officially an IMF soldier either. He'd need to tread carefully and come up with something until she became self-aware.

"I do," he finally replied.

"So, you are a soldier," Pocky said more than asked.

He nodded. "I am."

Their conversation in the library felt like a lifetime ago, but Lance knew what she was thinking. He could see the confusion in her eyes, yet her expression remained neutral. Though he wished she was self-aware to spare them this trivial conversation, he was ready to embellish with as much of the truth as he could. Bren, unfortunately, wouldn't be able to awaken her anytime soon. He'd already healed several people in one day, and Lance couldn't risk pushing their medic even further. Once Pocky was awakened, she would understand.

"Are you from Spec Ops, then?" Pocky asked. "I mean, it makes sense that Geara would've put one of you guys on the project. And you really do disguise yourselves well as civilians. Damn good." She flashed a proud smile, and a little chuckle sounded from her throat. "I totally bought it."

"I *am* an operative but from a different branch," Lance said. "Can't say anything further for the time being though. Okay?"

Pocky nodded thoughtfully. "If I'm not overstepping ..."

"Ask away."

"Sir, were you lying earlier to keep up appearances?"

"No. I told you the truth. The absolute truth," he said. "I know that doesn't make sense right now, but I promise it will. Just be patient with me. Once we get our team squared away, I'll explain everything. Clear?"

For a short moment, Pocky smiled, then glanced down at her boots. Sadness filled her expression, making him anxious.

"Pocky ..." Lance waited for her to look up at him. "I know it's a stupid question asking if you're okay, but I'm asking anyway."

Pocky nodded slightly. "I'm, uh"—she cleared her throat—"just wondering how Thomas is gonna pull through this. And Kai too."

Lance's shoulders loosened. It was just like Pocky to think of others before considering herself. She'd been shot, tied up, and beaten, but she wasn't thinking of that. She was thinking of the people she deeply cared for.

"Yeah, but—" Lance paused to clear his throat, which suddenly became tight. "You've had a bad day too. And ... I'm concerned."

Pocky touched her stitched wound for a moment. Her gaze darted to his face several times. "Yeah ... I might be emotional about it later, but for now, it just feels like a normal day on the job."

Just as Bren had warned earlier, Pocky was compartmentalizing her ordeal, but Lance didn't dare to point out that this had been far from a normal day. She wasn't being stoic or giving him an *"I'm a tough soldier"* vibe. This was more of a practiced routine.

Anger boiled within Lance as to how she'd come to be this way. He wasn't just angry about that. He was angry that he didn't protect her from the very beginning. He wanted to erase it all away.

She shook her head, as though she knew what he was thinking. "Sorry, sir. Didn't mean to make you concerned for me. I'm okay. Really."

Lance closed his eyes and sighed through his nose, trying to temper his anger and the overwhelming urge to hit something. He met her eyes. "Pocky, I'm gonna be concerned for you even after my last breath. That will never change," he said, voice low and warm. "And you don't need to be so formal around me. Nothing has changed between us. We're still—" Lance couldn't finish. What was her outlook on their relationship now? It could be a day—or longer—before Bren could help ease her awakening. Regardless of how much time that would entail, it didn't minimize his anxiousness for when she would remember him or his love for her.

Pocky's expression softened, then she held out her hands. Lance's chest tightened as he took them.

"Lance ..." Pocky said carefully. "Events like today can change a person's perspective drastically. But how I feel for you hasn't, and I'm open to where that'll lead if you are."

For the first time in what felt like forever, Lance smiled. His legs nearly buckled. No matter what they had been through in their countless lives before, he had an overwhelming sense that he couldn't live without her by his side. No matter what assignment they were given, he didn't care unless she was there with him.

"I have no reasons to guard myself," he said. "I want you. I want *us*."

Pocky blushed and looked away. Lance pulled her into his arms, savoring how good it felt to hold her. She wrapped her arms around his waist, and they didn't need to say anything else.

He put a hand on her head and stroked her hair, but his mind pulled him away from his elation and back to the entity inside her. Pocky obviously had no clue that the entity was inside her. How that even happened in the first place greatly unnerved him. Even more so, though, was that the Abnormals wanted her for it. There was still the fungus issue to solve too. Lance was more thankful than ever for Marker's team joining theirs; they were going to need the protection.

Pocky pulled away first. "I should get back to Thomas," she said.

Still holding her hand, Lance walked her down the corridor, letting himself relish how good it felt to touch her. Viper had returned and was waiting for him by the café.

When they reached Thomas's door, Lance faced Pocky. She pushed up on her toes and kissed him gently, leaving him wanting so much more. *Soon*, he promised himself. After the door closed behind her, he turned his attention to Viper. She smiled slightly but quickly returned to her default, emotionless expression.

"Where's Haize?" Lance asked.

"Down on engine level. The listing and collision caused significant damage," Viper said. "Says he's going to fix it. As good as he is, I don't think he can. The fucking ship is just too damn big for one man to fix. But the man *we* know is gonna try."

Since there were too many soldiers walking around for them to speak freely,

Lance nodded in understanding of what she was really saying, which was that Haize was self-aware too. He gestured for Viper to follow him. They walked to the end of the corridor for more privacy. When they were alone, he quickly turned, and they embraced. Just like with Bren, it felt tremendously good to hug his friend after so long.

After pulling away, Lance asked, "When did you awaken?"

"When I shot Stellan in the head and the bastard didn't go down."

Lance hadn't expected Viper to show up but was grateful that she had. "How much do you remember?"

"Not enough to need M to heal me," she said. "But I do have more tolerance than most."

"Still though, try not to push it."

"Yes, sir. Fucking hate it when we wake up like this."

It was always jarring to awaken on one's own; that was one reason why they had the Pre-Teams, to ease them into who they really were. Plus, the Pre-Teams would teach them not to absorb what wasn't necessary. Remembering other lifetimes was always tempting, but the capacity of their human minds could barely hold onto every second of their current life, let alone adding another.

Understanding that this wasn't the first time they were jolted awake, Lance sighed in irritation. "Agreed. Listen ... Pocky isn't awake yet like we thought."

"Shit." Viper's eyes widened. "What's your cover then?" she asked, knowing him too well that he wouldn't go back to being a civilian.

"Operative from a different branch. I didn't elaborate."

"Good call."

"What's the situation outside?"

"Thanks to Pocky's heads-up, the warships managed to get two subs before they split off. As you know, one still managed to sink the warship on *Gaia*'s port side. Because we were tethered to it, it almost took us with it. Thankfully the lines were long enough, and the water isn't too deep here. And thank fuck the shutters were down too, or we would be having a very different conversation. Other than that, no enemy survivors and the fleet is stable."

Lance furrowed his brows and rubbed his chin in thought before asking,

"Does the IMF have submarine technology?"

"We actually do," Viper replied with raised eyebrows. "Along with other surface combatants, and aircraft as well, but none of it is in production. We have no enemies, so why would we? Some elite commanders even feel the warships are overkill, but no one's arguing about it because it still showcases our power to the world with the obvious message of 'don't fuck with us.' But—and I know what you're about to say—they're not factoring in Abnormals and their fucking minions."

"That's a given, but I was thinking more of how Pestilence got a hold of both submarine and stealth technology."

Viper shook her head. "I was thinking the same, and I lightly broached Geara with the same question, which led to finding out that he's an Outworlder too."

Lance's eyebrows raised. "No shit." Though the Custodian had created thousands of Outworlders, remembering each other was just as complicated as remembering their past lives.

"Yeah, his team was assigned to Stellan, which makes sense now. He apologized for not recognizing us. And he truly didn't know that asshole was after Pocky, or he—"

"Uh-huh, I get it." They didn't need to rehash this again; there were more pressing matters at hand. "Did he have an answer?"

"Unfortunately, no."

"I need to speak with him. Can you arrange that?"

"Certainly," Viper said, then looked thoughtful. "Interesting turnout for our team. Right?"

"It really is. Security Chief suits you," Lance said with a smile.

Viper let out a small laugh. "Yeah ... I'm gonna miss it a little. And not just my place in the IMF but just being part of it period."

Lance nodded apologetically. He thought of Pocky and Bren and how they were going to feel about leaving too. Now that their team was together—self-aware or not, strange entities or not—they needed to get on track with their assignment.

"Funny how we all came together like this," Viper said, tilting her head. "This can't be a coincidence." Lance reiterated what Iza had told him earlier. Her eyes raised in disbelief. "Ah, fuck. Poor Iza. I can't imagine—" Viper paused, her eyes distant for a moment. "Nope, that happened to me once too. Fucking blows."

"Yeah," Lance nodded. Unlike Viper, he didn't care to know if he had a similar experience from another lifetime, but he didn't doubt that he probably had.

"Well, that explains why I was transferred onto *Gaia* four months ago," Viper said almost absently, then shook her head dismissively. "Got a plan, Cap?"

"Once I figure out what Geara's plans are, we'll have a proper meeting," Lance said. "But I want to stay for at least a few days so we can get our bearings, and we'll help clean up *Gaia* in the meantime."

"Yes, sir. Unfortunately, I already have bad news to report."

"I figured."

"First, we found Shox's escort. The guards are dead, but the medic thankfully made it—well, barely. And he wants to see Pocky."

"Friend of hers?"

"It's Trooper."

"Shit," Lance said with a sigh. "You can ask her but don't push."

Viper frowned, lowering her eyes. "I know their history, so I won't."

"What's the other?"

"Marker just reported that Shox is dead."

"Yeah, I figured Pestilence—"

"No, someone shot him. I—"

Down the hall, Thomas screamed. Lance let out a heavy sigh. Viper put a sympathetic hand on his shoulder. Pocky's words echoed in his mind. *Just feels like a normal day on the job.*

32

Gaia was en route to Way Station P51 to be properly repaired. Besides losing two warships, the remaining IMF fleet wasn't as battered, but the soldiers were still rattled. To be attacked by something unseen was rightfully unnerving. After speaking with Geara, Lance had learned that even though the IMF had the technology to build submarines and other advanced crafts, it wasn't shared among lower ranks. It still perplexed him how Pestilence got a hold of it, built it, and used it. But that was for Geara's team to figure out. His team was charged with contending with the fungus that was already out of control; they were years behind in fighting it.

Lance had decided that he and his team would stay on board during the journey. So far, the trip had taken thirteen days, but the time gave him a chance to formulate a plan for how they were going to proceed with their assignment. It also gave his team a chance to recover and awaken. Everyone but the twins were now self-aware. Though he hadn't shared yet what their next move was after *Gaia* docked, everyone—with the exception of the twins—at least was up to speed on how their team came together.

After speaking with Ruckers through a long-range radio, Lance learned that she'd been looking for their team ever since she had come across Iza. Some were easier to find than others.

Lance was the last to be found, and that was only after he'd applied for the project. Getting him on the project at the last minute hadn't been easy though, especially since it was designed as a trap for Stellan. It was still unknown how

Stellan knew it was meant for him, but that was for Geara to figure out. Ruckers would have tagged along and helped Iza to awaken them, but there was an urgency for her to rejoin her team. She at least indicated the Abnormals as the Protestors, which was one of many code words they used as a reference when talking among regular people. Lance thanked Ruckers graciously. Without her, he could only guess how the rest of their lives would have played out.

Night had fallen, and most of the soldiers were celebrating their final night in the Rec Hall. According to Geara, they would be arriving at their base by midday tomorrow. Everyone was elated and partied hard. As the party went on, Lance and Thomas stood against the wall, watching their team among the crowd. Bren and Viper were the only ones not present. He smiled as he watched them dance. Pocky's moves were liquid-smooth and flowed along to the beat. The others were awkward in comparison, but no one cared. All that mattered was that they were enjoying themselves, and they greatly deserved the chance to recharge. They'd all been working nonstop since the day after the battle. Lance didn't like dancing, but watching Pocky having fun was the only reprieve he needed.

"She always said she would have been a dancer if she couldn't have been a medic," Thomas said flatly.

Lance looked at his friend in disbelief. Thomas kept his gaze focused on the crowd, his expression unreadable. It wasn't the statement that had caught Lance off guard, but the fact that Thomas had even spoken. Ever since that awful day, the man was unreachable. They had tried to awaken him, hoping it would help, but Thomas refused any attempts. Bren was confident that Thomas would eventually come out of it on his own terms and said they all just needed to be patient.

Lance smiled, feeling optimistic that Thomas was finally coming back to them. He wanted to get Thomas talking more, but his radio went off. It was Viper. He had been waiting for this call.

"Go for Lance."

"Sir, Geara is ready. M, Marker, and I are already with him in C1."

"On our way in a minute. Call, out." Lance adjusted his hat. For a moment, he savored how good it felt to be in uniform again but had enough respect to know he hadn't earned it like the soldiers around him. He didn't take that for granted. "Hey, I have to go," he said to Thomas. "You staying?"

When Thomas didn't answer, Lance got Haize's attention and gestured that it was time for them to leave. The engineer got Pocky's attention and directed her toward Lance. He waved to her. They had planned this beforehand. The rest of his team would discreetly exit and join him in the meeting. Pocky would be none the wiser that she and Thomas would be left behind. He hated it, but it was what they had to do for now.

With a big smile, she happily made her way toward him, throwing in a couple of skip steps she timed perfectly with the beat. He laughed.

"Hey, you," she said.

"Hey back." Lance bit his lower lip.

"You know, I love it when you do that," Pocky said, beaming at him.

"Oh yeah? What else do you love?" Lance asked teasingly as he pulled her against him.

"Of you? Everything," Pocky replied tenderly. She had no memory of waking up after Bren had healed her, which turned out to be a good thing. She didn't even know she'd said those words to him before, and Lance couldn't help but laugh, making her puzzled with curious humor. "What?"

"You're a remarkable woman." He grinned but sobered quickly. "And I love everything about you."

Lance's chest tightened. He pulled her into a hug, and she molded into him, placing her head against his chest.

"Your heart is racing fast," she said as she pulled away quickly. "Are you okay?"

Lance's throat grew taut. He tried to swallow but couldn't. By outside appearances, Pocky seemed fine, but she was still unaware of who she truly was. Lance and Bren had tried several times to awaken her, but for some reason, she couldn't. They concluded it had to be due to the damage Ember—the entity within Pocky—had referred to. That, or the entity itself was somehow blocking her from becoming self-aware. She was as human as any of them could ever get.

This, of course, troubled the whole team. Pocky was alive and well, and Lance was grateful for that, but it still hurt that she couldn't remember herself or who he was to her.

Pocky placed her hands on either side of his face. "Hey, I'm serious," she said with a stern look. "Don't make me get my med pack."

Lance cleared his throat and rolled his shoulders, then took her hands in his. "I'm good. You excite me is all."

"I do?" Pocky asked skeptically. "That distressed look on your face says otherwise."

"Sorry." Lance shook his head, knowing he had to navigate the truth in some ways. "I'm heading for a debrief that involves a lot of crucial decisions for our departure tomorrow. Combined with everything that has been going on, I'm just a little stressed."

She nodded. "Yeah, I get that."

When they realized Pocky's inability to become self-aware, and with Thomas's current condition, Lance and the others scrambled for a plan to keep their team together that would make sense for the twins.

Geara had taken over the project and sent Naiko back to CCO Headquarters. The XO then redirected authority over to Lance and reaffirmed this as an order by their superiors. Geara then told the twins that the CCO and IMF were continuing their collaboration, and the team was being diverted to investigate the fungus as a high-priority project. Pocky, of course, was happy to serve and to still be with her brother. Though Thomas was unresponsive to most interactions, he thankfully at least acknowledged what they were doing.

Pocky relaxed and pressed her head against his chest again. Lance thumbed where a scar should have been on her forehead. Thanks to Bren, there wasn't so much as a mark. As he held onto her, a need brewed within him. They'd been intimate since the day after the battle, and he desperately wanted to take her back to his room right now, but the debriefing was vital.

Pocky pulled away and smiled up at him. "Alright, I'm going back to dancing. Might drink with some friends later too."

"Okay, I'll see you in my cabin later?"

Blushing, Pocky nodded, then turned her attention to Thomas. She braved to reach out to him, saying his name as she did. He turned away before she could touch him. Lance saw her chin tremble, then steady again. Thomas's avoidance was hurting her, but she was doing her damnedest not to show it. He hated to leave her this way, but he was already late.

"Hey, I'm sorry—"

Pocky refocused on him and forced a smile. "No, you do need to go. I'm sorry for holding you up. I'll see you later."

Lance reluctantly let Pocky go, watching her quickly disappear into the crowd. He looked at Thomas one last time before leaving the Rec Hall and making his way through the ship. Lance loved the man dearly, as he did everyone on his team, and he hated seeing Thomas go through this. He also hated how it affected Pocky. Lance just wanted to fix it all, to fix both of them. Especially since Thomas held crucial information about the fungus. He needed to get him awakened, and soon.

As Lance walked into C1, he took in his team. Bren sat next to Viper, who was tentatively watching their engineer scroll through a monstrous book. Geara spoke with Kaori and Marker, while Yana and Iza were absorbed in their own conversation. As Lance sat at the head of the table, Bren greeted him.

"Ah! Found it. Here, look." Haize excitedly passed the book to Viper, keeping his finger in the middle of the page. "The command code is right here."

Everyone's conversations stopped as they watched Viper squint at the tiny font. Her brows furrowed, then raised in disbelief.

"So, this verbal command opens that particular cabinet?"

"Yes, ma'am," Haize said with his usual cheeky grin. "Anything on *Gaia* that has a digital lock has a master verbal command code, just in case someone doesn't have their key card."

"And Pocky somehow remembered this one?" Viper asked, looking up at Haize. "Cause I certainly didn't."

"My partner has the amazing talent of retaining everything she reads," Bren answered. "Bet you a million coins she could recite every damn word from that manual."

"Huh," Viper mused. "Never knew she was capable of that."

"That and all the languages she knows," said Marker.

"Or how about her sight? It still boggles me how she could see those ships," Geara said, shaking his head.

"The fact that she can without her archives is what astounds me," Kai added. "I mean, what are we truly capable of if we don't have that?"

"Enough of this." Lance tapped two fingers on the table. "We need to get on with this meeting. Geara, you first."

Lance had been waiting for the XO to make arrangements for what they needed to carry out their assignment. Since they didn't have resources or funding, Geara insisted on helping them. However, Lance got the sense that the generosity stemmed more from Geara's assignment compromising his team and their help in taking down Stellan. Regardless of the man's reason, Lance was grateful for the help.

"Took a little time to get everything in order, and I've obviously been busy dealing with this shit, but you and Marker's team are now officially the IMF's Black Ops. For now, you report only to me, clear?"

"Yes, sir."

"I have an authorization code I'll give after the meeting. I've reserved ten armored vehicles along with five wagons for you to take. Once we're at P38, you can stock up with whatever you need from the depot. I also have a long-range radio so we can stay in contact. No matter how far you travel, you'll be able to reach me."

"Much appreciated," Lance said.

"Certainly. It's, uh, the least I could do."

"I understand. If you don't mind me asking, what's the fallout"—Lance gestured vaguely at the room around them—"to all this."

Geara rasped tiredly and leaned back into his chair. "It's a fucking mess, but it's my mess to deal with. I'm not looking good to my superiors, though, and might be demoted. I've promoted Marker to XO just in case I am."

"Sorry to hear that," Lance said, hating that he couldn't offer something more consoling.

Geara half shrugged, then continued. "According to one of the admirals I spoke with, the CCO execs caught wind of what happened and have dropped us for all current and future projects, which, when it comes to funding, is going to hurt us down the road."

Shit. Lance now fully understood why Geara could be demoted, even though it was from consequences that were out of their control. He could see the man's superiors taking this as an epic fuckup. He asked with sharp sympathy, "Did the admiral even disclose what actually happened?"

"Tried to but got nowhere. Plus, the execs felt we didn't have enough consideration to distance ourselves farther away from Daria Harbor or the Charter Channel when all this went down. In short, the execs felt we put civilian lives in danger."

"Those assholes really thought we could somehow plan a counter defense for an enemy we didn't see coming?" Viper asked in stunned disbelief.

"They certainly did," Geara said. "And it gets worse. A new military body was happy to reveal themselves and offered to take our place. Take a guess who."

"Pestilence's army." Lance clenched his fists, wishing he could have killed beyond what was in Stellan.

"Has to be," Geara replied with a nod. "But they wouldn't say who exactly is leading it."

"Fuck."

"And now they'll get the funding to grow?" Viper paled. "Oh, fucking shit," she muttered, putting a hand over her mouth. Bren gently grabbed her hand and held it in his.

They were all silent for a long moment, contemplating what that meant not only for their future and other teams but for the entire IMF.

Lance cleared his throat. "Geara, what're your superiors going to do?"

"They're recalling all personnel currently assigned to projects and returning them to the closest way station or base. They're also pulling all Strat Units across Theton back to our main headquarters. However, our OSARs will stay on task until further notice. We're going to have to keep our eyes wide open for any dirty looks from here on."

"Okay, and what are they wanting you to do?"

"They want me to stay in command of *Gaia* until she's fixed anyway. That could be up to six months, maybe a year. After that, I'm not sure. With Stellan taken care of, my priority now is to support you and other teams out there as much as I can with my rank."

"Again, that's much appreciated," Lance said.

Geara waved a hand dismissively. "It's. ... Yeah."

Lance nodded in understanding.

"And your plans?" the XO asked.

Lance updated his team and Geara on the details of where they were going to start. Yana already mapped what was publicly reported as infected areas, and explained where they would head to first.

"Kai, go ahead, please," Lance said when Yana was done.

"Yes, sir," she said. "I got all the test results back, and so I got an idea of how your biofluids are working against the fungus."

A week earlier, Lance had given Kaori a blood, saliva, and urine sample. Everyone knew his ability could kill Abnormals. Even though the fungus wasn't an Abnormal, it was still created by one. Kai had dived into her archives and linked the fungus to the Abnormal that most likely created it. Pham—or Phamine, as he was called—had to be the one. But the fungus was now a lifeform of its own, yet Lance's biofluids were still somehow destroying it. They had waited for Kai to give them an answer as to how.

"Go on," Lance said.

"The fungus is organic, yet has abnormal components to it. I'm thinking your ability adapted a way to kill it by using your biofluids. You can piss, spit, bleed, or ... you know ..."

"Yeah, I get it," Lance replied dryly.

"Whichever you use, doesn't matter, your fluids will eradicate it. I've tested the specimens we had, and they dissolved right after injecting them with your ..." Kaori didn't finish her sentence, but she didn't need to. They got the point she was pitching.

Lance let out a tired sigh. "So, that's fine on a smaller scale, but how can that be effective in mass-infected areas?"

"Once we get our boots on the ground and do some experiments, I can calculate that better," she said.

"Okay," Lance said, then looked to Viper. "Were you able to find out who killed Shox?"

"Unfortunately, no. All I could uncover was that the minion was left alone, but someone or the killer let him out. Because of the chaos, I couldn't get further than that. And whoever did it didn't leave any evidence. No gun, nothing, but it had to be a soldier. It was a clean shot to the eye."

Lance rubbed his chin. His stubble had grown longer than he cared for, but he'd deal with it later. After a long moment, he looked at Viper again. "So, we either have a rogue Outworlder or someone who took advantage of the moment."

"That's my conclusion as well. Besides us and a few other teams onboard, no one else has come forward, and their alibis all checked out."

"What about Trooper? Have you been able to figure out why Pocky intervened with his group?" Lance asked.

It was still a mystery as to why Pocky had gone after the boy and the people he was with, or even why Pocky—and not Bren—had received a distress message to aid them. They also didn't know why she—and not Thomas—received Bren's distress message. If they were next to each other, they both should have gotten it. Again, Lance and Bren assumed that Ember most likely had some factor in that but were unsure if they would ever conclusively know if that was true.

Viper fidgeted with her hands and shook her head. "I thought maybe Trooper was one of us, but he isn't. So, it has to be someone within that group he was with. Because he was so young at the time, I couldn't get much more than that."

"I can reach out to a team that can locate and check out the people he was with," Geara offered.

"That'd be great, thanks," Lance said to the XO. He then assigned everyone to list what they would need from the depot for their appropriate specialty. "We're way behind," he said, "but I believe we can mitigate the fungus issue and prevent it from causing further damage. We'll do our best with what we have."

It wasn't exactly an encouraging speech, but they all gave him some grace with an understanding of the burden they all carried on their shoulders: the fate of millions of lives. And it wasn't just for humans; it was for all life.

"Alright, get some sleep, people," Lance said. "We have a long day tomorrow."

By the time Lance got to his cabin, he was so tired his vision was blurry. He found Pocky asleep and naked in bed. After undressing, he happily joined her. She shifted and positioned herself under his arm and against his body. He savored her warmth and the feel of her skin against his.

Long before Lance had become the Dark Sun, he and Bren were designated to assist humanoids. Wherever they were needed, they went. Most of the time, that involved conflict or wars. He and Bren spent countless lifespans doing this routine, and it was why they bonded easily.

When the Abnormals started appearing and interfering within the Bubbled Reality, the Custodian asked for volunteers to be modified to counter them. Lance and Bren didn't hesitate. The Custodian listed the modifications of their choice to become. Bren wanted to be a healer and was changed to have the capability to heal. When they were first created, their form was akin to a translucent, single-cell lifeform. However, after Bren was modified, he grew into a planet-sized green sphere. For Lance, he became something much more than that.

Lance only understood himself as a warrior, a fighter, a soldier, and so he chose what made the most sense to him. However, he no longer wanted to be under someone else's command. He had asked the Custodian to make him not just a leader but something that could handle large-scale opponents. The Custodian granted his request and began his modification. Unlike the others, though, who had changed into planet-sized forms, Lance exploded like a supernova and grew to the size of twenty thousand galaxies clustered into one mass. He was no longer translucent but was now a glossy black sphere with blue flares emanating from his surface, instantly earning his name the Dark Sun.

The Custodian had transformed Lance into a force capable of eliminating Abnormals, literally wiping their existence from reality, hence why they feared him. After he had recovered from his modification, the Custodian then designed a team to follow and assist him. He and Bren watched as Yana, Haize, Iza, Kaori, and Viper were created. They were as ordinary as he and Bren had once been but were in every way capable in their own specialty. Pocky and Thomas came last. They started as a single cell like the rest, but the Custodian split them in two for reasons that were still unknown.

Lance was instantly captivated by Pocky. Though she was tiny, she glowed in honey-gold variations and flickered like a distant star. He didn't know then how instrumental she would become. And not just for him but for everyone on their team.

Lance held Pocky tighter and pressed a kiss to the top of her head. The love that developed between them wasn't common among their kind, but it wasn't unheard of either. He prayed to the Divine Universe that this entity inside her wouldn't alter the woman who literally gave him everything to live for, regardless of realities and lifetimes to come.

33

Pocky awoke to Lance kissing her face. He wasn't usually playful in this way, and she loved it. When he landed on her lips, he stayed there. They kissed slowly, deeply, like they had all the time in the world.

Desire bloomed within Pocky, and his body responded to her need. As he carried her through one explosion of pleasure to the next, Pocky relished how good it felt to be with him. How right it felt.

When they were both satiated, they held each other closely. Lance pressed his forehead against hers and repeatedly trailed his fingers from her breast down to her hip and back again. At first, it was soothing, but she pulled away as her skin became sensitive and ticklish. Her face heated as she tried not to laugh, but she relaxed again when their eyes met.

She saw so much of who he was in his eyes. She saw his love, his desire, his wants, his needs, his fear, and also his despondency. His eyes were darker now, harder than before. She stroked his face, wishing the past events hadn't changed the man she had met. But what happened had changed all of them. Especially Thomas.

Lance took her hand and pressed a kiss to the back. Being with him gave Pocky a great sense of security and a possible future, one where she wouldn't go down in flames as she had always thought. More than that, though, he showed her a kind of love she never knew existed. She knew familial love—that from a brother, from a best friend. But Lance ... his love was something she had never expected to experience. Seeing other couples together wasn't the same. This kind of love was something she never even gave a thought to, let alone wanting it or needing it.

Now that she had it, she never wanted to let it go.

"Are you okay?" he murmured.

Pocky smiled and spoke in a sultry voice. "I wanna do that again."

Lance huffed out a laugh, then pulled her closer. He still hadn't told her how he had become a soldier, but with everything going on, Pocky didn't push. She was excited to hear the story but patient for the right time.

Pulling away, Lance kissed her forehead. "We need to get ready."

They showered and got dressed. Lance shaved his beard back down to a stubble, almost matching his low and tight crew cut.

As Pocky was packing her duffel bag, a familiar yet invasive sensation rippled throughout her body. It felt like a pebble being tossed into a motionless puddle. She'd been experiencing these ripples ever since the battle and had no clue what it was or why she was having them. In all the medical texts she'd studied, she hadn't come across anything like it. So, she kept the occurrences to herself. It didn't seem to be harming her. It was just an odd shiver. She hoped it would go away eventually. But if it got worse, she'd have to consult a fellow medic. Someone she trusted besides Bren.

"Hey, are you okay?" Lance asked.

"Yeah. Why?"

"You were just trembling."

"Just felt a chill is all," she replied nonchalantly, then continued packing, hoping he wouldn't press. Thankfully, he didn't.

Another strange thing that had happened since the battle was that the pain in her shoulder was no longer there. It was just gone, like being shot had never happened at all. Pocky hadn't realized just how much pain and discomfort she'd been dealing with until now. Whether it was the Divine Universe giving her a break or if it was something else entirely, it didn't matter because she wouldn't take it for granted.

The last items they put on were their guns and hats. Pocky watched as Lance snapped the last thick strap of his gun holster around his thigh. The uniform suited him perfectly, again making her wonder how she hadn't figured out sooner that he was a soldier.

They headed to the café, where they met the rest of their team. Marker and his team were there too. Most were already eating and in good spirits. Her team's elation about getting on the road resonated within Pocky, and it eased her trepidation. Solving a potential famine crisis was going to be interesting, if not difficult.

The only one not enthused was her brother. Thomas sat alone with his back turned away from the group, slowly pecking at his food. After getting a serving, Pocky sat across from him and quietly ate, trying to desperately think of how to get through to him. She'd tried getting him out of his funk, but he wouldn't even look at her. He at least understood that he was a consultant on the team, but with his state of mind, she wasn't sure how Lance was going to utilize that knowledge. *"Time heals everything,"* Bren once said to her, and she hoped it would be true for their brother.

"Let's go!" Lance called over the team's conversations.

They weren't docked yet, but he explained that he wanted them to be on the main deck until they were. As usual, Thomas lagged behind and was the last to leave. Pocky lingered to be second to last, hoping her brother didn't notice she had done so on purpose. When Kai stepped into the corridor, essentially leaving them alone in the café, she about-faced and looked sternly up at him. He stopped abruptly but remained unreadable. When she didn't move, he looked away.

"I love you," Pocky blurted. They had never spoken those words to each other before. They never had to, but she didn't know what else to say.

Not wanting to wait for his reaction, she turned away. What Stellan did was sickening. It was Thomas's very nightmare that came true, but Pocky knew he'd do it again to save a life. She was so proud of him and proud to be his sister.

Pocky began to walk away but felt Thomas's hand on her shoulder. She paused, unsure what to do at first. She slowly turned, hoping it wasn't the wrong move. As he covered his face with his other hand, tears began falling from his chin. She closed the gap between them and pulled him into a tight embrace, sighing with relief as he wrapped his arms around her. No words were spoken because nothing needed to be said. She wasn't sure how much time had passed and didn't care. This was the first step to getting her brother back.

After Thomas cleaned himself up, they rejoined their team. They were hanging out by the corner of the port's stairs that led to the stern's well deck. Everyone cheered at their arrival. Pocky looked up just in time to see Thomas crack a slight smile before walking over to Bren and Haize. Pocky went into Lance's open arms before leaning her back against his chest. He folded his arms around her, and she reveled in how good that felt.

The day was beautiful, and they weren't the only ones enjoying the weather. The main deck was more crowded than usual. Soldiers flowed past them like the ocean. Some stopped and chatted for a moment before moving on, but the banter was all the same. Everyone couldn't wait to be on dry land.

Pocky's anxiousness died down tremendously. The unknown wasn't so bad when you were with the people you loved, and she loved every single person on her team. Her world couldn't be more perfect.

After a while, the crowd on the deck gradually dispersed until Pocky and their united team were the only ones there. It was a little odd, but she didn't put too much thought into it.

"Oh no, here she comes," Bren said with a groan.

"Who?" Yana asked, looking in his direction.

"Pocky's rival."

Everyone got quiet as they looked ahead. A woman with light brown hair and a dark complexion approached. Her hazel eyes seemed to burn with hatred.

Pocky just shrugged and tried not to smile.

As the woman settled against the corner of the bulkhead, her eyes drilled into Pocky. Lance loosened his hold, as though letting her know she was free to go. Pocky put her hands on his forearms, keeping herself in place. Everyone was silent.

"Pocky," the woman said with a mocking tone.

"Lawless," she replied flatly.

Lawless glanced up at Lance, then smirked at Pocky. "I see you finally know what a real dick feels like."

"Yeah, and you really need one in your mouth."

Pocky didn't hide her amusement as everyone clapped and cheered, but Lawless bared her teeth.

"Bitch!"

"Cunt."

Pocky slipped under Lance's hold and went after the woman. She pretended that she was about to throw a punch, but she couldn't hold her laugh in anymore. She threw her arms around Lawless, who returned her tight hug.

"Everyone," Pocky said, "this is my friend, Lawless." As she explained their ruse was a tradition ever since the academy, Lance looked amused. Bren, of course, was in on it and greeted Lawless with a hug.

"Fuck, I haven't seen you in forever," Pocky said. "How the hell are you?" Lawless's usual good mood shifted, and her face fell. Pocky frowned. "Are you okay?"

"Yeah, um ..." Lawless glanced at the team, then Pocky. "Can we talk alone?"

Pocky turned to Lance and didn't even have to ask as he nodded. "Just stay on the main deck," he said.

"Yes, sir."

As Pocky walked away with Lawless, she heard Lance's new radio click with Geara's voice, asking him his location. She continued along the port toward the bow. They'd almost walked to the restaurant before settling against the hull. It had been nearly two years since she had last seen Lawless, and it was good to catch up with her. Her friend's Strat Unit was working with General Rammer, who had just boarded *Gaia* for some kind of official business with Geara. She was a little curious about what the general's presence was about, but she knew her friend most likely wouldn't be privy to that.

"So, what of you?" Lawless asked as she looked around suspiciously.

"Nothing much," Pocky replied, again unsure what was going on with her friend, and decided to get to the point. "Okay, we can cut the bullshit. No one's here."

"Listen to me carefully," Lawless said, keeping her voice low. "Keep a neutral expression and act as though we're still having a casual conversation."

"Okay," Pocky replied with a nod.

"Is your gun equipped with rubbers or reals?"

"Rubbers."

"Okay," Lawless sighed. "I'm supposed to lure you into the Rec Hall. Two of Rammer's soldiers are there to take you down and sedate you. Don't ask, because I don't know. I'm just following orders."

Pocky was startled by this. With everything she had been through—a war, countless rescues, close calls, and even the last few weeks—she shouldn't be surprised by now, but this was new and unsettling. *Why the fuck does a general want to sedate me?*

She tried not to show her unease by disconnecting from her emotions and slipped into the soldier she was trained to be. "Yeah, I got you. Lead the way."

Lawless nodded, and they headed for the Rec Hall.

"So, I heard you play bass. That true?" Lawless asked, already knowing the answer.

"I do."

"Show me?"

"Love too."

Lawless reached for the door to the Rec Hall. Pocky looked ahead to her team before entering. She could see Iza and Marker were watching them, but the rest had their attention on something else. She had hoped to give Bren a signal or an expression to at least alert him, but they would all know something was up soon. She quickly formulated a plan to get back to her team.

As Pocky followed Lawless inside, she casually moved her hand near the butt of her gun as though she was scratching an itch. As her friend had forewarned, two men acted as though they were on their way out. Before either one of them could make a move to their guns, she pulled out hers and fired two shots at their crotches. Both men went down in agony and held themselves. She fired two more shots at their heads, knocking them unconscious. Two soldiers she hadn't seen before sprinted toward her from the back of the room. She ran out the door so fast that she almost collided with the hull. As she ran back toward her team, Iza and Marker hurried toward her, guns out. She stopped when she caught up with them, but they kept going past her.

"Put your guns down!" Marker shouted.

Pocky turned and watched the two men comply as Marker continued shouting at them. When she saw they had a handle on the situation, she turned her attention toward her team again. Thomas, Haize, Yana, and Kaori, along with more of Marker's team, weren't far off and quickly reached her.

"Sis? You okay?" Thomas asked between heavy breaths.

"Yeah," she replied, then looked toward Bren, who was still in the corner. With his gun drawn, his gaze stayed on whatever was going on down there. "What's happening?"

"General Rammer—Sis, wait!" Thomas shouted as Pocky took off.

Pocky ran and didn't stop until she rounded the corner. Lance, Viper, and a few other soldiers had their guns pointed at two men standing next to Geara. Based on their insignia, one was Officer Masters while the other was General Rammer. The general was bald and baby-faced with a butt chin. He had a stocky build with pale sunburnt skin. The officer—pointing his gun toward her team—was lanky with a dark tan complexion. His unruly short black curly hair and patchy beard made him look as disheveled as the loose uniform he was wearing.

An angry exchange of words was going on between Lance and the officer. The guy had a condescending expression, as though this was all fun to him. Rammer was unarmed. Pocky pointed her gun at him.

Geara slid in front of the general and held his hands out. "Pocky, don't! We're trying to explain."

The officer accompanying Rammer lowered his gun slightly and laughed. "She's just a medic—"

Pocky fired a shot into the officer's shoulder. He grunted as he dropped his gun and coiled away.

"I'm a soldier first! If you were a real one, you would know that!" Pocky shouted, training her gun back on Geara and Rammer. As Lance ordered Viper to deal with the officer, she couldn't comprehend why the XO was aiding a man who was trying to capture her. "Why are you ..."

Pocky's voice started strong, but her words faded as a ripple spread across her body. For a moment, she panicked, unsure why she suddenly couldn't move or speak. Darkness shrouded her vision, then exploded into an array of bright colors. She felt a crowd around her, and she smiled as music slowly gained momentum in her ears. She gazed ahead and saw the endless crowd jumping to the beat. She bounced with them, enjoying the sensation of being one with them. She didn't know why she had a lapse of time but got herself right back into the present moment.

34

Minutes before Lance's world was turned upside down, Geara had said he and General Rammer were on their way to speak with him. The general had boarded an hour before with an urgent matter. Whatever it was couldn't have waited until they arrived at the way station. Lance didn't think anything of the meeting until the general stated his true purpose for boarding.

"I'm taking Pocky into my custody."

Lance and his team had reacted simultaneously, drawing their weapons and making it clear that wasn't going to happen. Rammer tried to reason with him, but he wasn't having it. Besides, Rammer's escort was all too chipper about their objective to take Pocky.

Lance was amazed—captivated, even—by Pocky's willingness to fight, then everything instantly changed.

Her words slurred, and her gaze became unfocused. She went from alert to neutral, as if deep in thought. Lance made his way toward her but stopped abruptly when her blue irises turned to a grayish metallic color.

"Pocky?" he asked.

"Ember?" General Rammer said as he moved Geara out of his path.

Lance turned his gun on the general. "Don't you dare come near her."

"Sis?" Thomas cried as he made his way toward her. Bren grabbed him, holding him back. "Wait! What's going on? What's happening to her?"

"Hang on, Brother," Bren said.

Lance looked beyond his two friends. Everyone on his team was piling in from around the port side. An explosion of voices engulfed him for a moment.

"Shut it!" Geara shouted.

The XO's booming voice not only silenced everyone around him but also seemed to jolt Pocky—or whatever she had become—back into the present. Lance watched as she became aware that she was holding a gun and regarded it before looking straight at him. Slowly, she put her right hand out as though to stop him from approaching, then holstered the gun. She unbuckled her entire holster and passed it to the nearest person, who happened to be Geara.

Keeping his weapon trained on Rammer, Lance waited patiently for whatever was about to happen as Pocky observed her surroundings as though for the first time. When she refocused on him, he held his breath. *Please, still be in there.*

As though Pocky had heard his thoughts, she spread her hands out. "She's okay. I put her in a nice dream." Lance's chest heaved. She took two steps toward him. "We don't have much time. You have questions."

Lance struggled with hearing the entity speak through Pocky's voice. It was wispier, haunting even. He swallowed hard. "Your name is Ember?"

"Yes."

"What are you?"

"A bio-mechanical lifeform that needs several hosts before becoming mature enough to be on one's own."

"Why are you in her?" Lance asked, aware that his voice was becoming angrier, but he couldn't temper it.

"Rammer can explain that better than I can," she said, then looked to Rammer.

"Her previous host was compromised," Rammer said. "The team before mine that was protecting her joined up with your Pre-Team. Abnormals attacked them."

Lance's upper lip curled. "Is that why my team is fucked up? Why we were scattered?"

"Yes, but I don't know anything else except that we were deployed earlier than scheduled and have been looking for her since."

Lance looked at Pocky—Ember. "That doesn't explain why you're in my woman."

"As Rammer had said, my previous host was compromised, and I transferred into Pocky."

"You can transfer?" Lance asked.

"Yes."

"Great, then transfer into someone else," he demanded. "Give Pocky back to me."

Ember blinked a few times before saying, "If that's your choice, but I need to explain the consequences if I do."

"Go on," Lance said, dread building in his stomach.

"When Pestilence's parasites entered Pocky's body, I had to contain them, or they would have found me. She became aware of my presence and transferred me to her archives. I'm ... still amazed she even knew I was there. She saved me. But to be able to fit, I had to absorb her archives."

Lance's gut twisted. "Is ... is that why we haven't been able to awaken her?"

"Correct, and I'm sorry for that."

Lance took off his hat and rubbed his forehead. Everything about this was making him angry on a level he didn't know existed within himself. He refocused on the entity. "Can she get it back?"

"Finishing your first question will answer that. If I transfer to another host, I would take all her knowledge of you and everyone here with me. She'll only have this life and whatever comes after, but nothing of your shared history. Nothing from before will be there. That's the consequence. If you want me to transfer, I will, but I wanted you to understand the cost."

Lance's jaw dropped, and he almost fell back against the hull. All the blood drained from his face. Bren rushed to him.

"Don't fucking touch me," Lance snapped, stopping his friend in place.

"It's a terrible choice," Ember continued. "And I'm sorry for that too, but it's one you need to make soon. Whether I stay or not, she will be without her archives and the ability to awaken for the remainder of her life here."

"And what happens to her if you stay? What will she become from here and beyond?"

"If I stay, she becomes my last host, and I will merge with her. The process takes years, but eventually, we will become as one being. I need a long sleep before I start, though."

Lance's eyes darted over the floor as he tried to comprehend the future. He looked back up at Ember. "Will she be different? I mean, will she be different from who she is now?"

"Personality wise, no. In other aspects, yes. I don't have time to explain, but in short, after her life here has ended and she's returned to your home reality, she will gain all my knowledge along with her archives. Until then, she won't remember who any of you really are to her."

Bren stepped up to Lance. "Cap, that doesn't sound so bad. We can live without her knowing us for one lifetime."

General Rammer stepped up, desperation in his eyes. "Lance, no. You wouldn't want her to gain all that knowledge. Don't do that to her. Forget her past and let her build a new one."

Lance pushed Rammer's comments away as something else became more pressing for him to know. "How did you even know she was here?"

"It was me," Ember answered. Lance looked back at her, perplexed as to how. The entity again gauged his expression. "Now that I'm not fully concentrating on containing Pestilence's parasites, I used Pocky's archives to send a message to Rammer. She's been feeling me do so over the past few days but was unaware that it was me. There's not much time left. Make a decision. Stay or go."

Lance closed his eyes, trying to process what had been said. Thomas piped in with desperation hitching in his voice.

"Wait, if it's anybody's choice, it should be mine. I'm her brother. It shouldn't be his."

Ember turned her attention to Thomas. "Because I know Pocky better than any of you, I know factually that she would want it to be Lance's. It's why I'm communicating with him instead of you."

"But this should be Pocky's decision, not anyone else's," Kaori added.

"I can't ask in this state. She trusts Lance in making this decision." She paused, turning back to Thomas. "Brother, before you torment yourself with why this wasn't you, why I transferred into your sister instead of you, it's merely because she was closer." Ember paused and looked around at all their faces before continuing. "It could have been any of you, but she was the closest."

An eruption of voices engulfed Lance. He was too angry to be reasonable or considerate. He pointed his gun out toward the stern and fired. Everyone immediately got quiet. He looked at Ember, a blend of anger, fear, and sorrow brewing deep within him. She didn't offer consoling words as she spoke.

"I don't have much longer. I can't keep Pocky in the dream, and I don't want her surfacing in the middle of this. Departing from all of you is going to be traumatic enough."

"Wait, what?" Panic gripped Lance's heart. "What are you talking about? She's coming with us."

Ember sighed regretfully. "Lance, I ... She has to go with Rammer."

"What!? No!" Thomas shouted and tried to rush to her, but again, Bren held him in place. "Fucking let go of me!"

"Why?" Lance demanded, moving closer to her.

"Resources," Rammer answered. "You have a small team, while I have a fleet. I have ships, outposts, vehicles, currency. I have the means to be able to better protect her."

Without taking his eyes off Ember, Lance said, "I am the Dark Sun. I can protect you."

"Yes, you can protect me. But you can't protect them while you do." Ember pointed to his team.

"Fine," Lance said, then looked at Rammer. "We go with her."

"Lance." Ember reached for his hand. He allowed her to take it into hers. The twist in his gut turned up another notch. "You have an assignment to complete. You can't abandon that. You can't abandon your purpose."

"I can't abandon her! I won't!" Lance shouted. Being separated by death was hard, but being separated like this was so much worse. And not just for him, but for Thomas and Bren, and the others. He reined in his emotions as he spoke on. "I can do both. I swear I can."

"Lance, the Abnormals are coming for me. For her. I am too small to be physically seen, but they will dissect her to find me regardless."

"I can protect you from them. That's what I was made for."

"Not all Abnormals come in human form. Some are as tiny as a tick, sitting on a leaf, waiting for a victim to walk by. My knowledge is too dangerous for them to have. Rammer's fleet was made to protect me from them."

"They just want to know why they're here. Why not just give them that?"

"Do you really think they would stop there? If they gain my knowledge, they'll know how to destroy every living being. They'll know how to destroy the entire universe with everything in it, including you, and everything you love."

As a celestial being, the mere thought of Lance's infinite existence having an end sent a chill down his spine. The thought of that happening was unreal.

"How the hell does something small like you have so much knowledge?"

"Do you have seven lifetimes for me to explain it?" Ember asked, her jaw starting to tremble. Lance was speechless as he stared at her wide-eyed. Sweat beaded across Pocky's forehead, and her grip loosened in his hand. She turned to their medic. "Brengavion, please sedate her. Don't let her wake up to this."

Bren looked to Lance for an answer. He shook his head as he gripped her other arm firmly. "No. You stay in her. She stays with me."

"If you don't let us go, I'll have to transfer into someone else," Ember said clinically. Thomas let out a blood-curdling cry. Lance gripped his hold tighter but then loosened as Ember spoke on. "I'm sorry, but I can't risk falling into their hands." Pocky's eyes closed for a moment. She exhaled tiredly. "And I need to sleep. Please hurry."

It was an impossible decision. Lance found himself nodding once, then looked at Bren, who grabbed his med pack. Thomas began to protest, yelling threats and obscenities. Everyone's voices heightened, but Lance shut them out. He looked into Pocky's eyes. The bright twinkle in her irises began to fade.

He turned to Rammer. "She needs to have one of us with her. Please allow that."

"I agree," Ember murmured, her voice softer than before.

Rammer sighed through his nose, but Lance didn't give a damn if the general was annoyed. Everyone got quiet as Lance eyed them. "Iza, you go. Grab her duffel and med pack." Without replying, Iza quickly moved into action. He turned to Rammer again. "I'll put her on your ship."

Whether it was the emotions going around or Lance's killer gaze, the general didn't argue. Everything after that felt like a blur. Lance was completely numb to the chaos going on around him. He allowed Thomas to have a moment. He embraced his sister. Lance heard words exchanged between them but didn't listen to what was being said.

When Bren was ready to administer the sedative, Lance picked up Pocky's body and held her in his arms. He watched her eyes slowly close after Bren injected the sedative into her upper arm. Bren put his forehead against hers once it was obvious she was asleep. Lance wasn't sure at first what the guttural sounds coming from the man's throat were until he realized Bren was weeping.

Lance was on autopilot, and his view seemed to change drastically from one scene to the next. One minute he was on the main deck walking toward the stairwell. The next he was walking over the gangway from *Gaia*'s port door to Rammer's ship. And then next was being inside a small cabin that bunked two. Iza was talking, but he didn't listen to what she was saying. The next scene he was looking down at the floor and knew he was back on *Gaia*. It was lightly lit wherever he was, but he felt a strong breeze coming from the starboard side and figured he must still be by the port door. *Right,* he thought, remembering he had watched the ship detach and float away until he couldn't see it anymore. He wasn't sure how long he had been leaning up against the wall, but his hands were starting to hurt, and he didn't care why. He ignored the pain, or maybe more so embraced it.

Time had no meaning, but Lance became aware at some point that he wasn't alone. The heavy breathing from another person indicated that. Instead of looking up to see who it was, he played a guessing game of who it could be. The heaviness in the person's breath narrowed it down to the possibilities of a male. At first, his guess was Bren, but he immediately dismissed that probability. Bren had been closer to Pocky than any of them put together. She was his partner, his confidant, his best friend. The two had been through shit together that no one could come close to. As much as Lance wanted it to be Bren, the big guy was just as likely to be in bad shape. So, it definitely couldn't be him.

Lance then thought of Thomas and dismissed that laughable possibility too.

Thomas certainly hated Lance right now; he couldn't blame him.

He then figured it could be Haize or Marker. Maybe even Geara. But it didn't matter who it was, because Lance didn't want any of them. He only wanted Pocky safely in his arms.

He then realized why he hadn't bothered to look up to see who it was. It wasn't to play this silly game. The enormous shame he felt inside himself was too much to face any of them. He had failed them. He had failed Pocky. *If I can't protect her, how can I protect any of them? I failed all of them.*

"You didn't fail us," the person said.

Lance furrowed his brow in confusion. The voice wasn't Haize's, Marker's, or Geara's. It was too hoarse to recognize, but it wasn't any of them. Lance looked up and was shocked to see it was, in fact, Thomas. He was breathing heavily and sweating as though he had been running. Of all people, Thomas was the last person he thought would be in front of him.

"Why are you here?" Lance said, voice rough and raw. He grunted as pain shot from his hands to his wrists, but he kept his gaze on Thomas. His eyes were too much like Pocky's. Lance's upper lip curled in anger. "Why the fuck are you here, Thomas!?"

"I'm here ... for you," Thomas said, holding out one hand as though Lance would suddenly come after him.

"Fucking hate me somewhere else!" Lance spat.

"I-I don't hate you. I am mad. So fucking mad, but not at you." Thomas's voice cracked on the last few words. "I'm tired of ostracizing myself. So I thought, what would my sister do? What would you do, or Bren? So I'm choosing to be here for you. And ... to keep you from hitting the wall again. Sis would want me to do that."

Lance looked down at his hands. They were a trembling, bloody mess. Though he now understood why they were hurting, he still didn't care. Disgusted with himself, Lance sagged down to the floor. To his surprise, Thomas sat next to him. A comfortable silence filled the air between them, and he found himself oddly appreciating the man's effort and company.

How was Pocky faring? Probably the same as they were. *No,* he corrected himself angrily. *She's hurting more so.* They lost her, but she lost everyone and everything. She lost her brother, her partner, and him. She lost her team, her friends, her squad, the entire military, her job, her purpose, her life, her very being, and her freedom, and she couldn't even know the truth as to why.

Before he knew what he was doing, Lance was standing and felt Thomas holding him while he tried hitting the wall again.

"Lance! Stop!" Thomas shouted.

Thomas's voice brought him back to the present, and he realized they had repeated these actions several times already. But this time, Lance held back. He pulled himself from the haze of his rage. He let go and let the pain of losing Pocky sink into his bones. He gripped the back of Thomas's shirt, buried his head into the man's shoulder, and quietly sobbed before breaking into a scream. This hurt beyond any physical pain he had experienced in this life and beyond. Thomas held onto him and let him scream until he had no voice left.

At some point, they both sank to the floor. Sitting cross-legged, Lance held his head in his hands. He didn't have anything else in him. He didn't even know how he was going to stand up, let alone carry out his assignment without Pocky by his side. After another long bout of silence, a thought occurred to him.

"When did you awaken?" Lance asked quietly.

"Before Shox attacked us. I didn't remember after being drugged, but some-time well, after ... Stellan ... I remembered." Another long silence brewed be-tween them until Thomas whispered, "Lance?"

He made a low grunt sound in reply.

"I've got a plan."

"What?" Lance asked.

"To get Pocky back," Thomas said optimistically, then stood and offered his hand to Lance.

He took his friend's hand and let him help him up, ignoring the pain in his knuckles and arms. "How?" Lance asked, hating just even having a fraction of hope.

"Well, I'm one of your problem solvers for a reason. And I've come up with a few ideas in between your fits of"—Thomas waved his hand toward the wall—"rage. But first, we need to get you cleaned up. A hot shower, a hot meal, and Bren. You definitely need Bren."

Lance felt as though he had stepped into another reality. Awakened or not, the one person who was usually falling apart was now the one trying to help him. The change in dynamics had him disoriented. That, or it was blood loss. Either way, he felt undeserving of Thomas's kindness.

As Lance followed Thomas, he said, "Tell me."

Thomas smiled at him as though Lance was going to truly relish his next words. "I've never told you about my ability, have I? It's time you know what I can do."

Acknowledgments

I first have to thank God, the Divine Universe, Buddha, whatever you wanna call it, that made me who I am. There will never be enough in my heart to thank you for my life. It's been an interesting, messy, adventurous, nerve-racking, batshit crazy, beautiful journey.

I want to thank my husband, Chris, for all his support in every way that husbands do, but I truly feel he went beyond what the brochure offered. From listening to my brainstorming and thoughts, to my frustrations with technology, prying my hands away from the keyboard, making me coffee, and just supporting me through this whole process, and for believing in me, I could never have enough gratitude or give back for how instrumental you have been to me.

For my daughter, who literally gave birth to my vision of the Dark Sun (I wish I could explain what a triumphant, monumental moment that was for you and me), I'll always be in awe of your talent and your creative mind. I'm so thankful for you and for not being the teenager that everyone warned me of. You have made life way more fun.

I'd also like to thank my family and friends, who've been cheering me on and distracted me when I needed it. Your belief in me was much needed during tough times.

A HUGE thank you to my editors: Hannah and Jeanine. Exceptionally remarkable and brilliant women! I am beyond grateful for all your guidance and encouragement. And also thank you to my blurb editor, Jessie Cunniffe from Book Blurb Magic.

And thank you to the Reader. Yeah you! I truly hope you enjoyed the story and were entertained. That was my ultimate goal.

About the Author

GenXer, gamer, sci-fi lover, a nerd, and no apologies for who I am.
Favorite book: *Way of the Pilgrim* by Gordon R. Dickson (a classic sci-fi).
Favorite movies: *Aliens* and John Carpenter's *The Thing*. Favorite hobbies:
reading and writing. I've always loved writing stories, but a couple of years ago,
I took it more seriously, wrote a draft, and sent it to my developmental editor,
and as stories go, it changed my life. I am so incredibly thankful to her and the
journey that got me here. I honestly can't say or thank enough what my editors
have done for me.

You can follow me on Instagram @cristine_keller_author

You can also contact me at criskeller.thedarksun@gmail.com

I would love to hear your feedback.

Please, if you would be so kind as to leave a review, I would so be grateful.

Reviews are so important, especially for new authors.

Thank you again, Reader, for reading my book.

www.ingramcontent.com/pod-product-compliance
Lightning Source LLC
Chambersburg PA
CBHW021416110726
47901CB00008B/2188